Leo Giroux spent man
died in 1990.

By the same author

The Rishi

LEO GIROUX, Jr

Dark Ashram

GraftonBooks

A Division of HarperCollinsPublishers

GraftonBooks
A Division of HarperCollins*Publishers*
77–85 Fulham Palace Road,
Hammersmith, London W6 8JB

A Grafton UK Paperback Original 1990

Copyright © Leo Giroux, Jr 1990

ISBN 0-586-20529-2

Printed and bound in Great Britain by
Collins, Glasgow

Set in Times

To Ben Lackie

For a lifetime of friendship; for his enthusiasm, inspiring exchange of ideas, and for introducing me to writers who think sideways.

Acknowledgments

To Phillip and Margaret Vitti, Russ Kimball, Dorothy Tangusso and Ted Fitzgerald for their supportive efforts. And especially to Bob Vandal, a very informed person.

To the Reader

In the middle of the last century, the British Raj destroyed the cult of Thuggee in India. An estimated twelve million victims fell to the deadly *rumel*, or strangler's scarf, of the Thug assassin. Thugs killed for two purposes: to satisfy the destructive cravings of the goddess Kali and for robbery. They also believed that the victims would no longer undergo the almost endless cycles of reincarnation but would enter paradise immediately. Thus, members of the cult considered themselves to be saints doing holy works.

According to a secret file in Washington, DC, a resurgence of Thuggee in India in 1975 spread to Boston, Massachusetts, in the United States. The Thugs were trailed there by India's foremost policeman, Rama Shastri, who also had another reason for exiling himself: Prime Minister Indira Gandhi's so-called 'Emergency', when she jailed intellectuals, dissidents and rival politicians. With the aid of the former special operative for the US Government, Stephen Wrench, and others, the cult was successfully suppressed. Wrench's daughter Santha, whose mother was an Indian, was rescued from the Thugs, who had attempted to make her a 'vessel of Kali' through supernatural means. The Huzoor, or Lord of the Thugs, escaped mysteriously, however. He took with him the Scroll of Power that legend says was given to him by the sacred *rishis* (seers) of old in a hidden cave in the Himalayas. The Huzoor was an American, Kurt Leinster, a dark mystic who was chosen to be the adopted son of Kali on Earth. Since his phenomenal escape, no one connected

7

with the episode was certain that the day of Thuggee was truly over. In fact, in India, a few years later, there still existed a small Thug band, killing whenever possible.

But it was the revival of Thuggee on a grand scale that was most feared. That Kurt Leinster would reappear as the Great Huzoor of Thuggee . . .

PART ONE
Pursuit

There are chords in the hearts of the most reckless which cannot be touched without emotion. Even with the utterly lost, to whom life and death are equally jests, there are matters of which no jests can be made.

Edgar Allan Poe, *The Masque of the Red Death*

1

India, 1979 – The Ganga Riverbank, Uttar Pradesh

He waited and watched, rubbing his unique hands that were discoloured by birthmarks shaped like splotches of purple dye. The pilgrims had chosen their camp site a few hours before dusk, and he had observed them from the shadows of an abandoned mosque on a high knoll over-looking a small millet field and the stretch of savannah along the Ganga riverbank. Sometimes he watched with several others, sometimes with only one peer – another Strangler. He was, after all, Ajit Majumdar, the head of a Thug band, and had the reputation of being surly, often unapproachable. So he was alone during most of the long waiting time.

According to the precepts of the cult of Thuggee, Ajit was royalty. He came from a very long line of Thugs and knew the names of every ancestor for the past four centuries. He was nearly sixty, and, since his two sons had died in battle in an ancient Shakti temple a few years ago, Ajit had but a single grandson, in Varanasi, to continue the line. It was the one balm for the grief he felt for the loss of his sons. Thank Kali Ma.

And thank her, too, he had survived this long and with a body that still had tremendous agility. Only the face fitted his age – craggy, lined with deep ruts, and with eyes of smouldering antiquity.

Ajit thought of what he had seen when he approached the camp site after dusk. First, there had been two large tents where the merchants were to sleep. Ajit had counted

11

five of them, expensively dressed and bejewelled, one with an impressive stone in the centre of his turban that reminded Ajit of the Raj days when maharajahs were plentiful. The rest of the gathering were servants, fourteen in number. There were no women present.

Listening to bits of conversation, Ajit had discovered that they were pilgrims en route to Hardwar. Then, he had left his hiding place in the millet field and returned to the mosque.

Now Ajit Majumdar peered into the mosque doorway. He gagged at the pungent odour that wafted out into the night. The interior reeked of bat dung. Ajit managed the name of the next-in-command: 'Mohan.'

A tug at his sleeve. 'Yes, guru.'

'The *bele* must be prepared.'

Mohan disappeared, came back. 'It will be done.'

Three other men, the Diggers, left the mosque, went round the building to the left and descended the knoll.

'Merchants with their servants. There is much to plunder. Victims especially designed for the *rumel*.'

'Kali Ma be praised,' agreed Mohan.

Ajit Majumdar wet his thumb with his tongue, then dipped it into a small pouch. When he raised the thumb again, it was covered with *goor* sugar. He licked the sugar and repeated the gesture two more times.

Replenished, Ajit sighed. Yes, these were the best victims, he thought. They were wealthy, had things worthy of stealing. Robbery was every bit as important to the Thug as killing. It was an embarrassment if the victim had nothing of value on his person. But this happened to the best of Thugs now and then.

Ajit took the route of the Diggers, turning left round the mosque. Mohan followed.

The night was moonless. Only the stars hazed the way ever so slightly. Ajit could see the slope, a grey-patched,

12

whitish descent to the fringe of savannah that continued for miles and more miles up-river. Almost due east, a sarus crane trumpeted; from south of it came the rumble of a collapsing sandbank. Ajit Majumdar listened to the new sounds, the thud and chock of the pickaxes clawing into the soil at the knoll base. The Diggers were hard at work establishing the *bele*, the burial ground for Thug victims. He tried to find the Diggers' silhouettes in the night below, but they were beyond the starhaze, only sounds in a well of blackness.

Ajit turned completely around and faced the east again. The bushy millet field was outlined by the flickering light of the camp fires; two of them, one before the tents and one for the servants yards away. The entire savannah clearing was a long, ruddy ellipse. The fires grabbed and deflected the settling mist, lapped at the surrounding palm trees, and on as far as the riverbank and the Ganga itself.

In the centre of the ruddiness, two figures moved, sentries, each near sparkling tendrils of camp light. It seemed like a festival, a signal summoning: 'Come, children of Kali. Take up your silken scarves and celebrate. Nineteen throats for the *rumel*'s kiss. Kill for the love of Kali. Kill! Kill! Kill!'

He was certainly due some good fortune, Ajit concluded. The last two years, since he had gathered his Thug band, not much had turned out in his favour. For one thing, recruits were difficult to come by. Too much damage had been done to the Thuggee cause shortly before by a false Huzoor who Ajit had discovered only recently was an American. Rumour stated that not one drop of Indian blood was in the charlatan's veins.

But tonight Ajit breathed freely. Everything was so definite, more alive, filled with true meaning. Tonight, Kali Ma was with them, erasing the chaos of the past. Tonight was Order, Harmony . . .

13

The strides of the Diggers returning broke his reverie. The *bele* was finished, the sacrosanct ground. It was time to give the command. Ajit Majumdar headed for the entrance. Nearing, he wondered that his men had endured the sickly dung stench of their hiding place for so long. His band might be few in number, but they were the sturdiest and best of Thugs, and, giving the order, his voice was firm with pride.

Approaching from the northeast side, the Thug kept to the millet field's border as it curved back on itself, encircling a grove of mangoes. Beyond, in either direction, upstream or downstream, was the savannah, and a barely discernible track through the grove led to the clearing before the tents. In Ramasi, the secret language of the Thug, Ajit Majumdar whispered the plan to Mohan, who passed it on to Hasari, another Strangler. The band of thirty was to divide into two groups: Ajit Majumdar would lead six other Thugs to the tents while Hasari commanded the rest of them, who were to slay the servants sleeping on the stretch of ground. There weren't enough Armholders to handle all nineteen victims, and the Diggers and Scouts would have to compensate for the lack whenever necessary.

Ajit envisaged one Strangler and two Armholders, as usual, creeping up to a supine figure. His eyes searched, probed at the sleepers. One last check – was it a trap? The sleepers were very still. At the tents, the sentry was resting against a boulder. He smoked, and the red speck of the cigarette bobbed between his lips. On the down-river side, the silhouette of the other guard paced before the fire.

Moments passed. Mohan finally asked, 'Does the guru see danger?'

Ajit barely heard him. He was uneasy, suddenly . . .

14

'Guru, is there danger?'

A pack of jackals commenced their howlings in synchrony with another collapsing sandbank. It made Ajit start, and he barked, more to himself than to his men, 'Go!' He was squatting on his haunches and leaped and bounded now in a single flow of motion down the mango grove track and into the clearing. He sensed more than saw Mohan and the others at his heels. His fingers caressed the silken scarf that had been his turban. Ajit was a blur as he headed for the biggest of the tents.

His mind glimpsed his surroundings in quick flashes: the crackling embers and eruptions of flame and black smoke, the sentry still at ease against the rock, the shadow of a man undressing within the tent. Ajit's arm gestured; Mohan was to take care of the sentry.

Soundlessly, Mohan glided on. Another gesture and the five Thugs moved as one. The tent entrance was before Ajit. He balanced, his grip tight on the *rumel*, about to lunge beyond the tent flap . . .

The canvas rippled, and a small man dressed in an embroidered *shaluka* stepped out into the light. The man's right hand rose quickly, the gun it held erupted, and Mohan, about to lower his *rumel* around the sentry's neck, jumped with a loud shout of pain and slammed against the boulder.

Then came the din – more shouting, screams, flesh and muscle colliding with other bodies, gunshots. Ajit roared a command to retreat – it *was* a trap. The merchants, their servants, were the Kotwal, the police. Since a Thug could not spill blood, the battle was uneven. What were their *rumels* against guns and knives?

Ajit backed from the tent, but the short man saw him now, and neared. Their eyes met, and the Thug forgot his command. Hatred shredded his caution. 'Majumdar?'

questioned the other and advanced. Ajit arched his back to rush him.

Suddenly, he couldn't breathe. Arms, four of them, like metal bands crushing his waist, yanked him back. Ajit felt the ground give way. He was being raised high. Earth and sky whirled as he was flung far into a thicket.

For a second, Ajit lost consciousness. When he opened his eyes, he seemed encapsulated in something that was darker than night. The air was thick with the scent of musk. His ears still rang with a sound Ajit was certain he must have imagined: the clashing of bracelets, anklets. He tried to rise. Fingers dug into his shoulders, pressing him down. *Down*, he thought he heard, and shivered. The word was like a shard of ice.

Still stunned from his fall, Ajit decided it was too much to fathom now. Resigned, he thought: So, I am now a captive. It has happened before and is of no consequence. I shall escape when possible. I believe this to be true.

The battle caught his attention. Through a narrow parting in the thicket, Ajit saw a huge man shake off two Thugs. One leaped up again, crying, 'Kali!' and the man shot him in the shoulder. *They shoot us only to wound! Better death than such humiliation*. Ajit writhed against the four binding arms. If only he were free . . .

Then, there was talking nearby. One, no, two of the recognized enemy again, since the voice of the second talking man was also familiar. Ajit's head jerked up, and he noted another narrow parting closer to his face. He was still in that very black cloud, that strange cloak of nightness, and it opened slightly so he could see them.

'It was Ajit Majumdar, Gopal,' the man in the *shaluka* said. 'I know that's who I saw. I felt at first he would grapple with me, but instead he leaped away – in here, I think.'

The other was pounding through the thicket, brushing

16

foliage aside with a long knife. 'Then, he has fled. No man hides here, Rama.'

Now a third party spoke in English with an accent that wasn't British. From his profile against the garish camp light, Ajit saw it was the huge man. 'We've captured most of them. Six are wounded, two dead of theirs. Three wounded, none dead of ours. That's pretty good, Ram.'

'But not enough. Majumdar escaped.'

'We will pursue and find him,' stated the one called Gopal.

'We hope. Amazing how he evaded us so quickly,' replied the leader, Rama Shastri, Thuggee's greatest enemy.

They turned, left the spot hurriedly, and Ajit heard no more. His mind had finally cleared. Yes, how *had* he evaded the Kotwal so easily? And whose arms were holding him so fast if not those of the enemy? Was it two of his own men intervening . . . ? No – impossible. Ajit could feel a pair of hands now around his chest. He lowered his eyes.

For a brief instant, he thought they were chains of glowing insects. Bright and fluid, silver in colour. Sinuous, undulating. Then, as Ajit stared longer, the chain became an outline of arms and wrists and hands. And there were many bracelets attached to the lower arms. They moved and clanked against each other, with the silver erupting like fire crackling among embers. The fingers danced, it seemed, across his body, long, with nails that pointed, curled inwards and flashed from hidden light in the surrounding black cloud.

Kali Ma, Ajit thought in awe; this is no other than she!

And, as if in response, two additional arms moved out from behind him and swayed to an unknown rhythm, the hands gesturing, now fluidly, now fixed and posturing, speaking with supple fingers, while the bracelets clinked

17

to each motion and the hot, musk-scented breath of Kali was everywhere.

The arms released Ajit suddenly, and his eyes rose to see the rest of her, but the silvery outlines ended just short of the shoulders. There was only nothingness or more of that black cloud, with maybe the suggestion of two silver specks where her eyes might be.

But the command running through him like a string of ice was vivid enough: 'Leave now. This way.' Ajit somehow sensed he should go downstream.

2

There was no hesitation in Rama Shastri's search for the Thug leader. When he saw that all the remaining Thugs were captured, he ordered that they be brought to a makeshift Kotwalee near Kanpur, a short distance away. There they would await his return.

Shastri then nodded to Gopal, his personal aide; Stephen Wrench, the big American; a man called Shambu, who was an excellent tracker; and two other policemen with supplies. The group went to the area where Ajit Majumdar had disappeared. Shambu ventured out further with a long-handled flashlight that gave an intense beam.

'If we don't find Majumdar, he'll only reorganize again. A man like that won't stop until he's dead,' said Rama Shastri, 'or alive and captured. I'll settle for either but for nothing less. This must be the very end of Thuggee in our time.'

He heard a soft cry from the millet field. When the rest arrived there, Shambu was waiting. He pointed to a row of crushed panicles. 'See, I believe a man has fled through this recently,' he told them. Shambu went ahead along the route of bent and twisted sheaves, and they followed. The condition of the millet told of a man in a great hurry pushing fiercely against the barrier of stalks. This led them in a nearly straight line to a descent into a water-filled gully.

Shambu knelt, his light flush on a group of footprints. 'Notice, Kotwal Shastri, the shoe of his right foot has the imprint of a slice cut into the leather of the sole. Possibly something was stuck there and was cut out with a knife.

Now, that is a real designator. He is much like the tiger with two claws missing from one of his pads. If the ground ahead be soft or wet again, we'll look for this telltale sign.'

The others listened intently while the tracker spoke more of his thoughts aloud: 'The man has the energy that comes with great fear. Look at the depth of the print, the force of his tread as he speeds to freedom. And the destination is south, no doubt of it.'

'Don't be so confident' – Shastri stressed the meaning of the Hindi word *Thug* – 'These *deceivers* are always going right when you expect left or vice versa. Be alert for any trace of Majumdar suddenly backtracking in the opposite direction.'

Now they were moving through the vast savannah. Small night creatures scurried from their path. To their right, from a village on a cliff of hard ground that had endured the monsoon floods, came the noising of cattle. Mingled with it but barely detectable were the pad and sniffing of a dog nearing rapidly.

Shambu stopped, faced the sounds and aimed the flashlight beam at the animal's eyes. Ganga bank dogs were often very wild and dangerous. This one growled a while but finally, after much pawing of the ground and snarling, dashed away.

The pursuit continued. The starlight had dimmed even more; the darkness verged on Stygian, slowing their pace considerably. Ahead, a sandbank slid into the river with a roar.

Stephen Wrench jumped. 'Christ Almighty!'

'The collapse wasn't as close to us as it sounded,' Gopal told him. 'It is the way sound carries here at night.'

Again Shambu: 'Kotwal Shastri!' The tracker had reached a mudflat. And more footprints. 'He leaves the shelter of the thickets and trees. Closer to Mother Ganga.'

'He is seeking a boat,' concluded Shastri.

To a man, they turned and faced the great river. They saw a churning sheen as it snaked around countless islands along the Uttar Pradesh bank. They heard the congested waters, thick and yellow with silt and detritus, erupting into semi-solid rapids and whirlpools. The sheen extended to the mudflat, the streaks of starlight flush on the display of prints – bird, animal, and man.

But Ajit Majumdar's trail suddenly veered from the bank in a broad arc back to the savannah.

'Ah, the telltale Delhi shoe again. Again and again. See the cut in the sole,' Shambu chirped excitedly. 'He sped along most of this. The imprints in the mud, the soles especially, dig in deeply, as with a man running fast, and there is barely a heel imprint . . . Although, note – right here he paused. We see the entire track of both' shoes. We can read his thinking: Should he continue along the bank or return to the savannah and cover? And here he sets forth to that banyan tree . . .'

Shambu pointed at the tree, and his finger moved even beyond the savannah growth to a sugar field where the stars reflected strongly. The field was connected to a long, thin stretch of high land running through the beach and out into the river for some distance. And still beyond that were the lights of a rail bridge.

Shambu renewed his tracking, followed the arc of Majumdar's flight.

Rama Shastri called him. 'Let us go this way.'

'But, Kotwal . . .'

'Humour me, Shambu.'

Shastri had reached the end of the flats. Below, a yard's distance away, the Ganga climbed up the bank cluttered with clay deposits, thick like molten lead.

He then followed the bank, heading for the stretch of

21

elevated ground. No one spoke; only the flutter of a group of scavenger birds broke the silence.

Before the jutting land finger of clump grass and dry beach, they found the indentation of a boat's keel. It had rested on the flat, the mud outlining where it had canted on its leeward side. Close by were the imprints of cone-shaped traps for setting under water. The boat had been moved not too long ago, judging by the remnants of bailed-out water, still distinct as little pools and minute rivulets.

Shastri stepped round the trench left by the keel to the side where the beach rose and meshed with the higher ground. 'Now turn your light here.'

They had already discovered the prints of one man, the boat-owner, probably, and these showed again. But then . . .

'How did you know, Kotwal?'

Shastri didn't answer. He knelt before the new prints, saw they emerged from the darkness of the incline. He directed Shambu's torch up the rise. The prints were clear, descending from the high ground.

He finally said, 'Our friend, the nicked Delhi shoe . . . Majumdar went into the savannah for probably at least a mile. That would make his ruse convincing enough. Then he doubled back by wading through the river. The prints are still damp on the dry red clay of this slope. He left the river on the other side, scrambled over the point of land and came down to the boat. Most likely, he hired the fisherman owner to take him upstream or maybe across the Ganga.'

He knew they all wondered how he could be so positive about the Thug's direction. Except Stephen Wrench, who was almost as familiar with Thug thinking as he was. Yes, Steve would understand visceral feelings about things. Shastri spun round, climbed the slope and stared at the

22

bridge lights. This particular one, an immense rail bridge, had piers that were sunk one hundred feet deep in the river bottom, he recalled.

'Where does the railway go?'

'Back and forth across the Ganga, Kotwal.'

'I mean on the other side. Does it go north or south?'

'North. All the way to Hardwar.'

'So it is north.' Shastri walked along the high ground projecting out into the river, passing under the pendant branches of a banyan tree, then a run of pipals, until he came to the tip of the peninsula, nearly a quarter of a mile from the bank. There was much bubbling below, a pair of whirlpools. 'North again,' he said to the ancient river. 'Is it possible . . . is it again . . .?'

Rama Shastri shivered and left the point hurriedly. At his heels was a sulking Shambu. 'Don't take on so,' Shastri snapped. 'You're an expert at trailing a man, but I have witnessed Thugs outwit the best of us. They are inspired, you might say, have an inner faculty, a sense that aids them when they're at bay . . .' And he shivered once more at what he had said.

He headed towards the spot where the boat had been beached, aware he was the second fugitive that night. He was racing against his thoughts, fiercely concentrating on the moment, the very instant. As if the present were sanctuary from what had been and what might be.

Shastri found Stephen Wrench, Gopal and the two policemen resting on the slope. Wrench was lighting his briar. Gopal had already lit his. Shastri's hand reached into his tunic pocket and withdrew empty. Force of habit. He had stopped smoking months ago. He sat down and listened to Gopal's droning voice narrate their first encounter with Ajit Majumdar.

'He was leading the Jumaldehee Thugs then. We had captured him and his band at Hyderabad.' The words

23

were lost in a plethora of memories, of much evil and terror that had spread from the Himalayas to the heart of New England in America. Shastri looked at Stephen Wrench's profile flickering out of the darkness as he drew the match light into his pipe bowl. Their eyes met and Shastri knew that his lifetime friend was remembering, too. Mostly about Santha, Wrench's daughter, and the threat all this had been to her sanity and life and, worse, her very essence.

Shastri missed the camaraderie of men smoking and conversing, and it made him suddenly irritable.

He stood again, left the slope, walked to the beach's edge. He had to make a decision soon. As if in answer to his need, voices came to him from the river.

'Who are you?' he called out in Hindi. Then he added, 'This is the police.'

He strained to hear. No voices. Silence.

'Shambu, show them your light, man,' Shastri growled. Once more he shouted across the waters, 'We are the police. I, Kotwal Shastri, demand that you answer us!'

Shambu's light searched, and found the stern of a boat and the bow of another, very still behind the first. They were floating; no one steered. These fishing boats were loaded with nets shaped like bags.

'I saw a head bob,' Shambu reported. 'They are hiding from us, Kotwal.'

'Perhaps it's the language, Rama,' Gopal suggested, at his side suddenly. Gopal cupped his mouth. 'Show your-selves or suffer the Kotwal's wrath,' he called, in Bihari.

When they heard only the slap of the waters against the clinker-built boat sides, Stephen Wrench added calls in Marathi and in Urdu.

Finding the silence intolerable, Gopal waved his gun. 'Heed now, you low-born curs of the river. Here is a language you will recognize!' He fired over the heads of the hiding men.

Before the echoes of the shots had subsided, voices were begging: 'Please, oh merciful one. By this sacred home of Mother Ganga, refrain from doing harm to us' and 'We implore you to consider the fears of defenceless fishermen. We did not know if you were dacoits disguised as the Kotwal and his men!'

Shambu's flashlight exposed the boatmen behind their poles, guiding their crafts towards the bank.

'That is much better,' said Gopal, and he proceeded to question them. The replies were quick enough – no, they hadn't seen another fishing boat with conical nets. Shastri interrupted and gave the order. He was personally requisitioning the use of their boats for a while.

Shastri, Wrench and Gopal climbed aboard the first boat; Shambu and the two policemen took the other. 'Head upstream along the opposite bank,' barked Shastri. Then, 'How far upstream were you heading?'

'Perhaps most of the way to Fategarh, Kotwal. There are *tengra* and *lachi* fish there. The other day, my son' – the fisherman nodded at the boy perched upon the nets in the stern – 'saw a *gaunch*, the freshwater shark, even.'

The river was slowly brightening in streaks; light glanced off bits of mica. Another jackal pack began to howl vociferously, as if in protest at the coming dawn. The temperature had risen, foreboding another daytime peak of at least 115 degrees. Today the merciless hot wind would blow again from the western desert.

Stephen Wrench commented on the prospect between curses. He wasn't certain which was worse: tracking a criminal in just-premonsoon season or during the rains and floods themselves.

Rama Shastri smiled thinly. He too was rapidly feeling his tolerance shred, but it wasn't because of the weather.

His eyes hungrily searched the river, which was beginning to accumulate its usual bustle. More boats were about now, mostly heading downstream, country boats with upturned bows and square sterns. Two of them were lashed together, sharing the same sail, a ragged banner of communal harmony.

The approaching bank showed a vast grey flatland with splotches of brassiness. Shastri saw a pair of spoonbills poking for frogs. A blur of black and white avocets flashed by on the wing. Shastri turned again to the upstream flow. Still no other fishing boat.

But this was the route Ajit Majumdar was taking; it had to be, Shastri insisted to himself. Shastri knew, dammit, that Majumdar chose, no, was *compelled* to go north. And the reality of these deep, demanding spurts of instinctual knowledge depressed him.

The sense of being trapped in an undertow was all too familiar.

Rama Shastri sat, paralysed for a moment, perched on an upturned basket, with only his eyes moving, darting beyond the bow, then to the bank, then back upstream again. Never once did he face Stephen Wrench. Those same disturbing instincts had already informed him of what his friend was thinking.

'Keep using that light,' he urged Shambu, who was at the gunwale of the second boat. The beam seemed to sweep away the faint smudges of lingering night.

The boats moved slowly. That and the repetitive landscape left an impression of many hours. It was Gopal who first saw the beached boat. Canted on its side as before, except that this time the sail wasn't furled. Shastri commanded that they head for the craft.

As they neared, a cloud of gulls and cormorants fluttered from the unexposed side. They were working at the bait in the conical nets. Something else slunk from the bow's shadow, then stopped at a few yards' distance. Gopal fired his weapon; the jackal barked with pain and limped towards the high grass encroaching the flats.

'There is death here, Rama,' Gopal stated.

The boats closed in on the bank. As soon as wading was possible, Shastri, Wrench, Gopal and Shambu went over the side. The two policemen were directed to stay with the fishermen.

Wrench arrived at the boat first. He gripped the gunwale and pulled it back on its keel with ease, since the clinker wood was not heavy. The brassy dawn had ignited the beach now, and both the boat and the big man looked as though they were of the same metal. It added pallor to Wrench's jawline where he was unshaven and a sullen opaqueness to his eyes. When Shastri joined him, Wrench grunted. The *brrrt* of the flapping sail was like a punctuation to the sound. There was nothing to say. The body, doubled up in a fetal position against the sailing thwart, explained everything. The face was turned upwards, however; eyes wide and staring, mouth open.

Shastri imagined what had occurred. Majumdar had used his *rumel* on the man instead of making the payment he had promised for being ferried across the Ganga. To ensure that the body would remain undiscovered for a while, the Thug had then raised the boat on its side.

Wrench reached in, grasped the corpse under the arms and started to pull it out. Shastri and Gopal helped with the man's legs, and soon the body was flat on its back on the sand. Shastri squatted and examined the bluish discoloration around the neck. A great deal of force had been used to leave such a cincture mark.

He heard Wrench grunt again. It said to Shastri that they had failed to save at least one victim from Kali's kiss that night.

Shastri stood looking for Shambu. The tracker had left

27

the mudflats and was climbing to the high grass. Shastri smiled. Shambu had found the Delhi shoe again. The Kotwal knew already where Majumdar was heading, but he allowed Shambu to continue, and, when Shambu called, he went forward as if Shambu's new revelation was unknown to him.

'A fine job,' Shastri praised the other when they stood on the slope together staring down at the footprint. Shambu grinned widely. 'Now let us explore what exactly Ajit Majumdar is seeking.'

Taking binoculars from a case attached to a crossbelt over his field jacket, Rama Shastri studied the horizon. For a long time he concentrated on a point in the northwest. Finally, he handed the binoculars to Shambu and from a wallet extracted a neatly folded square of paper which he spread out on Shambu's back.

'Move the glasses northwards,' he was saying. 'Follow the railway tracks until they are blocked from view by a small knoll. You are familiar with this area, Shambu; is that a suitable camp site during the afternoon sun?'

'The elevation isn't very high, but there are many indentations along its base, niches with shadow, if my memory is correct, Kotwal.'

'Excellent.' Rama Shastri drew a circle around the contour lines of the elevation on the topographic map. He then refolded it. 'Now then, let us return to the others.'

As they did that, 'You believe, then, Kotwal, that Ajit Majumdar is waiting in the shelter of the elevation for a passing train?'

'Yes, that is where he went, I'll wager. But as to whether he is still waiting – well, that is another matter, I'm afraid. A train may already have passed through,' Shastri sighed, 'but we must go there nevertheless and be certain.'

'Trains do not move rapidly in this area, sir. When the Ganga overflows, it often erodes the earth and loosens the sleepers. Thus, they must move slowly. It would be quite easy for a man to climb aboard.'

They crossed the mudflat and found that Wrench and Gopal had carried the body to one of the fishing boats. The beached boat had also been set upright on its keel and turned around with its bow facing the river. Everyone was helping, including the two policemen and the fishermen. One of them was now tying a tow rope to the boat's bow.

'Listen carefully,' Shastri told the policemen. 'The body must be delivered to the village from which we originally set out. After that, both of you must go to the railway bridge, telegraph a description of Majumdar to Hardwar, and then wait for a train crossing to this side, stop it and take command.' He gave one of them the topographic map. 'The rest of us will be at the position marked on the map by then, hopefully. If not, then stop the train again and wait for us. But make certain from the beginning that the train is going all the way to Hardwar. Understand?' Shastri spilled coins from a small pouch into his cupped hand. 'And pay these boatmen for their trouble this morning.'

Stephen Wrench touched his arm. 'Ram, let's talk.'

Shastri nodded. 'I'm uncomfortable,' Wrench admitted, once they were alone. 'The trail has been easy to track. Too easy. I can't help feeling everything has been designed that way.'

Shastri winced. 'Yes . . .' He muttered, half to himself. 'The Design.'

Wrench hunched forward. 'Has it all started again, do you think? I'm certain that's what you're wondering, Ram. It's happening again! Goddamn, I can feel it – those convenient footprints, the way the bastard's heading

29

north. Kurt Leinster went north, didn't he? Isn't that what you told me? North up the Ganga, as far as the goddamn Himalayas . . .?'

'Maybe it's coincidence. Consider: Majumdar must escape in some direction. Why not north?'

'You're not convincing, Ram. Hell, it's not as if we've never dealt with this before. You and I have been part of the Design before.'

Rama Shastri stared about him. The thought returned that the roles had reversed themselves that night. Were they the hunted now, not Ajit Majumdar? 'Come, Steve, we must go on,' he said softly, with understanding. 'We mustn't imagine too much, you know. We must think of facts only and forget the past.'

Then Rama Shastri headed for the slope, evading his friend's eyes.

3

It was exactly 9.42 A.M. when George Buchan's Porsche turned in from Route 20 into the Kitteridge drive. Santha Wrench, eyeing the clock on her writing desk, estimated she had another twenty minutes before she had to make an appearance downstairs and continued to reread the letter she had just finished writing to her father. The open bedroom window wafted in the sounds of the Porsche door shutting and a man's tread on gravel.

Santha put down the letter, rose and went to the window. George was standing in the shadow of the porte-cochère, looking up. But she remained invisible to his view, pulling back even further behind the lavender curtains. Let him think she was in the shower or dressing, Santha decided. George would want to speak to Annette alone for a spell, anyway. Santha returned to her desk.

She continued her reading.

. . . and to describe the exhilaration, the great release one feels, as just that sounds so typical, but I really can't think of a better description at the moment. Anyway, when Annette took me flying, I decided almost immediately that I should take lessons as soon as possible. The prospect has awakened new confidence in me. Annette said it did the same for her when she started and has continued to do so since. I'm pleased more and more that I chose to live with her these past months. Her uncluttered and unfettered (I almost used the cliché word 'liberated') nature has reflected new vistas of life and experience for me.

I said uncluttered. So many people have an undertow, a sub-text to them, and you're constantly wondering who or what they

31

really are. Annette has her own secret world, her private self, of course, as we all do, but with her it never seems to interfere with relationships. I feel that I know everything about her that I should know, that I'm not being cheated in our friendship. In short, we communicate with total trust and respect.

So I warn you, Daddy, when you return you may have to go flying (at least once) with your daughter, the aviatrix.

Now a grim topic. Lately I've been corresponding with Krishna Pandey in Delhi. I have known him since he attended a kindergarten on Curzon Road, around the corner from Grandfather's house. One day he took ill, and his nurse, who was escorting him to kindergarten when it happened, brought him to Grandfather's door. I was staying there that morning so we met. He felt better shortly after Grandfather's ministrations, and he and I pored over those wonderful books with their many colour prints on the shelves of the waiting room. Very extravagant of Grandfather. Magazines would have sufficed as they do in doctors' offices here. But it was Grandfather's home, after all, and that made a great difference.

Krishna and I have remained friends ever since. You would've met him, Daddy, if you had been home more often in those days. He's a newspaperman now and works for *The Times of India*. Needless to say, he was one of the newsmen imprisoned during the Emergency. So you can imagine, Daddy, how closely he has been watching events since the Janata party took control a few years ago. As you already know, I'm sure, both Morarji Desai and his replacement have been ineffective as PMs. Now, Krishna claims Indira is on her way back. I don't recall who said the will to power is strong, but with her it fits like the proverbial glove. Please tell Uncle Ram to be careful. Whether the real threat is Indira or her son, Sanjay, is unimportant. Uncle Ram was the one who got away, remember, and they may be inclined to repeat with another Emergency if reinstated and seek revenge on him for getting off scot free last time.

If you ask me, Indira is the one who has managed to do that most of all. Her acts during the Emergency fill me with disgust and shame for my own sex. I realize that women are new at this game of leadership but I expect more, somehow, since they have had time enough to learn from the stupidity and inhumanity of the countless male dictators of history.

Well, now, I'm being a Soapbox Santha, aren't I? But please, I implore both of you, Daddy, Uncle Ram, be very careful.

I love you both so very much.

Santha

She folded the letter pages, placed them in an envelope and sealed it. Then Santha left the writing desk again and paused before the full-length mirror resting on its pivots in the corner beside her bed. Today her clothing was an East-West mix, with an *angya kurti*, a combination of a pinkish-roseate blouse and a tortoiseshell waistcoat, while her matching roseate ankle-length skirt was totally American. She wore sandals, imitation Oriental in design but made in southern California.

Santha wondered whether she should wear her multicoloured *bangri*. But she had worn the glass necklace so many times lately that she immediately dismissed the idea, concluding that her zircon earrings and the two bracelets on her right wrist were enough decoration.

It was still difficult to break free from her deceased mother Kamala's influence. Recently, her father had explained why Kamala had insisted so strongly that Santha dress as Western as possible. Kamala had been concerned lest Santha be ill treated in the States, as Anglo-Indians were in India. The derogatory Indian names *kutcha butcha* (half-baked bread) or *teen pao* (three-quarters) might have an American equivalent.

The Anglo-Indians in turn developed their own snobbery. Especially towards 'pure' Indians. The women wore Western dresses and only one or two bangles. They cut their hair short, too, but in regard to Santha, Kamala overlooked that custom. The natural beauty of Santha's hair was rare indeed, and her mother couldn't help but respect that. Some things were just too inherently sacrosanct to be tampered with.

33

Santha kept her opinion to herself. Stephen Wrench might not have appreciated her comments about Kamala's naïveté. The truth was that neither Western clothing nor coiffure nor paucity of jewellery could hide the fact that Santha's skin colour fringed on duskiness. The ancient Dravidians had left their seal on her, WASPy American father notwithstanding.

That alone was sufficient to engender prejudice here.

Santha Wrench laughed softly. Taking a brush from her dresser, she ran it through her shoulder-length hair. It fanned, billowed out, a blue-black mesh. Static crackled with each stroke. Staring at her reflection, Santha admitted she loved her darkness. Her complexion seemed to trap her white side just beneath the surface of her skin. It was like a glow throbbing from within the dusky patina, while her hair, eyes, lashes accentuated her moods. When Santha laughed, their blackness cast a dancing shadow across her features; when she brooded or felt sorrow, the blackness hung, still and deep, almost unfathomable.

She stopped brushing, reinspected herself. Pleased at what she saw, Santha Wrench replaced the brush on the dresser and left the room.

The east window to the corridor and stairwell was a blazing lozenge. The newel post looked so filled with sunlight fire she nearly hesitated to touch it. She passed through the blinding light, a silhouette for an instant, and descended the stairs.

Voices in the dining room, muffled by the stairwell wall, carried enough volume and rapid staccato for her to sense that George and Annette Kitteridge were arguing. It's about me, I bet, Santha thought, and suppressed a giggle.

The parlour was cool, a soothing place with lowered shades and the thick grey bulk of cabinets with their extensive shell collection. Santha passed through to the dining-room door and opened it.

George was standing, his back blocking Annette from Santha's view. His shoulders were hunched, and they jerked as he spoke. He was agitated, all right.

'. . . damn unfair, Annette,' he was saying. 'I've never restricted her. Ever.'

'From what?' Santha asked in a mock-serious tone.

George turned and Santha's eyes darted to Annette Kitteridge, seated before her finished breakfast, her mouth line curled at its ends in bemusement. Then Santha heard George's appeal: 'I've never stopped you from doing things, have I?'

Santha raised her hand and tweaked his beard. 'So true, love. But from what?'

'From flying, dear.' Annette's patrician face became sober. 'I think George is worried about whether you're ready for such stress.'

'What stress?' Santha sat before the sliced grapefruit that was already prepared for her. She reached for the spoon jutting from the sugar bowl. 'Flying has just the opposite effect on me. I find it very relaxing. And besides, I'm not one of your patients, George.' Oops, Santha told herself – one shouldn't walk into a debate about oneself. One easily loses control then. Now you're irritated, you stupid girl. No way to begin a beautiful morning.

'Annette, why have you done this to me?' George accused. 'Santha will believe I'm intent on grounding her. She'll chew me up every time a plane flies by!'

'Well, it's not that bad.'

'You don't know Santha.'

'Am I really that difficult? A remark like that really has me piqued.'

'See what I mean? She's on the defensive . . .'

'Like hell I am.' Santha nearly spilled the sugar. 'But what *about* my plans to fly, George?'

She already knew the answer. George Buchan, her lover, was also a psychiatrist, and he was concerned about her current mental condition. As to whether she was fit enough mentally to fly planes, he had good reason to be concerned, she admitted. About three years ago, Santha had undergone severe mental trauma. The reasons were something she could barely speak about still. Santha had recovered, but four months ago, a near-paralysing terror began to grip her whenever she was alone in her flat in Boston. At George's suggestion, she had moved in with Annette.

George's rationale behind the idea was clear: Dr Annette Kitteridge was another psychiatrist. The two women had met a year earlier and, despite a wide difference in age, had become close friends. For one thing, Annette never tried to 'psych her out', as Santha put it, since Santha wasn't a patient. Her age placed Annette in the role of surrogate mother, however. Both women were aware of it. Annette, who had no children of her own, was delighted to have a 'daughter'. The fifty-three-year-old widow badly needed someone to dote upon.

Yes, Santha couldn't blame George, since what had happened to her had been such a terrible thing, such an awesome and maddening adventure that she could recall only some of it. The 'events' that she didn't fully remember, like that nightmare in the house on Gray Park East in Cambridge, worried her. What exactly had happened to her there? What?

Pulling from her reverie, Santha bit into the grapefruit. The tangy flavour brought her back to the sensate world.

'I made an agreement with Santha,' Annette explained, 'that I wouldn't play doctor with her. It's so easy for you and me, George, to fall into the trap of analysing our friends and loved ones. It's one of the hazards of our job. Now, I'm sure Santha knows that we discuss her when she's not around, but I don't want her to feel uncomfortable about it. And let me say I resent your attitude about her wellbeing as regards flying. She was euphoric the other day when I took her up. As a pilot myself, I understand that euphoria.'

Santha suddenly wished it would end. *George knows everything*, Santha thought, *or enough so that it's not mental illness in me he's concerned about. It's possession, something taking over that's not scientifically plausible. He's unsure it's really over, isn't he?*

She had never told Annette about it. George, however, had described the Thug cult thing to Annette and told her how Thugs had captured Santha. But he had stopped at the other part, the business that wasn't supposed to be real. How could he have told Annette about that?

So no one was to blame, neither George nor Annette. They were each concerned about different things. Santha said, 'Please, both of you, this is unimportant. I don't feel upset in the least. Let's not spoil this delightful day.'

Later, as George drove Santha to Boston, he said, 'Who does she think she is, protecting you from me that way!'

Santha smiled. 'I know. A fine way for a psychiatrist to act. So human, so nonprofessional. Oh, understand, George, flying was something meaningful she wanted to share with me. But you questioned her right to do so by worrying about my fitness. It was as if you accused her of not having thought that out beforehand.'

'It's not been that long since your feelings of pending . . . well . . . evil.'

'But even they weren't as bad as two years ago. At least, I wasn't mentally transported to another place.' She

37

shivered. Then she clung to his arm and tried to smile. '*Kesari*, the flying seems good – expansive. You're just afraid I'll demand you come up with me.'

He grinned. 'Maybe so.'

And she released him, gave him a playful sock on the shoulder.

Finally, George turned off the Massachusetts Turnpike on to the Copley Square exit. Santha's eyes were closed; she concentrated on her feelings. Beacon Hill was where the trouble had begun, and now they were returning there. Every Saturday, like today, she came to the Hill to check up on her father's apartment and her own. After that, they sometimes went to Otis Place, where George lived.

To make love.

Santha watched his profile. His bearded jaw looked tense, the mouth was pursed, with the lower lip slack, as if weighted down by one too many burdens. It belied all that old, rawboned New England Yankee stock that made him so tenacious. Her *kesari*, her lion, never surrendered to Fate, she had discovered during her earlier ordeal. George had stayed with her, fought for her against what caused the strongest of men to pale. His education at Harvard hadn't taught him how to be so unswerving in the face of such terror, Santha knew. The quality was deeply rooted in him, and that made him a real find in this age of noncommitment.

They found a parking space near Charles Street Circle and walked along Storrow Drive, still silent. The passing traffic whished by; sometimes the noise was strident – a horn, a dog barking from the Esplanade, a low-flying 737 heading for Logan Airport. When they reached Pinckney Street, she checked her father's mail as they entered the large, four-storey building with its wind-stained awning. In the lobby, on a small table, were the newspapers and magazines delivered during the week. Santha quickly sorted out the ones addressed to Stephen Wrench.

They then climbed to the next floor, the stairs winding around the lift with its criss-cross bars that Santha always thought of as a cage.

The flat was at the end of a short hall. Extracting her father's key from her bag, she unlocked the door. They went past a bathroom and along a narrow corridor, and emerged into a massive living room complete with floor-to-ceiling bookshelves, a fireplace, and windows facing the Drive and the Esplanade. Everything, the desk in the corner, the television, the sofa and coffee table, and the armchair next to one of the windows, looked dust-free. Santha went to the kitchen, off the corridor on the left. That too was spotless. She then checked the bedrooms and a small 'retreat' room with a sewing machine and a console with a combination radio and record-player. It was all acceptable. The rugs were vacuumed, the curtains clean. Her father's cleaning woman did her work well.

Santha returned to the living room, sat on the sofa and faced the weeks of mail on the coffee table. A lifetime ago, it seemed now, she had lived here with her parents. She missed the simplicity of that time, when life was a crystal with many-faceted meanings to be explored. It held no threat then that the foundation could suddenly give way and one could fall into another reality, a place decreed, predestined by Something without light and hope.

Her eyes centred on the desk photograph of her on her twenty-first birthday, standing before the Esplanade's Hatch Shell with Kamala and Stephen Wrench. Their very small family, close, secure. And now there were two.

'Daddy!' she whispered with a start.

George, who was poring over the latest *New Yorker*, looked up.

'I just miss Daddy,' she told him. 'For a second I felt I might . . . lose him. Before he returned. It would be devastating if he never came back.'

When he left he was in good health, she reminded herself. And he's safe enough with Uncle Ram.

'I don't exactly know what he's doing there,' she continued. 'He won't tell me, of course. His letters are little more than commentaries on conditions in India these days. I suspect there's more than that.' Santha stood. 'Let's leave here, George.'

He took her hand, pulled her close and kissed her. The kiss was neither long nor hard, but a soft thing that dissolved the melancholia she felt. 'Oh, *kesari*,' she said in his ear. 'Sometimes I'm so alone. Within me, I mean. And then you drive the feeling away.'

'You're not alone, whatever happens.' Then he added, 'I'm with you, remember?'

She nodded. Outside again, they went to the corner of Brimmer Street and headed along it towards the Boston Public Gardens. She had missed the Hill often during these past months, its quaint aura of a village within a city. Also, what were landmarks to her: here, a few town houses from the Pinckney residence, Admiral Byrd's widow lived; there, on the opposite side, before the Lime Street corner, was the home of the naval historian Samuel Eliot Morison.

Lime Street proved to be cool, almost balmy. Its narrowness brought the house shadows closer together. Pleasant shadows, they were a solace, a comfort; they seemed to hug her. Little wonder she couldn't bear to give up her little flat here, no matter what happened to her within its walls.

Santha unlocked her door. She darted to the windows and raised the blinds. In the light, her living room appeared strange. Usually it was a clutter of books, records or cassettes lying about on the floor, chairs, the mantelpiece. Nearly all of these things were at Annette's, however, and the place looked barren.

George, who had taken the mail from the outside box, handed it to her. There was little of interest, junk mail mostly. Santha quickly flipped through the pages of the latest *Smithsonian*. She then hurried through the rooms, eager to leave. Santha hungered for George's body, suddenly. She could barely wait.

In the bedroom, she paused momentarily, thinking perhaps they should make love now. There was only a mattress on her bed, and to love without sheets and at least a blanket to nestle under afterwards was too unromantic, in her view. Even her dresser top was free of the usual stuff. The room was almost drab. Except, of course, for the amusing columns of hand prints from ceiling to floorboard near the bedroom door.

Back in the living room, Santha chirped, 'Everything's fine. Let's embark, my love, to – '

She gasped. At George. Frozen in mid-stride, she gaped, her hands trembling.

'Santha!' Thinking she was about to fall, George placed a hand on her back for support.

'Shit!' she screamed. 'Not again! Shit! Shit!'

She pulled away, literally ran to the bedroom. She pointed at the wall. 'George, when I did that, I only made two columns of hands.'

He stared and went to the telephone. A second later he slammed it down. Of course, it had been disconnected while she was living in Wayland.

'We can use Mrs Tangusso's phone a few houses down,' she was saying. Her anger was like a pulse across the room. That's so much better than panic, he thought gratefully, and followed her out.

* * *

The two men who came were in plain clothes. George and Santha were surprised – they had expected the standard patrol car and uniformed officers.

'I'm Lieutenant Cavanaugh. This is Captain Condorelli,' said the man with sandy hair and eyelids that drooped slightly. He was the one who asked all the preliminary questions. Santha showed him the third column of hands that looked exactly like the others.

'I only made two columns,' she emphasized. 'I scraped off the wallpaper, stained my hands with a mixture of shoe polish and poster paint – brown – and created the two. It was a joke. A bit of rebellion, too, you might say. I knew it would upset my mother.'

'Could you clarify that?'

For a moment Santha eyed Captain Condorelli, wondering why someone as high-ranking as he should be present. He was a wiry man of average height with the dark hair and eyes of a Calabrian. His expression was soft, even whimsical. Like an Italian elf – if that was possible – about some mischief, she concluded.

'In India,' she continued, 'where I was born, peasant women plaster walls with cow dung. The process leaves hand prints like decorations. I created a facsimile of those prints on my wall as an "in" joke. My late mother didn't think it was at all funny, since her family had been above that by caste and education. She wanted me to clean off the wall. It embarrassed her, I think.'

'And there were only two columns? You're sure of that?'

'Absolutely.' Santha paused. Then, 'The thing that bothers me most is how close to my own work the third column is. The hands are about the same size as mine. They're feminine-looking hands, too. See for yourself. Someone broke in here and very painstakingly added column three to shock me, I feel.'

'Over the phone, miss, you said you had some idea of who it was.'

'Well, not the person, exactly. But I'm certain it was someone who is either Indian or a Westerner who has been there and knows what the hands mean.'

'It's a feeling you have, then.'

'Yes, a very strong feeling. *Someone has turned my little joke against me.*'

Captain Condorelli bent towards her from his perch on the arm of a living-room chair. His eyes were intense now. It was startling. 'Who? Why would they do that?'

'I don't know. But they've succeeded, if shaking me up is what they wanted. And I sense that's it.'

'Sense?'

'What else can I go by? I don't know anyone who would do this to me. At least, not recently.'

'But there was someone earlier? Someone who might have done this to you?'

George added, 'We both knew someone a few years ago whose sense of humour was extremely bizarre. He was expert at manipulating people through their fears. He – '

Condorelli nodded. 'Yes, Kurt Leinster.' He noticed their silence. 'I should explain. I'm the head of Intelligence for the Boston Police. We have you in our computer and when you phoned – '

'Computer?'

'Yes, Miss Wrench. Our Intelligence Division has kept a file on you and anyone else involved in the case of the Stranglers' cult years ago.'

'Am . . . am I suspect?'

'Not at all. But you were their prisoner for a while.'

'And you think they're behind this?' From George.

'We don't know. But this kind of thing seems to fit our

psychological profile of Kurt Leinster. And he did disappear under mysterious circumstances.'

'But . . .' Santha was having difficulty breathing. She closed her eyes and waited. Finally, 'But the cult, these Deceivers – Thugs – were like one all-encompassing mind. Any one of them could have done it.'

'Why not Leinster?'

'No, that's impossible.'

'Why?'

The statement was shouted, vehemently: 'Because it mustn't be, that's why!'

'I didn't mean to upset you. If it's any consolation, your father came to me before he left for India. He asked me to use my resources to help you, if necessary. Of course he needn't have asked. We don't want the cult to rise again, either. Last time, an entire church congregation was murdered, as you know.'

The silence returned. As Santha stared at him, the whimsical look returned. 'We'll have our fingerprint people go over this place. But I doubt we'll be lucky.'

She wet her lips, then asked, 'Did Daddy say . . . that he thought Kurt was still alive?'

'He admitted that he didn't know. I've known Steven Wrench for at least seven years, and I've never seen him so worked up about a man. It impressed me. As usual, though, Leinster is a mystery. There seems to be a murky area, something that is always left unspoken about him. Can you clarify that, Miss Wrench?'

He watched while she hesitated. Santha concentrated on a ball of fluff near her music centre, and thought, I should get Daddy's cleaning lady to come here this week.

Then: How can I lie to this man? He'll know it's a lie, for certain. But again, how can I possibly tell him the truth about Kurt? He wouldn't believe me.

Santha tried, however. 'He wasn't like other people, you see.'

He waited. He urged, after a while, 'How was he different?'

Santha inhaled deeply, exhaled. She wished George would come to her aid. That he would explain, instead. Damn you, George . . .

Softly, so low that even she could barely hear herself, 'Kurt Leinster was . . . in touch with the supernatural.'

4

Beacon Hill, Boston

'Somehow I don't feel any safer. Even with Police Intelligence concerned about me,' Santha Wrench admitted.

They were at George's flat now, at Otis Place. It, too, was on Beacon Hill, near both Lime Street and Pinckney Street. Santha thought of the town house as being 'tucked into' the small court. It always made her feel hidden and protected. It was only illusion, she knew, and that saddened her the more.

There was no hideaway, no place to run from the cult of Thuggee and Kurt Leinster.

Santha had told that to Captain Condorelli. She had also stressed that she didn't know whether Kurt Leinster was still alive, and if he were, then the terror hadn't ended.

Because Kurt was . . . And here Santha had watched the two detectives carefully. They had listened attentively and hadn't coughed in embarrassment or shared a 'knowing' look with each other. Not once.

Her statement that Kurt Leinster was a kind of dark mystic, spiritually linked with the dreaded goddess Kali, had caused no negative response, no scoffing or denials. Santha concluded that this fiddling with the hand patterns was very similar to Kurt's brutal, sardonic humour. He played with people's minds and souls in much the same way.

There had been no more questions afterwards. Captain Condorelli had given her a card with his name and phone number, saying, 'Please call me immediately if anything else like this happens.' Then the officers left.

She hadn't even asked them whether they believed her, nor had they revealed anything that proved they did. Now she asked the question, 'Were they just being nice to me?'

'I don't think so,' George replied. 'I think they listened with an open mind. I don't believe they wanted to make a decision about the truth of it. You can't blame them. They deal with facts. But, nevertheless, I don't think they thought of you as lunatic fringe, either, Santha.'

She sipped the lemonade he had brought her from the kitchen. And . . .

'Could it be Kurt?'

'I don't know, darling. I can't tell any more than anyone else can.'

'George, you were one of the last people to see Kurt that day . . .'

'Yes. I saw what I think I saw. But who knows for certain? He was before that godforsaken altar at Gray Park East. You were unconscious at his feet. There was fire, smoke everywhere . . .

'He had with him the scroll that Hanuman said was so important, and then those huge ebony arms, massive, gigantic, seemed to come down from the ceiling to pick him up. Then more smoke – darker, billowing – and he was gone.'

George's eyes had widened, as if he were witnessing it all again; his voice had become a whisper. His silence was like a hush that punctuated the incredible account.

'I still can't believe what I saw,' he added at last.

Every line in George's face was taut. He had undergone a series of events that very few men had experienced, and now the idea that the evil might occur again strained his temperament. His imagination lay in his hobby, painting, and it had never left that part of his nature, transferred itself to everyday reality.

The stuff of dreams, pleasurable or nightmarish, was in the unconscious, the psychiatrist that he was told him. No doubt something in him still insisted that what he had seen at the altar of Kali was delusion.

The living room, with its fine old furniture, reflected his wealthy and prosaic New England background. Generations of Buchans before him had faced reality without idols and superstition but, rather, with all the Unitarian concentration on the rational. The door to the right led to the office where he helped patients challenge anything which weakened that reality. The Age of Enlightenment and science had long proven there were no demons or angels. There was, particularly, no dark goddess that involved herself in the affairs of men.

Unlike Santha, George had no heritage, no roots that included such fantasy.

Santha suddenly wanted his world more than anything. Now, at this moment, what George represented was freedom from the arcane, from an unjust and amorphous creation that held no natural law or rational view. George Buchan was something solid and real to cling to. And she did.

Santha rose and crossed the room to him. She took his wrists, pulled him closer and kissed him. She didn't utter a word, but her look, her body spoke clearly: *Make love to me. Please don't wait*.

The plea was of compelling intensity. George couldn't have refused if he had wanted to. The kiss summoned all his manhood before he realized it. He was hard immediately, from her hot breath, from the meshing of her body with his just by contact. But then, the hunger must have been there in both of them, an almost pitiable hunger.

How much they had needed each other was suddenly

so clear at each touch. Santha's desire verged on the frantic, except somehow she managed to control it enough that her caresses were smooth and soft.

Her fingers deftly unbuttoned his shirt while her lips followed with a series of kisses down his chest to his navel. She dropped to her knees while George unbuckled his trousers. When they fell, Santha gripped the top of his underwear and pulled. Now the erection was exposed, the tip flush with her mouth. Santha Wrench forgot the comfort she had desired from him and lost herself instead in just giving. Whenever he tried to respond by making love in some way, she held him back and continued rapturously mouthing his penis. Again and again, Santha ran her lips and tongue over his stem. George breathed heavily and cried out. Santha persisted, feeling his foreskin against her tongue as she moved her head up and down. When he shouted he was about to come, she was ready. Digging her nails into his buttocks, she braced herself while he convulsed and emptied himself into her. Moaning loudly at the liquid fire that coursed through her, Santha was overwhelmed with her own release.

Finished, she remained at his groin for a while, running her fingers over his testicles and backside. 'Oh, *kesari*,' she murmured, 'I never tire of this and you.'

'Then marry me,' he said.

Santha sat back on her haunches. 'Soon.'

'You've been promising that for two years,' he complained, lifting her up. He nibbled at her ear.

'When Daddy comes back,' she assured him. 'Right away when he returns. You'll see.'

Santha returned to her chair. There were reasons why she hadn't married George, and she had explained them to him more than once. She must be certain first that she was truly free of . . . Well, Kurt Leinster must certainly be dead. These many months had been without a sign.

She remembered the pattern of hand imprints again. Standing, she said aloud, 'It can't be Kurt. I won't believe it.' Santha paced. 'If only Daddy and Uncle Ram were here. They'd know what to do.'

George shook his head, his mind still preoccupied with their lovemaking.

'I'm sorry, sweet,' Santha said, noticing. She went to him and stroked his beard. 'I don't mean to be so unromantic. I . . .'

He smiled. 'The change of mood was too fast. That was beautiful, Santha.' Then, 'What about Swami Hanuman?'

'Huh?'

'The Swami. He would know if Leinster is alive. He has a way of knowing those things.'

'Yes,' she agreed, with a sigh of relief. 'He would, wouldn't he?'

'That's right.' George was on his feet, too, tucking his shirt in. 'We'll go now, Santha. The sooner we settle this . . .' He didn't finish and headed for the door.

The sun winked out behind a cloud trail as they left Beacon Hill; its quaint and diversified rooftops were draped in shadow. The many chimneys, vanes and ventilators looked murky to Santha when she gazed back, a haze of randomly placed silhouettes. The Porsche crossed Longfellow Bridge with its 'pepper and salt shaker' minitowers, then into Kendall Square, and finally slanted off along Hampshire Street. They were by-passing Harvard Square, on their way to North Cambridge.

Without being conspicuous, Santha studied George's profile. She was trying to probe his private thoughts about having to turn to Hanuman, the Swami, for help again and felt guilty. Oh, give George his due, you silly girl, she chided herself. George no longer considers this to be Indian mumbo-jumbo. He was with the Swami when they rescued her that day. He knows, goddammit; George knows you were never insane.

It's you, she accused, who don't have enough faith in people like George. You should have told Annette Kitteridge the whole story long ago, for example.

His eyes turned to her for a second, and she smiled. Her mind wasn't so free, though. That guilt, that unnecessary burden of guilt, still lingered.

Swami Hanuman had explained it to her once, why it had happened to her and how she hadn't been responsible. The truth was she had no extreme defect of character that made her more vulnerable to supernatural influences, he told her. Kurt Leinster, supreme guru and high priest of modern Thuggee, controlled by the force of Kali, had picked her because she was psychically receptive to their invisible manipulations and physically beautiful. It was what they needed in a human vessel on Earth; those were the characteristics which inspired that crazed and bloodthirsty sect.

They had almost succeeded, too. They had nearly consumed her, taken the identity that was Santha Wrench and replaced it with . . . She couldn't remember what, exactly, thank heavens.

They were moving through the North Cambridge side streets toward Massachusetts Avenue. When they parked near the courtyard with its familiar triptych of doors where Hanuman and his disciples lived, George said, 'This doesn't look good.'

Ahead there was a group of people standing before the stone steps and door on the left. A huge van was parked before the building, and two men emerged from its back with a pane of glass. George and Santha climbed out of the Porsche, and, while George paid the meter, she went ahead.

In the midst of the group bobbed the long straight hair

of Nirmal Kapur, Hanuman's favourite *chela* and famous rock star. Next to him Santha recognized Molly Doyle, another long-time disciple. The rest were strangers. Everyone was talking at once, and only Nirmal stopped when she neared. He looked at her without surprise. Santha worked her way around broken glass scattered about the courtyard.

'You expected us,' she said.

'No.' Nirmal nodded at George as he approached. 'But, seeing you two now, I can't help thinking I should've. Considering . . .' His hands gestured at the broken windows on every floor of the building. 'Man, it was difficult explaining this to the police. They just left.'

'They think it was a bomb,' Molly Doyle cut in. 'Fucking dummies. I explained that it was a negative spirit, a mystical entity pissed off 'cause it was trapped in the Master's house.'

'And they couldn't hack it. Thought it was bullshit,' added Nirmal.

'Fucking dummies,' Molly Doyle repeated.

Bits of glass crunched beneath Santha's sandals as she climbed the steps.

'Something wild has been happening to you, too,' Nirmal stated rather than asked. 'It figures, from what the Swami said a while ago.'

She stopped. 'What was that?'

Nirmal imitated Hanuman: he squinched his nose and added a lilt to his English. 'The Mother has not forgotten us. All these months and we suddenly experience her rage.'

Santha hugged her arms. She felt cold. She turned quickly and went through the open door.

The parlour, unkempt as usual, looked the worse because of the detritus from the windows. The glaziers were replacing the glass while a woman named Adelaide swept around them. Santha noticed that the semi-naked Pucks attached to an old clock had been chipped by a fall from the mantelpiece. She particularly liked the Pucks. They were so out of place in the Swami's home. A photograph in a frame was tilted on the wall. Santha recognized the lean body of Hanuman's late guru, Vishnarma, standing before a village hovel somewhere in Madhya Pradesh, she had been told by Nirmal.

He was continuing his story as they left the parlour and went down a hall. 'I was walking past the door to Bapu's meditation room about eleven-thirty when I heard a noise like a cross between thunder and a loud tearing of fabric . . . except they weren't separate. They were in sync, you dig? And then, trailing it, came a great shout echoing from some vast tunnel or chamber – and the wind.

'I mean something like a cyclone. The two big doors flew open, then, with a slam and broke free of their hinges. I was hurled back against the wall, and this . . . thing whished by, invisible but full of vibration and cold, so that even though you couldn't see it, you felt its vibration.'

'It made my teeth hurt.' Molly was suddenly there again. She cupped her breasts, jutting from her sweat-shirt. 'And these, too. Like someone thwapped 'em with a two-by-four.'

'Man, I lost my breath. Like Molly, I was in pain, too. I could see inside Bapu's room, though. He was still in meditation and totally unruffled. But I wasn't so lucky. I was flat against the wall with all that pressure on me and cold – there was frost in my breath and the tip of my nose.

'Then I saw where it was coming from. On the wall behind Bapu was a hole, a black funnel that went in, in and on endlessly, it seemed. Well, what had come out had come from there.'

They had stopped before a doorway. Santha and

George stared at the warped wooden doors on the floor. Their hinges were torn free, scattered here and there. George picked up a piece. The metal had been cut clean through, separated from the rest of the hinge. Cold lingered on the object's surface, and it pained his fingers. George dropped it.

They entered the room. Large, it was empty of both furniture and people. The ceiling of the room was missing. Ropes dangled from the ceiling of the floor above, their narrow shadows running along the succession of windows on the south side. Rumour had it that the Swami sometimes climbed those ropes and meditated up there. He liked heights.

'That was where the fissure was.' Nirmal pointed.

They all stared at the wall. There was no sign of a rent now or a deep funnel.

'Bapu says that the gap wasn't in the wall, anyway. It was a hole in space.' Nirmal's long, straight hair shook with his head. 'Think of it – what a scene! A fucking hole in space!' Although born in India, he had long since adopted American street slang. 'Let's go find Bapu.'

Swami Hanuman was in the kitchen. He wasn't wearing one of his colourful turbans. His shaven skull reflected the overhead fluorescent; it made the head look shrunken on an already diminutive body. Santha thought of a child with wizened features.

He was seated at a table, a half-filled teacup before him. His eyes were closed. Santha whispered to Nirmal that he was asleep and maybe he shouldn't be disturbed.

'Bapu,' Nirmal said in an ordinary tone. The eyes opened. Nirmal looked at Santha as if to say *See!*

'The Mother has not forgotten us. She has gathered nearly all of us here,' Hanuman said.

They understood him. Only Stephen Wrench and Rama

Shastri were missing from the original group that had struggled against Kunkali, the Maneater, in the past. Molly Doyle had left them earlier to help Adelaide with the housekeeping. Santha was the only woman present now.

'But first,' Hanuman announced, 'we shall have more tea and our midday meal.'

Santha sighed; she hadn't realized how hungry she was. It overcame her, a wave of nausea and fatigue, and she collapsed into a chair.

When her head cleared, George was pressing a glass of orange juice to her lips. 'Quick nourishment,' he told her.

Other *chelas* whom Santha didn't recognize were placing salad and fruit bowls on the table. George was explaining why they had come, and she felt grateful he was taking over. Everything, even talking, had become extremely taxing.

The *chelas* had left. Now there was no reason to be secretive, and Hanuman confronted her fears directly.

'You seek to know if it has started again. I can't say with certainty that it has or hasn't. But this I can tell you: Kunkali, the dreadful Mother, had prepared a trap for me.'

Hanuman told them of what had happened during his meditation that morning.

'This time my astral body had a task to do, and I arrived at a place, a plane of Creation, where I was to meet my dear Master, Vishnarma. The colour of the landscape was ochre – hills, valleys, mountains, flowers, all the same monotonous hue, with shadows shifting and blending across the faces of the high reaches. There was one particular cliff edge, very straight, high and smooth, you understand. The shadows were especially magnified here, and they passed by and into each other, walking people, some dancing, and now and then an animal, usually large, pachyderms, I believe they were.

'I attempted to detach myself from the surroundings. The sameness of everything was disquieting, and I sensed danger in it. As if this world was a huge maw that could swallow me up if I weren't careful. A strange sensation, an inexplicable one.

'I searched for my Master. That he was waiting for me I assumed, since it was always so whenever I found myself on one of the infinite astral planes that is the stuff of Eternity. I constantly imagine them to be like the set of a drama, the theatrical stages of the gods, whose curtains or veils are lifted by cords – or, better still, gossamer threads. Creation is filled with delicate strong things, gossamer with power and force beyond our limited understanding. All is grace in motion, but, even more important, all is grace in stasis. Inertia is dynamic there. That is the sacred paradox.

'Now I wandered aimlessly, never so much so before in my meditations. As in a dream-state, I was moving in circles, it seemed, rediscovering the same troublesome landscape again and again . . .

'When my Master's voice spoke into my consciousness, a whisper in my inner ear: "Say these three prayers aloud until there is no need:

> Vishnu, who has incarnated as Kurma the
>   Tortoise, help me.
> Vishnu, Parasurama, Rama with the Axe, help
>   me.
> Vishnu, Prince of the Ayoda, help me."

'I proceeded to do this immediately. Over and over again I repeated the prayers, until the air became blurred and liquefied, and my next step brought me to an elevation of greensward with a blue-white sky above, and on the apex of the rise was a towering black wall. I recognized it immediately as the fortification before the garden of Kunkali, the Sleeper, the astral Dreamer, that lies reclining in her Bower of Skulls. I had been here before, knew this place well. Here I had once caused a drunkenness to overtake her, with the help of my Master.

'Who was waiting, as he had promised, surrounded by a bright blue nimbus, as is fitting for such a holy servant of Lord Vishnu. I sensed he was about to tell me that I must scale the wall again and enter that foul garden, but my purpose in doing so was as yet unclear.

'I never learned what it was. Indeed, it was at that moment that the Mother made her move, but I did surmise that my master Vishnarma felt it urgent to summon me there and that I was to learn or rather to acquire information in some way concerning her new aims, her new machinations as regards perhaps Thuggee again, the sacred Rishi scrolls . . . and the missing Huzoor.

'But the black wall, that incredibly dense and impenetrable thing, dissolved and became a gigantic funnel with the outside edges pursing like lips and inhaling the very atmosphere, the entire environment into itself.

'That sensation of being swallowed up was becoming real, suddenly. I was lifted off my feet and hurtled back into the funnel's mouth, back and back, deeper and deeper into it.

'My Master was gone, his protective blue nimbus gone with him, and I fell into that endless well of blackness. But as fear rose within me, so did the logic of repeating again my three prayers. I spoke – no, I bellowed – them against the roar of that force and the smothering rage which I knew sprang from Kunkali herself. I bellowed, shouted and shrieked them until my body reversed its momentum, and, after a long, long time of dizzying speed in which my breath seemed to stop, I hurtled free. Like a missile shot from a cannon, I flew into that blue sky I mentioned earlier and finally awoke from my trance.

'Well, needless to say, part of Kunkali followed me, and, finding itself trapped by the blessings of Lord Vishnu, which are everywhere here, in the corridors and rooms, it fled in its agony and wrath, breaking the windows and dissolving itself in the world outside.' Hanuman paused. 'That she was ready for me, prepared for any assault I might make against her, is clear. And she took the offensive. She struck before I could speak with Vishnarma. This worries me . . .'

Santha let George continue. 'Kali has already got something up her sleeve. She's set something in motion.' He said the words as though they were distasteful things, illogical facts that should not be.

'I cannot say for certain. But that would appear to be the proper conclusion.'

Santha Wrench reached out, her fingers grasping Hanuman's wrists gently. 'And what was done in my apartment connects, doesn't it?'

Hanuman shrugged.

Santha needed to know more. 'And Kurt? Kurt Leinster. Is he dead, Bapu? Is he?'

'You are demanding that I tell you what I do not know, my child.'

'Oh, please, Bapu . . . What does your wisdom say about these matters?'

Hanuman's eyes rose until she thought they had disappeared and were replaced by yellow-white discs reflecting the fluorescent.

'If he is not dead, then he was taken by the Mother to a place no human soul should know.'

After a silence, 'What place? Please tell me!'

'Where Kali rests and where souls are forged, reshaped

58

like malleable things. No soul could dwell there without such change.'

'Is he transformed? Is he a monster now? An unearthly creature . . . a demon?'

The eyes returned, became riveted to Santha's; for a moment, she thought she would faint.

'If he lives, he is no longer . . . just a man.'

'If he's alive, then he's like her, isn't he? He's a creature of hers, I mean. More powerful than he was before, more deadly . . .' She couldn't finish. Santha covered her face with her hands and shivered.

George placed his arm around her. He looked at Hanuman, then Nirmal, appealingly. The guru and his *chela* remained silent, however.

The fluorescent sputtered and flicked on a few times, flickering light, then darkness, light, then darkness . . .

5

India, the Bhabor

It is as I have believed, Ajit Majumdar thought. I have vision. I have great wisdom. I am to be the Huzoor.

The freight car stopped for a breath's time, then jolted and stabilized. He sat with his back flush to the pile of *chudders*, moving side by side with the brief halts and starts. The ride was a slow one; the train wheezed, coughed, stumbled, and somehow fought on and moved again. Its mechanical will was like that of a very old traveller who had lost interest in what he was doing and desired just to stop and rest.

Ajit was elated, however. Yes, all was so predestined now. He was the chosen one.

The Huzoor, the One Lord of Thuggee.

Who could doubt it? Mother Kali had appeared to him. True, he had seen only her hands and eyes, but what other man had been so blessed? She had guided, saved him from Rama Shastri and the police. *He was that important*. The supreme head of Thuggee – imagine that!

And how well she had directed him. Even to a killing. Once he had reached the boatman on the opposite bank, all sign of her had disappeared. However, later, when the boatman's job was done, he had had the presence of Kali in his own hands, in the cold tricklings of thought within his mind. *Kill*, the command had come, and his mottled hands had swelled and throbbed and shaken until he gripped the *rumel* and thrust the loop around the other's neck. Then did he have his first and only victim that night.

I am not alone, Ajit told himself. I think with her thoughts, see with her eyes. Which was how he had trekked to the rock Rama Shastri had seen through his binoculars. When the train passed, its speed on the gradient was a bare eight miles per hour. Majumdar ran along its side and jumped into the open freight car.

Looking around, he saw rows of *chudders* piled to the ceiling, except for two rows in one corner, which were rugs. Majumdar chose an aisle between the cloth piles that was near the slight breeze from the opened door.

The train crawled along and Ajit dozed. After an hour or two – there was no way of telling – he was awakened by a voice speaking in Bengali. Ajit rose, and stared at the corner with the rugs.

A small man in a very grimy *kurta* was saying, 'Thou hast made me endless, such is thy pleasure. This frail vessel thou emptiest again and again, and fillest it ever with fresh life.' Then he saw Ajit and bowed so low his turban was askew when he raised his head again. This time his words were in Hindi: 'Forgive me if I disturbed your slumber, fellow traveller. I am G. Natarajan, nephew to S. Mukerji, who owns everything you see in this car. I am not a thief, as I trust you are not. I but enjoy travelling in this fashion.'

Ajit tried to hide his hands. They were throbbing so much that they were painful.

'You heard me quote the opening lines from Tagore's *Gitanjali*. I too had been asleep. You see, I always say those words when I awake. Some choose to pray – I quote the great Tagore.'

Ajit remained silent. He wished the time to wield the *rumel* would be soon. Very soon. This strange man spoke much too much. Surely, he had been a monkey in his last incarnation. Surely . . . Kali Mother, he was beginning again!

'How shall I address you? You don't reply, O man of no expression. There, that is a name. It must serve, since even if you be an idiot, you are endless, as I am endless . . .'

Kali Mother, be it not so, prayed Ajit.

'Are you bound for Hardwar or Rishikesh? Are you a holy man, perhaps, a saint?' G. Natarajan turned his back. Ajit's pulsating hands rose. *Kill*. Then the man faced him again. Ajit grimaced, in agony to lower the *rumel*.

'Fear not if you are only from the sweeper caste. The poet says next: "This little flute of a reed thou hast carried over hills and dales, and hast breathed through it melodies eternally new."'

The man examined Ajit's face. 'I see you don't understand Bengali.' He went to the open door, back turned. The fingers, misshapen, enlarged from the pulse and throbbing, gripped the silken scarf . . .

Then again this chattering monkey turned.

Kill! – like stabbing icicles.

Kill! Kill! – in Ajit's brain.

G. Natarajan turned the final time. His slight body fought for balance as the train jolted. His last sentence began, 'I see that we are brothers . . .' And the *rumel* descended.

Limestone and then more limestone. As far as Ajit Majumdar could see. And small sun-flashing patches scattered randomly or a snaking narrow line – water, more like a memory of the Ganga than the river itself. This and scorching heat, despite the lateness of the afternoon. Boulders of every size cluttered the empty bank which joined the Garhwal Hills. Some of them had rolled close to the dry river bottom during the monsoon floods. Heat and thirst, a vast barren place of baked earth and oppressive silence.

Only demons could thrive here.

No life here like the riparian world he had left behind. No *sadhus* meditating in niches in the banks, or little boys fishing. The islands too were much higher, barely a foot of water surrounded them. Wooded with shisham trees, their tufted snake-like branches drooped with bleached grasses tossed there in the rainy season.

An eerie view, it spread out before him, broken only by the jungle in the hills.

Why had Kali Ma told him to leave the train? he asked. Why couldn't he have left it when it arrived at Hardwar? There was shelter from the sun, and food and drink, at Hardwar; here there was only the potential for death.

This awesome wasteland, what could it possibly do for him? Nothing good, that was certain.

After killing G. Natarajan, Ajit had taken some of his *goor* sugar and resumed his sleep.

When he awoke, Ajit noted that the sun had begun its western arc. He watched through the chinks in the freight car walls. The car was intolerably hot; sweat kept dripping from his brows and blurring his vision. Although the train was moving much faster now – at least forty miles per hour – and he went to the open door and faced the fanning breeze, it wasn't enough.

He had nearly tripped over Natarajan's body when he did this, and he had kicked it aside to get to the opening.

Then, staring at the dead man, he apologized for not burying him, as was the Thug custom. For an instant, he considered pushing the corpse out of the car, but of course he couldn't, since that wasn't at all proper. Finally, he decided to drag Natarajan to a corner behind the column of rugs. It would have to suffice; that was that.

About an hour later the train slowed again. They were

nearing the Bhabor, where the Ganga bed was exposed for miles. Like a bolt coursing through his ganglia, he was commanded, 'Go!' Ajit Majumdar jumped free immediately, and now here he was, weakened by the merciless sun, parched, very hungry . . .

Verging on collapse. Beyond doubt doomed. Why?

He prayed for night, then laughed bitterly. How foolish, since in this dreadful place the heat wouldn't leave the ground for many hours. His swollen lips could just barely utter his favourite mantra to Kali Ma. Why was she forsaking him, he asked again and again. Was this a test of his strength, of his faith, of his right to be Huzoor?

Ajit heard a sound from the bank and the jungle. Probably one of the wild animals rumoured to dwell there coming forth boldly from the bush, since hopefully night must fall soon. Why was he so concerned with night? You are an old fool, he chided, to think it will be easier to die at night than at day.

'At least I will quench this thirst!' he declared to himself, to the emptiness, to his goddess, if she was still with him, and fell prone to drink from a muddy trickle along the cracked face of the Ganga.

The taste was foul, however, and he spat most of the water out. He paused before lowering his head again. And paused longer, listening.

Ajit Majumdar heard, 'I greet you, wanderer, and offer you food, even purer water than Mother Ganga can provide.'

The Thug rose to his knees and covered his eyes from the sun while he searched for the source of the voice.

An emaciated man waving a long switch. Behind him were two bullocks attached to a strange high enclosed cart with curtains on its side.

Ajit stared suspiciously at the figure. Stories were told about the residents of the Garhwal area – that they were very unfriendly, even towards their closest neighbours. And here was one greeting him, a total stranger.

Nevertheless, the thought of food and drink urged him towards the cart. Ajit clambered up the rocks before the bank and finally stood facing the driver.

'I am called Raghubir. I am a maker of bullock carts from the wood of the shisham.'

Ajit spoke, gave his name. His eyes never left the strange structure that the animals were pulling. It was decorated in garish orange, yellow and green. The curtain was old, tattered in spots. Ajit saw that within the high box-like compartment a woman lay, stretched full length, her foot dangling over the edge of the cot. The foot was naked and large, the ankle covered with at least five circlets of beads.

Raghubir warned, 'Don't look too long lest she look back.' His voice was very low. 'Come up here where we can talk in safety.'

Safety? Ajit hesitated. Raghubir held up a goatskin of water. Ajit joined the driver on the seat of plane wood.

Raghubir flicked his switch at the dusty backs. The bullocks moved. 'Let our voices mix with this noise. I think she sleeps, but why chance it?' He gestured towards a small carved trough fitted in an area behind the seat. 'There is food here, for what it is.' Ajit searched back. It was mostly fruit, and he had to brush away the cluster of flies around it. He bit into a mango and chewed slowly.

'You must understand, Ajit Majumdar, I am beholden to you for joining me. I am in great need of a companion – in great need. This trek to Hardwar, none of it is of my volition. I must go, you see.' So *sotto voce* that the Thug had to read his lips: 'She demands it, the one behind us, that my poor beasts work so hard to freight her there.'

Another man who talked too much. But even though Ajit's fingers often neared his *rumel*, they never swelled.

He sensed that for the inexplicable plan of Kali, he must endure this. And the more pleasant side of it all was the ride and food and drink.

'She is called Mrinalini Pal. She is of my village, but not related – may the gods be forever worshipped for that blessing. She is the curse on our village. All fear her, all run from her stare. She has the evil eye, and such it has been since her birth. The story is, friend wanderer, that her parents sought to destroy her when she was a babe, so afraid were they of her gaze. But as they set about to drown her in the Ganga – right hereabouts during the monsoon – Mrinalini opened her eyes and they froze. It is no wonder both adults died of severe afflictions before the year ended. The father became blind and fell from a height one day. He should never have looked into those eyes . . .

'The mother, she was ravaged by a beast, a tiger who carried her in his mouth to her doom high in the Garhwal Hills. I can testify to that truth. I saw it, was a few feet away when it happened. There was nothing I could do, you understand. I was a small boy then.'

Ajit said, 'She is but a woman.'

'Ah, but Kali is female too, wanderer.'

'There is wisdom in that. But I have never feared a woman. Never.'

'She is more than a woman, perhaps.'

'Pfah!'

'Our village has tried placing black pots outside in the fields to stop the evil eye. This did no good. She was able to move about as she wished, and she even entered our homes at any hour she desired.'

Night was with them now, and Raghubir stopped the cart. 'Let us camp,' he urged, and in no time they had built a fire. The stirrings and cries of animals were everywhere in the jungle. Ajit kept turning to the brush behind him wonderingly.

'Tush, wanderer Majumdar; fear not the night creatures. Fear instead' – the other pointed at the curtains on the cart – 'her. That she might emerge. I fear her greatly, which is why I sought your friendship on this dreary journey.'

'Pfah!'

'There, you are at it again. Let me tell this tale, then, while we cook our flour and drink this tea from Darjeeling.' The bullock driver hunched forward, the firelight flickering at his emaciated face. 'Once a *sadhu* came to our village, a most holy man with the signs of Vishnu on his forehead. For many weeks he remained with us, fasting, meditating and turning his prayer wheel. Mrinalini did not approve, and she often sat before him in the lotus position, as he was, and glared at him. Then one day he told her that his Path and her Path were in opposition. She stood, and her terrible eyes spoke with her reply: "My spiritual Path is of Kali the Destroyer."'

'Kali?' Ajit repeated.

Raghubir nodded. 'That night there was much screeching and many cries of agony. A wind passed through the village and it spoke strange words with a rasping noise that made one shiver. The next morning the holy man was gone. Swallowed up, we believe, by the forces that Mrinalini unleashed upon him.'

Ajit was quiet. The other yawned, and announced, 'Now I shall sleep. Under the cart I will place myself. If she leaves her bed, then she can't stand above my exposed body. You should sleep there, too, wanderer.'

The Thug snarled his contempt. 'Never. It is not fitting that a man should fear a woman so!'

Raghubir saw immediately that Ajit was not to be

67

challenged. He nodded and scurried under the cart as he had said he would.

Now Ajit Majumdar, secure in the knowledge that he had seen the eyes of the goddess and endured, curled close to the fire and slept without worry.

Yet later, in the early morning hours, he was awakened by a low growl. The fire, he noted, was a small glowing ring, but the embers cast enough light that an approaching form stood out clearly before the cart. The bullocks, too, were restless, pawing the earth and snorting.

Ajit could barely breathe. Before him was one of those tigers Raghubir had spoken of, and the big cat was easing forward on his belly. At first it had intended, no doubt, to attack the cattle, but now, apparently concluding the man would try to prevent that, it chose to deal with him first.

Ajit's eyes searched desperately for a weapon, a thick branch, perhaps, that he could set alight. Yes, a torch would do it. But there was nothing in the clearing, not even a sizeable rock to throw.

He instinctively closed his eyes, expecting the cat's leap any minute. Then came the sound of feet thudding on earth, big heavy strides, the clamour of many anklets. Ajit looked again, gaped at long fingers gripping the hot coals. They were hurled at the tiger, which scrambled backwards from the shower of red-hot projectiles.

Ajit raised his head, awed at the sight – a towering woman in a sari the colour of flame. She was the tallest woman Ajit had ever seen, and also the most fearless. The tiger was holding his ground, fangs bared, his growl a steady protest.

The woman didn't stop moving. She went on without pause, her head bent towards the creature. She is staring at him, Ajit thought; her eyes are centred on his. He couldn't see her face, but he knew somehow that this was what she was doing. It had to be. She neither spoke nor gestured; she moved, hunched forward, nearer, nearer . . .

The beast spun suddenly and disappeared into the jungle.

The woman turned and walked up to Ajit. He saw her eyes for the first time. His breath caught again, and he was about to lower his own, since to face her was painful. However, he noticed Raghubir's head sticking out from under the cart. Ajit willed himself to keep looking. His temples throbbed, sweat drenched his scalp and neck. The tendons on his neck stretched from exertion.

Mrinalini Pal snickered and went back to her bed.

Gasping, Ajit managed a prayer: Mother Kali, her eyes are almost like your own and no one can bear to gaze too long on yours. What does this mean? Is she one of your own or merely a gigantic female demon? Why am I here with such an abomination? Answer me, O Kali Ma. Do so now, since *this woman I do fear indeed*!

Ajit Majumdar waited. The jungle night became restless again. Brush stirred, leaves shook, the earth had a suggestion of movement, of quake. A sultry wind lapped at his glistening brow. It was as a caress, and though Ajit wondered still at its meaning, he slept a deep numbing sleep without dreams.

6

India, Hardwar

Gopal shook his head despondently. 'If Majumdar is hiding in that multitude, Rama, then we will never find him.'

He was referring to the mass of pilgrims at Hardwar's Har-ki-Pairi ghat, the footprint of Vishnu. The spectacle of so many people, breathtaking as it was, held that depressing threat that is so common at large Indian gatherings: in the last century, over four hundred people had been crushed to death during the bathing ceremonies at this same ghat.

'Yes,' Shastri agreed, scanning the sea of faces with his binoculars. 'If Majumdar is among them, he is well protected and hidden.' It was impossible to pursue a criminal amidst those sweltering, pressing bodies.

Rama Shastri, Stephen Wrench, Gopal and Shambu were behind a wall separating the ghat area from the rest of the city. The morning sun had emerged fiercely from behind the Himalayas, dissolving the brief respite of pre-dawn coolness.

Lowering the binoculars, Shastri rested his elbows on the wall, clasping his hands in frustration. The thousands milled below him, around the temples and bridges to the false island with its contradiction of blessed ghat and an ugly Occidental tower and clock. Thousands, standing nearly atop each other, a bare inch between them, their noise a drone if you were close to them long enough.

The tower made everything more grotesque, of course.

A gift from an Indian car manufacturer, the tasteless municipal clock jolted one's meditation on Eternity back into the twentieth century. Time versus the infinite; the mortal coil defying the spirit; the world, the flesh against India.

Yes, India claimed to have more shrines, more sacred places than any other country. He wondered how many in that crowd this morning felt pangs of hunger. No amount of bathing, even in the most holy of waters, could relieve them.

He shielded his eyes. The sun's glare was painful. Gopal had sunk to his haunches in the wall's shadow. 'In my youth,' Gopal said, 'the sun was a friend. Now it is a beast tearing at my carcase. Wah, but I grow old.'

'Ageing is not a luxury I allow any officer,' reprimanded Shastri. 'I expect soon you will replace me with these glasses and search out Majumdar, if he is here. You and I are the only ones who know his face, Gopal.'

The other nodded, rose and took the binoculars.

Stephen Wrench, Shastri noticed, was surprisingly calm. He stood tall, like an old Raj memory, his pith helmet greying his profile. In truth, he was anything but Raj. His eyes snapped at the scene before him, eager for action but nevertheless under control. Wrench was leaner than when he had left America months ago. It suited his direct, energetic temperament. Wrench had mixed well with Shastri's men, a very un-American trait. And even more so was that he accepted India as she was. Not that he approved of everything. But whatever his true feelings, Wrench left India's problems to India to solve.

Only once had he questioned Shastri's methods and that was recently, on the train ride to Hardwar.

They had hailed the train, which had two of his men already aboard. They were quickly brought to first class by a railroad official and then given tea and some semblance of breakfast. It was here that Wrench appealed to Shastri. He bent forward, speaking softly, so that Gopal and Shambu wouldn't hear: 'There are indications,' he began, 'not just little hints but goddamn hit-you-over-the-head facts, Ram, that have been spinning in my head. I feel as though this is so much *déjà-vu*. Who's leading whom in this chase, is what I keep asking myself.

'For over two years, I haven't had this feeling. But here it is again, and already there are questions. Why has it been so easy to trail Majumdar? Hell, we found tracks right up to the spot where we hailed this train. We know for sure, because of that Delhi shoe of his, that he leaped aboard the train that's running ahead of us. Now, it could be that Majumdar's a damn fool, easy to follow, and – '

'I understand, Steve. Or we are being played with, directed to do this.'

'I've read it in your eyes, Ram. The uneasiness that it's happening again.' Wrench bit into his pipe stem. 'My point is, we ought to break your rule. You've never told any of your men about the supernatural monkey business side of all this. Well, I don't think it's fair to Gopal and Shambu. Hell, they're officers and less apt to fall apart in a superstitious frenzy than the other men, I should think. What I mean is, suppose this trip leads into something extraordinary? Well, these two haven't been properly briefed on what to expect . . .'

So Rama Shastri told Gopal and Shambu the entire story of what had occurred years ago. He stated first that there was a supernatural force behind the earlier Thuggee uprising.

Gopal, who had sensed as much, said nothing. Shambu repeated in a whisper, 'Supernatural!'

'Yes,' Shastri continued in Hindi, since Shambu's English was limited. 'Steve and I and . . . others actually saw manifestations of Kunkali.'

72

Shambu's breath caught. He made a clicking noise.

'Kunkali, yes. The Maneater, India's goddess of destruction. It makes you shudder, Shambu. The thought that she exists, has appeared on Earth in our time, shatters one's peace, doesn't it? Well, it has done the very same to Steve and me in the past. We have asked, How can a policeman ever hope to combat such an unseen nemesis? There are ways, however, so listen carefully.'

Three years ago, Shastri narrated, when he had fled near-incarceration during Indira Gandhi's 'Emergency', he went to America. He flew to Boston to be with Wrench and his daughter, Santha. Upon his arrival, he soon discovered that the Thug Huzoor, the Lord of the cult, had brought his leading Stranglers there as well.

'Strange but true, this Huzoor wasn't an Indian but an American named Kurt Leinster. The hazy story Thug prisoners told was that Leinster, while in India, was directed to a cave deep, deep in the Himalayas, near the ice cave called Gomukh, the Cow's Mouth, from which the Ganga emerges. Here Leinster was taken to the place of the ancient *rishis* and given a scroll granting him the power over all Thuggee. The means by which he was chosen are at best hearsay but Steve and I have seen a portion of this scroll. It truly exists.

'Now, it happened that in America, Leinster sought to transform Santha Wrench into a vessel of Kali on Earth. What that meant wasn't entirely clear to this moment; but without doubt, Leinster, who through the scroll was now Kunkali's son, as he saw it, did plan to unite with Santha. She was to be his consort or wife.

'To achieve this, the Thug band kidnapped her one night and brought her to their hidden temple ashram in Cambridge, which is across the river from Boston. Steve, myself, Santha's lover, police and government officials, and a guru called Hanuman rescued her after much difficulty. The Thugs were either destroyed or captured, but – heed this – Kurt Leinster escaped with the sacred scroll. The very arms of Kunkali lifted him free of the burning temple. Where? No one knows for certain. Hanuman has stated he believes the Huzoor was taken to the goddess's domain.'

Shastri paused. 'Hanuman is probably correct,' he added in a matter-of-fact tone.

He cleared his throat and waited for Gopal and Shambu to ask questions. When they didn't, Shastri explained further.

'Now, this Ajit Majumdar was connected to the Thug uprising when it was in India. After I was reinstated as Kotwal, Steve joined me in this pursuit, to end these cult practices totally in our time. You must have something to add, Steve.'

'You bet. In the beginning, Ram and I thought Majumdar was just leftover business. At present, we're not so sure any more. We think that possibly this whole chase has been designed – '

'Designed?' asked Gopal. 'How "designed"?'

'Like we're puppets in a play, goddammit!' Wrench had switched to English. 'We've had the feeling before, a sensation that, offstage, Kali is pulling the strings.'

In Hindi, Shambu asked: 'Am I correct? You say our karmas are interlocked with Kali's will?'

Wrench nodded.

'Then, how is it possible to overcome such power? Karma is fixed, Kotwal.'

Rama Shastri thought fast. This was exactly the kind of religious conundrum he had wanted to evade. With irritation, he replied, 'But there is more to this karma than you have read into it. Although Kali can control human wills from a great distance, Hanuman, the guru, showed

74

us a method that worked to prevent this. We must be united – the four of us – as one will against her.'

They had all settled into their thoughts after this, and the many miles passed by, a blur of desolation outside their window. In time, some of them slept. Rama Shastri couldn't, however. The idea that history might be repeating itself was too disturbing, much too haunting. Like a curse that carries on in time. Like a curse, like a curse, like a curse, the thought continued in unison with the rhythmic pulses of the train.

Then, at Hardwar Station, the authorities showed them G. Natarajan. No, there was no sign of Ajit Majumdar on the previous train. Majumdar must have left the freight car earlier, aware that the police would be awaiting him at the journey's end. Nevertheless, he would still come to Hardwar, Shastri reasoned, more by hunch than logic. He and Gopal worked on a drawing of the Thug's face. Gopal held it up, proud of his skill. 'That's him,' Shastri agreed. He then assigned his other policemen to join the locals in searching other parts of the city. Shastri wanted only Steve and his two officers with him.

Rama Shastri turned from his memories as the reverberation of a loud noise disrupted the spectacle at the ghat. The first indication of it was from somewhere above the concourse behind him, a sort of pumping sound with a stutter, and, as a vast shadow and heavy breeze accompanied it, he looked up.

It was a helicopter, a large one. Shastri could see the faces of young men and women staring down through the plexiglass windows. The vehicle banked even lower, and the multitude beyond the wall swayed atop each other as the rotor's wind tugged at them. Screams and more screams came from below the wall as one pilgrim after another was nearly crushed beneath the weight of the swaying mass. Meanwhile, the group in the helicopter waved in greeting. Then, as the machine circled, Shastri saw the pilot's face express concern over what he was doing. Without hesitation, it suddenly rose and swept away from the ghat, out over the Ganga. Within seconds it was disappearing upstream towards a gorge in the Siwalik Hills.

'They are of the West,' Gopal said in disgust. 'Rock musicians or cinema stars heading to Rishikesh, where one of the gurus there will embrace them.'

The bustle below continued as before. The *nais*, or barbers, continued to shave the nostrils, heads and ears of the ritual bathers. Limbless beggars crawled, lepers scurried for alms. Brahmins debased by one circumstance or another sold horoscopes. Others recorded each bather in books, along with their caste. Anointing oil, sandal-wood paste, and clay for *tilak* marks on the forehead, to cool the brain, were provided to those in need of them.

A cow-dung and ash-coated *sadhu* chanted loudly, seeking to be heard above the din. Worshippers of Vishnu wore their hair in mud-packed beehives. Three vertical stripes were on their foreheads, two white on the outside, blood-red in the middle. All the while bathers drank the waters, made their libations and launched boat-shaped baskets filled with marigolds and sweets encircled by rose petals.

Shastri heard the prayer to the Seven Sacred Rivers:

> *Gange Cha! Yamune chaiva!*
> *Godavari! Saraswati!*
> *Narmade! Suindhu! Kaveri!*

Then, *Ja le asmin snnidhim kuru*, May you all be pleased to be manifest in these waters.

Rama Shastri sighed and turned his head away. He had

little patience with this personification of Nature. He looked across the concourse. To his far right, a bullock cart of unique structure emerged from a side street between a series of ugly godowns covered with even uglier billboards. Wrench slouched next to him, wiping his brow. Then he groped for his pipe.

The cart had stopped, Shastri saw, as it reached the wall at least sixty yards away. From the cart's back, a tall box-like affair, a woman stepped down from a curtained litter. She went to the wall, where a holy woman, a *sadvi*, sat in the lotus position. Shastri recognized the *yogini* from her earlier wanderings among the bathers. They had greeted her with joy, he recalled. Indeed, she was very popular with them.

But what held his concentration more was the gigantic size of the standing woman, who was now shouting and waving her arms at the *sadvi*. They seemed to be angry gestures. Now the driver of the cart was shouting at the big woman, while his companion, on the driver's perch, looked on.

Rama Shastri asked Gopal for the binoculars.

Through the glasses he saw the wrathful female face, fierce beyond imagining. A strange, disturbing giantess, who made him tense his grip on the binoculars' casing. He focused on the *sadvi*, who remained unperturbed, and, when he returned to the standing woman, he quickly left her and sighted on the two men.

And straightened. And pulled the binoculars from his eyes . . .

And shouted, 'Ajit Majumdar!' Then again, as if the trio around him hadn't heard the name the first time, 'Ajit Majumdar!'

Rama Shastri started to run. Simultaneously, the concourse erupted with a new sound, a roar that came from his left like a tidal wave of cacophony. He couldn't help

77

but look, and saw an uprush of people coming along the entire reach of the concourse. They were heading for the wall, led by a guru and a handful of disciples. Shastri lowered his head in an attempt to increase his speed. Somewhere behind him, Stephen Wrench cursed, 'Such rotten luck.'

The wave of shouting pilgrims proved faster. Like a wedge, they crossed Shastri's path, and he had to push at each cluster, demanding – this was a police business. Some gave way. Some flailed at him with elbows and arms. Shastri felt panic rise in him. Was Ajit Majumdar to escape again? He lowered his head still more, attempting to butt through, if necessary.

Raghubir was at it again. Ajit had never known a man to comment on everything like this before. They had just turned from the side street on to the concourse when the driver complained about the advertisements on the surrounding hoardings.

'Cinema, Sher Bidi advertisements towering above this holy place. What has happened to India? And the flying machine we heard, overlooking the Footprint of Vishnu. What indeed has happened?' He pointed behind him, 'And now Mrinalini will emerge to do what mischief?'

A pounding on the walls of the litter. The tall, rickety cart shook from the force of it. 'See, Ajit, she is already impatient for trouble. Ah, what an unfortunate wretch I am!'

He halted the cart. Raghubir prayed silently, eyes closed, waiting. Ajit stared, listened. The clatter of Mrinalini's jewellery preceded her. She appeared then beside the cart, her eyes centred on the concourse wall. The ghee in her black hair shimmered. It looked alive and separate from her, moving at its own volition. Approaching an old *sadvi* at meditation, Mrinalini began to rage.

'Old fool, you are no saint! Were you so, you would be able to stop these intruders from the sky. You would turn your eyes upon their machine and cause them to crash in flames for their sacrilege. You have no power, no venom, you false saint!' Her words rang along the concourse, her arms rose high, her hands were bent inward like talons. Ajit thought of a great predatory bird of bright plumage. Her sari flamed more brightly under the relentless sun.

Certain that Mrinalini was about to make a scene, bringing attention to herself and thus to him, Ajit began to leave his perch. Raghubir also stirred. 'The mad woman!' he cried. 'I think she will strike the holy one!'

Ajit paused as though hypnotized by the idea. He could feel the hatred emanating from Mrinalini. He couldn't see her face, only her broad back, but the hatred was like a ring of radiation around her.

'Are you a fiend, woman, that you would persist in this?' shouted Raghubir. 'Stop – or you will have us in jail within the hour!'

The word 'jail' broke the spell for Ajit. His eyes bore into the rushing crowd ahead, running across the concourse. Jail? Police?

And 'See! See!' – the commands again, the warnings, the icy grip of the thoughts . . .

Alert, ready to spring, the feral Thug probed the countless faces. Until his eyes met what he feared most: Shastri pushing his way through the blur of flesh and bone. Shastri's eyes were probing, too, his jaw grotesque and savage as he bellowed at the mob, demanding they part, make way for the law.

Ajit Majumdar leaped free of the cart and headed back to the hoardings. His spindly legs rose almost to his waist as he bounded towards the side street. Ahead, past the corner with the old one at his prayer wheel, on down, down into the darkness between the godowns. For this was hot pursuit of the worst kind, with the unswerving Rama Shastri at his heels. The great Kotwal himself. He who never sleeps and fears no Thug.

Still he seemed to crawl. Pain darted through his side. Ajit blinked at the array of stars blotting his vision. He was faint. Had his spirit diminished? Had his heart burst?

Mother Kali – was this the end?

He staggered at the corner, panting heavily. The prayer wheel had stopped turning. Something grabbed Ajit's ankle, and he sprawled on the greasy stones. For a moment, consciousness left him . . .

Ajit came to as he was dragged through a narrow door. He was in echoing darkness, a corridor in one of the godowns, he was sure. Bony hands pushed at his shoulder blades, moving him on with their strength. Soon he was beneath streamers of outside light from a casement window.

Then Ajit Majumdar studied the visage of his rescuer.

It was the old one who had been at the prayer wheel. The head was like a long, lean mask of yellowed parchment. The dome was hairless, the frame skeletal, covered solely by a loin cloth.

Ajit shuddered. The eyes were closed. They opened suddenly, and the Thug backed with a screech. '*Wait!*' He felt a numbing in his brain – so very cold. The figure moved out of the light.

Ajit Majumdar gritted his teeth to curb their chattering noise. He wasn't certain, due to the dim lighting, but he thought he had seen two empty sockets instead of eyes! And the thought-command the old one had given him was from Kali! Was she speaking to him through the *sadhu*'s body?

His mind stilled. He heard voices, muffled, at a distance, and he struggled to learn what they were saying. The words acquired sense, meaning . . .

'He went down this street. I'm positive, Ram.'

'Then come with me, Steve. You, Gopal, Shambu, search the area. We can't let him escape again.'

Footsteps heading away . . . Silence.

Ajit Majumdar remained where he was, sweating profusely. The only movement he made was to edge cautiously away from the casement light.

Gopal and Shambu searched the area around the hoardings with no success. They stood before a billboard with a soft-drink advertisement, chagrined at their lack of success. Then, from the concourse wall, came the sounds of an altercation. It was just beyond Raghubir's cart; people had formed a semicircle, and there was a great clamour from its interior.

'Wasn't Majumdar on that cart?' Gopal said. 'Everything happened so fast I'm not quite certain.'

'Yes,' replied Shambu. 'He was seated next to the driver, and when he saw us running in his direction, he leaped free.'

'Then let us question the driver. Perhaps Majumdar has a hideaway here and the fellow knows of it.'

The two walked forward. A woman at the edge of the crowd saw them, noted their uniforms and rushed to their side. 'Oh, you must stop this terrible thing,' she begged. 'There is a mad woman in there. She is determined to destroy the saint, Deva Pavati, who was in meditation. The people have formed a ring around them in the hope of preventing the tragedy, but – ' There was a loud commotion and the crowd backed away. 'Aiieee! I fear we are too late.'

Gopal nodded to Shambu, and the two went up to the group, demanding they be allowed through. The onlookers immediately complied, and the two policemen found themselves facing an unforgettable sight.

First, Raghubir was on his knees appealing to Mrinalini that she stop this 'sacrilegious display' and return to her village in Garhwal. Otherwise, some god, if not the authorities, would surely punish her.

The giantess ignored him. She paced back and forth, confronting the crowd by hissing, spitting at them. Then she would interrupt this, face the squatting *sadvi*, and demand she rise to face her judgment.

When the *sadvi* replied, the people became silent, she spoke so softly. 'What demon has you, child? Can you not see I commune with the spirit of this place?'

'Ah!' ranted Mrinalini. 'How I detest all you passive saints! You are the curse of India, I say!'

At this, some of the onlookers expressed shock, imploring Heaven to protect the sacred Pavati.

Who in turn held up a frail hand, announcing calmly that Mrinalini was a poor possessed child.

Which angered the giantess even more. She stared at everyone, and even Gopal's hackles rose at those eyes. Mrinalini promised, 'Some day I shall go through the gorge to Rishikesh and destroy every ashram, every pathetic saint within them. It is not saints that India needs but fire.'

That was enough for Gopal. 'You are under arrest!' he told her. Shambu stepped into Mrinalini's path. Looking at her now, Gopal felt a strong revulsion he couldn't explain. He read the same in Shambu's face.

'By the heavens, there is a demon in her,' the other said.

Before he could continue, Mrinalini's long arm reached out, fingers of steel gripped his throat and shook him. Gopal saw Shambu turn very blue. He rushed at her, gun in hand, planning to club her fingers with the butt.

But Mrinalini was prepared. With amazing swiftness and grace, she sidestepped his lunge, raised her left leg and kicked him in the kidneys. Then she flung Shambu away. He spun and spun until he hit the wall and collapsed.

Gopal managed to rise to his knees. He still had his gun, and, seeing her massive legs in motion again, he thought to shoot her in the thigh. His view of everything shifted, though, and before he realized it, he was being raised over her head. Gopal convulsed, firing the gun into the air, once, twice. Then there was the terrible sensation of flying. She had hurled him at the crowd. Gopal landed atop bodies that hadn't been able to flee in time.

Groggy, he tried again to rise. He groaned when he saw her venture to seize him once more. But she stopped in mid-stride and looked down at a hand that had gripped her wrist. Gopal, thinking he was dreaming, followed the withered arm to an emaciated chest and a parchment face on the stalk of a neck. He watched her follow the ancient across the concourse. Then he fainted.

'Are you with us yet, Gopal?' the voice said over and over again. For a time, Rama Shastri's face was unclear, then Gopal refocused, and sight and sound returned with a surge that caught his breath.

'Here, old fellow, take it slowly,' Shastri was saying.

'Shambu?'

'Still unconscious. Steve's with him.'

Gopal sat up. 'A huge woman,' he murmured.

'I know. Witnesses told me. Where did she go?'

Gopal rubbed the back of his skull.

'It was a dream,' he concluded.

'What was?'

'Very old man . . .'

'A *sadhu*, perhaps?'

'Yes – like that. He . . . took her away.'

'I was told that, too,' Shastri replied bitterly. Then, 'The giantess was in the cart that Majumdar rode.'

'She was indeed.'

'I saw her leave it. Through the binoculars.'

'But the old man . . .'

Rama Shastri helped him stand. 'We searched for Majumdar, with no luck. Heard the gunshots and hurried here.'

'Is she connected to Majumdar?'

'I'm not sure. But the old man . . . the *sadhu*. When Kurt Leinster climbed to the Cave of the Rishis, it was an old *sadhu* who led him there.'

'The same?'

'I don't know.' Then, 'No, dammit, I do, Gopal. I sense it so strongly. We were lured this far that we would know. It is a kind of challenge. The *sadhu* will guide someone up there again.' Shastri was staring towards the towering Himalayas. 'It is Majumdar he is taking this time . . . And perhaps the woman.'

'To what purpose?'

Rama Shastri was silent. He offered his shoulder to a wobbly Gopal and led him back to the wall. Gopal looked around them. The crowd was still there, subdued, numb. Some were administering aid to the injured. Wrench was to their left, slowly raising Shambu to his feet.

Gopal turned to Rama Shastri. His superior was still gazing at the distant peaks. He knew that Shastri was thinking of that place of dark beginnings – the secret, hidden Cave of the Ancient Rishis.

Rama Shastri suddenly lifted his right hand in a fist and shook it at the north . . . and Gopal knew the challenge had been accepted.

7

Hardwar, India – a week later

The wind shifted, and for an instant Ajit Majumdar
thought that the shadows did the same. The small darker
outlines on the vast white stretches remained fixed, however. Static, immobile, the *sadhus* sat on the glacier slopes
in meditation. Always that way, into the night sometimes.
When did they sleep? he wondered. Mile after mile, he
had seen them dotting the landscape.

They had passed one at his morning libations, beneath
the small cataract of ice water pouring from a glacial
orifice. Amazing to see these men, barely clothed, up
here where cold ruled. But then again, their own guide
wasn't any different. The low temperature was like an
illusion to him. It didn't exist.

The wind shifted again and Ajit gasped. His lungs
ached with the pain of breathing. Here, his body reactions
reflected his age. Every step was an ordeal; his muscles
were useless, his bones rickety. His yak's-wool coat wasn't
warm enough. His eyebrows had miniature icicles jutting
from them. The scarf that covered the lower part of his
face did little to keep the frigid air from his nostrils. Ajit
was convinced he would surely die from this terrible
climb.

He had lost track of the days since they left Hardwar.
Was it more than a week already? Two weeks, perhaps?
His memory was a blur like the wind-driven snow that
would suddenly rise and haze his view. What did it matter,
after all? He would die soon. He would freeze, be as a

statue standing alone somewhere in these eternal mountains, the symbol of a foolish man who died because he trusted his goddess.

Ajit Majumdar, Thug Strangler, had lost faith.

It had happened first in Hardwar. He remained in the dark passage of the godown. Thus Kali directed, and he heeded. And waited. Rama Shastri's men searched nearby; Ajit heard their scurrying, their voices, sometimes only a thin partition away, it seemed. But still he waited.

When the *sadhu*'s steel fingers gripped his arm without warning, Ajit jumped. The *sadhu* pulled at Ajit's tunic. The Thug followed. Ahead was the casement window light. Again he was in its light. At the same time, the *sadhu* disappeared and returned with someone else. Ajit nearly wailed aloud. The *sadhu* had brought Mrinalini Pal with him. She was obviously another chosen one.

That was the beginning of his crisis of faith. Now there was this impossible climb. True, Mrinalini had proved to be an asset. She was the one who had gone forth to seek the proper clothing and supplies and had returned with every necessity for the climb. How she had managed it was a mystery Ajit never sought to solve.

Again, she carried the heavier packs on her broad back. She proved a marvellous beast of burden. Agreed, though, if she hadn't been present, the supplies would have been much fewer. Probably, Ajit could have carried them with ease.

However, he had to admit the climb would kill him anyway. The ordeal was too great for him. He wasn't like this ancient master, in control of forces within himself that subdued the elements. He was only Ajit Majumdar. A man. A Thug Strangler serving Kali, true, but nevertheless a man.

Then there was the incredible sensation that distance

86

had somehow telescoped, shrunk, you might say. That they were headed for Gomukh (the Cow's Mouth), the source of the Ganga at the Gangotri Glacier, 12,770 feet up in the Himalayas, Ajit knew for certain. Where else would the source of all other things spiritual be?

If this was so, then the famed ice cave was at least three hundred miles beyond Hardwar. Now they were nearing the end of their journey. There were landmarks, shrines en route he had heard of, that convinced Ajit of their present location. They had already passed the shrines of Gangamata and Sri Kedarnatheswara, which displays the ninth of Siva's twelve *lingas*, the temple of Lord Badari Narayana (Vishnu), and also, at the beginning of their trek, the temple of Mansa Devi.

These Ajit had learned of from others, and he recognized them in passing by, more and more in awe that the sometimes long distances between them seemed so short.

Yet everything was already so unreal and so illogical on this trip. The choice of Mrinalini Pal, for example. Why had Kali Ma forsaken him so? And, telescoped as space might be, he was no better for it physically.

The wind whipped at his eyes, mocking him. All Nature held him in contempt, since he couldn't equal the strength, the stamina of the giant woman before him. It had been this way since Hardwar. First the *sadhu*, then Mrinalini, finally him, Ajit Majumdar. He didn't trust her at his back.

Besides, he admitted bitterly, he didn't move fast enough to take the second lead.

Ajit stared at a new holy man in meditation. The figure was seated on the rim of a mountain's shoulder overlooking a valley that sloped down in a series of rib-like projections. The valley had turned green from shadow, but there was no grass; at the most, a smear of algae on rocks. The mountain base was a mass of detritus. The force of glaciers determined this part of the landscape. Sometimes there was a distant crackling or roar – ice and avalanche reverberating everywhere like the condemnation of the gods.

Ajit felt an urge to appeal to this *sadhu* communing with the heavens. He didn't want to die up here, in this forsaken place, from the merciless conditions or the sadism of Mrinalini.

She had tried to maim or destroy him more than once. It was an obsession with her.

The first time they had slept in a cave overnight was when she began to threaten him. He had sat down, exhausted, rubbing his arms and legs to help circulation, then Mrinalini unslung her rucksacks and hurled them down. They barely missed him. He jumped to his feet, ready for trouble. But Mrinalini walked away, giggling. That night he barely slept. Especially since the darkness carried her low laughter to him now and then. It made him tense each time, since he expected an attack from her any second. She had left him alone, though.

The following evening, at their camp site, a very fatigued Ajit was preparing the camp fire. As he bent over the kindling, a great heat near the side of his face nearly seared him. Ajit pulled away in time to miss the full impact of a blazing torch made from the branch of a dead tree and a rag soaked in kerosene. Mrinalini had acquired the kerosene at Hardwar for making fires easily.

This time the *sadhu* stepped between them and gave the mental command *No!* Ajit and Mrinalini turned their backs to each other. The altercation was over.

Now, moving over the hump of ochre-faced glacial rock, Ajit became aware of the gelid surface of the stone; he must go slowly lest he slip. Ahead, many miles ahead, but scintillating in the iced blue dawn, was a glacier with a towering escarpment behind it. Was it the Gangotri Glacier and its neighbour, the Shiv Ling peak?

From this distance, the peak was spangled by glassy blue layers around its girth and beneath its white crown. Black specks whirled and glided high about its highest point. Lammergeiers, the bearded vultures, Ajit recognized.

He was still struggling along the hump when a slow-moving shadow passed over him. Ajit looked. One of the lammergeiers had descended to this level. It glided into the blue lozenge of sunrise and then out of it to Ajit's left side. He became nervous – the vulture was very near. Ajit could see its profile and the unblinking right eye. The eye was naturally fixed on a point beyond itself, but when Ajit wasn't looking at it, he felt that the eye had turned to watch him.

At intervals, the Thug looked at the bird, hoping to catch it in the act of observing him, but each time the eye was centred on the world beyond its beak.

The creature smells my death, thought Ajit Majumdar. His time was about to happen. Very soon.

On and on the trio climbed. The wind grew fiercer, the shadows shorter and deeper. The sun was less blue now, a whitish radiance that sparkled off the drifts, off the ochres, greens, pale blues and deeper greys of the patches and shoulders and straight drops of rock.

The lammergeier glided more than flew, lifting eerily into the brightness, becoming lost for a time; then, like a weightless thing, floating back to their level, never lower, and continuing alongside them. Like a fourth party, hovering, hovering . . . waiting . . .

They were close to the climb's end when Ajit stumbled and slid towards the peak's edge. He dug his hands into the small snow mounds, his fingers leaving a trail of grooves as he slid further. He stopped just short of an abrupt cliff face. Far below was a black sliver, a gorge that snaked around the base. He searched for the vulture. It was gone. He raised his head at the sound of a heavy tread. Mrinalini peered down at him from above her face covering. Her eyes were black, alive with the zest of what she would do. The blinding sunlight flashed under her hood on to the quick of those eyes and Ajit cringed.

She meant to be his executioner.

Mrinalini raised her foot to stamp on his clinging hands. The flutter of large wings, a screech, and a large shadow darkened the snow. Looking again, Ajit saw the huge bird spreading its wings before Mrinalini's face. She fell back, squatting in a drift, a hand to a bloody cheek.

Once on his feet, Ajit saw that the lammergeier had settled again into its flight pattern. He walked ahead of the alien woman, no longer afraid. In truth, his heart sang.

From that time on, Ajit Majumdar's vigour increased. The thought that he was more important to Kali Ma than Mrinalini Pal sufficed to fill his spirit with greater endurance. Years peeled away from him, and he was able to be second in the single-file climb through the Himalayas.

The lesson was clear: Mrinalini was to master whatever hatred she had for the Thug. A hatred whose motivation, although unclear, seemed to be rooted in her need for power. In her village, Mrinalini had always controlled everyone near her. She had expected to do the same in her new calling as one of Kali's children.

With this problem solved, Ajit Majumdar now had the peace of mind to ponder other things. That night they camped in a cave on a precipice overlooking what Ajit had believed to be the Gangotri Glacier. Now, standing at the cave entrance, he could see the cascade of water in the distance at what he estimated to be a near-mile below and towards the southeast. The outpouring of water was like a flickering white veil in the moonlight. In the night sky the stars were clear, their glow glazing the high snow belts.

With this tranquil world about him, Ajit tried to probe another mystery. Years ago, from Chundra Bala, the foremost guru of Thuggee at that time, he had heard of another trek to a mystical cave where dwelt four ancient *rishis*. It was located here near Gomukh, the Ganga's source. Bala claimed to have been led there with the false Huzoor by an eyeless *sadhu*.

The similarity of this story, which he had believed to be a fabrication, to his own current adventure was shocking. It implied that Bala's account was not only an accurate one but that the then Huzoor – an American, not an Indian – was also the real thing. Not an impostor at all.

Ajit Majumdar couldn't accept it. Now that Kali had proved again that he was special, a favourite, he returned to his prior conclusions about himself. He was to be the true Thug Huzoor of the age. He had been brought this far to be initiated by the ageless seers to that lofty title.

If he could only communicate this to his guide, he thought; but something always made him refrain. The *sadhu* was unapproachable. He was dissociated from him and Mrinalini in a beyond-life way. No, the guide would never answer his questions, Ajit felt. Never.

He faced the cave, searching for the *sadhu*'s skeletal outline at the smoking fire. He saw only Mrinalini's broad features through the haze. She was staring at him, but the contempt, the leer was gone. For once, the force in her eyes was subdued.

Ajit heard something dislodge out on the ledge at the cave mouth. A section of drift had loosened and fallen below, a few yards away only. Through the crisp night, Ajit saw two silhouettes at the curving ledge boundary before it turned past the escarpment wall beyond his view.

The silhouettes were of the *sadhu* and the lammergeier together. They were concentrating on the distant white torrent, Ajit thought.

Ajit Majumdar shuddered. The source of all Creation seemed to be in that onrush of icy waters. More than a river had been born there. It was too great, too awesome and breathtaking for Ajit's consciousness. His mind reeled. He had to leave this tranquillity, to sleep. The night had become expansive, like the legendary mouth of Brahma inhaling the entire world. Ajit left the entrance and returned to the shadows and his bedroll.

The next day they reached their destination. It wasn't easy. Ajit Majumdar thought this the most difficult, most perilous day of the journey.

Instead of heading for Gomukh, as he had thought they would, the trio crossed a long natural bridge abruptly east. It placed the Shiv Ling peak at their right shoulders. They stopped before mile upon mile of moraine. Then they began a descent into a crevice whose black line snaked and veered back towards the Gangotri.

Ajit Majumdar hesitated once he looked into the descent. It appeared they would have a gradual immersion into a passage of total night. Aware that Mrinalini was watching him, he moved on down the sloping grey shale.

Shortly, Ajit noticed that the walls of the crevice above him seemed to be coming together. The twilight he passed through darkened rapidly. Once the sound of wings descended with him. Before the creature disappeared into the Stygian depths, he saw its form briefly. His heart pounded in his ears. Ajit thought he saw a woman's head with long trailing hair, a woman's breasts attached to wings, and taloned legs. Had the lammergeier revealed its true nature?

What followed was a journey of the blind. He and

Mrinalini might just as well have been eyeless like the *sadhu*. Sight was a disadvantage, actually. One could *see* the pitch-black of everything. Which added to the nightmare.

That they were deep underground was certain. Every sound echoed and re-echoed. The place was a cavern that, judging from the range of the echoes, was so vast it spurred alarm that they would lose themselves from one another.

The *sadhu* moved somewhere ahead, soundlessly. There was no way of knowing whether they were still at his heels. In time, Mrinalini's enmity for Ajit forgotten, she called to him, only to discover him a few feet beyond her reach.

Soon, besides the overwhelming darkness and stench, they heard water dripping from above, very, very high. Were they beneath a distant roof cluttered with icicles? The dripping noise multiplied and multiplied. Then, when the drops struck, they splashed loudly. Never once did the drops land on Ajit and Mrinalini, however.

They reached a river, finally. At their right it roared on, the din implying great rapids churning over rocks and something that cracked and split. Ajit thought of massive shells.

The stench increased. There was suddenly much scurrying over their legs. Things squealed, croaked, cackled, hissed and snapped. Mrinalini shrieked. Then Ajit. Hands were tugging at their clothing; there was breathing, close and rancid-smelling.

Ajit cursed, fought them off. What he hit was cold, slippery and brittle. He thought he was breaking bone, from the sound of the impact. The more he smashed at them with his fist, the more whatever they were fell apart, even splintering, he sensed.

That he was fighting dead things, he was convinced.

The odour of decay, of death, was thick in his nostrils. He could hear Mrinalini battling behind him. The ruckus of it echoed, once, twice, three times, and he lost count. There was no vocal sound from the 'dead ones', as he explained them in his mind.

As they faced each onslaught, the two continued to walk on. There must be an exit from this underground tomb, he told himself. This couldn't continue forever.

He was right. He was still swinging his arms when he realized there was nothing but emptiness in his path.

Gasping, he paused. Drenched with perspiration, he wiped his face with his sleeve. Then he sniffed and sniffed. The air was sweeter now, fresh and natural. The underground river had calmed; it lapped gracefully against surfaces.

'A light! A light!' he heard the woman say.

Ajit focused. Yes, he saw it, too, a sepia glow. It was like the sun, bright to his eyes after all that blackness. Then he saw the *sadhu* walk into the glow, and he willingly trailed behind.

It was impossible to see the entire cavern in one glance. It was also impossible that it was here beneath the mountains and glaciers far above. And far it must be, not merely far from the Himalayas but from that which is of Man, Ajit Majumdar concluded. Yea, this was a heaven, an unearthly place. This was a dream.

It was at the end of the sepia-tinted route. The light had changed to a breathtaking opalescence, a play of colours that taunted the eyes. It was almost too beautiful for them to withstand.

Indeed, I must have died to witness this, he also concluded. Truly, this is paradise.

The cavern was like the large throne room of a palace. There was a dais with a stone ramp leading to its centre.

The ramp scintillated; thousands of precious stones must be embedded in its surface. There was something resembling a throne at its end. It was glassy and angled throughout, like a prism. It reflected things, colours shifted through the crystalline surface, continuously changing. Behind it was an entire wall of the same feldspar substance, and immersed within it was a form, a human form, barely detectable due to the reflection and refraction of light.

Other shapes were in the cavern. They seemed to be recognizable geometric forms, to a degree, then some new angle would appear, and the shapes became impossible to look at. The sight of them hurt not only his eyes but his total consciousness. They weren't meant to be, should not have existed, is what he felt.

All this was too much for Ajit. His eyes turned swiftly away, groping, searching for something tolerable.

He found it. A massive square pillar covered with what looked like brass. Four figures in bas-relief, old, bearded, in the lotus position, stared out at him. The *sadhu* was standing before them. He moved. Ajit blinked. He thought the man had suddenly walked into the pillar. No, Ajit thought; he either went round it to the other side or somehow he climbed up.

He surveyed the area above the bas-relief. The column's height was beyond evaluation. The cavern's ceiling was somewhere high in the opalescence. The column disappeared in it. The brass coating continued up its length. On its surface was writing in a language and a script Ajit was unfamiliar with.

He was still observing the writing when he heard the voice. So near to him that he jumped. He gaped. One of the figures in the bas-relief was moving. The brass mouth opened and spoke. Ajit couldn't understand what was being said except that the aged droning voice was reciting.

Ajit was certain of this, the way the words flowed, one after the other. Perhaps it was a mantra or . . . perhaps it was what was in the script above.

Ajit Majumdar watched, listened and trembled. Despite what had already happened, he was totally unprepared for what he saw. The brassy head moved, the lips opened, the long beard dangled, swayed, the robe-covered arms pointed up to the lettering or towards the throne. Ajit heard Mrinalini Pal gasp behind him.

On the voice droned, as if it would never stop. Two thoughts came to Ajit while he remained transfixed before the pillar. One, that if the *sadhu*'s head had united with the four brassy figures, then he had been of them originally. Second – and this thought was a gift from a source beyond him – that the four images in the bas-relief were the ancient *rishis*.

Ajit and Mrinalini stared at one another in the silence that followed. Mrinalini, he noticed, looked pale; but then, he couldn't tell if that was the result of the surrounding opalescence.

He sighed. The scattered objects were losing their disturbing geometrics. Now there were shapes he could accept – squares, triangles, circles – all intermeshed with one another and brightly coloured. He sighed again; a strange paradise, unfathomable, but nothing he couldn't live with.

If this was his initiation into the sacred state of Thug Huzoor, it wasn't very difficult. So far, he quickly warned himself.

Ajit spun at the tinkle of jewellery. Not Mrinalini; her towering outline hadn't moved.

The sound came from the throne area. More delicate tinkling, followed by a *chock, chock* duller noise, and finally what he recognized as the rattle of bone bits. Ajit

96

had heard animal teeth make a similar sound on a necklace.

His hackles rose. The silhouette of a four-armed figure was moving slowly down the ramp. Each of the four hands was gripping something black with a curved edge. The figure moved gracefully, raising one leg waist high before it descended. The second limb then caught up with the stride, barely bending at the knee. The arms in turn had their own rhythm of motion. The two upper crossed over the neck and face, then separated, while the two lower remained constantly away from the body, alternately raising and lowering themselves at the elbows. It was a kind of dance.

Ajit Majumdar knew who it was before it neared sufficiently to be seen with clarity.

Kali Ma. He mouthed the name with his lips but couldn't quite say it.

Her jewellery increased its tinkling, while the skulls of her girdle struck each other. The jewellery – long earrings, bracelets, anklets – scintillated, gem-like pieces, so thin they were as wire traceries. Her eyes were silver, then green, then bright ruby flame. Her sensual mouth, carmine, full-lipped, curved with irony. The breasts were full, large and uncovered. The skin black, with a restless sheen that flowed with every step.

The face held his attention most, though. Kali was in her most beautiful aspect, and Ajit's entire self worshipped. The objects in her hands whirled faster, faster. They were pickaxes, the sacred symbol of Thuggee.

It is now, Ajit was certain; now she comes to me. Now I am to be the one.

But instead, the apparition turned, once it reached the ramp's end. With unimaginable speed and strength, it hurled the four pickaxes simultaneously. They flew accurately, objects imbued with a direction of their own, into the four corners of the glassy wall behind the throne. It burst in a radiating shower, a thousand miniature prisms. A tremendous gust of frigid air came from the break and nearly toppled Ajit and Mrinalini. When it settled and Ajit could see again, his heart seemed to stop.

A tall, naked man stepped out from the opening. His skin was extremely pale, his hair almost white, his eyes (which appeared so close, despite the distance) a cold blue. It was the false Huzoor. *No! Not false!* He heard the rasping command this time: '*Bow to him.*'

Ajit didn't hesitate. The terror he felt from the voice was enough. He fell prone.

Then, '*Bow to your Lord!*' he heard again, louder. Ajit realized it wasn't meant for him. Mrinalini Pal was resisting, because the Huzoor wasn't an Indian. He heard the tinkling; the chocking skulls approached, then passed him. The smell of musk was heavy. And of things burning, like a cremation fire.

Despite his fear, Ajit moved his head to see behind him.

He saw Kali's back, rigid, expressive of her wrath. Mrinalini Pal's eyes were swollen with horror. The two faced each other, and Ajit heard the terrible voice say, '*You are mine. You are his now.*' Kali seemed to be as tall as the woman. The four arms rose and embraced Mrinalini.

For a very long time the cavern was filled with screams.

PART TWO
The Mark

We watched the face of the beast, and saw the soul of Fleete coming back into the eyes.

Rudyard Kipling, *The Mark of the Beast*

8

One morning, Santha Wrench thought she was being followed. She spotted the man when she left the Kitter-ridge drive on her way to work. He was seated in a parked car reading a newspaper. The thing she remembered about him was that he was hatless and towheaded. It reminded her of Kurt Leinster and disrupted part of her day. Try as she did to exclude him from her thoughts, the memory stayed with her until lunch. Then, her boss, Dr Kim, joined her and they went to the School of Architecture cafeteria to eat. Dr Kim's constant chatter about her impending trip to Peru and the ruins of the Inca city Machu Picchu changed Santha's mood.

The second time, a week later, the man was in Good-speed's, near the corner of Beacon and Park in Boston. Santha was there with George, looking at prints, when he came in. She paused for a moment, curious about him. He was examining a set of Bret Harte volumes. He finally bought them and left. Santha immediately scolded herself for being so paranoid.

The third instance, however, quickly changed this diagnosis.

Leaving Symphony Hall one evening, she spotted him in the crowd. He was supposedly reading a billboard advertising Jean Pierre Rampal, the noted flautist, but Santha knew better.

'That man' – Santha nodded in his direction – 'at the poster, has been following me for days.' Santha told George about the other times she had seen him. 'Now, you really can't call that coincidence, can you?'

George frowned but was silent. He didn't speak until they were in the Porsche. And only after Santha said angrily, 'Please, George, don't treat me like a fool. I tell you, he's been following me . . . or us, I suppose.'

'I'm sorry, darling.' George took a deep breath. 'It was a secret. Captain Condorelli didn't want to upset you unnecessarily, but that's Kearney, one of his men.'

'Are you sure?'

'Of course, I am. I met him and Abel and Belanger, the two others assigned to trail you.'

'Three of them?'

'Certainly. One man can't do it all the time.'

'And you met them? When?'

'Two days after we saw Condorelli. He phoned me and I went down to his headquarters.'

Santha was quiet for a while. George Buchan became nervous. 'Santha, he was very concerned about your safety. He asked me some more questions . . .'

'What questions?'

'About the time you were kidnapped. About the Stranglers, whatever I knew about the Thuggee cult. He was only thinking of you. He asked me what I thought about having his men tail you. I replied that it was a good idea. Then he introduced me to the three men. You're not upset about it, are you?'

'I wish I'd been told, George.'

'Well, he felt it would make you self-conscious. After all, there might be nothing to worry about. And you have been affected by the break-in. It was two weeks before you went to your apartment again.'

'This Kearney hasn't exactly been invisible. I noticed him immediately when I saw him again. It was his trademark.'

'Trademark?'

'I meant what they call "distinguishing characteristics".
He's a towhead, George.'

He understood what she implied.

'This Kearney was parked outside Annette's drive the
first time I saw him. When I saw his hair, George . . . For
a moment I thought it might be Kurt Leinster.'

'I never thought of that when I was introduced to him.
The other two – the ones you haven't seen – aren't
towheads. In fact, Jerome Abel is a Black.'

'Sometimes I think I'll be staring at towheaded men all
my life. Do you think he's still alive, George?'

'Do you know how many times you've asked that
question?'

'That many?'

'Enough to worry me.' He took the Massachusetts
Turnpike from Copley Square. He seemed to have forgotten the matter, but after a mile he said, 'I don't believe
he's dead.' Then added quickly, 'But *where* he is, I can't
imagine. That day . . . the place at Gray Park East was
an inferno. I saw arms, gigantic arms, Santha, pick him
up.' He shook his head. 'I still can't believe it. He was
like a doll in those huge ebony hands. Then there was
smoke . . . and he and the arms disappeared. Just like a
magician's act.'

Santha watched George's jaw jut out. The dashboard
light made his beard glisten. 'No, I can't think of him as
dead. But where can he have gone after a disappearing
act like that?'

'To where *she* dwells,' Santha told him. 'He was rescued
by *her*, wasn't he? She took him to *her* special place.'

'The Land of Things That Go Bump in the Night.'

'Yes, where nothing human exists.'

'He was human.'

'I suppose so. Since human beings are capable of any
heinous act imaginable, I must agree, I suppose, that he

was, or is, human. If you saw him, talked to him while he was the Huzoor of Thuggee, you'd wonder plenty about his humanity, George.'

'I saw him from the balcony a little later.'

'Yes, and I was unconscious. I wish I hadn't been. I'm very grateful that you and Daddy and Uncle Ram – oh, that all of you – rescued me, but, well, if I'd been conscious, maybe I would've got my licks in, too . . . I don't think I'd have hesitated to kill him, George.'

'I understand. I wanted to kill him myself then, I remember. When I thought of the deaths he and his followers were responsible for, when I saw you there before his altar like a human sacrifice . . .'

Santha placed her head on his shoulder. 'My *kesari*. It took something supernatural to save Kurt from you that day.'

They had reached the town of Wayland and were close to Annette Kitteridge's house.

I am so fortunate, Santha thought, so lucky to be loved like this. The fresh hay smell from a horse pasture on their left relaxed her, and her eyes rose to the clear spread of stars over the countryside. There was meaning in her life, and it was good meaning, filled with the spirit of two great, although diverse, cultures. Santha was suddenly glad to be herself, to be free enough to choose the best of these two worlds and add them to her being. It was everything worthwhile not to be fatalistically trapped by the machinations of a blood-lusting goddess. This love around her, this new meaning, was a cocoon that protected her from the clutching fingers of yesterday . . .

Santha pulled her wrap tighter about her shoulders. There was a chill in the air suddenly.

They pulled into the drive. The porch light was on and another shone at a first-floor window near the southeast corner. Annette was awake, probably reading in bed.

Once parked, Santha didn't stay long with George. They both had busy schedules the next day. She left him with the strong reassurance that she was no longer piqued about the police surveillance. She kissed him warmly and long and waved a final time from the porch steps. Then she watched the Porsche drive off and listened afterwards to the sound of the crickets that quickly filled the ensuing silence.

Upstairs, she did find Annette in bed, reading. Annette said, 'I got home late and missed most of the Pops concert on the radio. My car radio's on the blink, so I had to wait until I got home. How was it?'

Santha shrugged. 'Well, it was the Pops, you know – more talk and clinking of glasses than music. I certainly wasn't in the mood for overtures like *La Gazza Ladra*. Too damn bouncy after a hard day's work. And the piano concerto was my least favourite one – the Rachmaninoff c minor. You know, the old mood music for *Brief Encounter*. Much too soupy for me.'

'That's generational, my dear. I loved *Brief Encounter*.'

Santha smiled. 'It was nice enough, nevertheless. Being with George.'

My God, Santha thought later, that was a little like reporting to your mother after a date. But she didn't mind. Not really. This was all part of her good fortune, of being loved and cared for so much. Santha went to bed and was soon asleep.

'I believe this the best India exhibit I've ever seen,' said the woman in the strange white sari which splayed out beneath her arms in a fan-like design. Santha wondered about it but hesitated to comment lest the woman think she didn't approve.

There was very little room to move, Santha noticed. The exhibit was a great success, and everyone who was there was extremely well dressed. Santha stared at the countless artifacts: miniatures, sculptures, coins, the famous illustrated book *The Akbarnama*. There were also musical instruments, clothing, jewellery, wall paintings and reliefs. Somewhere, softly, the sounds of Ravi Shankar were pumped in like Musak.

Distraught, Santha searched for her boss, Dr Kim. There was much she couldn't understand. The main issue was how this project had been undertaken at the Peabody Museum without her help. Wasn't her job there as an Indologist significant enough! She had handled other India exhibits for them in the past and received high praise.

Then again, how had the museum managed to set up a large display overnight? Yesterday, when she left work, these rooms were filled with Mayan culture artifacts and some models of Early Man surviving attacks from sabre-toothed tigers, and maps of their migrations before the continental drift.

And last, when and where were these items on display unearthed? Although many closely resembled early Indian objects already known and in other museums, none of them had she ever seen or read about before.

It seemed impossible that anyone as learned as she was in the subject would have missed knowing about them.

She must question Dr Kim immediately.

But, search as she did, Santha couldn't find her. She asked a few employees if they knew whether the doctor was present. They didn't, sorry, and returned to their tête-à-têtes as if eager to ignore her.

Passing a bronze dancing Siva, almost a facsimile of the one in the Victoria and Albert Museum, she paused. The difference was that the Siva's foreground arms were placed to the right instead of the left when you faced it.

Then again, what of the illustrations of *The Akbarnama*

that Akbar the Great had commissioned to be created concerning his life? The illustrations weren't the ones she was familiar with, especially the one where Akbar is restrained from strangling his faithful relative, Raja Man Singh. Instead, it showed Akbar trying to equalize the bravado of the suicidal Rajputs whom he had just conquered, by announcing he would fall on his sword. Raja Man Singh had prevented Akbar from this, and it was why the Conqueror, in his unreasoning anger, was attacking his friend.

Santha remembered she had thought of the incident as what she called an example of the 'saving-face syndrome' so common in the Far East. She had also dubbed it 'macho self-destruct' when describing the scene to George.

Was this *Akbarnama* a different edition, then? Had more than one been discovered, and why hadn't she read or heard about the discovery?

'Now, you must translate this for me.' The Indian woman's fan-like sari brushed Santha. Santha jumped. The ribs that extended the sari felt like fingers poking. Such an inane style to adopt.

'It is in this glass case.'

Glass case? Here it was – near the life-sized statue of the Jaina Saint Gommateśvara's phallus that was unaesthetically too long. The colossal image at Mysore was much more in proportion. How had she missed the glass case on a pedestal at its left?

Santha stared at an ancient scroll. This, too, seemed familiar. Her scholarship came to the fore. She stated, 'It came from the North, I'm certain. The Himalayan districts. The material is the inner bark of the birch tree. See how well pared, how smooth it is? In Southern India, the leaf of the talipot palm was used instead and . . . But isn't there a description card to verify this . . . ?'

'Not at all. I've looked everywhere,' replied the woman. 'But please to translate.'

'Well, the language is Vedic Sanskrit and the script very early Brāhmī. It reads from right to left. Later Brāhmī is the opposite – left to right. Since Semitic scripts are read the same way as early Brāhmī, it is believed by some that this was the original influence.'

'Then you are familiar with it. Translate . . . please.'

Startled by the urgency and command in the woman's tone, Santha observed her more closely. She was a beauty, with skin like the rind of a chestnut. The features were flawless, the hair sparkled due to a jewelled comb snugly holding coils of scented black hair. The smell of marigolds. And the irises were black too, truly so, except for tiny silver traceries. She smiled at Santha, displaying very white, even teeth. Then her hand rose to touch her neck, and more expensive jewellery flashed.

'Please translate, please,' she implored, and the pupils widened as if taking in all the light of those stones.

Santha Wrench turned again to the case. She was about to begin when she remembered. It was a jolt of memory, a succession of images that made her back from the case. Such a scroll had been the basis of Kurt Leinster's power over all Thuggee. 'I'm sorry,' Santha lied. 'This is beyond my capabilities.'

'How unfortunate.' The woman took her arm. 'It appeared so very ancient and interesting. Like that lovely mountain view.'

Santha frowned. They had wandered into a smaller room with a lighted wall. Or rather, a lighted mural, very realistic, of ice-capped mountains. At the lower left was a glacial wall with a man in a loin cloth bathing beneath a waterfall. There were others around him but ill dressed for the obviously cold climate.

The woman's chatter echoed around Santha. 'Now, this

must be where the very gods dwell, wouldn't you say? Come – let us investigate together.' The words trailed in the icy wind. Santha could smell the water, could hear it pouring forth while voices recited mantras. Over and over again.

The floor crunched. Crunched? The snow covered her naked toes, her ankles. Naked toes?

Had she been dressed this way, in a translucent night-gown, at the exhibit? Santha felt the landscape stimulate her. The cold, the ice, the voices coming from all that vast space of white and blue and icy iridescence.

She was about to speak. The woman directed her. 'Not to the left, dear, but right. Right direction, the Proper Path is what we are seeking, Santha Wrench.'

'I didn't tell you my name,' Santha managed.

'Oh, it was on the list of names of the museum staff. Santha Wrench with her Harvard MA in Indology.' There was mockery in the tone.

'I must go in. I'm only in my nightdress. It's much too cold.'

'We are going in. And you *are not cold*.'

'We shouldn't be here. There are no mountains outside the Peabody Museum.'

'Of course there are, Santha. You should have observed more carefully.'

'This wind – it makes the nightdress hug my body. I'm not dressed for this wind.'

'Walk only a little more. Just beyond this turn in the rock . . .'

Santha had been dragging her feet through the ankle-deep snow. The vastness had left the landscape, the mantra-singing pilgrims and the bathing *sadhu* were gone. There was a vast silence instead and a wall of ice where their figures were mirrored in a blurred way. They went round the wall.

109

Santha saw the maw of a cave.

'See, we're going in,' the woman told her.

'Who are you?' Santha asked.

'Don't you remember?'

'I don't. I can't recall ever . . .'

'Think hard, now.'

'. . . meeting you before. Ever. In India or America.'

'Liar.' They began to enter the shadowy opening.

'I don't lie . . .'

'We know each other, I tell you.'

'Where are we? I sense we're not alone.'

'You're right, Santha. The Right Path, as I said.'

'I shouldn't meet people dressed like this.'

'Don't drag your feet, Santha. You must move faster.' The woman slapped Santha on the flank.

'Stop – that hurt!' Santha cried.

'Then faster.' Again the woman slapped. Santha jumped. The pain was terrible, but it shocked her into thinking hard. Into remembering. Back there her memory had saved her, but then it had disappeared again. What she had to remember was something she was constantly aware of, something she knew when everything was normal. She knew this woman, she knew her, she thought.

Another blow. Santha flew across the cave and had total recall.

'Yes,' the woman said. She had read Santha's mind. Santha then faced her, knowing what would happen.

The woman unravelled her sari. The perfect teeth showed in her malignant smile. The fan-like effect collapsed as if deflated. It had hidden what now emerged as the cloth fell. Two other arms, jerking like mechanical things, began a stride like a dance. The naked goddess moved on, nearing Santha Wrench. It was a deliberately slow stride, the leg raised high, the knee bent, the foot

110

descending and the other leg, once its need to balance the stride was over, continuing it.

And with every move, the jewellery – bracelets and anklets – clinked from their dead weight, metal striking metal, and stones, ruby-red like blood clots in their settings.

Kali! Kali! Yes, she and Santha had met before. Sometimes the goddess had been far uglier than she was now. But the malevolence was always the same. Blood-lusting Kali.

The palms of the upper arms met above her head, the palms of the lower arms pressed together between her pendulous breasts. The neck snaked left to right, right to left. The eyes followed suit and the silver traceries enlarged, covered the black irises, and then coated the rest.

Santha had seen enough. She turned and bounded further into the cave. She was running down a corridor with smooth rock walls that glowed softly. Ahead an outline appeared. Santha stopped, listening. She could hear only her own heavy breathing. The outline neared. Santha squinted to see more.

Santha tried to plan, to think. In her terror she had gone blank for a moment. Strategy evaded her. There was little she could do, with Kali so close behind her.

Then why can't I hear her? she suddenly wondered.

Instead, there was breath. Soundless breath, the barest cold that she felt along the back of her neck. She knew instinctively it wasn't the *usual* cold of the ice, of the place. Santha hadn't felt that en route, not for an instant. The climate was as something detached from her, like something in a wintry scene in a mural. Something that couldn't be felt, and she realized, my God, that's what I'm in, a painting, that's what. And that was the most disturbing part of all.

The scream in her shattered the impact of the breath but not the pain of the fingers that dug into her shoulder and spun her around. The scream continued with the face that rose before her as if springing from the ground. The scream continued as her mind registered it wasn't Kali this time but someone else.

There was another grip, strong but softer, another breath, warmth almost too sweet for breath.

'It's Annette, my dear. Annette, Santha – can't you see?'

Santha collapsed in her arms. She could hear Annette, but the other face was still there. It moved, a glowing, bodiless globe, away from the bed and across the room to her writing desk. The glow wisped and streamered, an ignis fatuus elongating itself. It had shape, a neck, chest, everything, a whole body now.

'Santha, can you hear me? Santha, this is Annette.'

'Annette,' Santha whispered. But Annette wasn't here in this mountain cave.

The body had definition now. Beyond the bed. It registered, finally. She was no longer in the mountains. There was no cave, after all. No snow and ice. No Kali. Especially, there was no Kali.

'Santha!' Annette calling again. Somewhere. Not here, though. A man instead. The one. The man, naked and tall and white with blue eyes, disrupted at intervals by a flicker of that same silver. That alien silver.

Hanuman had warned that he was no longer human. Not exactly human. She had forgotten that.

He came forward. She knew her scream had died. She no longer heard it. She was almost calm, almost. Almost, not afraid, for some reason. Almost brave, courageous.

It was her hatred, she suddenly decided. This man, this

intruder into her psyche. This creature who was barely human.

'You have no right to be here!' Santha shouted.

He said something *sotto voce*. Santha blocked her ears. 'Get out of my mind!' she cried again.

'I have returned,' the lips said.

'You keep away from me!'

'I have returned,' one more time, and Kurt Leinster was no longer in the room.

'Dear. My poor dear.' She was in Annette's arms. Annette was seated on the bed, holding her, stroking wet strands of her hair. Santha was drenched with perspiration. 'You had a bad dream, didn't you?'

Santha didn't reply. Instead, she burrowed her face in Annette's shoulder and wept hard and long.

9

'You could've purchased that lovely beige and white frock, Santha,' Annette Kitteridge said. 'I would've helped pay the extra if you didn't have enough money.'

'I decided against it,' Santha answered her. 'The blouse was enough. The frock wasn't quite suitable for work. A professional woman soon learns to wear clothes that aren't too suggestive. It was cut too low, and I have enough clothes for after hours at the moment.' She bit into her finger sandwich. The tuna salad was fresh and suitable food for her tea. They were eating at the Birdcage, the restaurant at Boston's Lord & Taylor's. Her dream had left her so drained emotionally that she had taken the day off from work. It was Wednesday, Annette's free day, and they had decided to have a shopping spree. This was after many hours of discussion, after Santha had revealed everything about Kurt Leinster and Thuggee.

'I need time to digest this,' Annette had said. 'Why don't we go out today and have fun, forget for a while? I find that a break, like some frivolous girl-shopping, settles the little grey cells when they've been overburdened. The mind needs to break the circuit temporarily.'

It had been small talk since then. Santha was beginning to wish that it hadn't. There was inner release in telling it to someone. The deep, tight-coiled thing within her, the part that had remained shocked and numb long afterwards, was finally loosening. Still, she was pleased to have one of Captain Condorelli's men around. Her eyes roamed to the other tables, hoping to see Kearney again.

He wasn't there or beyond the thin white wire, part of the Birdcage decor. The decorations on the ceiling, more wire with imitation flowers, gave the place the look of a bower.

Santha turned to her left at a man's laughter. Three people, two young men and a woman, were enjoying some joke. That they were Pakistanis, she recognized immediately. One of the men looked back at her with open admiration and a boldness that disquieted her.

'Something wrong?'

'One of those Pakistani men has decided he owns me,' Santha explained in a low tone. Then she giggled. 'It's the Muslim way. They lust more than other men.'

Annette looked confused.

'Oh, don't think I believe that,' Santha told her. 'It's just a common remark made by Hindu men.' She now spoke with an Indian accent. '"All these terrible Muslims do is lust! Lust! Lust!" That's what they say. Classic projection, as you or George would say.' Her face became very serious. 'Sometimes, when I see strangers from the subcontinent, I become nervous.'

And, she thought, Well, Santha, here's where the small talk ends. Her eyes still searched about her, saw a totally bald small man with a black froth of beard was talking to a very quiet girl in a checked dress. They were sitting near the two-tiered dessert trolleys loaded with Napoleons, whole cakes and petit fours. Perhaps if Kearney wasn't nearby, one of the other two was. What were the names George had said – Abel and Belanger?

She saw that Annette was waiting and continued, 'Kurt Leinster enlisted the services of Indian subcontinent Thugs, both Hindu and Muslim. They were brought here – teachers, gurus to the Western recruits around Boston. So these Pakistanis could be otherwise than their surface appearance. They could be part of Leinster's newly

115

imported group of Stranglers, or Bhartote. That's the Indian name for them.

'There are also Sotha, or Deceivers, whose speciality is to make friends with who-ever have been chosen as victims. Another rank, Chamolhi, are the Armholders, Legholders, or whatever might be the job of keeping the victim still for the killing.' Annette shuddered. 'I'm sorry, I had to become very knowledgeable about this heinous business, I'm afraid.'

'That's all right. Please continue, Santha.'

'Why did you need the time to digest this? Was it the supernatural side to it?'

Annette's long, lean face narrowed more as she pursed her lips. She tilted her head, obviously thinking about what to say next. When her silvered perm bobbed slightly, Santha knew she had come to a decision. 'I don't think so. You see, George prepared me to some degree. Couldn't help himself. He mentioned something about paranormal events. Now, I have great respect for George Buchan both as a doctor and a rational human being. I figured that if he was convinced that the events actually happened, that was good enough for me. That opinion hasn't changed since then.

'Chiefly, I wanted to think out how I could best help you. I've concluded I should begin by believing you entirely. So I do. I'm not, I must admit, even remotely a religious person, but I've always accepted the fact that there are mysteries. Only the biggest of fools believes that everything can be rationalized.

'Personally, I've never been strong about Jung or R. D. Laing or any psychological theorists who shift the focus from the person being treated to mysticism, metaphysics or a troubled society. One can't treat a god or a devil or an insensitive environment. But one can help another person to cope. But the truth, I'm afraid, is that we

116

scientists are never as objective as we often convince ourselves we are. We are all too easily influenced by our own prejudices or those of our peers.'

'My adopted uncle, Rama Shastri, had the same difficulty. His police training fought the fact of these other-worldly influences whenever he encountered them. I'm afraid he still does, the poor darling. But the truth is, these influences exist.' Santha sipped her tea, waited a spell, then added, 'Last night's dream was an example of them . . . Yes, Kurt Leinster is very much alive, Annette. Last night, he showed me, told me so . . .'

'And you say he once sought to make you a vessel of Kali? Could you explain that more fully to a rather unimaginative WASP like me?'

'Oh, he desired me as a man would too. But his principal interest was to have Kali's spirit enter me. My body was to be the vessel, and it was to be filled with . . . her. Kali would dwell in me, control me, act through me. I was to be put into a trance, I suppose, and – '

'Hypnotized into believing you were the goddess of destruction.'

'It was more than hypnotism . . . you don't understand what I'm saying, do you?' Santha curbed her impatience. 'What difference does it make anyway? The results are the same. I would act like Kali.'

She became very quiet.

'Go on.'

'Per-haps' – the words were stammered – 'be-come . . . transformed. Change . . . physically.'

'Is that possible?' The question was asked tactfully.

'I saw Kali. I have learned that my father, Uncle Ram, George, Hanuman and Nirmal Kapur all saw her. They seem to me to be reasonable men. If she could appear that way before others, couldn't she also take over my entire being? Why is one thing more believable than the other? Or perhaps you really believe that we were all victims of mass hypnosis. Isn't that the usual pat jargon that's used for any inexplicable phenomenon?'

'Santha, I didn't plan to offend you.'

'You haven't. I realize that acceptance of the irrational doesn't come easy for you. I rarely talk about this concern, believe me, but allow me to share with you my biggest fear. I can't remember some things that happened during my captivity by the Thugs. There is a deep, deep feeling I sometimes have that I actually might have changed, been transformed because I *was* a vessel of Kali for a spell. I've asked Daddy, Uncle Ram, George . . . They say they don't think so. But Swami Hanuman – and *if anyone knows, he does* – thinks it did happen.'

'Did he tell you that?'

'No. He just never answers my question, that's all. And that's convincing enough.'

'Santha, would you like one of the desserts?'

'No.'

'Neither would I. I've been thinking I'd like to go up today. The weather's just right for it.'

'You certainly switched subjects abruptly.'

'I know I did. I'm sorry. I didn't mean to be rude, but I think I should slow down about this. It's so contrary to my view of the world . . .'

'Yes, I would like to go flying, if that's what you were leading up to.'

'It is.' Annette reached across the table, pressed her hand. 'Be patient with me – I'm trying.'

Santha nodded. She understood. Some things had to be experienced as well as seen, to be believed. With concepts like mass hypnosis, some people would never totally trust what they saw. It would take more for Annette to be convinced. Which didn't seem very likely. Santha had just made up her mind to return to her own flat very soon.

* * *

118

Kearney watched the pair follow Santha and Annette. Once out of the Birdcage, the pair turned on to the corridor the two women had taken. Kearney stepped in front of the man and woman. 'That's far enough,' he said, and he showed them his badge.

'I don't understand,' the small man fidgeted.

'C'mon, now. I spotted you two following Miss Wrench and her friend from Wayland a few hours ago. Both of you are going downtown.'

'You can't do that. You must have a warrant.' The man turned to the girl. 'This ass hasn't even read us our rights.'

She nodded.

'Listen, Mr . . .' Kearney grabbed the other's arm.

'Mr Croce. Victor Croce. And this is Mauna. Now, take your hand off me.'

Kearney frowned. He had asked for back-up a short time ago, but Abel wasn't here yet. Kearney was usually cool when in action but he was now sweating. He couldn't understand why, but these two had him all nerved up. Why? There was something about them, goddammit.

'You are troubled,' Croce was saying. 'That is because of the light that surrounds us. It is blinding.'

'What light?'

'The light you can't see, of course. But it is here, nevertheless.'

Kearney felt that the man was stalling for time. Where the hell was Abel? Belanger had been in a car outside, waiting to tail the Wrench girl and her friend. It was the end of Kearney's shift when he decided to call HQ to send Abel over. What the hell was keeping him from showing up?

Croce said, 'Forgive Mauna for not speaking. She has taken a vow of silence.'

Kearney stared at the girl. What the fuck was she – a nun? No, she belonged to that crazy Thug sect, he bet,

119

and they'd do things like that, they would. Goddamn religious fanatics! Kearney placed himself between the two, holding an arm of each now. He was about to say more when something hard pressed against his spine.

'Don't stir,' a nasal voice demanded, 'or I'll waste you right here, so help me.'

'Quick, into the men's room,' Croce commanded.

'Now,' Croce rubbed his hands, 'we aren't likely to be disturbed, with so few men in this building.' Mauna had remained outside. She was to warn them by rapping on the door if someone was about to enter.

'My back-up's coming any minute, buster,' Kearney warned. 'You'd better quit while you have the chance.'

'Oh, yeah?' The gunman raised his .38 to Kearney's temple. 'Get in that stall. Go on – now!'

Kearney walked into the stall. The gunman hit his skull hard with the grip of the .38. Kearney fell.

'Now prop him up on the lavatory seat.' Croce pulled a silk scarf out of his pocket. It was neatly folded.

'I told you I should carry this gun with me for a while yet.' The other grinned, his bony, chinless face forming a wide V.

'Yes, Thin. We were lucky. But it's a two-edged sword. See, the blow broke skin and he bleeds. Not a good sign – spilled blood.' He quickly unfolded the yellow scarf. 'Now, keep him propped up while I do this.'

An hour later Jerome Abel explained, 'I couldn't get free of the downtown traffic, Captain. Never saw it so piled up.' He approached Kearney's body to look at the scalp wound. 'They knocked him cold and then strangled him. Right?'

'That's what they did, Jerome.' Vincent Condorelli turned as a uniformed policeman walked in and said, 'The

120

medical examiner, forensics and fingerprinting just pulled up.'

'All of them at once. Well, that's a relief. I don't want to stay here longer than necessary.' Condorelli added grimly, 'Imagine if they'd chosen the ladies' room to do this in. At Lord & Taylor's it would be no small panic, believe me. This way, the women customers needn't know. Did Kearney give a description of them when he contacted HQ?'

'Yeah. A little guy, bald, black beard, middle-aged, and an average-looking blonde, very slight, mid-twenties, maybe. Checkered suit coat for the guy. She had . . .' Jerome searched his pockets. 'Shit, I think I left my notebook in the car.'

'That's good enough. Let's get that over the radio right away.'

'Yessir.' Abel hurried out.

Condorelli sighed, looking at the body of Kearney sprawled on the toilet seat. It appeared to be about to slide off any minute. 'Hurry up, boys,' he told the photographers, who arrived first. 'He won't stay in that position forever.'

Damn, he thought to himself, but I'd like to believe there was a third party – another man. How could a middle-aged runt and a slip of a girl ever get Kearney like this? I always thought he was better than that. Damn, but there had to be a third party.

'How do you feel?' came over the headphone.

'Better every minute.'

Annette winked at her. She was flying her Beachcraft Bonanza again, her grip on the wheel steady, her profile rapt. That was the word for Dr Annette Kitteridge now, Santha thought. It was a beautiful thing to observe. She wondered then how she herself looked here, drifting among the cirrocumulus, the famed mackerel sky.

Santha settled against the green leather cushions, letting her imagination soar with the plane: she was in Annette's seat, Annette where she was – just in case – and Daddy and George or Daddy and Uncle Ram were in this four-seater, all with her while daredevil aviatrix Santha Wrench climbed and climbed.

Annette read the altimeter aloud: they were beyond seven thousand feet and over New Hampshire. For a moment a voice cut into the cabin with a series of crackles. It was Manchester Control asking her to verify her altitude, then giving her a transponder code. Annette replied about the altitude and dialled in the code numbers. Manchester volunteered the latest weather report. There was something in the northwest, they said, some thunder and rain expected, but not for another hour. Then a final clink and the intruder had left.

Annette banked the right yellow wing slightly, and Santha saw the green-blue-brown pastel that was foliage, here another colour mix, a grey-whitish meshing. Houses? There, a long, narrow stretch of grey . . . it must be the highway. Off its shoulder – that squiggle . . . water? A river? A lake? With mountains? Yes, Santha was certain they were mountains, way beyond the squiggle.

Santha pulled her head back, and a fibrous white mass hurtled against the cockpit window. She gasped, then laughed. It was only a cloud, hanging together by its thready self.

'We're nearing Conway,' Annette said, her voice crisp and vibrant in the headphone. 'We'll go beyond it for a few minutes and then circle back.'

Santha nodded. She remembered the mike. 'Fine!'

After that Santha went into a reverie. The steady drone of the Bonanza helped it along, a kind of background music. She felt grateful again that Annette had never been her therapist. The flight would never have been possible in that case. George had once wanted Santha to become her client, but somehow the fates had decreed otherwise. There was a thrill to having such an interesting woman friend who did fabulous things like fly planes.

Her mind then turned to George Buchan. Perhaps she could convince him to take up flying, too. Think of all the places they could go then – Maine, Martha's Vineyard or Nantucket, Cape Cod, upper New York State – in practically no time at all.

Almost two seconds of total silence passed before Santha noticed it.

It was broken only by the sounds of Annette trying to switch on the fuel tanks. Still there was the shocking silence.

Annette said, 'Goddamn, this is impossible! Everything's stopped. She's gone totally dead on us.'

'How can that be?'

'Everything's cockeyed . . . What the hell's . . . ?' The headphones stopped working. Annette took hers off. Santha followed suit.

'Well, that means the radio's out, too.' They could hear each other now, without the engine noise. 'This is crazy. What's keeping us up!' She tried to switch on the fuel booster pump again. 'Has to be more than the fuel pressure. Everything's crazy dead.'

Suddenly the Bonanza lurched. The cockpit interior gave out a wrenching noise; rivets were being strained. Then, the plane plummeted. Santha shrieked. Down the Bonanza went in silence except for the wind resistance against its fuselage. Desperately, Annette worked at the controls again, her face streaked with perspiration. Again and again and again. The Bonanza finally lurched once more, upwards this time, and the plane levelled off and stopped.

'We dropped at least a thousand feet, the altimeter says.' Annette wiped her face with her sleeve. 'But what's keeping us up now?' She paused, passed her tongue over her upper lip. 'When we fell, I could sense the controls tugging me. As if we were over a magnetic pocket. And now it's as if a column of air were holding us up. Oh, goddamn, here we go again!'

This time Santha knew it was over. The gods would not be kind and level them again. Faces flashed before her eyes. Loved ones. Dear, dear George, Daddy . . . Uncle Ram . . . The cabin walls rattled. Somewhere behind her, in the rear of the cockpit, a bolt snapped.

Santha was about to pray when she heard a loud thump on the fuselage window. Santha's hair rose, ends rigid. She was staring at a face, dark and grotesque, with eyes that virtually screamed in her brain. Over and over again, the same words . . .

The face disappeared.

Santha breathed in deeply, waited a second and said calmly, 'We'll be all right.'

Annette turned her head, then swung back as the engine came to life. She gripped the controls and quickly pulled the Bonanza out of its dive. The panels lit up again; everything worked perfectly.

Santha heard, 'How did you know? Santha, can you hear me?'

'. . . yes.'

'How did you know we'd be okay?'

'I saw . . . her.'

Annette waited.

'She was peering in at me through the cockpit window. Her ugly face was squinched up, pressed against it. Her eyes screamed that there was no place to hide from her.

124

No place. Ever. That's when I knew I couldn't die – not like this, anyway.'

'Did she say that, too?'

'No. But I knew. She made this happen just to prove a point. Even up here I'm not safe. You believe me, don't you? You don't think it's because I saw one too many *Twilight Zone* shows?'

Annette's reply was immediate: 'I believe you, Santha. I have to. After what we've just been through, I have to!'

10

Near Allahabad

Rain. Monsoon rain. This was the rain that killed. Flood
rain. Plague rain. Rain with the dark, dark cloud face that
rolled in from the sea. Rain in the shape of torrents,
hazing the view and greying the world.

Sometimes it's even a black rain, Rama Shastri thought,
a day like night. He left the window, silently watching
Stephen Wrench fill his pipe. They were at the makeshift
Kotwalee near Allahabad. Except for the main house,
which had been meant for the officer in command and his
family, the other buildings, little more than barracks,
were jerry-built for survivors of the Sepoy Mutiny in 1857.
The grounds had been used for every kind of activity since
then. Rama Shastri, hearing of the site, had adopted it as
a home base in his search for Majumdar's Thug band
along the Ganga.

Wrench had just announced that perhaps he should be
returning to America soon. His instincts told him that
Santha might be in need of him soon, he explained.

'We've learned to trust our strongest feelings, you and
I,' Wrench stressed. 'Ever since this neo-Thuggee cult
first appeared. I doubt our current suspicions are wrong,
Ram. If Ajit Majumdar has been led to that legendary
Cave of the Ancient Rishis, the very same one that Kurt
Leinster was taken to years ago, then the world's in the
soup again, and Kali's stirring it with her ladle, you can
bet.'

'But I know Majumdar. I can't imagine him as the new Huzoor. He's not leader mentality – not on that scale.'

'Then maybe the big woman's the one. The blind *sadhu* took her with him. Or' – Wrench dragged on the pipe stem and made a face – 'maybe it's much worse. Much, much worse.' He placed the pipe in an ashtray and took a packet of pipe cleaners from his pockets.

He cleaned his pipe for a few moments, dragged on the stem again, and seemed pleased with it. 'Maybe *he* was at the Cave. Waiting.'

'We're dealing with suppositions, Steve.'

'Ram, you believed enough at Hardwar. We waited two goddamn weeks up there, hoping they'd return. You smelled it, as sure as the hound picks up the scent of the fox. Don't turn sceptic on me now.'

Shastri shrugged. 'Perhaps Leinster *is* alive. Perhaps it's still his play. I know you're right, but I think I don't want to believe it.' He returned to the window. The thunder had started again. The grounds flickered brightly for a moment. Monsoon lightning that could continue for days. The torrential onslaught drummed on the roof.

Leinster. The Chosen One among the chosen. Shastri understood very well why Stephen Wrench worried about his daughter. Santha was to have been the Huzoor's prize, his consort, Kali's vessel – all in one. Leinster had tried to achieve that once. If he wasn't dead, then he would try again.

'No doubt about it,' Shastri said aloud.

He looked at Wrench refilling his pipe. Wrench was brooding, troubled. Rama Shastri thought how good this time had been, the two of them together . . . alive because of the chase, the tracking down. As in their youth. How blessed they were with such a friendship, sharing mutual interests as policemen. They were a team and more . . . They were as brothers.

'Now that Kamala is gone, Santha's all I've got.' How many times had Wrench said that these past weeks? Kamala. Love for her was something they had once shared, too. Long ago. The lightning flashes seemed to punctuate the thoughts. Long ago. Long ago.

There was someone at the gate.

Rama Shastri saw the grounds guard's kerosene lamp bobbing as he held it aloft. When the lightning brought the day back, he saw two figures holding an umbrella over a third, who was between them. He saw in the quick colourless light what might have been a sari or a kimono. There was apparently much discussion. Finally, the guard let them in. As they crossed to the Kotwal's residence, Gopal met them. He was with Shambu and another guard. They all headed towards the veranda, muffled, hunched figures hurrying to be free of the lashing rain and mud.

Gopal was the first to enter Shastri's den. He signalled to Shastri that he wished to speak privately. Wrench, preoccupied with his pipe and his thoughts, didn't notice.

Rama Shastri crossed the large room and stopped before the huge cedarwood doors. Gopal spoke in low tones, and Shastri gave a start. Then he thought for a moment, gave a command and left Gopal.

'We have a visitor,' Shastri announced to Wrench. He said no more, sat behind his desk instead, and made a mental effort not to shuffle his papers. He suddenly felt very vulnerable, very brittle, and his palate was dry. He looked again at Wrench, who still hadn't stirred, grateful that he wasn't alone.

The door opened. Gopal entered first; behind him came a woman holding a dripping coolie hat and an oilskin. Rama Shastri willed himself to remain still, expressionless.

He hadn't seen her for three years. Soaked as she was, her dramatic sense was still honed. She placed her hat and raincoat in Gopal's hands with such aplomb that he forgot to protest. 'Ah, Mongoose,' she said, walking forward as she enunciated each word with perfect diction. Her name was Ileana Heng, Rama Shastri's former mistress; jumbled memories of past intimacies crowded his consciousness. He quickly shifted his eyes to Wrench for balance.

Steve had never liked her. It wasn't personal, however. It was her effect on Shastri that concerned him. Ileana was addicted to opium.

Shastri found himself searching her features for any ravaging effects of the drug. To his surprise, she looked more striking than when she had left him. He watched her sit in one of the big leather chairs facing him. When she crossed her legs, the decorative slit up her dress exposed her thigh. The brooch at her throat sparkled. It was the only jewellery she wore, but it was enough to impress.

'Ah, Mongoose, your men have forgotten me. The guard at the gate was so unco-operative.'

'He was supposed to be. These are very troubled times.'

Ileana took a package of cigarettes and a tin of matches from a small pouch attached to her wrist. She extracted a cigarette, placed it to her lips, struck a match on the arm of the chair and lit up. Watching her, Shastri thought of sex. That was the way she always moved, he recalled, sensual to the last flicker of her eyelids at day's end. And even beyond that, he reminded himself. When he had first seen her, she was asleep. It was then he had known she must be his.

'It was unexpected that the guard acted so,' she was saying behind the snaking of exhaled smoke. 'As if I were a total stranger. After all, I remembered he was from Lahore. Really, anyone can come from Lahore, and still I remembered it. Surely, I must have been much more memorable than that, back when you and I . . . Have your men been ordered to forget your Ileana?'

Shastri said nothing.

Now her voice was reprimanding. 'You haven't even searched for me, Mongoose. Not once. And how long have you been back in India? Six, seven months?'

Then she looked at Stephen Wrench for the first time. He had remained slouched in his chair, his eyes barely open. But Wrench had never stopped observing her, Shastri knew. Ileana's mouth formed a shocked O at the sight of him. Resentment surged in her eyes. As quickly, she suppressed it and faced Shastri again.

'I'm hurt you didn't search for me, Mongoose,' she continued as before.

'I did make inquiries. It wasn't easy, but my man traced you to Sri Lanka. You were living with a male relative of the Prime Minister, Mrs Bandaranaike. I saw no reason to interrupt your sojourn, so I let things remain as they were.'

It was Ileana Heng's turn to be silent.

Then she finally spoke. 'No matter.' She gestured briefly to Wrench. 'It is all much too private to explain here . . . But allow me to remind you, did I not inform the press when you fled from Indira's clutches to America? Did I not say you were chasing villains? Did that not prevent Indira from extraditing you because she would lose face after my story? Also, did I not help to expose a government spy in your household, a dreadful *babu* boy? Yes, I did these things. I have protected you much, Mongoose.'

'I am grateful.'

She examined his face. Then, 'Ah, so you are, I see. Now be even more grateful when I tell you that what you seek at the moment is at Varanasi.'

Wrench straightened.

'Varanasi? What do I seek, Ileana?' Shastri asked evenly.

'A man named Ajit Majumdar. A Thug. Others who are allied with him. A seven-foot woman, perhaps. Though why one would flee the police with so conspicuous a figure is beyond my understanding.'

'And where did you hear of this?'

'Where? Why, the news is at every port, every railway station! One has merely to bribe the right policeman to discover what is sought. When your name was mentioned as the official behind the manhunt, I learned your where-abouts. Then, thinks I, what better way to serve my beloved Mongoose than to probe in areas unopened even to police spies for information about Thuggee practices . . .'

Ileana paused. She waited until Shastri's fingers beat a tattoo on the tabletop. 'Well?' he demanded.

'I am pleased at your impatience. I now have your undivided attention.'

'Steve's, too.'

She ignored Wrench. 'There is a certain pig, a Bengali who has fled Calcutta, whose name is Hasari Chandar. He had the unique profession there of selling human embryos to American laboratories. Very lucrative, I must add.

'I was led to this *cochon*, Hasari, since he is in constant communion with all matters disgusting and nefarious. He now dwells in Varanasi, that most holy of Indian cities, and, like the evil grub he is, keeps chiefly away from the temples and bathing ghats, but instead is found on one of those streets that slope down into such darkness between the buildings that some sections never know the sun. There I was led to him and there he told me that the ones you seek are also in Varanasi.'

'How do you know he speaks the truth?'

'He took me to a certain tea shop. I saw this man Majumdar. At least, he fitted the description I had been told. You must admit, Majumdar with his birthmarks is unique enough . . . But later we followed him and his companions to a warehouse deep in the shadowy district I mentioned. Through a window I saw the seven-foot woman. It is amazing, fantastical. She truly is, Mongoose.'

Shastri had to ask the next question: 'And you travelled from Varanasi to here to warn me? In this monsoon?'

'Oh yes, Mongoose, oh yes.' He thought her eyes darted to Wrench for a second. 'You are always my Mongoose and I must protect you. But I would be that much better in dry clothing. Perhaps Gopal would direct me to my quarters . . .?'

'Yes, arrange that with him.' Ileana knew that Shastri meant his quarters and smiled.

When Ileana Heng had left the room, Wrench asked: 'Does she call you that all the time?'

Shastri winced. 'Mongoose? Most times, Steve.' He looked at his friend. 'You needn't suppress your laughter. Go on, let it out, if it makes you feel better. I wonder what sobriquet she'd have for you? Gorilla? Bear? Buffalo?'

'Probably Boar. And she'd make a pun on the word. BORE. Her English is superb, Ram. You taught her well.'

'Oh, her French is good, too. And a few other languages, besides. But that's where her level of civilization ends. She has never forgotten the enmity between you two. Ileana never forgives, as her Buddhist doctrine teaches her to do. Not that she ever thinks of her religion much, I wager.'

The lightning outside lit up the den. For an instant, they were a still photograph tinted yellow. After the room became dark again, the thunder returned, the torrent hurled itself at the windows and throbbed on the low flat roof. They had lost their electricity ten minutes before and hadn't bothered to light the kerosene lamps.

'Do you believe her?' Shastri knew that Wrench had waited until he couldn't see his eyes before posing that question.

'Yes, I do. Ileana is resourceful and has . . . protected me in the past.'

The lightning again. Wrench's face was almost ghostly. 'Then we go to Varanasi?'

'We? I thought you'd decide that way, Steve.'

'America can wait. It doesn't look as though Leinster's behind this, anyway. Ileana would've seen him, don't you think?'

'Not necessarily. But whatever the case, Ajit Majumdar is there for a reason. Perhaps recruiting Thugs.'

'Well, if Leinster's alive and in India, my little girl is safe from him for a while, at least. Yes, I'll go with you.'

'Tomorrow, early morning, Steve. And we might have the monsoon in our favour. Remember, it was during such weather that Siraj-ud-daula attacked Fort William at Calcutta and thus imprisoned a hundred and forty-six English captives in the infamous Black Hole.'

'Damn, anything's better than just waiting here.' Wrench rose. 'Even if it's a trap.'

Rama Shastri agreed. He was almost certain it was a trap, but he refrained from speaking about it. Other matters clouded his thoughts.

Later, when Shastri stood at the door of his sleeping quarters, the cloud lifted. Someone was beyond the door; he could see the kerosene light between the louvres. When he entered, Ileana sat up behind the mosquito netting over the bed.

'You were so long, Mongoose,' she said.

'I had to issue orders to my men. We leave at early morning.'

'So soon?'

'Yes. Perhaps the element of surprise will be with us if we move fast.'

Ileana moved the netting aside. Rama Shastri forgot about everything else. He sat next to her, stared at her slender, naked body. The lamplight flickered across her breasts. It seemed a lover's caress.

'You were hungry for me, Mongoose. I could tell that the first moment you looked at me.'

He took off a boot, let it slip gently to the floor. 'I've missed you, yes,' he admitted.

'It has been much too long.' She breathed on his neck. Her hair was scented; a perfume, not oil or ghee.

'I too have missed you. While I was in Sri Lanka, too. It was not as your spy told you.'

'Oh.'

'It was a cultural affair. We were not lovers. He was an important man who needed a grand hostess at the table to be witty and intelligent for his guests. Very important people, Mongoose. He had a wife, but she wasn't suitable for the task, of course.'

'Of course.'

'Don't do that, Mongoose. You know I'm a learned woman. You have taught me all I know – languages, culture. Very literate. I also enjoy banquets with famous people, you know that. Was I to mourn your leaving me forever?'

'I didn't expect or want that.'

'I was determined not to be a *femme fatale* – no Emma Bovary or Anna Karenina. I suffered without you, Mongoose. I was no Estelle who had been taught to reject love. You see, I've remembered all that I've read.'

'I'm pleased.'

'I am no common *dassis*, no *rum-johnie*. No Bubu of Montparnasse. I'm no . . .'

'I'm convinced. You're showing off now, Ileana.'

She laughed, starting to unbutton his tunic. 'I like to remind you of what I've learned. When I read *Pygmalion*, I said to myself, "Ah, this is about Mongoose and me. Has he not raised me beyond what I was born to? Did he not leave a sizeable annuity for me when he went away so that I would not be reduced to life on the streets?" Then, when I saw you needed me again, I returned.'

Shastri fingered her long sleek hair. 'You're still as beautiful . . .'

'Why, of course. I said to myself, "Ileana, you must take care of yourself. He will be back. He may believe this love between the two of you isn't worth a hill of beans, but . . ."'

'Where the devil did you read that?'

'I didn't. It was the American cinema.' She lay back and pulled him towards her. 'Mongoose, embrace me. It has been so long.'

Shastri kissed along the line of her neck and down to her nipple. There he lingered and the nipple hardened. He moved his face then between her breasts, and his body eased over hers and he waited. Ileana spread her legs. The tip of his erection met her vulva and everything transformed itself, heightened, became stimulation. His entire nature was affected. The air itself titillated his skin, and his nakedness seemed increased. The electric fan, now working again, breathed ecstatically on his flanks. Thoughts submerged, were replaced by a totally erotic consciousness. It had been too long. His penis slid into her with a life of its own. He flowed with the rhythm and now the room meshed with them until he felt himself coiled in space, poised, taut with a wondrous expectancy.

He would in time be tossed free, hurled into her. All of him in, in, mouth open to mouth, breath to breath, the explosion of his penis life into the dark moist unknown place that was Ileana. He was discovering her, discovering her, discovering her again, again and again, and . . .

Ileana moaned. He found her sweat and licked it from her cheek. She spoke. He distinguished her words of crazed rapture, begging him never to stop. 'Oh, Mongoose – ah, ah, ah, ah, oh – I want your come in me. I want you to spill it all . . . In me, Mongoose . . . Ah, oh . . . oh . . . eeiii, Mongoose, I am . . .' Shastri's time soon followed. The lingering expectancy dissolved, and he lost himself in the uncoiling of his need. His breath caught, held, all of him was released in her . . .

Later, curled next to him, she told Shastri that it had been their greatest moment together. Then Ileana braced herself on her elbow so she could study his face. 'Now I must tell you about a great thing that I have done.' And she did. When he smiled and held her closer, she ended with, 'I live to please you, Mongoose.' And finally slept.

For at least an hour Shastri let her remain in his arms. He relived the first moment he had seen her, in a Lashio dive, asleep on opium. Her mother had been a half-Chinese, half-Burmese exotic dancer, her father a Roumanian jewellery merchant. Shastri had taken Ileana from the den despite Stephen Wrench's protests. She had become his mistress for what seemed an eternity until the Emergency. Now they were together again. Ileana had returned to him, sought him out. Had travelled through a monsoon to be at his side. Think of it.

'*Bajke bajao, khabadar*' – it was the rickshaw coolie's cry, but it was whispered. It was strange, in his dream the coolie didn't shout.

'*Bajke bajao, khabadar.*' Again the warning cry, 'Look out,' again in a whisper.

Rama Shastri looked for the coolie, the rickshaw. He saw nothing. He heard the whisper a third time, and felt Ileana stir and leave the bed. Shastri realized he was awake. This was no dream.

Now he heard Ileana dressing. Shastri opened his eyes a little and saw her hurry to the door with something in her hand. The corridor outside was dark, but he could feel a presence there, waiting.

Once the room door was closed again, Rama Shastri slipped into his trousers. He took his gun from its holster. Reaching the door, he opened it slowly. When convinced that the corridor was empty, he left the room.

He found that he was breathing heavily. Thoughts, questions mostly, crowded his mind. What was this about? What was Ileana up to? Viscerally, he knew it was serious, that there was danger. He couldn't escape the memory of someone waiting at the bedroom door for Ileana. Someone who had whispered the coolie's cry – three times! Why? What was the reason for such an unusual thing?

That it was a signal, he knew. That it was more than a signal, he was positive.

Rama Shastri turned right, since there was nothing but a wall to his left.

Perspiration beaded his forehead as he tried to recall what it was that Ileana had had in her hand when she left. The memory kept slipping out of focus. He asked himself the dreaded question, Was it a weapon she carried? If so, why?

Shastri came to the corridor turn. Ahead were the officers' rooms and Steve's . . . He suddenly ran. Swiftly down the corridor's length, past Gopal's room, past others. There were sounds behind the doors, men jumping out of bed, shouting . . .

Shastri left the corridor and sped across the alcove to a small hall off which Wrench had his quarters. Then he heard a loud bellow. Rama Shastri leaped into the darkness.

Arms encircled his waist. Shastri's momentum carried his assailant along. His gun arm moved up, then down with all the force he could muster. The assailant groaned, his grip loosened. Shastri butted into a new barrier, a man's chest. He felt spittle on his face as the new antagonist fought for breath. Another pair of arms slammed down on Shastri's shoulders. As he stumbled, a noose slipped over his head. It tightened, digging into his neck, and Shastri panicked. He fired his pistol again and again at the dark mass of face and weight before him. It cried out and the noose loosened.

Shastri tried to call, 'Steve! Steve!' but couldn't. His vocal cords seemed paralysed, his throat was afire. He had reached the open door when another shot echoed loudly in the small area. Shastri turned briefly. In the beam of flashlight the first assailant lay dead, another *rumel* in his hand. Shambu held a smoking gun, Gopal the light.

Into the room darted Rama Shastri. The flashlight followed and Gopal aimed it at the bed. Stephen Wrench was standing in his shorts, holding Ileana against the mosquito netting. Her arm was high behind her back, her wrist trapped in Wrench's grip. He pointed to a knife on the floor with his free hand.

Shastri struggled with his thoughts – the effort of the chase, the surge of adrenaline throughout his body had temporarily blanketed his thinking. But now the many questions to be answered tugged at him. His senses were violated: the monsoon hammering was fiercer and the storm was like a raging creature stamping on the roof; the pungency of heavy sweat assailed his nostrils.

'Why?' he barked at Ileana. He yanked her hair, raising her head. 'Why?' Ileana gave him an oblique look, confused, hesitant. Then she turned away, faced Wrench and tried to lunge. Wrench never relinquished his grip.

'Too much pipe tonight,' he said.

'No,' Shastri cried impatiently. 'She stopped the opium two years ago.' He added, when he saw Wrench's disbelief, 'She told me and I believe her. She . . .' In frustration, he went to Gopal. 'Can they tell us anything?'

Gopal nodded at the two bodies. 'This one barely has a chest, Ram. You shot him at point blank. Five bullets. Shambu saved you from the other. Point blank again in the back of the head.' He held up two *rumels*.

'Who were they?'

'They escorted Ileana here, Ram.' Shastri started to pace. The men shuffled and coughed restlessly in the small area. Shastri stopped. 'Steve, one of them whispered the rickshaw coolie's call, three times. Ileana then left my bed, dressed and went with them, the knife in her hand. It was a signal . . .'

He went to Ileana, motioning to Steve to let her go. Shastri grabbed her arms firmly and placed her where the light was directly on her face. He whispered, 'Ileana . . .'

Her eyes passed through him.

Shastri said her name, again and again. She didn't respond.

'Hypnosis,' he stated. 'The call was a hypnotic summons. Perhaps it breaks the trance, too. Ileana . . .' His voice rose. '*Bajke bajao, khabadar.*'

Her head and shoulders slumped. Rama Shastri watched the head shake slowly. Then she lifted her face. 'Mongoose,' she murmured, 'must we rise so soon?'

'Yes,' he replied softly. 'It's time to rise.'

'Oh, but I slept so deeply.' Ileana paused, staring at the

faces surrounding her, the walls, Stephen Wrench in his underclothes. 'But this isn't your room, Mongoose.'

'No, it isn't.' Shastri told her everything, slowly, gently. His eyes met Wrench's; the big man appeared convinced.

'It must've happened sometime when you were with that Hasari Chandar fellow. Someone hypnotized you. Do you remember anything?'

'No,' she told him, after some effort. She gasped. 'I could've killed you . . .' Ileana bent to pick up the knife. 'I don't carry such things.' She flung it on the bed.

'You couldn't harm me. I suppose the claim that a hypnotized person won't do what they consider wrong held in this case.'

'But I was a different matter altogether.' From Wrench. 'You'd kill me if you could, wouldn't you?'

Ileana listened, waited a moment. 'This proves it,' she agreed coolly. 'However, I would never be such a fool in my normal state, Stephen Wrench. It would mean alienating Mongoose.'

'That's reasonable,' he admitted.

'You have always been between Mongoose and me. He has left me more than once to be with you. You have never approved of or liked me. Isn't that true?'

Wrench shrugged.

'Ah,' and there was some disgust in her tone, 'you have great pride in your civilized demeanour, Stephen Wrench. Such simple, primal feelings as jealousy and hatred are beneath your precious policeman's nature. Why do you stay here in the Far East, then? Does it make you feel even more superior to observe someone like me? You are an American, but you might just as well be one of the Britishers, who used to believe they owned us all.'

Shastri cut in. He sought to redirect her wrath. 'This Hasari, he helped to arrange this incident?'

140

Ileana's eyes were wide. 'Yes,' she agreed. 'Let us deal with him, then.'

Shastri breathed evenly again while she ranted about Chandar's duplicity. With a wink at Stephen Wrench, he took her arm and directed her to his quarters.

11

Varanasi

The raid on Hasari Chandar's residence occurred shortly after twilight two days later. He lived a short distance away from the temples and ghats of Varanasi (Benares) in five affluently furnished rooms above a *sonar*, or goldsmith's shop.

In no time, Rama Shastri and his men forced their way past the servants in the outer rooms and into Chandar's private area. He was at play with two young girls, new arrivals to puberty. All three were naked; the girls screamed in fear, and Hasari screamed in protest. The girls were immediately ushered out with their clothing, while Shastri ordered Hasari to stand as he was.

'I have rights, you understand,' Hasari protested. 'I'm rich. I have friends in Congress. You will all suffer greatly for this.' He became quiet, however, when he saw Ileana Heng. Then made one final effort, a half-hearted plea for decency: Could he have his clothing, please.

'I suppose,' Shastri began.

'No!' Ileana stepped forward. 'Let him stand that way in his shame.'

In truth, Hasari Chandar had a handsome face and a hard, lean body. An Indian Adonis, he was never so modest before the ladies, but now his nakedness made him feel vulnerable. Particularly with Ileana facing him, a gleam in her eye suggesting mockery, contempt and . . . something worse. That she was in a vindictive mood, he

142

was certain, since he volunteered without any prodding on anybody's part, 'It was beyond my control.'

'How is that?' asked Shastri.

'They would have killed me if I hadn't obeyed.' Hasari studied the group of men in the room. 'How can this be? You aren't all policemen. Some of you are in beggar's clothes. Who are you? I demand to know!'

'Who would have killed you, Hasari?'

'I don't know their names. But they were a powerful lot. And fierce. Oh, very fierce. Very . . .' He saw Wrench. 'This man is no Indian! Why is he here? He is dressed as an Indian but isn't! I demand an answer.'

'Tell us more about these others.'

To Shastri: 'And who are you? Please identify yourself.'

'My name is Rama Shastri. I see you have heard of me.'

'Oh, yes. You are very famous. A great policeman.' He pointed at Ileana. 'But tell me, why does the great Rama Shastri take orders from a mere woman? Why must I stand this way before her? It is humiliating.' He moved to take a robe that was neatly folded on a *charpoy*. Shastri motioned to his men. They neared Hasari, weapons raised. Hasari remained still.

'Why – why do you obey her?' he finally stammered.

Shastri held up a finger. 'Once,' he explained. 'I obey her this one time. It is expedient. Tie him down.' The men seized Hasari and placed him in a chair. Then one fetched a rope and they bound him to it.

'Now,' Shastri informed him, 'I must know if you are speaking the truth. I have no time to spare, and the lives of my men depend on it.'

'But I am telling the truth. I drugged this woman with tea when she came to me. Then *they* took her into the next room.'

'And hypnotized her.'

143

'If you say so. I was not present. Later, they told me to point out this Majumdar to her.'

'I must be certain about you.' Shastri shook his head. 'It is expedient that I break even my own rules. You are in her hands now, I fear.'

He turned and left the room. His men followed. Ileana stood alone, still dripping monsoon rain on Hasari's expensive rug. She raised her arm before his face. Hasari shuddered. Ileana held the knife in her hand.

'Christ, Ram! Listen to that! What is she doing?'

'Don't worry, Steve. She's been told what she *can't* do. That's the important thing.'

'Ram, I don't understand you. Torture has been against your principles all these years . . .'

Shastri placed his ear at the door. 'Any minute now, Steve. You see, Ileana is making him bleed a little. Just a little. Oh, to Hasari, if I know my man, it will be a veritable arterial fountain. But I assure you, the cuts are superficial. Of course, Ileana is playing the cold-blooded female, out to sever his manhood.'

'Yeah. Well, let's hope she doesn't overplay. Listen . . . Christ! He's calling to us, Ram. Go in now, before she forgets your directions.'

Shastri looked at his chronometer. 'One moment longer.'

'You know, I think you're enjoying this. Have you gone crazy? Look at your men, for chrissakes. They don't approve. It's written all over their faces.'

'Yes. Most of them are upset that they're not doing the job instead of her. You know the Indian police mentality. They love torture. If it wasn't for me, my men would've resorted to it long ago. In countless cases. Ah, the time is up.' Shastri opened the door.

Only to pale at what he saw. Hasari was covered with

144

blood: on the sides of his face, the nipple areas on his chest; some of his pubic area had been shaved; and two rivulets of blood streamed down his inner thigh.

'I am dying,' Hasari cried.

'No, you are not, pig,' Ileana told him. 'You bleed easily, that is all. That is all,' she repeated to Rama Shastri to reassure him.

Shastri went closer and examined the cuts. They were indeed superficial, except for two, one on each cheek.

'Well, he may not be as handsome as before,' she explained. 'But, Mongoose, justice must be served a little.'

Hasari started to babble in a low, droning voice. His eyes were closed, and there was spittle on his lower lip. Shastri ignored him.

Ileana was saying, 'He knew more, of course, and in a short while he told it. He is not a brave man for one so corrupt. Somehow, I expected more defiance, more panache under stress. But, you see, it was the threat to his handsome visage and, of course, to his genitalia. That is all this man is worth, Mongoose – a pretty face and a penis. Ah!' She turned now to Hasari. 'And you thought me just a *chee-chee* Eurasian girl.'

Shastri said impatiently, 'What did he reveal, Ileana?'

'The ones you seek are at an old abandoned Kali temple down this very street. Now, Mongoose, every night they stay there. At this hour they are at worship. You can't miss the temple, if you seek it out. There is a hoarding on the side facing you as you descend the alley. The temple has been in disuse for a long time. Closed in the Raj days by the Britishers because of . . . well, no one seems to know for certain. The rumours are that human sacrifices happened, to appease Kali . . . It is fitting that these Thugs would be there, isn't it?'

'Perhaps too fitting.'

Ileana looked at him in wonder. Shastri didn't explain. 'There is more yet,' she continued. 'Hasari – when once the knife almost slipped near his groin – willingly confided that there is at least one of Majumdar's men acting as a sentinel at all times. Often it is a boy – Majumdar's grandson – who is skilled at snake charming. Whenever he senses approaching danger, he plays his flute. It appears a normal thing to do for a snake charmer. But in reality it is a signal to those within the temple.'

'Very good.'

'I have done well, haven't I, Mongoose? But now this has increased my concern for your safety. These people are most awful, very evil. Hasari has begged that you protect him because he has betrayed them. I told the pig that my great Mongoose has more important things to do than save his worthless life. Is that not correct?'

'Not correct,' Shastri told her. 'We will protect him.'

He joined the others.

'You heard?' he asked Wrench.

'Yes. But I still can't help feeling we've been set up.'

'Let us consider then that it is happening as before. On a plane of existence, a dimension or astral plane coterminous with ours here on Earth, Kali watches all that we do. Since this astral plane has no space or time as we think of them, she can travel around the globe in less than a second to eavesdrop on or affect her prey.' He paused. His voice had been low so only Wrench, Gopal and Shambu could hear him. 'Now, perhaps this very time is the best moment to strike. If she is being worshipped by her followers somewhere on this street, then she may be much too preoccupied to know what we're about to do.'

'You hope.'

'Steve, I have to. We've no alternative.'

Wrench thought about that for a moment and agreed. He, Shambu and half a dozen other men were in disguise.

146

Shastri's plan was that they would attack in two separate groups. Wrench and the disguised men were to be back-up in case of a trap.

Shastri left two of his men with Ileana and Hasari. He hurried from the place, desiring no emotional partings. Everything between himself and Ileana had happened too quickly. Shastri wanted time, some detachment for himself.

The wind and rain lashed at him on the unlighted street. They were high above the right bank of the Ganges, above the temples, the *dharmsalas* where the pilgrims rested, the ashrams, mosques and famous bathing ghats. Even on this stormy night the gongs and bells of a religious event could be heard in a temple. A flicker of light showed beyond the screen of buildings like the final glow of day before the encroachment of this omnipresent darkness. There was little difference when the sun rose, though. The alleys of Varanasi are very, very deep, and soon the sky above is barely discernible.

This nigrescent world was filled with stalls and shops, most empty and unlit at this hour. The protest of cows echoed up to them. The narrow way was congested with them, homeless and without masters.

Rama Shastri asked, 'Where did Steve disappear to?' He could barely see Shambu's face.

'Across the way. With the *fakir*.'

Shastri walked to the other side. In a stall, nothing more than a hole excavated in a wall, he saw his friend conversing with an old Hindu about his bed of nails. Bemused, he listened.

The Indian was saying, 'The money is more than sufficient. You are a thunder of charity, *sahib-logh*. At least, I believe you are so, although you dress like a simple *bheesti*. You offer enough rupees for my bed of nails that I may retire. For a while, at least.'

'You may have the bed again later. I but want to rent it for the evening.'

The *fakir* looked out at the downpour. 'Your Hindi is as good as mine, *sahib-logh*, but my understanding is small. This is no night for *fakirs*. To be true, I have not been on my bed in many days. Only in sunshine, when the foreigners – not as clever as you, *sahib-logh* – pass me by and say, in their ignorance, "Surely, this is a very great holy man. Let us give him rupees, that he may survive." Indeed, to be so holy has been more profitable than a few I've seen who have college degrees.'

Wrench laughed. 'Heed me, you old rascal, or I'll yank your long beard. Don't worry about my using the bed properly. I don't intend – '

'There are things you must know, whatever your intent. You have paid enough to know secrets, and I must feel that you are properly informed, or I shall pass my restful hours with much worry.'

Wrench smiled at Shastri. 'Well, we can't have that. So ease your mind.'

The *fakir* had extracted a grubby vial from somewhere in his dhoti. 'Here I have oil and a special kind of herb juice. It is the same preparation my teacher of this career made for me. First, one of the many smiths in Varanasi made the bed of sturdy pikes. There must be no doubt that they are real pikes, you understand. Next, I rub myself with this preparation, and it numbs my senses. It is only good for two hours, however.'

'Only two? I'll remember that.'

'Two hours on nails seems to be a long time. Two hours again before sundown. That is enough to make a profit. But use the oil and herb juice before you lie down. Otherwise, you will scratch or puncture yourself and must

148

see a doctor. There is never any profit in seeing one of them.'

'I understand. Here is the money. Fear not, I will obey your instructions.'

'Here, take the vial, O sea of benevolence.'

Wrench took it; then, seizing the bed of nails, he returned with Shastri to the waiting men.

'This will make my disguise more authentic,' he told them. To a man, Shastri's people smiled. They were fond of this unpredictable American.

12

It was agreed that some of the disguised men would filter down the alley first. When they neared the temple, they were to disappear temporarily in the many nooks of the surrounding buildings.

Stephen Wrench went alone, using the bed of nails as protection from the rain. It was no burden for a man of his size; his only worry was to maintain balance on the sloping stretch of mud, refuse and waste, human and animal.

The stench made him curse. Not that Wrench wasn't used to the odours of Indian cities; but this alley, with its abundance of cows, was even more vile than most. Besides, when they weren't wandering about, they would settle into the mud, blocking the way. A few times he had an urge to kick them, but he was supposed to be a Hindu *fakir*, and to harm India's most sacred animal was extremely perilous.

At one place the alley was so narrow he had to squeeze between a wall and one of the beasts, which had simply sprawled across the alley to die. Often one of India's 220 million cows ended in this fashion. Sometimes the many cow hospitals endowed by wealthy merchants to solve this dilemma lacked room.

Finally, the long alley became clear of obstructions and he was able to move faster.

The darkness was total most of the time. Starlight – there was no moon – was unable to penetrate the steep gradient. Now and then, someone shuffled past him. He was unable to determine whether they were friend or foe.

Knowing that the other disguised men were also about did little to ease his mind. Such darkness was the perfect setting for a Thug strangling.

A few kerosene lamps blinked here and there. Usually prostitutes' stalls. Their voices called out, and once a woman stood in his path with a lamp. She wore what might have been a very shortened sari; it was impossible to tell in the scant lighting. The lamp was held at such an angle that he could see her naked bottom. He heard her whispering her price. When he passed her, she called out angrily, '*Tum soor ka butcha*' ('You son of a pig').

Now very little rain thudded on Wrench's bed of nails. The buildings seemed to bend inward, almost forming an arch for the alley. Some had balconies. On one, two monkeys attached to a railing by leashes were chattering and screeching.

Wrench wondered whether he was nearing the temple.

Two torches in sconces lighting an ornate door answered his problem. It was at least twenty yards ahead. He could see the hoarding on the side, and he didn't know how anybody could read it, even in the day.

The torchlight splayed across the alley like bright, nervous fingers. Wrench entered an opening at his left. It gave him a good view of the temple front.

One of Kali's little joints, he thought grimly. She had many pleasant aspects, he was aware; but this little out-of-the-way temple had to be for the Maneater. Kunkali. This was not the same creature one prayed to for a successful child delivery.

It still awed him that anyone could worship her. Nothing in Stephen Wrench's nature could accept what she represented. He scraped the dung from his sandal as he watched, as if the goddess and the filth he had picked up on his walk were the same.

Yet, he had to admit, he loved India. So much of his

life had been spent here years ago that he had somehow adopted the country as his own. After all, he had met his late wife Kamala here. And his daughter Santha was born in New Delhi. Here, too, his friendship with Rama Shastri had budded. For him, India held memories of love, of exotic adventure. He frowned. After all these many years, he was still the dreamy-eyed boy who had read too much Kipling.

Grow up, Stephen Wrench told himself. Put away the toys. You're in India now to stop this terrible thing. Permanently. It had already reached across the ocean once and nearly destroyed Santha in Boston. It had tried just very recently to use Ileana Heng as his assassin.

Face it, man, he railed, Thuggee doesn't play fair. *It will use anybody it can* to achieve its heinous goals. This is no schoolboy's game.

Then he chuckled. Kali had tried to separate him from Rama Shastri through death. Together, they must pose a pretty big threat to her. The more he dwelt on that, the more it pleased him. To think that he and Ram, at their age, should be so strong a force! It was fabulous to think about. It was like being a hero. He had never thought of himself that way – a powerful force for good. Never, ever.

Wrench started.

'It's me,' whispered Shambu.

Wrench lowered his gun. 'Do you piss as quietly?' he said.

For a second Shambu seemed nonplussed. Then, 'Kotwal Shastri is coming any moment now.'

Wrench relaxed and leaned his palm on one of the 'nails' of the *fakir*'s bed where it leaned against the wall, and nearly bellowed with pain. Fortunately, the skin was unbroken. Rubbing the palm, he concentrated on the temple facade.

152

'See, they have arrived,' Shambu said in Wrench's ear. His breath smelled of strong spices.

Emerging into the quivering semicircle of light were Shastri, Gopal and a dozen men in uniform. They paused before the entrance, silhouettes before a flickering, dreamlike backdrop. Shastri gave the order. One group went between the front columns, another seven men were deployed to a porch on the left that led to a columned hall. The hall was on a high plinth that jutted beyond the main entrance, which allowed Wrench to see it from his position.

As soon as they disappeared, a lone shadow stretched across the facade. It settled somewhere near the temple and placed another, smaller bulk of shadow before itself. Wrench immediately thought of Ajit Majumdar's grandson with his snake in a basket. Now, with the cover off, the shadow put a thin black streak at an angle to its head.

The strains began, a reedy sound that rose slowly and then descended more rapidly, then a repeat of the same again and again. Not a melody, only a monotonous succession of notes. Nevertheless, it had an aura of gloom like a fragment of a threnody.

'Now we do our part,' Wrench planned. Shambu listened to what he proposed and left. Wrench waited a few minutes and went out into the alley. He left the bed of nails against the wall; he no longer needed it. Slowly, he walked towards the rim of the lighted area. Behind him, he heard others walking. Shambu and the rest of the men, he knew.

He was about to move on, then stopped in mid-stride. The strange dirge had ended. Wrench watched the enormous shadow on the temple rise and pick up the bulky object. Wrench wondered whether there really was a snake in the basket, since it hadn't emerged to the music. The shadow began to climb the temple columns, the top

153

half becoming foreshortened while the legs grew longer and longer.

Then he saw the boy. He wore a turban and a loin cloth, nothing else. The boy looked about warily as he passed the temple, heading in Wrench's direction. Wrench tensed, unsure of what to do. But the boy suddenly veered to the side of the temple and disappeared behind the hoarding.

Wrench quickly signalled the others to follow and went to the spot.

Shambu was the first to reach him.

'Shine your light here,' Wrench directed, his hand groping at empty space behind the hoarding. The beam exposed a niche with an ornately decorated entrance. Beyond was a small stairway.

When Rama Shastri heard the flute music, he had three of his men cover their rear. Aware that they might have walked into a trap, they remained close together. Thugs could kill only with a *rumel*, and in order to do so they would now have to confront the policemen face to face. Fanatical as the sect was, he didn't believe they would unnecessarily hurl themselves into a wall of gunfire.

Shastri felt they must be nearing the sanctuary. They were in a long passageway with reliefs of divinities and dwarfs carved everywhere – on the columns, the walls and even the pierced stone windows. The torch lighting was sparse, the sconces placed at longer distances from each other than usual. Shastri was sure the great blots of darkness were placed there by design. Thus, he commanded his men to avoid walking close to the columns or niches.

Since these Thugs could melt easily into shadows and spring forth with their deadly *rumels*, keeping to the open central area of the passage was the safest procedure.

Shastri raised his head and tried to pierce the balcony darkness above the sconces. For some yards now, there had been surrounding balconies. The balconies made him very uneasy. They are following us up there, he thought, moving stealthily along with us. We are seen but we cannot see them.

The balcony stretched the entire length of the temple, Wrench estimated. At first, the short stairway had led to an enclosed passageway; but now they were in an open place that extended beyond the balcony rail to the opposite wall and another balcony. Immediately, Wrench had ordered everyone to move doubled over so they wouldn't be seen above the balcony's edge.

He found it to be an extremely uncomfortable way to move. Pain shot up his calves and thighs. This was much easier for a younger, slighter man, so he motioned Shambu and some of the others to go on ahead.

Besides, while resting he could think, work out strategy to fit these new conditions. But nothing came to mind. That Ram and company were somewhere below was all that he was certain of; the rest he would play by ear, as usual. He needed more information; then he could deploy his own men properly.

Wrench didn't have to wait long. One of the policemen who had gone ahead returned, and said that Shambu wanted to see him. Wrench followed the messenger. He found Shambu and his group hugging the balcony wall before a turn where the temple widened into a rotunda.

Shambu pointed round the corner. Wrench looked and held his breath.

In the dim lighting was a long line of black lumps. A band of men hugging the balcony wall as he was – very, very still and waiting.

Shambu nudged him and pointed to the temple wall

opposite the balcony of the rotunda. There, in the haze of a shaded kerosene lamp, sat the boy on a *charpoy*. The wicker basket was at his feet. Wrench had to adjust his eyes to the scene before he realized he was looking into the doorway of a small room. It was part of the side of a niche in the wall, and, fortunately, it was the side facing them. If it had been on the blind side and he and his men had moved on, they would have been in the boy's sight, unawares, and the boy could easily have given the alarm.

Wrench pressed his head against the carved stone and shut his eyes. So it was another set-up, he thought, a trap. And probably more intricate than he could imagine. Swami Hanuman had explained it years ago: 'Kali has the advantage most times. She moves about her plane of existence, observing the ways of men. She can view any part of the Earth she wishes, telescoping space and time on her plane that knows neither. Only the strength of the group can defeat her, and decision-making that is both spontaneous and adjusts to the situation as it is.'

Then a mere mortal like me may have a fighting chance, Wrench concluded.

The sound of a gong, sudden, jarring, gave him a start. Wrench looked below, through the gaps between the balcony carvings. Below, at the far side of the rotunda, he saw a dais. There was nothing on it except two incense braziers. He saw the two lines of smoke climbing upwards but was too distant to pick up the scent. The echo of the gong still reverberated along his ganglia.

Footsteps, and Shastri and his men came into the rotunda. The area was brightly lit; the torches gave them a ruddy cast. Simultaneously, Gopal and his group came in from the outside passage. They met, fused as one force. The voices of Shastri and Gopal echoed up to Wrench, even though they spoke in low tones.

* * *

The gong sounded, so unexpectedly that it made them all jump, to a man. They were about to enter the rotunda when it rang out. Instead, they gathered even more closely, expecting an attack, fearing that it had been a signal.

As the seconds piled up, Shastri began to understand its purpose. It was two things: a challenge, a pronouncement that something was waiting for them; and more of this war on the nervous system.

He ordered that they continue and that they keep alert to the shadows. The rotunda, however, proved a surprise. It was extremely well lit. Sconces capped by long curling flames were placed not only on the walls but on every wide squared column as well. Inscriptions and reliefs, mostly of Kali battling the demon Raktavīja, were clearly delineated. There were hardly any shadows. No dark crannies.

They tensed at noise to their left. Gopal and his men came through the side exit. He reported quickly; they had seen no sign of anyone on the columned porch. In the glare, Gopal's face was waxy, strained.

With their strength doubled, they moved slowly between the two rows of columns that ran through the centre of the room leading to an empty dais ahead. The reason for such strange architecture baffled Shastri. But then again, Indian temples had often been built in very innovative styles, he knew.

As they walked, Shastri studied the balconies on both sides. They were still up there, he thought; they must be. The columns blocked his view for a moment. Then he quickly looked up again, hoping to see that telltale flicker of life. Again, another column . . . And again, stepping out from it and making another quick scrutiny.

By the time he reached the cleared semicircle before the dais, Rama Shastri felt a bit silly. He should have known that Thugs would never expose themselves so easily.

Suddenly, his men were stirring, breathing heavily. The gong again. It rumbled and rang and echoed until their ears hurt. Apparently, the gong was very big and nearby. The loudness of the sound was a violent invisible wave bouncing off nerve endings. Jaws tightened, teeth gritted.

Gopal growled, 'They defy us, Rama.'

'Yes, it is a kind of sport.'

Gopal turned round, surveying the entire room, including the ceiling with its intricate patterns.

'Spirits don't strike gongs or burn incense. The balconies are the only place they could be.'

'Or behind this shrine, if shrine it is.'

'But there are no statues.'

'Precisely. I believe the wall behind the dais is a false one. It moves, I'll wager.'

Someone cried out behind them: 'Kotwal, there is much mist, suddenly.'

Shastri looked. Clouds, whitish and opaque, were rising from the floor behind him. In seconds, he and Gopal were separated from the others. There were no death cries or coughing, though. 'Keep close and come forward,' he commanded. 'It's not a gas.'

The ground before him shook with a deep grating sound. Shastri spun round.

He had been correct about the dais wall. It had moved aside and now the rest of the sanctuary was clear. In the shadowy background, fire licking at its feet, was a statue of Kali. Then a small gilded staircase with figures at its top, barely discernible because of the subdued lighting. There was motion. Shastri saw a man's sandalled feet, then *cudidara* pyjama trousers that tapered near the ankles.

Take another step, Shastri nearly shouted aloud. Show

158

us your face again – if it is you! But it was bad form to show his excitement and anger. Shastri bit his lip until it bled.

The moment the mist started to cover the floor below, the Thugs crouching on the balcony moved. One by one they silently crawled along the balcony floor until they reached a hole where a large slab had been removed. Wrench and Shambu hadn't noticed it before Wrench counted them; eight had disappeared.

'Now the boy,' he said. Shambu darted to the opposite wall and crept along until he faced the open door. The boy was still on his *charpoy*. He had been left behind, apparently, since he was too young for a Thug's work.

Shambu's expression was of great alertness. Wrench wished he would hurry; he must get his men down that hole.

Shambu left the wall. In one bound he was at the doorway, in another he was atop the boy, his palm pressed firmly against the boy's mouth. Then, with his free hand, Shambu punched. The boy slumped. Shambu proceeded to bind and gag him.

Wrench signalled the men to the hole. Slowly, silently, they lowered themselves to the narrow stairway that led down through the heart of one of the stone slabs supporting the balcony. Wrench joined them when he saw Shambu rush to the opening, carrying the boy's basket. Wrench had no time to ask why.

The nearly vertical stairway wasn't easy to descend, and the heat and musty air were stifling. Fortunately, the stairway was very short, and Wrench and his group found themselves in what must be the temple cellar or storage area. They were bombarded by a plethora of odours – oil for the braziers in large urns, grains, spices, other food-stuffs in extremely large burlap bags, cow dung for heating or cooking fires.

But it was the extension of the square columns above that held their attention. One of the first policemen to reach this level told Wrench he had seen men enter two of the columns in single file.

'Then that's the trap,' he replied, *sotto voce*. 'The columns are hollow, with stairs or ladders inside. The buggers intend to emerge from them and strangle our comrades. The mist will help hide them, too.'

They approached one of the columns the policeman had pointed out. Shambu, grinning, told Wrench, 'The boy did play to a snake, after all.' He held the basket to Wrench's ear. 'Listen.'

Wrench did, agreed something was alive in there, and quickly grasped Shambu's meaning.

He placed his hands on the column. Now, let's hope this doesn't make too much noise, he prayed; God help us – we've got to be fast.

The stone moved. 'Now, Shambu!'

In the brief seconds that he held the stone panel open, Wrench saw a pair of brown spindly legs on a staircase. Shambu opened the basket and emptied its contents into the gap.

There was a loud shriek when the expanding hood of the cobra blocked the view of the legs as Wrench closed the panel.

The upper garment of the man on the dais was a *kurta*, the Indian long-sleeved tunic, white like the *cudidara* pyjamas. A yellow *patka*, or decorative sash, and turban of the same colour completed his dress. The rest was all memory to Rama Shastri.

Hair verging on albino white; eyes, the blue of them heightened by a mysterious silvery flickering that leaped across them, as if he were an android whose internal workings had gone awry. Shastri had an image of things short-circuiting; of Life feeding on itself; of pulses alive, of pulses dead, fusing into that silvery static. Silver – was that the true colour of Evil?

The face was lean and pale. It might have been handsome once. It also might have been interesting and intelligent. It might have been all these things, and it must have been human. But that part seemed vague, only suggested now. Instead, the face was a force, filled with energy, a pale meshing of quick.

The humanness was almost gone.

And what was left was a strange, alien beauty, hedonistically alive with the joy of itself, of its own wrongness, of its warped, arcane perspective, of its discordant note.

'Rama Shastri, thank you for arriving on schedule. I was concerned that I would have to seek you out.' The voice was resonant, self-assured. 'It is so much more convenient to kill you here in India than later in America.'

'So you are returning,' Shastri replied, slowly raising his gun. One shot and this would end at last.

'Yes. I have work to finish, remember.' Kurt Leinster raised a hand. 'I suggest you lower your weapon. It would only mean . . . her death.'

Each sentence was spoken so evenly that his final two words didn't register with Shastri. It was Gopal who grabbed his arm. 'Look, Rama. Behind him.'

Two figures were descending to the dais, a man and a woman. The man was Ajit Majumdar. He held the woman in a vice-like hold, his *rumel* ready for her throat.

'Ileana!'

'Yes. It was simple to overcome her police guard.' Leinster shrugged. 'All is in order except the whereabouts of Stephen Wrench. But he will be found . . . in time.'

'With all Kali's power at your command, you still can't master everything on the chessboard, can you?' Shastri taunted. It was forced bravado, but he wanted to distract

Leinster from Ileana. Shastri's eyes darted to her for an instant. She looked calm. Am I to lose her now? he asked himself, and fought the godawful pain that swept through him.

'This bores me,' Leinster announced. As if in punctuation, there was the noise of stone on stone; then the sound of struggling behind Shastri; a groan, the thud of a body falling. And then a repetition.

'Shoot, you fools!' Shastri cried. But the mist was thicker now. His men couldn't see whom they were facing, friend or foe. More struggling, and a third man was strangled. Gopal rushed back into the mist.

Shastri, however, froze. He couldn't leave Ileana. He saw Kurt Leinster's eyebrow cock in mockery, and he knew the command to kill her would come any second.

A terrible scream shattered his preoccupation, then another scream and another. They sounded hollow, echoing from a distance. Leinster's face revealed concern. Majumdar shifted, trying to pierce the opaque cloud visually. More screams, the din of men scrambling for their lives.

Ileana leaped. She couldn't pull free of Majumdar, but she took him with her. They fell together, rolled across the face of the dais. Leinster raised his arms, mumbled something, and the mist began to shred.

Shastri rushed up the dais. He fired at Leinster, but the man wasn't there! Shastri turned to the two prone figures. Ileana was kicking at Majumdar's face. Not daring to shoot lest he miss and hit her, Shastri leaped instead at the Thug and swung at the turbaned head. The gun butt smashed against the Thug's temple. The man's eyes widened, and then dulled, and he slumped.

Shastri grabbed Ileana's arm and dragged her down the dais steps. Once assured she was temporarily safe, he faced the battle behind him.

His men were shooting without hesitation. The mist was dissolving, and the Thugs were toppling beneath a barrage of gunfire. The stench of cordite was everywhere. Shastri understood in an instant what had happened.

Three, four of the square columns had openings; stone slabs were on the floor. Through these secret panels the Thugs had obviously emerged, hidden by the thick mist. Except there were contradictions. At one of the openings, Leinster's men were sprawled, and crawling over their bodies was a seven-foot cobra. At another column, Stephen Wrench and his group were entering the room.

A blur at his left. Shastri ducked, and a Strangler slid off his back. He looked into the raw, fanatical eyes, at the gritted teeth; at the swollen hands like throbbing dough clinging to the ends of an oily yellow scarf. These men were possessed. Shastri had seen the same kind of swollen hands before.

Rama Shastri braced to shoot, but a *rumel* descended over his face. Once at his neck, it tightened. Shastri swerved, his eyes bulging. He had a quick impression of Ileana at his feet, terror in her eyes at his plight. Shastri bucked again, trying to force off his assailant. Through the red haze of his vision he saw Stephen Wrench trampling forward, aiming, seeking a clear shot. *Please, Steve – do it now!*

The explosion somehow seemed louder than usual. The room spun afterwards as if in reaction to the long-drawn-out echo from the blast. Then something replaced the echo, a voice indistinct, the words trailing down the long shaft Shastri was in; they were like a rope he could cling to. And raise himself. And raise himself.

The first sensation was the terrible pain in his throat. He knew he couldn't speak. He tried, but it was like a series of gargles.

'Keep still, Ram,' Wrench urged, a boom of thunder in

his ear that made Shastri start. The room reappeared, a chaos of fierce gutturals and gunfire that ended abruptly.

'I think they've had enough,' Wrench remarked. His great arm was around Shastri's waist. 'Steady now, Ram. Look, they're surrendering.'

Shastri counted slowly. There were at least thirteen Thugs on their feet. They were holding out their *rumels* in surrender. Strewn about them were bodies – the dead, the wounded. Eight of the policemen were standing. None on the floor was alive.

It was too great a toll to pay, he thought.

Shastri sighed, and prepared himself to give the next command . . . when the gong changed everything. And although Shastri couldn't see him when he turned to the dais, he knew the Huzoor wasn't finished with the game.

The hush was ominous, each man in the room listening to the last lingering breath of the gong. Like a dying man who would not die.

Finally, a murmur that became cries, shouts, the infamous Thug call itself: 'Kali! Kali! Kali!'

The hairs at the base of his neck stiff, rigid, Shastri gaped. He was still regaining his breathing pace after his near-strangulation, and he breathed with a slight wheeze. For a moment he almost felt himself suffocating again as he stared at the statue of the goddess – moving.

She moved! First, Leinster had disappeared into empty air and now this! He saw Wrench out of the corner of his eye. The man's bull neck jutted out between his hunched shoulders like a rabid dog's. He almost thought he heard Wrench growl.

The statue, once half-immersed in shadow, came fully into the light. Anklets, bracelets, necklace and girdle of skulls – all accompanied her movements, a mad cacophony of metal against metal, bone against bone. Her two

164

upper arms displayed the *rumel* noose and the pickaxe. The other two arms remained fixed at right angles to her body.

'Kali! Kali!' The screams rebounded from the sloping supports of the ceiling. 'Mother! Kaliiii!'

'Oh, for chrissakes!' Wrench kept repeating.

Shastri understood what he meant. This moving statue was rallying the Thugs to fight again. To the last man. 'Shoot! Don't hesitate,' Shastri commanded, and it passed from Gopal to the other officers: 'Fire at any sign of attack!'

The creature was nearing the edge of the dais. From her height – it was at least seven feet, Shastri estimated – she glared down at them. Her dark body rippled as she took each step, the muscles on her legs, arms, neck shimmered as if coated with oil.

Shimmer? Oil? Shastri backed, stunned. Something was out of order. When he discovered what it was, he said aloud, 'The lower arms. They don't glisten. They don't even move.' He shot from the hip. He knew where to direct his bullet, and his aim proved accurate. The left lower arm jumped at the elbow and dangled a few inches from the floor.

The elbow was shredding, exposing what looked like plaster of Paris and cotton stuffing.

Wrench yelled, 'She's a goddamn phoney! Ha, ha, you buggers – she's nothing but a phoney Kali!' And he spun to the despondent Thugs and laughed in his triumph.

It broke their spirit but not that of the ersatz goddess. She shrieked at them and bent to lift one of the incense braziers.

'That is the giant woman of Hardwar,' Shambu said. 'Don't you recognize her, Gopal?'

The woman seemed to change her mind. Without warning she hurled the pickaxe at Wrench all in the same motion as she turned from the brazier. He was obviously the bigger, easier target, and he certainly didn't expect it.

Nor did anyone else except Shambu, who threw himself against Wrench's chest. Wrench slipped, fell, and the pickaxe's point speared through Shambu. One could hear the sound of his spine cracking from the force.

Wrench was the first to reach the dais. His excess weight proved to be more of an asset than a setback. He had hurled himself from the floor, using his strong calves like springs. He virtually flew after Mrinalini Pal, a juggernaut of muscle-power and rage. That she was a woman in no way impeded his attack.

It froze her for a second, too. Such fierceness was something she apparently never expected. She leaped to the brazier again, however, and swung it at Wrench's head.

He met it with his shoulder. His jacket burst into flame, and he rolled across the dais, pounding at the fire. Mrinalini headed for the other brazier, to use it against Wrench while he was alone. A bullet richocheted off the metal surface, and she bounded back. Rama Shastri took aim again. Mrinalini threw herself from the dais towards the back wall and plummeted out of sight.

That was when it registered that Ajit Majumdar had been gone all this time as well. Shastri, now on the dais, crossed it and saw that it ended at a slope that led to the cellar below. So this was how they did it. When Shastri had turned his back, Kurt Leinster had merely gone down the slope. The same with Majumdar. It had all been trickery. Dramatics and clever trickery.

Shastri set his feet apart for good balance and slid down. He was half-way across a low-beamed room when Wrench and Gopal came down. Shastri saw a ladder in the dim lighting from somewhere above. He started to climb.

There was a trap door leading to the roof. It wasn't entirely closed. Shastri could see light filtering through. There was also rain; it dripped on his head, pounded at the trap like the fists of crazed children.

Reaching the barrier, he shoved with one free hand and shoulder. The trap rose, flew open. Shastri climbed out.

Gun in hand, he groped his way through the storm. Across the way from the temple's rear was a cow shelter. He could hear the animals protesting the monsoon. Behind him Wrench and Gopal came running.

They reached the roof edge. Lightning flashed, lighting up the shelter roof a few feet below the temple. At the far end were three figures. Leinster looked back, his white face hovering like that of a disembodied ghost. Darkness returned.

Wrench had already jumped the distance. The other two joined him. This roof was tin and tarpaper between beams, and it nearly gave beneath their weight. It was also slippery, treacherous, but they ran anyway, unheedful of danger.

Panting, they stopped and looked from the shelter's edge to another alley. The lightning came again, knifed into the alley for a moment. The area below was empty.

Wrench managed to be heard above the cattle din beneath them. 'Now we've got to begin the chase all over again.'

Rama Shastri and Gopal remained silent. It was their way of expressing the futility they felt.

13

Cambridge and Boston

Billy Dangerfield was playing the *tabla* drums. Seated in a folding chair at the front, Nirmal Kapur listened, waiting for the feeling to come, that special inspiration that would buoy him into the proper complementary improv. Wasn't that the way the old jazz men used to put it? The musicians had to complement each other. Like colours.

So he listened, eyes closed as in meditation.

Behind him to the right, where the synthesizer stood against the studio wall, sat Esmeralda. Thirteen years old now, she had been with Nirmal and Billy since she was nine. She was a prodigy, and together the trio had left their mark on the music world.

They were improvising on a new sketch of Nirmal's called *Gandhi's Dream*, his most spiritual effort to date.

Nirmal's fingers began to move along his guitar. It was like a caress, and the notes, chords and Indian *ragas* flowed as if in response. The *ragas* were especially melodic, suggestive of serenity and love. The *tablas* became subdued, the background now. Esmeralda, after some meditation of her own, spun round on her stool, pushed a disc in on her synthesizer, and the drone note so common in Indian music came alive, high, almost to the end of a contralto's range. The drumming grew louder again, and both sounds worked at sustaining Nirmal's melody.

He stood, his lank hair splaying from the sides of his head as he arched his back, and ran across octaves and heptatonic scales, jumping from Western to Eastern sounds and back. It was already an amazing and unusual performance, and it had barely started. A feat of skill, instinct, endurance and incredible precision. His eyes were still closed; his was an intense concentration.

And in mid-stride up another scale, Nirmal Kapur stopped. Dangerfield and Esmeralda played for a few seconds longer, like superfluous chatter. Then they stopped, too.

Billy Dangerfield was about to speak. Esmeralda shook her head, two pigtails flying. Billy watched the wall clock. After five minutes he coughed.

Nirmal opened his eyes. It was the only motion he made. The rest of him stood, frozen. 'It's too tight, too forced. I can't get in free fall.'

'That's crazy, man. You were doing just fine. We all were, right, Esmeralda? Right. Trouble is, you count on inspiration too much. The sweat counts too, you dig? This is work, brother, not just play.'

Nirmal put the guitar in the case and turned off the amplifier. 'We don't rehearse today.'

Billy Dangerfield waved his arms. 'For cryin' out loud! It's only three weeks till concert time. Three mother weeks.'

'Yeah, three mother ones,' piped Esmeralda.

'I'm sorry, people.' Nirmal unplugged the guitar and closed the case. 'I've got other things in my head lately.'

'What other things? It ain't that bimbo works at the Coffee Klatsch, is it?'

'Bimbo is right,' Esmeralda stressed.

'You sound like an echo chamber, do you know that?' Nirmal told her.

'Well, is it? Is it that bimbo 'lizabeth?'

'No. No.' Billy shook his head. 'She pronounces it "Elspeth". Shit.'

'Yeah, Billy. Shit. Shit.'

'I'm getting out of here.' Nirmal picked up the case. 'Take her home, Billy, will you? Same time tomorrow.'

'That 'lizabeth's supergross, Nirmal,' Esmeralda shouted.

He didn't look back. 'Tomorrow.'

Nirmal hurried down the narrow staircase outside the hall. He didn't want to change his mind. He needed space, time by himself. Nirmal Kapur had a problem all right, but it had nothing to do with women. He paused at the entrance for a moment, looking through the greasy window glass at the hubbub of Central Square, Cambridge. As usual, a couple of winos were drinking out of their paper bags. They always loitered near the front door. As he opened it, a tall, rangy, grubby drifter with a beard joined them.

Nirmal passed the first two, who surprisingly didn't ask for a handout. The third stood directly in his path, however, and said, 'Thurnauer.'

Nirmal brushed past him. The man rushed forward and caught Nirmal's arm. 'The name's Thurnauer. Bernie – '

'Look, find another live one.'

'Please, listen, I'm – '

Nirmal tried a tough-guy voice. He had been to the Bogart Month Festival at the Brattle theatre a few times. 'See here, guy, you better put yourself into a detox if you know what's good for you.'

The man blinked. 'You've got me wrong.'

'Sure. Sure.'

'I'm not a drunk. I don't need detoxification.' He held out a wallet. 'See.'

'Police?'

'Yes. Undercover. Please . . .' He led Nirmal to a parked car. Nirmal looked inside. A well-dressed black man was at the wheel. Thurnauer had opened a back door. Nirmal still hesitated.

'I'm Lieutenant Jerome Abel,' the black man said. 'I guess I should've approached you instead of Bernie.' He showed his badge and smiled.

Nirmal climbed in. Thurnauer followed.

'We are going to see Captain Condorelli,' Abel explained further. 'He has something to show you.'

'Now wait a minute. I think I should know a little more first.' It suddenly occurred to Nirmal that he should have been more careful. He looked beyond his guitar case at the face in the rear-view mirror. Suppose these people were fakes? Damn, he hadn't been thinking right lately. 'Man, how do I know . . . ?'

'What?' asked Thurnauer. Nirmal moved himself into the far corner. Thurnauer smelled in those dirty clothes. Even from where he sat in the front seat, the smell wafted back to Nirmal.

'Well, I'm a kind of celebrity. At least, I'm getting there. Celebrities are prime targets for kidnapping.'

Abel and Thurnauer looked at each other.

'See?' Abel said. 'I should've been the one.' He turned to Nirmal. 'We're police, all right. And this has to do with Thuggee. You're familiar with that, aren't you?'

Nirmal nodded. He looked very unhappy.

'OK, now, kid? So relax. It's nothing so bad as kidnapping.'

'That's your point of view.'

'What's that mean?'

'Of the two. Being kidnapped is the lesser evil, dig?'

Abel and Thurnauer looked at each other again.

The black and white images flickered brightly, almost too white at times. The scene had been photographed at night with infra-red film. Nirmal could barely believe what he was seeing. No wonder the Swami was in trouble, no fucking wonder.

'Now, please don't tell me that's the Indian rope trick,' Captain Condorelli said.

They were such polite policemen, Nirmal thought; I've never thought of American policemen as polite before.

Abel and Thurnauer had taken Nirmal into Boston, to the Intelligence Division headed by Captain Vincent Condorelli. The captain made every effort to help Nirmal feel at home in the large briefing room. Through the open door came the sounds of their master computer. Condorelli's dark, smiling eyes had flustered Nirmal at first, but then the captain asked about his music.

'You're a rock star, aren't you?'

'Not exactly. I do play rock, but I combine it with Indian classical, European classical, even some jazz.'

'It's like a collage, Captain,' offered Belanger.

The captain looked as if he didn't know what a collage was. Nirmal eased them out of that gracefully. 'In a sense. You see, so many people believe that things like Eastern and Western music contradict each other. The intent behind my work is to prove such thinking false. They can link, connect with each other. Dig?'

'Then perhaps, Mr Kapur' – Condorelli suddenly got to the point – 'you and, uh, Mr Hanuman, is it . . . ?'

'Yes.'

'Perhaps both of you can help us. We tried to contact him, but we were told that he is' – Condorelli tried to keep his voice level – 'in meditation.'

'Right. The equivalent of that is a priest at his orisons. You know – prayers.'

'I see.' A nod.

'Meditation for an Indian holy man can last a much longer time, however. Like whole days . . . weeks.'

'Don't they eat?'

'Their disciples give them sustenance. You see, they're often in a trance.'

172

'A trance?'

'Yes – and the Swami has been seeking that state for some time now.'

'He hasn't succeeded?'

'Something is wrong. There is obviously a counter force preventing him from seeing Vishnarma.'

'Who?'

'Vishnarma, his late master.' Nirmal breathed deeply and tried again. 'Let's think in Western terms again. Christians pray to Christ, some to His saints. All of them are deceased, you know. Oops! Or were. Christians believe Christ was resurrected. But He had to die first. Dig me?'

'OK, I see your point.'

'Not all of it yet. Swami Hanuman meditates, goes into a trance. Then his astral or spiritual body goes to the heaven, I guess you can call it, where Vishnarma dwells.'

'That's a bit more complicated than praying to someone.'

Nirmal waited, checking whether Condorelli was laughing at him. He couldn't tell. Nevertheless, he continued, 'Anyway, the Master hasn't been successful in a while in his attempt . . .'

'What master?'

'My master. My guru. My teacher – Swami Hanuman. Vishnarma was *his* master. Got it?'

'Yes. Does Mr – uh, Swami – Hanuman usually succeed?'

'Oh, all the time, man. He and Vishnarma are rapping all the time. 'cept lately Kali has scrambled everything.'

'You mean like scrambling a transmission, a radio message . . . ?'

'Loosely speaking.'

Condorelli wet his lips and asked, 'Kali – she's the Indian goddess behind Thuggee?'

'You got it, man.'

'And she exists?'

'You got it. Guess you haven't heard that before?'

'Not true. There have been others . . . Santha Wrench was one.'

'So she told you the entire story.'

'Yes, what she claims is the supernatural part as well.'

'Do you believe her?'

'I'm beginning to.' Condorelli turned to his men. 'Put out the lights. Let's get the projector going. Let's see it again. And this time, I'll explain how the scene was filmed.'

The screen on the wall lit up. Before it was the movie projector.

'This was taken a week ago at a stake-out. The house was a centre for drug traffic. About 10.30 P.M., my men saw a group of figures crossing the lawn. This is what they filmed.' Condorelli sat down. 'OK, Jerome.'

It looked like the back lawn of a sizeable house, Nirmal concluded, and, as the picture focused on the lawn, it too proved sizeable and well cared for. Now the camera centred on a large oak tree with far-reaching branches and thick foliage like thunderheads piled atop one another. Beneath the tree stood six figures. All men, Nirmal thought, from the quick snatches of profile that were visible. They were clustered very close together near the trunk of the tree.

Finally, two of them left the hiding place. They scurried, bent over, up the incline and settled in the grass at a point a few feet from the house's left wing. Then there was a long wait; the camera showed that very spot again and again, and nothing happened.

The two figures seemed to be waiting for something.

The camera returned to the tree as if the cameraman became impatient. But the other four, braced against the trunk, were just as still. The camera passed over faces – a small bearded man, one with a long thin face. The picture jerked, seemed to tilt at an angle. The picture centred on the two men in the grass again. And something new.

What it was Nirmal couldn't determine at first. Because of the infra-red, the focus was soft with quite a few whitish flashes that were distracting. When it finally cleared, there was a shuffling of feet and some coughing in the room.

The new presence resembled a giant snake. That it was sentient was obvious, in that it uncoiled and gradually slithered upwards, its surface glistening. It had no head, though. Shaped like the cut end of a rope, its tip undulated on and on until it stopped and hovered a few feet from a first-floor window.

The perplexing question was: What held it up? It was much too wide to be a rope – perhaps six inches – and the oily surface suggested a gigantic worm, except there were no segments.

'It's not a snake, and it's certainly not a rope,' said Belanger, in a voice that hinted he had said the same thing each time he watched the film. Maybe he was hopeful someone would suggest what it could be.

But no one had a theory.

Now came the most amazing thing of all: one of the men started to climb the writhing thing. In the close-up view, he shinnied and grabbed hold of the shimmering surface.

'That looks damn smooth. Why doesn't he slip?' asked Jerome.

'The surface could be sticky,' put in Thurnauer, who had been quiet since their arrival.

Nirmal thought that a good explanation. He saw the second man start to shinny up. From the tree another pair darted to the base of the snake-like thing. The camera jerked, the scene tilted momentarily. Then it straightened, and the focus was on the first climber. Seated on the flat end of the 'snake', his legs bent and hugging its sides, the man reached out to the first-floor window. Slowly, he raised it, and climbed into the building.

The window remained open. The second climber repeated the same performance. Numbers three and four of the men were climbing now. The final pair darted from the tree to the colubrine ladder. As the final one rose, Nirmal remarked, 'I think that one's a girl. I was fooled, at first, but from this angle . . .'

'I think so, too,' agreed Condorelli. 'That's long hair tucked under the cap. Of course, nowadays it's hard to tell, but I think only a girl would bother to hide her long hair.'

'And the hands – look at them.' Nirmal was excited.

The camera stopped. Nirmal went over to the screen. 'I've seen this before. Swollen hands.'

'Why are they?' From someone.

'They're filled with extra power. Ordinarily, Thugs strangle in pairs or trios. One or two to hold the victim's arms and legs. The second or third one is the Strangler. However, for the sake of greater efficiency in this new cult, Swami Hanuman says, Kali grants more power to the hands. The Strangler can now do it all by himself or herself, if necessary.'

'That was how it was a few years ago?'

'Yes, Captain. The Thug meditates, empties himself and lets the goddess take over. She gives him more juice, his hands swell.'

Thurnauer left the back of the room and came forward. 'You see, sir, these neo-Thugs reach a state of nonbeing, absence of ego, of self; then they're all ready.'

So, Nirmal thought, they do have a resident expert.

'You have to remember this is a religious cult. That's

why they're so fanatical and so deadly.' Thurnauer studied the figure on the screen. 'She looks slight to me. Not up to the strength it would take to use a *rumel* correctly. But if what Nirmal says is true . . .'

'I've seen hands like that before – on other small recruits,' the Indian repeated. He sat down. The camera whirred on.

Nirmal saw the girl disappear into the house. The camera moved again, searched the entire structure. There was only one light, on the ground floor near the front. The camera settled on that, but not even a silhouette showed on the drawn shade.

Suddenly, the camera darted to the upstairs windows. The figures were climbing out and descending via the 'snake'.

'Less than five minutes. Four minutes nineteen seconds, to be precise. That's all it took,' Condorelli muttered, half to himself.

The six reached the ground. They went back towards the tree and then separated into pairs. They were gone. The camera went to the 'snake' again. It seemed to be melting. Finally, there was nothing. The film ended.

The lights went on. Condorelli's face looked as if it had the whitish cast of the infra-red. 'One of my men tried to tail one of the pairs. It was impossible. They got away too fast.' He sighed. 'We lost them . . . Then my men reported that there was no sign of activity in the house. We were already certain something uncommon had happened there, although there had been no noise, no screams, shouts or gunfire.

'I rushed down with a back-up team. We went in.' His face darkened, and the pale cast left his features. 'There were five members of a drug ring in there. Five big hombres armed to the teeth. They were all dead.'

'Strangled,' said Nirmal. It wasn't a question.

'Every one. And not one milligram of drugs was missing, as far as we could tell. Nothing had been taken. Aren't Thugs also thieves?'

'You've got it. But this might have been a trial run. You know – a class practising.'

'Practising?'

'Yes, like in school. A field expedition.'

'But why these pushers? They were armed to the teeth. Why not some easier group, like normal, everyday citizens?' asked Jerome.

Nirmal shrugged. 'Who knows? Maybe they figured that way there'd be no publicity. Like, the police aren't apt to publicize this, are they?'

'You bet. We don't look so good after this,' said Belanger.

Captain Condorelli gave him a scathing look.

'Well, that's the way I see it.' Nirmal scanned the faces. He knew they could barely believe him. 'When you speak to the Swami, he'll have more to offer.'

'Will you talk to him?'

'Soon as possible, Captain,' Nirmal replied. 'But I can't guarantee you when that will be. You see . . .'

'You already told me, son.' Condorelli ran his fingers through his thick hair. 'Abel, give him a ride home, will you?'

'Nothing's changed,' Molly Doyle said when he arrived. 'Six days – Jeez.'

'He's all right. And maybe he succeeded this time.' Which was something nobody would know until Hanuman came out of his trance. Molly was so quick to expect the worst. Nirmal went to his room, showered, and put on fresh jeans and a T-shirt with a decal of himself playing a guitar printed on it. One of the souvenirs sold at his

178

concerts. He only wore it at home. In public he preferred to be as invisible as possible.

Nirmal joined Molly and Adelaide in the kitchen and ate sparingly – lentil soup and a salad, with tea. Molly was talking at top speed to Adelaide about 'the horny fuckface that keeps staring at my teats in basket-weaving class. Now I'm sorry I even saw the adult ed centre ad. Shit, it's hard to concentrate with this sleazebag lookin' at me that way.'

'You're getting upset again,' Adelaide Jaworski told her. Adelaide hated scenes. 'Besides, you ought to be flattered. I know what he's doing is sexist, but sometimes that's good for a girl. I should be so lucky.'

Nirmal chuckled.

'What's so funny?' Molly wanted to know.

'You,' he said. 'You don't fool anybody.'

'Hey, you stop that now!' Molly went to the sink and threw her utensils in.

'We're losing c-control,' Adelaide stammered. 'It's b-because of the Master. We're l-losing control of ourselves.'

'You mean, he is!' Molly pointed at Nirmal. 'You heard what he said, Addy. Do you have to be a dumb fuck alla time?'

Nirmal shook his head. 'Don't mind her, Addy. Her head's always full of crap.'

Adelaide started to cry.

'Jeez, I'm gettin' outta here.' Molly left the kitchen.

'You should've let her be,' Adelaide told him as she wiped tears with her sleeve. Her big body shook, and she was having trouble breathing. 'She's afraid of men; you know that.'

Nirmal stared into his tea. He knew Adelaide was right and he felt guilty. 'Shit,' he said under his breath. He rose, and placed his cup and saucer into the sink. 'I'll do the dishes later. Don't touch them,' he added, in an attempt to make amends.

In the hall, he went to Molly's bedroom. The door was closed. Nirmal knocked, then tried again when there was no answer. He called Molly's name, once, twice, a third time. Finally, he shrugged and walked away.

Now he found himself nearing Swami Hanuman's meditation chamber. It was true, he kept telling himself; he had not been himself since his master had had difficulty. Realizing how dependent he was on the Swami, Nirmal Kapur felt even more terrible. Neither Hanuman nor he had intended it to turn out this way when, years ago, Nirmal had come for help. At that time, Nirmal's life had been drugs and nothing more.

But – and now he had to ask this question – what if the Master died? Could this change that had happened to him continue? Was the change deep enough? Indeed, was there anything to him that was separate from his teacher? Nirmal didn't know; and the fact made him feel even more abandoned, adrift with swirling eddies surrounding him and rapidly eroding the small foundation he stood upon.

It was an image Nirmal hadn't expected after all this time, after the guru's great teaching.

Nirmal entered the room. He always loved the great space of the place, with its hanging ropes. The amazing sight of the Swami dangling high above, near the ceiling, his toes clinging to the rope, while he meditated, was missing. Instead, Hanuman was grounded so his disciples would be able to feed him. Light from the windows seemed to pass through the diminutive form in the lotus position on the small carpet.

Nirmal went forward and stared into Hanuman's eyes. He saw only the whites; the pupils were gone. A cold sensation travelled along Nirmal's spine to his neck. It was eerie.

He wondered if Hanuman had found Vishnarma. He wondered . . . about the crash of breakers and the sea smell. Nirmal turned from his master.

Standing on the beach, Nirmal gaped at everything, at the great turquoise sea. It had no horizon, went on into infinity. Frothing breakers came charging in from everywhere. The din they made was painful, hurting his ears. This was an assault, he thought; Nature here sentient and fierce beyond belief.

Frantic, his eyes rose to a distant, colourless sky. His hands rose above his head. Perhaps it was an appeal. Nirmal was moving unconsciously. It was impossible to collect his thoughts.

He wanted to leave this landscape. The beach was blinding with its total whiteness, and the long reach of it made the pain increase. He trembled; arms, legs shook so he could barely stand; the noise grating inside his head was his teeth rattling.

God, he wasn't created for an experience like this! Such a happening was for Swami Hanuman, or Santha Wrench, who was psychic as hell. This wasn't the kind of thing that should be happening to him. He was only an ex-junkie, a composer-musician who was determined to stay straight. He had never sought out-of-the-body experiences, never ever wanted them, and certainly never subscribed to the belief that everybody should have one. And even his experiences under drugs had never been so total.

Nirmal stumbled, fell to his knees, then more on to his back, and rolled against a boulder bristling with red lichen. He willed himself to be still. But again his entire body shook, and again he rolled over the sand. Nirmal cursed himself in disgust, tried to stand, discovered he could, and then realized his lack of balance hadn't been due to his trembling.

The ground had quaked. So very much it had quaked that he had toppled on to his back.

There had been a loud reverberation too, but he had thought it was the sea. Now that the quaking was over, he could tell the difference. Nirmal scaled the boulder and felt somehow better, standing on its top.

He faced the frothing combers. They hurtled and eddied at and between the small chain of rocks. He turned, and to his great wonder saw a wall of jungle. Somehow, Nirmal didn't think there had been one there earlier, but he wasn't quite certain.

The jungle was quiet. Perhaps because whatever had caused the quaking came from that jungle, and that left everything else in it – animals, birds and insects – noiseless.

The terrible silence that spoke so loudly. The quiet that comes with waiting. The stillness of awful expectancy . . .

'Nirmal, my *chela*.'

The three words were like thunder in the hush. Nirmal started, sweat blurring his vision. He shook his head, and, when his eyes cleared, he saw Swami Hanuman emerging from the bush at the edge of the jungle. Nirmal leaped to the ground.

'What is happening, Bapu?'

'My faithful *chela*, you are here.' Hanuman held Nirmal's arms warmly. 'It is as it should be, then. Your true and unblemished spirit has brought you to me.'

'But Bapu, I'm very frightened. I am neither brave nor worthy enough for this.'

'That is not for you to determine, my *chela*. Now we must prepare ourselves.'

'For what?' Nirmal looked around. 'What was that quaking? What monster . . .?'

Before he could finish, the sound came again, and with it the splintering of trees. They held on to each other for balance.

'This way,' the Swami urged. He ran along the beach. Nirmal followed. 'But what comes, Bapu?'

'She . . . It is *she*.' Hanuman pointed. Nirmal looked, and nearly stopped in his tracks. An entire section of the jungle was being trampled – trees fell, brush parted. Nirmal saw something very high, very massive and very black heading towards the beach.

In his ear, Hanuman's voice guided him. 'Do as I do, *chela*.' And Nirmal raced to his master, who was now a speck in the distance.

It was a long run. White glaring sand made geysers beneath his feet, little spurts and billows that rose in the air like mist and stung his eyes. Ahead, the speck became larger, and soon he was at Hanuman's heels. He started to turn his head.

'Try not to look back, Nirmal,' he heard. The gentle voice steadied him. 'It is better to look away.'

'She is that terrible to see?'

'Not in her present form. She is but a gigantic black elephant. But it nevertheless is paralysing to observe such an anomaly.' Hanuman veered closer to the crashing waters.

More running. 'Note we are climbing.'

Nirmal panted a 'Yes'. Behind, the beach was trembling, the skyline shifted, the sea was at an impossible oblique angle. The trumpet of the elephant suddenly resounded everywhere, even to the infinite horizon. It seemed to echo from the sky instead of thunder.

Hanuman was correct about climbing. Without warning, the beach had become a slope. Steeper and steeper. Up, up, as in a dream. If so, the stitch in Nirmal's side was too painful, the sweat on his body too thick, the pump of his heart too loud to be a dream. Were dreams ever so detailed?

The trumpeting again. The quake, the pound, the thump, thump of the colossal pachyderm shattered the very geometries of everything. This dream, this heavenly plane, this world had become inconsistent. Not only did the beach become a slope, actually a cuesta, but its moderate side led to a valley that replaced the jungle.

Hanuman led them to the steep ledge. They reached the drop, and Nirmal yelped at the high, steep escarpment and the comber-coated rocks below.

'Jump, *chela*.' The voice in the ear again.

'Jump?! Oh, Bapu!'

'Trust me.'

Obviously, Hanuman was waiting for him to move first. Nirmal closed his eyes and leaped. He felt himself dropping, but slowly. He was a feather. He dared to look. To his left, the Swami was drifting with him. Nirmal was euphoric. He started to rotate slowly, and he bent his head back. The sky moved with him, a wash of blue and white gently rocking on an invisible pivot.

No longer afraid of the plangent beach line beneath him, he surrendered to the descent. He closed his eyes again and reopened them immediately. The very atmosphere shattered, he felt. The pounding, the trumpeting, all that had slipped from his memory returned, magnified tenfold. The heavens grew dark, as if a shadow had fallen across them. Two fissures like lightning broke through the roiling blackness. Something gripped his waist and then shot out to Hanuman, and the Swami almost disappeared.

Nirmal finally understood what had happened when he saw the tip of the elephant's trunk nearly cover Hanuman totally. It curled only once around his diminutive body. Its width was so great that one curl was all that was necessary.

The blackness above became delineated. He saw now the great flapping ears like the wings of a giant pterodactyl. Heavy gusts of air and sea whirled around whenever the ears moved. *Thwup, thwup*, they flapped like rhythmic thunder.

The eyes, bright, an effulgence of Evil, bore into his, and he screamed as his consciousness began to shred. Colours spun, he was in a whirlpool of chromatics.

Blue won. An ethereal blue, a fireball of blue incandescence spearing the sky.

Spearing black Kali!

Nirmal stared. The serpentine blueness that had suddenly sprung from the sea had cleaved the head of the fantastic pachyderm. The huge face was splitting in two down the centre of its forehead. Nirmal continued to fall, Hanuman again at his side.

'Thank you, my master,' he heard the Swami pray, as close as a breath in his mind.

Hanuman had found Vishnarma at last!

The blueness followed them, delicate mist that was a balm. Nirmal felt its healing touch. It went through him as if he were a wraith.

The last thing he heard was a new voice that said, 'Indeed, he is a faithful *chela*.'

Nirmal awoke in the meditation room. Hanuman was still in a lotus position, but he was out of his trance. Neither spoke for a while; both understood the meaning of their experience.

And when they did speak it wasn't about that. There was no need.

14

Varanasi

Two days had passed. Two more days of monsoon and
the shelter of Hasari Chandar's house. Rama Shastri
listened to Ileana Heng repeat her question for the third
time: 'Am I not enough for you, Mongoose?'

He refused to respond.

She waited, then left the *charpoy*. Naked, she moved
across the room and knelt at his feet. Her long black hair
draped over her breasts and splayed like silken tassels.

'How many times do you think I will endure this? This
man controls you. He plans to return to America, and
now you tell me you must go there, too. First, there was
his wife, Kamala, who was dearer to your heart than
myself. Now, it is this daughter . . .'

'It isn't like that.'

'Then how else is it? She isn't your child. If she were, I
could understand, but . . .' She stood up, crossed to the
chair opposite, took a cigarette from a box on a lacquered
table and lit it with a lighter. She then crossed her shapely
legs, inhaled and exhaled, her eyes following the smoke
trail to him. 'You are determined to leave. I can tell. You
are not listening. Perhaps you prefer me behind the
mozzinet.'

'I've indicated nothing like that.'

'If you will not listen, why am I here, then? You raise
me from the level of a common *dassis*, then you push me
down again. I suppose I should be more grateful. Forgive
me, Mongoose. Without you I would be in the Cages in

Bombay, maybe. I owe you my life. Without you I am nothing.'

'Without me you did very well,' he reminded her. 'You even put away your pipe.'

Immediately, he wished he hadn't mentioned that.

'Ah, Mongoose, I wanted so to please you. I thought that would make you very happy.'

'It did, Ileana.'

'But not enough. You still plan to return to America.'

'I have to. Santha Wrench is in danger. This Thug Huzoor, this Leinster, admitted he planned to go there and . . . You saw yourself what he was like.'

'Talk. Talk. He was lying, seeking to make you go there while he continued his evil ways here.'

Shastri shook his head. 'Would that it were so, my dear.'

He stared at the room, wondering why he had chosen to use it. Hasari Chandar had been set free when the Thugs came for Ileana. Two more names, the men he had left with her, had been added to the list of dead policemen. For some reason he couldn't fathom, they had let Hasari go. Perhaps they considered his betrayal of them as part of the trap they had set for Shastri and the others. Which was true, basically. Thus, perhaps their feeling towards Hasari had been impersonal.

Whatever the motive, Chandar had fled. And since Shastri had to take care of the cremation of his men here in Varanasi, he had decided to make use of the best quarters available for Ileana.

The decor was depressing, however. Much of the place was covered with erotic paintings, carvings, hangings and murals. Some were recent and reflected Hasari's preference for very young girls.

A low rap on the door. Shastri, who was partially dressed, motioned to Ileana. She crossed to the *charpoy* and disappeared behind the netting. Shastri put on his *kurta* and went to the door.

Gopal was waiting. He handed something to Shastri. 'This was wedged under the front door. A chit, it looks like.'

Shastri fingered the small oilskin packet. He extracted letter paper, folded, and read the first few lines. 'Is Steve in the building?'

'In the drawing room.'

'Tell him I will be there shortly. I also want you present.'

When Shastri returned to Ileana, he heard, 'Now I am behind the *mozzinet*, as you would like. Why did you educate me, make me articulate, only to suppress me?'

'You have never been inarticulate. Even when you knew only one language. And certainly never suppressed.'

'How can you be sure I won't resort to the opium pipe if you leave me stranded again?'

He was already prepared for this. He countered, 'That is not my responsibility, Ileana. Now I must leave. Business.'

As he headed for the drawing room, Shastri weighed the possibility of her following through with her threat. He concluded she would smoke again, but, whatever the outcome, he mustn't let her blackmail him emotionally. He had to go to America. And soon.

The aroma of Stephen Wrench's pipe met him before he entered the room. He had been reading editions of the *Hindustan Times* dated two months ago, and they were stacked at his feet. He sat near the arching fronds of a potted plant. To his left was a large lacquered screen heavily decorated, but this time minus the erotic depictions. Gopal was standing, and Shastri gestured that he sit. Shastri remained on his feet, however, and announced, 'This letter is from Kurt Leinster.'

'That sonofabitch . . .' began Wrench.

'. . . has cheek,' Shastri ended. 'And plenty of it. Why don't I read it aloud now, and we'll see what his point is.'

They both nodded. Shastri read without hesitation. He wanted to drive Ileana's threats from his mind, concentrate on police business, the sole thing he should be concerned with.

There was no heading to the letter.

Rama Shastri read the tight scrawl:

I want to establish here and now that your fates are sealed, gentlemen. You can't change any of it. Kali Ma has decreed it and so it shall be. Once too often you have thwarted *her* plans, and a terrible death will be your end, both of you.

But first you will witness the transformation of Santha Wrench. Her father and the avuncular Rama Shastri will witness woman become goddess. Then that same vessel of Kunkali will demand the deaths of her own loved ones. What a delicious irony.

This is no idle threat but a prophecy. I, Huzoor of Thuggee, he who has received the sacred Scroll of Power in the Cave of the Ancient Rishis, do pronounce this sentence of death and blight upon your kind. I prophesy this, so beware, be warned, and expect the doom that awaits.

'Egocentric bastard,' said Wrench.

Well could it have been written when the fools you are intruded, defied the sanctity of my temple – 'Abandon All Hope Ye Who Enter Here'.

'Smart ass. The same precious smart ass.'

Shastri's voice drowned out Wrench's remarks.

I don't expect you to heed this. The policeman's mentality limits itself. It lacks the poetical vision necessary to embrace ideas like the emergence of the avatar. For it is such that I am. I have been to the abode of my Mother and back. I have brought a

189

new fire to the Earth. The fire of Kali, the ancient truths, the placement of all humans in the proper order of things. Namely, the divine ones who are part god, part men; their gurus, followers and acolytes; and finally the slaves, the sacrifices.

Evil, mad – you are already thinking this of me. I say you are mad because you will not accept the true reality. You are evil since to deny that which has been created is a great crime.

But only a matter of time and your end will come.

There was no signature.

Gopal said, 'The man is possessed. Can he actually believe this?'

'I'm not so convinced as you two that he isn't a bit of what he says. Where has he been all this time but in Kali's abode? He certainly disappeared from the face of the Earth for a while. And if he came from some supernatural hiding place, then one can well believe some part of him has changed . . .'

'Become divine? Come on, Ram. What happened to your agnosticism?'

'No, Steve. Not divine but demonic. I'm only trying to point out that this raving lunatic, this egocentric maniac, does have unusual powers.'

Wrench stood up. 'He's no more than a charlatan. With his Kali with the phoney arms.'

'Yes, that's more of the elusiveness of Kurt Leinster. If you recall, he loves theatrics, he even wore a false face, make-up, when he first reorganized Thuggee years ago. The phoney Kali is very much like him. *But*, he could and has conjured the real thing when necessary. He is in communion with the living goddess, or a kind of usually untapped life force that produces Kali and her demons. An area of evolution unknown before. After all, Nature never concerns herself with good or evil. But it is probably very demanding, takes all of his energy to do it. So, instead, he made the Amazon play the role.' He paused.

190

'Mrinalini Pal – that is the name the cart driver gave us at Hardwar.'

'The killer of Shambu,' Gopal reminded them.

Wrench went to the window, listening to the tympani outside. They knew he was thinking of Shambu, who had saved his life. And that of his daughter. The monsoon seemed to reflect the future – wild, windswept, the raging onslaught, the voice of the eternal storm. Waiting. Waiting for them.

'Waiting for Santha,' he concluded aloud. This was the second time Leinster had spoken of her. 'I must go home.'

15

Cambridge and New Hampshire

Phyllis pulled the curl out of a strand of hair and rubbed it even flatter against the fabric of her dress at the shoulder. 'I want to go back to Danvers,' she said. 'It's too hard living on the outside.'

'Do you really believe that?' Dr Annette Kitteridge asked. 'Or do you think you were in the hospital for so long that you became institutionalized?'

Phyllis blinked. She wasn't prepared for the question. 'I miss my friends on the ward,' she blurted, after three brisk puffs on her cigarette. 'It's hard to make friends on the outside.'

'Have you tried?'

More puffs. Phyllis looked at the clock. 'Can I go now?'

'Did you try to make a friend?'

Phyllis nodded.

'And . . . what did she say?'

Phyllis turned away. 'It was a guy,' she said softly to her left, as if there were a third party standing there.

'A man?'

Phyllis finally swivelled her eyes to the doctor. 'Yeh. He was alone, sitting on this bench on Comm Ave.'

'Did he speak to you?'

A nod. 'He seemed to want to talk to me.'

'Did that surprise you?'

'Yeh.'

'Why?'

'Men never seem to want to talk with me.'

'This one did.'

'Yeh. He liked me, too, I think. In the beginning, anyway. He told me about himself and asked me questions. About me. We talked for two hours almost.'

'Two hours! He must have been interested in you.'

'Until the end. Then I think he figured it out.'

'Figured what out?'

'That I was in a mental hospital before . . . He put it all together in the end and couldn't wait to get rid of me. He liked me until he worked that out.'

Dr Kitteridge looked at her watch with regret. 'I think our time is about up.'

Phyllis tried to say more, but her lips only seemed to gulp air like a stranded fish. Now she wanted to talk, but the fifty-minute hour was over.

'We'll continue our discussion about this man next week,' Annette tried to reassure her.

Phyllis's shoulders slumped. She went to the door, stopped, looked back.

'Next week, same time,' Annette told her in her best voice. Phyllis nodded and left.

Annette Kitteridge wrote into a notebook on her desk: *At our next session, must ask Phyllis about the man she met.* She paused, tapped her pen against her chin, then added: *This is progress. In the past, Phyllis has denied herself any conversation with men because she desires them so much. For once she* overcame her fears *and talked with one for* nearly two hours.

Annette pondered the words she had underlined. Phyllis had made a decision not to panic; she overcame her terror. The amount of time was important, too. 'For two hours almost.' That was a long time for Phyllis to sit there and not up and run.

Courage is a decision, Annette decided in writing, *a rational progression that weighs and evaluates its fear and then decides to face it anyway.* She thought about it again, then added: *This isn't what I mean but very close. Courage is a mechanism? An instinctual surge that* . . .

Annette shook her head. Leave it alone; it will come to you later, she thought. A mechanistic impulse, an instinct – someone else must have written that already. Besides, that's a regression. A conscious decision is what you want, no matter how fast that decision was made.

Annette wanted to do a paper about the decision to get well. She had observed her clients doing that for years now. Continuing life's meaning, surviving, living with the terror – Annette's thoughts switched to Santha Wrench.

Could I go on with something inexplicable at my heels? she asked herself.

The July sunlight bevelled through the bay window behind her desk on to the curving side wall with its framed diplomas and ignited the pink curlicues of the trimming. Below was the loop of the Charles River and the Cambridge Boat Club facing the colonnade of Harvard Stadium.

Annette Kitteridge stood, stretched her rangy frame and looked at the view. She saw students reading or sunbathing along the riverbank, and she remembered her own student days when she had done the same. It was the kind of day when one hungered for the past.

Then there had been no mystery, no loose threads. Everything had an explanation, and if it didn't, she had always known that sooner or later there would be a solution. Everything was always connected to something else, somehow. Nothing ever, ever came into existence out of its own being. Nothing.

She never knew then that she would end up childless, either. Or that she would meet Santha and be as a mother to her; fill that life-long empty void within herself.

How easily, how swiftly it had all happened. Nature

abhors a vacuum, the philosopher said, and her relationship with the young woman had occurred with that immediacy that comes from a very long duration of great need.

Fulfilling the rules of 'natural law', though. So clear, so logical – surrogate mother, the reverse-surrogate daughter. Everything fitted the text, nothing to disturb the foundations of 'reality'.

Nothing mind-boggling . . . like a magnetic pocket that wasn't there.

Annette's trained consciousness, with its roots in the loam of cause and effect, had worked tirelessly at that 'magnetic pocket' for over a week now. Since the very day, if not the hour, that her Beachcraft Bonanza had nearly been yanked out of the sky.

She had even returned to the spot, to see if it would happen again. This was after she had checked the meteorological charts of that memorable day and the geodetic and topological maps of the region. She had to fly to the place again, and when she did, nothing happened, of course. A part of her already realized this; why, she had flown safely over that area three or four dozen times in the past. Which was why she hadn't reported the incident in the first place. It was not a repeatable phenomenon; not a magnetic pocket at all, or a vortex or any other natural event that would pull or hurl or suck a plane to its doom.

When she did tell Santha, the girl shook her head with understanding. 'It's difficult to accept. Evil is a force. It exists. In its rawest form it can do a thing like that.'

'There was something below the plane, pulling it down. I felt it in the controls, I – '

'Whatever it was is irrelevant. Yes, it was there, perhaps, and it was at the cockpit window with me . . . And then it was gone. And gone when you returned again.

You see, *it was only meant to be there to speak to me.* And it did, very clearly, very convincingly.'

As time passed, believing that it had occurred at all became more and more difficult. Annette admitted this to Santha. 'If I adopt your methodology, Santha, it makes the scientific method look like so much obfuscation.'

'When we speak of the supernatural, it is,' Santha agreed, to Annette's surprise, if not shock. 'The problem is, you want me to prove that it was real. I refuse to because I can't, honestly. So you've taken on the burden of proof like a true scientific martyr. Since you can't believe, you've set out to disprove it or to rearrange it to fit some logical explanation.'

Annette smiled at the memory of the words and Santha's affronted look. She was expecting more honesty than this, the look demanded.

A soft rap on the door. Annette opened it slightly. 'I'm leaving for lunch now, Doctor,' her secretary said.

'Thank you,' Annette replied and left the door ajar.

It was time for her lunch too, but still she lingered. There had been a phone call for Santha from India the previous night. Santha's father, Stephen Wrench, was returning to America. Annette recalled the few times she had seen him. Had he stopped grieving about his wife's death? she wondered. Her actions became automatic while she fantasized. She took her bag from the desk drawer, then went to the cupboard. Stephen Wrench was attractive, she thought, and a widower. Perhaps . . .

'Now, don't be manipulative,' she scolded the image of herself reflected in the long mirror behind the cupboard door. 'All this because you want a daughter so badly.' No, she quickly assured herself. Stephen Wrench was exciting enough on his own merit. Had he never had a daughter, she would have found him intriguing.

Annette examined her figure, turning slowly round. She

was pleased with what the reflection told her. She reached for the summer jacket on the hook, and had just put it on when she heard a sound.

Two men had walked into her office from the anteroom. The smaller man smiled affably. 'Ah, Dr Kitteridge,' he began.

The familiar *brrrriit* noise. Woods. Branches against car windows. *Brrriitt. Crack!* There a twig broke.

More motion. Jumping. Springs straining. More bouncing, the jumping was very hard on the stomach. Why didn't they stop?

'Bear more to the left, Thin. More to the left. That's it.'

'This route'll raise hell with the suspension.'

'We may be observed from the turnpike.'

'I don't see it that way.'

'Thin, trust me. Nothing in this looks like it appears.'

'I already figured that. But I still don't think the cops are on to us. Aw, look, Vic, I don't really belong to this ashram thing. In the beginning it was only a hideaway. Now I'm in so deep and I don't understand what's going on.'

Fully awake now, Annette listened. She didn't remember everything, but enough to know she should remain quiet. That was what she felt deepest – be very quiet. Pretend to be unconscious and listen.

Besides, her head ached. They had knocked her out with chloroform. The wooziness lingered. That alone guaranteed she be still, to recover.

Annette could smell country air. The low temperature, the dampness, had to mean it was beyond nightfall. They had been travelling since early afternoon, and wherever they were now had to be a sizeable distance from Boston.

'She still out cold?' asked the male voice she could tell was the driver's, the one called Thin.

Hands grabbed her. The man in the back seat next to her said: 'She should be clear of the chloroform by now.' Fingers wound themselves in her hair. Her head was raised, then lowered. 'She remains in the lap of Morpheus.'

'You were pretty quick with that soaked rag, Vic. Good thing. I could see she was looking for a chance to break free. Can't trust these long-legged bitches . . .'

'Yes, she is a clever one.' That would be the small man. The first of the two to speak to her in her office. It rushed in now, the memory, everything . . .

'Ah, Dr Kitteridge, so here you are. And here we are.'

The small man had made the announcement as if they had been longtime friends finally reunited.

'You have no right to come in without knocking first,' she snapped.

'Tra-la, Thin and I have no time for etiquette, Doctor. You're to come with us.'

'I am – what!' she cried. She saw then the gun in Thin's hand.

'Please, Doctor. Thin can be unreliable. He has killed before. It would upset me as much as you, the spilling of blood, when killing is contrary to my faith.'

'Well, we can't have any spiritual traumas, can we?' Annette replied, heading for the door. There was little else she could do but banter. It didn't ease the terror she felt, though.

As she neared Thin she hesitated. Something eager in his eyes glued her to the floor. 'Move,' he gritted, pressing the gun muzzle into her midriff. It spurred her on.

Unfortunately, they met no one she knew on the way to the lift. Nor in the lift itself. It was uncanny. Dr Annette Kitteridge's office had been in that building for thirty-three years. Everyone, from Maintenance to the dentists on the sixth floor, knew her. Yet that day not one of them was around.

The three of them went down alone in the lift to the basement garage. It was then she began to panic. Annette had had some strange hope that escape would be possible in the presence of others. Now . . .

Also, they didn't go to her car but instead to a dusty old Buick near the garage entrance. The finality of the little man's opening of the back door made his mock attempt at a warm accompanying smile seem ominous indeed.

'It's a beautiful day for a drive in the country,' he added. Again Annette paused. A hand pushed against her spine and backside roughly, and she went in with a screech. Sprawled on plaid upholstery with an oily smell she could not place, Annette set about to turn. Instinctively, her hand went first to her dress, which had risen to her thighs.

The ladylike instinct proved her downfall. Vic, the little man, leaped on to the back seat and, in a kneeling position at her elbow, lunged with the chloroform-soaked rag. His grip was surprisingly strong. With his body pressing against her chest and arms, he was able to hold the rag in place over her nostrils until Annette spun into the whirlpool of unconsciousness.

Now, revived, despite a headache and a lingering dizziness, she heard clearly, distinctly, 'Very clever. I think I should double-check her condition.'

Hands roamed over her clothing. This time, they remained fixed on her breasts. Then one of them went in under the fabric of her blouse. The fingers dug under the cup of her brassiere. Annette sprang up, her arm rising to smash into his nose.

Deftly, the man pulled away. He laughed, a high-pitched sound that angered her more. 'Now that's an improvement,' he said.

Annette took a deep breath. Through the dashboard window she saw the Buick's headlights funnelling along a path through a field of high grass and stalks. The funnel seemed to lift beyond the route in the distance and leave the stalk tips bright, glowing like a horizon line at the last breath of sunset. The car moved more smoothly, and she was able to see the sky vastness that open space unfolds and a few stars. They made her feel terribly melancholic and twice as trapped, somehow.

'Where are we?' she barked. Let it out, that's right, she spurred herself, before you slip totally into a depression. Farm odours, manure, humus, gathered produce answered that it was farm country.

'We are in New Hampshire.'

'Where? Why? I demand . . .?' Annette stopped. The man had placed a gloved hand before his mouth. He was laughing behind it, damn him!

Annette chose to ignore him, to treat him as she would a very sick client who was enjoying a sadistic joke on her. Ahead the lights met a succession of others. A building, a huge house with many lighted areas – windows, a front porch, a sprawl of illumination as from a pole with arc lighting.

'You see,' from the man, 'we have a destination.'

'The ashram,' the driver added. His voice held a forced attempt at reverence.

'You are familiar with the word, of course.'

'What word?' she baited.

'You mock me, Doctor. But I'll play the game. An ashram is a hermitage. Yes, a place to meditate on matters spiritual. See how bright it is. Like a beacon waiting to

200

guide us to the solace of the Holy, the Divine. But that, too, is illusion, I fear.'

Annette said nothing.

'Ask me what I mean,' he suddenly insisted. 'Go on, please. Humour me.'

'All right,' she decided, speaking between gritted teeth. 'What do you mean?'

'The light is illusion, I say. It may sound melodramatic, but I must confess . . .' He suppressed a high giggle, more like a lurking wheeze, she thought. '. . . yes, I must tell you, lest your hopes rise unnecessarily. Ours is – a dark ashram.'

'Oh,' she said, after a while.

'Darker than night, than pitch. I am speaking of God's Very Own Shadow now. If Man has a shadow side to his nature, who is to say that God doesn't?'

Annette concluded that this dialectic was intended to impress her. A typical sociopathic stand, a pose to warn her that she was dealing with her peer, and even more.

Again, Annette had no intention of answering him, and besides, they had left the field and were climbing a slight incline, in the arc-lighted space. As they neared the house, Annette heard the repetitious strains of sitar music. To her surprise, the car veered left, away from the house, however. For a brief moment before they turned, she thought she saw the silhouette of a woman in the highest window. Something was wrong in its outline, she realized, a serious aberration, but she couldn't quite grasp what it was.

The Buick moved on further left, went down a gradient. The headlights flashed on a massive barn; the car stopped in the sloping pocket before the barn door.

The man Thin tooted the horn. Twice. Then a quick slap to produce half a blast. Arc lights near the roof blazed on, and one of the barn's great doors was pulled

201

back. Annette Kitteridge stared at the man in the doorway. His features were indistinct in the glare. The barn's interior behind him was a bright sheen.

That this was the journey's end hit her with the force of a blow. Stunned, Annette stared at the doorway. It was like a block of cool fire.

This is it, she kept thinking; this is my prison. The world she had fitted into so comfortably but a few hours ago was slipping away.

Vic Croce was in no hurry to leave. He wanted to talk, to elucidate. The ego of the monomaniac, she analysed.

'There are twenty-two years of tradition behind this ashram,' he was saying. 'It has been in existence that long. A place of pause. Sanctuary from the world for those who would meditate. Entirely self-reliant. We grow our own food, you understand. We sell some of it to pay for other necessities. We have managed to survive well, we Vedantists . . . I beg your pardon, former Vedantists, I should say. We have given that up now since the dreams came. The dreams changed everything.'

He waited. Thin tapped the wheel with his fingernails. His eyes were fixed on Annette. She could see them in the rear-view mirror. Uncomfortable, she turned to Croce. 'Dreams,' she repeated.

Immediately, on cue, 'I was the first to have them. Later, there were others . . . The very same dreams. Like clone dreams. How is that scientifically possible, Doctor?'

'Nothing comes to mind.'

'Precisely. More of that inexplicable phenomenon we read of every so often. But I was the first, among the fifty-three here . . . *I saw* her *first. Her*, you understand.'

'I'm afraid I don't.'

'And I think you are a liar, Doctor. Either to me or more so to yourself. I am positive Santha Wrench explained everything to you. It's very simple, once you accept the simplicity of it. She exists. Kali is as real as you or I. I would evaluate it as even a greater reality than the two of us.'

When she didn't respond, 'That was what separated, split us Vedantists. Kali came to us in our dreams, tutored us in what was to come. The Vedanta masters were to be replaced by He Who Was To Come. Now that very He will be here – tonight or tomorrow. Whichever, it will be soon.'

Thin coughed.

'Oh, yes,' Croce agreed. 'We must go in. The rest I will narrate later.'

The door at Annette's side opened. She looked up at Thin. His eyes reflected something like disgust. She couldn't tell whether it was at her or at Croce's procrastination.

Her stomach felt as if it had a tight fist in it. The fist moved around. Painful, painful. She thought she might vomit or faint, and she took in great gulps of air as she stood.

That settled her. Some. The car door slammed behind her. Croce moved forward and stood before the background of cool fire.

'Come,' he said.

16

Wayland

Santha Wrench crumpled the cablegram. Even the fact
that Daddy and Uncle Ram were flying here couldn't fill
the mind-boggling emptiness she felt. It was as if her
consciousness had been ripped from her mind. Some
violent hand had seized her awareness, her link with
surroundings and loved ones, her life's meaning.

Annette was missing.

Taken away from her. Kidnapped. Forced to leave
Santha's world.

'I'm cursed,' she cried out. To a man, they looked at
her. George took a step. Santha extended an arm, palm
upward. 'Stay away. I'm cursed!' she told him. 'Keep
away from me!'

The time was 8.45 P.M., and she had been aware of
Annette's disappearance for almost five hours now. At
four in the afternoon, she had phoned Annette's office,
only to find that she hadn't been seen by her secretary
since lunch. When Santha hung up, she became
uncomfortable about that. She then phoned George
Buchan, who reassured her that Annette was probably
dealing with an emergency involving one of her clients.

Nevertheless, Santha contacted Annette's secretary
again at five o'clock. No, she was told, the doctor had not
returned nor had she phoned in.

Santha worked a little late that day and was about to
leave the museum when she received a call. It was
Annette's secretary. She had gone to the building's garage

for her car and noticed that Dr Kitteridge's Toyota was still in its parking space. It struck her then as very strange that, if the doctor was in the building, she hadn't appeared at her office, not once. Concerned, the secretary had contacted Security, who in turn questioned the man at the entrance booth. He hadn't seen Dr Kitteridge's car since the morning, when it came into the garage.

That was enough for Santha. She turned to George again for help. He notified Captain Condorelli's division immediately.

George drove her home that evening. Shortly afterwards, the captain arrived with Thurnauer, Abel and two other men. As the time increased without a sign of Annette Kitteridge, Santha began to lose control. Even a cablegram from her father stating that he and Rama Shastri were heading for the States immediately couldn't curb her grief.

George Buchan suggested that Swami Hanuman be brought to Wayland at once. 'She needs much more than just psychological help,' he pleaded. Condorelli gave the order to Abel: 'Get the Swami. And that disciple of his,' he added, groping for the name.

'Nirmal Kapur, Captain.'

'That's it. Bring him, too.' He told George, 'That's in case I can't follow the old guy. The kid can interpret.'

'Sir,' Thurnauer said, 'I've heard Swami Hanuman lecture. He's pretty damn articulate.'

'My man here gets around,' the captain informed George. 'Undercover. He's mixed with every kind. Hippies in the old days. Yuppies and mystics. Addicts, pushers, perverts. Nothing makes him queasy.'

Thurnauer listened intently, stroking his beard. 'The less prejudice the better, Captain. It shows, otherwise, and they smell cop.'

'You've got him on the defensive,' one of the men quipped. 'Can't you see, Cap, he's sensitive.'

Thurnauer glared and sank into an armchair.

Santha meanwhile had been in the next room, brooding over a cup of tea. It was shortly afterwards that she announced she was cursed. It interrupted Thurnauer's final retort that he had learned everything from Condorelli, who had once been undercover too. It was all nervous banter, George understood. There was tension about the fate of Annette Kitteridge. All the more so since they had never expected she would become a victim of the Thug cult.

If that was what had happened, of course.

Santha had no doubts. She ranted, 'It's like a curse, I tell you. Annette is close to me, and they – *he* knows that! They – he had you worried about me, but it was her he wanted first.'

'Why would that be, Miss Wrench?' Condorelli asked. 'What's the logic behind it?'

'Psychological warfare,' she explained, while she hugged her arms and shivered. 'It undermines me, that's why. He took her away to shred what balance I have left.'

'You mean Kurt Leinster?'

'No other. And I almost dislike myself for cringing this way. His nature is really so warped and petty. He lacks the majesty of the literary villain, and, as I recall, that's what he hungers for most.'

'Sure. And Hitler saw himself as a great Teutonic warrior,' agreed Thurnauer.

'But it's Leinster who has the power, don't you see? Not you or me.' Santha raised her hands to heaven as if she were battering at an invisible foe. 'The gods are on his side!'

'This is where it gets over our heads, gentlemen,'

warned George. 'Now you know why I wanted the Swami to be present.'

'Well, Leinster has Kali's blessing, George,' she railed at him. 'You've seen that for yourself. First, as she nears, you hear the bracelets, the anklets. Not just two, like the ones you see here on my wrists. But countless – ten, fifteen, perhaps – all clinking against each other. And the skulls – let's not forget her girdle of skulls – you hear them too.'

'Santha . . .'

'And the smell of musk. Oh, come now, George – inform these good men what to expect. It's only fair, George, the decent thing to do. Because this is Kunkali, the Maneater, we're talking about. Not any little ol' demon. This is Kali Ma.' Santha's arms jerked, her eyes rolled. 'Mother, Dark Mother, perhaps what Shakespeare meant by "that sulphurous pit". Kaliii, Kali-iii. Hear how plaintive that call is.'

'Stop it, Santha.'

'No, George, I won't! These men should know about her. Then, if she appears some day, night, hour, a minute from now, they'll be prepared. If that's ever possible. That's what Kurt Leinster has backing him, Captain. Behind every great louse there's a . . .' She collapsed into a chair. 'And now he has taken poor Annette.' Santha lowered her head and heaved great, racking sobs.

When Swami Hanuman and Nirmal arrived, George had long since sedated Santha and brought her to bed. Captain Condorelli and his detectives were silent at first, as if in a spell at the presence of Hanuman. George made the introductions, and still there was silence. George coughed, then told the Swami about Santha.

'Excuse me, sirs.' Hanuman gave them a slight bow and went upstairs. The captain gave a 'that's all right', but his words trailed behind the departing figure. He looked back at George, who explained, 'There are elements he must look for . . . that he can determine better than we.'

'Something your Harvard training didn't allow for.'

'Nor your own training, Captain,' George replied, a little put out at the other's reverse snobbery. 'I think we all get the rhubarb on this one. What the Swami is looking for isn't in any text or manual, I'm sure. Nevertheless, he is a kind of diagnostician. He witnessed Santha in the past when she was possessed. It was something akin to the wild imaginings of a horror novelist.'

'Yes, like what she was briefing us on. The signs of the goddess Kali . . .'

'You're correct. But there was more. He particularly remembers one incident when he saw her. Besides the sounds that Santha mentioned, the musky smell, there was an unnatural coldness. I was pretty close to her that time, and my exposed extremities – nose, hands – turned blue. There was even frost on my eyebrows . . .'

The men listened to every word. There was surprisingly no coughing, no averting of the eyes, no cynical upturning of the mouth, no chuckling. They were well trained, these men. However, George could tell which of them truly believed. It was more instinct than anything. Thus, it was Thurnauer to whom he directed most of his description.

They were in the parlour: George, Nirmal, the captain, Belanger, Abel and a man named Haskell. They had been at the Wayland house for two hours now, still unruffled, men used to waiting. The captain had already asked the routine questions – was Dr Kitteridge prone to disappearing for hours, did she have any lovers or private friends that she might be with? Or extremely disturbed patients who would abduct her? A description of Annette had been sent to the police throughout the state and all the

208

bordering New England states as well. All airports were being watched.

'Why Dr Kitteridge, do you think?' Condorelli rubbed his chin with a knuckle. 'What's the point?'

'You heard Santha say it – psychological warfare. They want to break Santha's resistance down. She and Annette are very close, like mother and daughter.'

The captain strained, gazing at the ceiling. Every so often he heard a footstep, the creak of a stair.

George noticed. 'Hanuman's checking the whole house.'

'For what?' From Belanger.

Nirmal, who had been quiet since his arrival, explained: 'For presences.'

'More of what we can't see?'

'Right, Captain. For example, the goddess herself could be present.'

'So I gather.' Condorelli slapped a thigh. 'Every time I look at myself in the mirror these days, I ask myself, "Am I really doing this? Chasing phantoms?"'

'There are stranger things than you or I have ever thought of, Captain.'

'So I've heard, Thurnauer. But I keep thinking of poor Kearney, dead in the men's room at Lord & Taylor's. He was killed by living, breathing people. I can deal with that. But I just don't have the imagination for the rest.'

'Then why do you tolerate us with our *imaginings*?' George Buchan challenged.

'Dr Buchan, you're a recognized psychiatrist. I don't believe for one moment that, until your encounter with Kurt Leinster and his gang of fiends, you ever considered a goddess to be much more than a symbol. Am I correct?

'Yes. A symbol. Nothing more than a pictograph of an idea in Nature or in Mankind.'

'And Stephen Wrench hinted as much when he came to

see me before he left,' Condorelli continued. 'Now, Wrench can be a pretty matter-of-fact sort of guy, like any good policeman. These are the things that keep me tied here listening to all of you. Yet . . . I'm a man with a religion. I'm a Roman Catholic. Now, there are things like the transubstantiation of bread and wine at Mass that I never question. Because I believe in it. That's how simple it is.'

'Precisely,' a voice from the doorway said. 'Belief determines perspective. One may believe in one thing but not another. Both things might be very real, however.'

'OK, Swami, I can follow that. But I've done some research on Kali. Why, at her worst, she's something out of nightmares. Are nightmares real?'

The little man walked into the room. He appeared even more dwarfed by the size of the men around him. 'I can only beg of you, Captain, and each of your men, to reserve judgment about this. It could mean your lives.' His eyes commanded attention. There was poise and power behind that look. 'I have been throughout the house. *Nothing* is present. Within this residence or within Santha.'

'Could I ask how you can tell?' Belanger asked.

'I can *see* if anything is present.'

'Yeah, sure. You're like that Peter Hurkos that's helped the cops so much. I read about him. He sees things, too.'

'I saw nothing. Santha is safe at the moment. She is but emotionally upset. Very normal, very understandable. When she awakens I will speak with her. Perhaps I can calm her.'

He stopped talking. Some of the others set about asking more questions, but he held a hand up. 'Please . . .' His simian features squinched for a moment. 'I expected an assault on Santha in the usual way. As before. Possession through her psyche, her thoughts and emotions. This abduction of Dr Kitteridge suggests a new strategy, however. It concerns me greatly. We are dealing with the Mistress of the Deceiver. That is what Thug means – Deceiver. She is a mistress of the convoluted, the unexpected. She is treachery personified. To confront Kali is to encounter a series of trap doors. Everything changes, is no longer what it seems to be. So we must be very alert, we – '

Haskell, who was seated near the open window, tensed. 'Excuse me, Captain,' he interrupted. 'There's somebody outside. On the lawn.' His voice quivered.

Condorelli went over and looked through the screen. He saw an outline in the porch light. It was near a tree where the lawn sloped from the drive. He started, and his mind fantasized that it was an apparition. Then he shook himself free of the image. 'How did she get past Donello, my man at the entrance? Where the hell is he?'

He went to the front door, and his men followed. Thurnauer, directly behind him, said, 'It's a woman. In a sari.'

'A what?'

'A sari. It's what Indian women wear, Captain.'

'Holy Christ, but she's tall!' From Abel.

'Well, let's find out what she wants.' Condorelli felt Hanuman's strong grip on his arm. 'Please, let me, sir. This woman must have a message from whoever kidnapped Dr Kitteridge.'

Condorelli nodded. 'Abel, find Donello.'

Abel left.

'OK,' Condorelli told Hanuman. 'But I don't like this. It's too damn cocky. Who do they think they are!'

'Exactly. They are certain they can get away with it. It is the Thug way. They are confident. After all, they are the chosen of Kali.'

'Freakin' fanatics,' Belanger added.

Hanuman left them. Condorelli immediately followed, then stopped when he heard Hanuman's 'careful . . . please.'

The Swami reached the tree. The woman stood as if transfixed. She towered like a great carved image, her face criss-crossed by bars of shadow from the oak's branches.

'Whom do you wish to speak to?' the Swami asked in Hindi.

'I won't be able to understand them!' Condorelli was upset.

'I'll translate,' Nirmal said at his side. Condorelli started; he hadn't realized the Indian was present.

'Captain.' Abel rushed forward. 'Donello's missing. Not in his car. Nowhere around.'

'Well, look again. Belanger, you go with him.'

'You are the one,' the woman replied. 'I was directed to come to you. To say that my master wishes you well. He has no anger towards you.'

Hanuman remained silent.

'My master says, "Tell the guru he may withdraw from the fray." He wishes none of the ill fortune that can come from the death of a holy man by the *rumel*'s kiss.'

'This is nonsense, deceit. A lie.'

The woman moved for the first time. She jerked her head at his words. The light filtering through the branches exposed her eyes burning through the lambency.

'Cursed little man, how dare you speak thus to me?'

'I speak what must be said. Twice now, Kunkali has sought to destroy me. This talk of peaceful intentions is the most obvious of deceits. I thought your master more subtle than that. No, I think he fears my capacity to endure these attacks.'

'Are you so great a guru that you can withstand even *her* wrath?'

'My master, Vishnarma, is easily your master's equal. Together, Vishnarma and myself, the lowly Hanuman, can withstand any evil *she* may perpetrate.'

The woman sank into the shadows again. Her tone was calmer after a while. 'Then let it be known that we of the *rumel* have returned. We challenge you and these others to prove who is the greater. Now tell them that the woman who dwelt here will die if I am overtaken. There is another – the man who was guardian of the road hither will die as well.'

When Condorelli heard Nirmal's translation, he ordered, 'Haskell, find Abel and Belanger. Tell them to cool it.' Haskell left. 'Tell her,' he cried out to Hanuman, 'that if either Dr Kitteridge or Donello is hurt in any way, I'll trail them to the ends of the Earth, if necessary.'

The woman here spoke in Anglo-Indian. 'Tell the *burra-sahib* to *jow*! *Jow*. Into *sakht burra mem* place. Or everything *oolta-poolta* for memsahib doctor and *choki-dar*! *Jow! Jow!*' Her arms were waving at Condorelli and his men, pointing towards the house.

'What's she talking now? I can almost understand her.'

'It's patois – Hobson-Jobson. Some English, some Indian slang. She wants us to go into the house and stay there until she leaves,' Nirmal explained.

'Like hell.'

'Captain, she says either we do it or both Dr Kitteridge and your missing man will pay for it in the worst way.'

Condorelli kept shifting his weight from one foot to the other. Decisions weren't easy. Everything was so different, a departure from what he had been trained to expect in situations like this.

'We don't make deals. Tell her that.'

'Captain,' Nirmal urged, 'just let her go. Otherwise, the doctor, your man . . .'

'I know, I know.'

Haskell appeared with Abel and Belanger. Abel said, 'Sir, there's a mini-bus parked near the next property. We think Donello might be in there . . .'

'Get into the house. Everyone!' Condorelli decided. 'Quick, before I change my mind.' And screw things up, he said under his breath.

As the men moved, the woman told Hanuman, 'Why do you interfere? What can a holy man do in a war?'

Hanuman didn't respond. He was listening to something else.

'Then I go,' she announced, and in one stride was past the Swami. The second stride was never finished. Instead, she spun about to her right and reached out her long arm to grip Hanuman.

However, even before she broke stride, he had moved backwards and kicked out at her hip. She was hunched forward, stretching to grasp him, when the blow landed. Big as she was, it carried enough force to send her staggering.

Simultaneously, all in one continuous flow of motion, the guru leaped straight upwards. His strong, muscular legs propelled him to the height of a thick branch above his head. Dangling from the branch, limbs wound about it, was a figure with a scarf forming the loop of a noose. Hanuman seized the Thug's shoulders and ripped him from the tree. Then he let go and the Thug hit the ground head first.

The Thug yelped into the night, and Condorelli, who was last to enter the porch door, turned and witnessed the end of the thwarted assault. He was about to send men to Hanuman's rescue when the guru came down the slope unharmed and told the captain, 'I'm fine. Let them go. It is the only course to take.'

Condorelli watched the woman pick up the semi-conscious Thug and sling him over her shoulder. She headed down the drive.

'Abel, Haskell, follow her,' he commanded.

'Wait,' Hanuman pleaded. 'Do that and she'll know. Heed what I say. Let them leave. Your man will be alive, as she promised.'

'How can you trust her?'

'In this I believe her. You have no idea how quickly someone can be killed by a Thug scarf. Heed me – let them go.'

Condorelli thought of Kearney again. He told Abel and Haskell, 'I can't chance Donello's life.'

Minutes later they heard a vehicle stop, a door slam, and the sound of the motor again. After it receded in the distance, 'OK, now go and look for him.'

'If the mini-bus was theirs, Captain, I got the licence,' Abel said. He and the other men hurried to the entrance.

While he waited, Vincent Condorelli went back into the parlour. He looked at Hanuman and Nirmal and scowled.

'You two better be right.'

Shortly, someone ran up the drive. Abel came in, breathing hard. 'Sir, Donello's OK. We found him on the roadside. Out cold. But he's coming to all right.'

'What about the mini-bus?'

Abel became grim. 'It's still there. Gee, I thought . . . I mean, it seemed probable . . .'

'Yeah,' the captain cut in. 'Well, nothing seems probable in this case. It wasn't very probable that that Amazon would show up on the front lawn. I mean, do you realize what they just did? They assaulted a special investigations detective, stood out there for God knows the reason why, tried to kill the Swami here, and got out scot free.'

'The reason they came here,' Hanuman said, 'was to convince me to detach myself from this matter. Two attempts had been made on my life and I had survived. They are worried.'

'OK, they are, are they? Hell, they didn't try to make a deal for Annette Kitteridge.'

'These aren't your ordinary kidnappers.'

'Then we're no closer to finding her whereabouts.'

'Rest assured we'll discover everything we need to know.'

'How's that?'

'We . . . I have been challenged in this. They will confront us again. Probably on their own ground next time. *Bele* ground. Sacred ground where they bury their victims. There, the force of Kali will be strongest. I will be lured there. You can believe that. And with me as bait, you will find them.'

Condorelli closed his Calabrian eyes. He wished Stephen Wrench were back. Wrench would be a big help. He was a policeman, too. Somehow, the captain knew things would be better then. Right now, all he had was the word of a mystic to go by. God help them.

17

'F is Foxtrot, dot dot dash dot. G is Golf, dash dash dot.
H is Hotel, dot dot dot dot. I is India, dot dot. J is
Juliette, dot dash dash dash.' In a very low whisper,
Annette Kitteridge ran through the pilots' phonetic alphabet and Morse code. She had just finished reciting the
portable traffic control light signals – colour and type, on
the ground, in flight. Thanks to her photographic
memory, reviewing her *AOPA Handbook for Pilots* had
kept her emotions under control.

Annette had been doing this since awakening. Not
knowing where she was was part of the panic that had
threatened to overtake her when her eyes opened. It was
the same room, the very bed they had left her in the
previous night. That is, if she had slept through only one
night and not more than that. There was no way of finding
out in this place, she discovered. There wasn't a clock in
the room and her wristwatch was missing.

Annette remembered the brightly lit barn, and how
Thin, at Vic Croce's nod, had blindfolded her shortly
after they entered. Which had baffled her, since the barn's
interior appeared similar to that of any other barn. She
was urged forward then, walking amid animal sounds and
odours and the smell of hay and manure. At one point
she picked up the permeating scent of oil and axle grease
and nearly fell on the slippery pathway. Her right hand
contacted an extremely large tyre, similar to the kind used
on tractors.

They must have walked the entire length of the barn
before they stopped. Thin, she guessed, was close behind

her. His gun prodded her whenever she paused. Footsteps, possibly the little man's, moved ahead. Without warning, there was a deep rumble and the ground quaked slightly.

Thin pressed her forward again. Annette encountered a filmy substance, she remembered, and, thinking it was spider webbing, she nearly screamed. No, I will not give them the satisfaction, she told herself, and went on, past the film into what she surmised was a vast draughty area.

There was more walking. Thirty, forty yards; then, from the claustrophobic echoes, a long narrow corridor. At the end of it was her bedroom.

Another pair of hands gently directed her to her bed. The fingers of the hand, Annette sensed, were long and slender. Hair, long and straight, touched her face as she sat on the edge of the bed. She was sure this new person was a woman.

When the blindfold was removed, Annette saw she was correct. Up to now, there had only been men, the two who had abducted her and the handful she had seen when she first entered the barn. Somehow, the young, slender girl-woman before her, in a plain grey dress without ornament or belt, something merely draped on a figureless body, the face pale, framed by the elbow-length colourless hair . . . somehow, this drab female figure gave Annette temporary hope.

Maybe this person could be nurtured into a friend. Certainly, the smile she gave Annette was warm enough.

'This is Mauna,' Vic Croce introduced. 'She is neither deaf nor mute. She has taken a vow of silence.' He waved at the room. 'This is the new addition to our ashram. It may not have all the comforts of home, Dr Kitteridge, but I don't believe you expect that from us. Is that accurate?'

'I don't know how to answer that,' Annette managed.

'Ah, Doctor, I expected more protest, much more indignation.'

'Would it produce results?'

'Frankly, no. Oh, bother . . .' Croce looked at his watch. 'I must leave you now. Sometime in the near future I look forward to explaining more about the history of this place.' He waved again. 'But I must leave. He has arrived – our Huzoor – I've been told. He has sent someone to your Wayland home with a message.'

'What sort of message?'

'It pertains to another matter. The messenger is a most interesting personage, I'm informed. You will meet her later . . . And, of course, our Huzoor – the Lord and Supreme Master himself. You see, I am merely a trusted lieutenant. To each his own place, Dr Kitteridge. Tra la – Thin and I must go now. Sleep well.' And as he turned, Croce laughed again, his high giggle that so infuriated Annette.

She kept her control and concentrated instead on her surroundings – a blue-grey-walled room, the texture of which seemed unusual. Annette passed her fingers over the surface and found it to be very smooth stone. There was little else of note – a chest of drawers beside the bed, a small table with a porcelain bowl. No mirror, no pictures on the wall. Austere.

Mauna, who had left the room, returned carrying a bowl of thick soup, the spoon made of wood, and a cup of herbal tea.

Annette discovered she was hungry. The soup was a combination of creamy asparagus and various other cut vegetables ranging from carrots to lentils. The tea was also pleasant. Sleep came soon after.

Now, since her awakening, Annette Kitteridge realized the tea had most likely been drugged. Her sleep had been too immediate, too absolute.

'S is Sierra, dot dot dot. T is Tango, dash. U is Uniform, dot dot dash. V is Victor, dot dot dot dash,' she continued. 'W is Whisky, dot dash dash.' Her mental calisthenics were working, crowding out her depression. Awakening to this cubicle, the stone walls, was enough to depress anybody. Wasn't this after all the old terrorist ploy? Control every aspect, every cubic centimetre, of the victim's environment; then proceed to alter the consciousness. People in a prolonged state of captivity were known to adopt the philosophies of their captors. Well, not she, if she and her old *Handbook for Pilots* could help it.

'Now, when I finish the alphabet, I'll do the digits, one to nine, and then do everything all over again,' she told herself.

Mauna came into the room.

Annette watched her through slitted eyes. Mauna in turn stared back for a while, then disappeared.

'Four, Fow-er, dot dot dot dot dash. Five, Fife, dot dot dot dot dot. Six, Six, dash dot dot dot dot.'

Mauna returned with a bowl of food and a cup of steaming tea. She hadn't been fooled. 'Eight, Ait, dash dash dash dot dot. Nine, Niner . . .' Annette sat up with a start. Mauna had pinched her thigh. Hard.

'Well, little sweetheart, a good morning to you too!' Annette barked.

Mauna smiled, and gave her the bowl of oatmeal and the tea.

'Is this drugged too?' Annette demanded to know.

Mauna shook her head.

There was cream already in the oatmeal. 'This isn't my favourite cereal, by a long shot.' Annette shrugged, and ate. She ate half the bowlful, drank some tea, and asked, 'I realize this is doing things in reverse, but where's the bathroom?'

Mauna motioned Annette to follow her. They left the

room and went down a corridor with similar stone walls of blue-grey. The corridor was well lighted. Annette hadn't seen a bulb or a lamp anywhere. The mysterious lighting was eerie.

They arrived at a room. There was a hand-built latrine but no wash basins. 'Don't people wash here?' Annette asked, but Mauna only turned away and left the room. Annette stared again at the wooden latrine with its open circles above the pit below. She could see no toilet paper, and was about to scream for Mauna, then gave up.

Back in the room, hours passed. Now and then, Annette thought she heard voices, but no one appeared. Only Mauna glanced in at intervals.

Dr Annette Kitteridge turned to analysis. Subject: Mauna. Example of child-woman, age approximately nineteen, brains washed by cultist philosophy. Similar to other fanatical religious groups of the time except that, unlike Jesus freaks or Moonies or Hare Krishnas, this cult believed in garrotting victims for the Hindu goddess Kali. The victims in turn were guaranteed entry into paradise. No more reincarnation. Total bliss if you went out via the Thug's silken scarf.

So Santha Wrench had told her. Santha. God Almighty, she missed Santha. Was that why she, Annette, had been abducted? A hostage to exchange for Santha Wrench?

Annette felt she must do something quickly. But what? Try to penetrate Mauna's shield? A vow of silence. Pretty intense. Pretty austere.

How can one deprogramme someone who holds an ersatz, beatific vision of life and its reincarnated beyonds? And what of you, Annette, she asked herself, are they reprogramming you? If so, there was the consolation that that should take time. Time, time, time. Her eyelids became heavy. Annette Kitteridge slept.

When a hand roughly shook her awake, she nearly

wept. In her dream, she and Santha were flying again, free and smiling. Now it was as if the dream plane had crashed to earth. It was so unbearably sad that there was no Santha in the reality she awoke to. 'No!' she cried, staring at the long nut-brown face with black riveting eyes.

Annette turned her head away and closed her own eyes in an attempt to return – high, soaring, Santha breathless and carefree with the climb. It had meant – escape.

Fingers gripped at the ribbon that tied the neck of her blouse, and pulled her up from the bed. The ribbon tore from the fabric, the grip was so strong.

Annette looked again.

This man was an Indian and not young. His breath was offensive; the back of his hands had purplish birthmarks. His body straddled her, the *kurta* he wore was stained. He pulled back, and Mauna's face appeared. She held a cup of aromatic tea.

'It's drugged, isn't it?' Annette gasped. She tried to squirm free, but the man held her arms. His fingers were like steel bands.

No one answered. She stared at the cup. She thought: They could have fooled me into drinking this. *They want me to know what they're doing!*

Annette pressed her lips against each other. She shook her head, murmuring behind the closed lips, *Uh-uh*.

The man's hands left her shoulders and gripped the sides of her face, prying her mouth open with his thumbs. The pain drove her to scream. Mauna saw her chance and poured the tea into the open mouth. The tea was a bit more than lukewarm. It had a bitter taste that lingered. Annette tried to shake herself free, and some of the tea poured down her chin and neck into her blouse.

Gasping, she swallowed despite herself. She choked,

and tried desperately to spit or vomit it back out, but the moment the drug settled into her system, she felt listless.

A surge of terror made her flush, like blood rushing to her head. She was rapidly becoming numb, and no matter what they did to her, she wouldn't be able to respond correctly. There was no way to fight back now. Her spirit was diminishing, dissipating.

She was forced to stand. It was difficult, with the drowsiness and weakness she felt. She was drowning in a tranquil sea of albescence. The whiteness permeated everything, a glow along the corridors they dragged her through. People were partially delineated silhouettes.

Annette made an effort to break free, to protest. But only her thoughts seemed involved. Her lips moved, but there was no sound. Other voices drifted to her through the white wispiness. They talked of the Master, of his mother. Someone chanted in another language. Every so often the word Kali burst into her ear as if someone put his lips there and shouted; yet no one had.

Kali! It was familiar. Santha had talked of Kali. Kali – the name was as all-permeating as the misty veil across her vision.

Then the corridors were gone. She was in the centre of a room, spacious, far-extending – as large as a city square. It was enclosed, though; Annette knew there were walls, a ceiling, none of which she could see. Still, they existed, she was certain.

Kali-i-i-i, the name stretched out, accompanied by music. Vibrating, repetitive music from India. Annette recognized that, too. Like that musician played – what was his name – Ravi . . . Ravi . . . Ravi who?

She could barely remain on her feet. The drug left her with the minimum of balance, of co-ordination. She had no strength to resist. If they were trying to intimidate her through drugs, they were succeeding.

And where were they? Where was everybody?

Annette walked across the hard, cold floor. She was in her stockinged feet. The upper part of her blouse was shredded, and she clung to it, held it flush to her breasts. Stumbling, she forced herself to move on, although she could no longer reason why.

The vastness, the emptiness, made her more helpless. The music came from everywhere – front, back, right, left. Or was it all the drug? She wished she could explain it clearly. Her life had been dedicated to the clear explanation of things, of people, of events.

Annette raised her head and brushed her hair from her eyes. The vastness was changing, stretching itself on and on ahead of her like an infinity plane in a Dali painting. Where before her sense had been bombarded by dimensional expansion on every side, now it all seemed linear. Annette recognized it as the drug's effect, but that did little to soothe her logical need for normal space with predictable limitations.

The milkiness eased. Layers of wisp sank, dissolved from her visual range. The sudden clarity made her blink. To her left sprawled a figure; beyond him there was a smoking crevice with something like a rope dangling inside its opening. The wispiness had centralized at the opening in puffy clouds like smoke signals.

Hesitant, but nevertheless curious, Annette neared the figure. She saw it was a young man, Caucasian, dressed in nothing but a tattered dhoti. He had stirred, sitting on his haunches, covering his face with his hands. His chest and back jerked with deep sobs.

Dr Annette Kitteridge had seen enough people weep in her lifetime but rarely with such total sorrow. She knelt beside him. 'Can I help?' she asked softly.

The weeping continued.

Annette touched his arm. He was a prisoner like her,

she sensed. His body showed signs of deprivation. He was so thin she could see his ribs; his back and limbs were moist with sweat, marked with bruises and blotches of grime.

'Please, can I help?' Annette asked again, eager to forget about herself for the moment.

He raised his head. Though ravaged by intense suffering, the youth had a sensitive, attractive face. Annette guessed his age to be no more than seventeen.

'There is no help for me,' he told her, while tears trailed to his chin and fell in droplets. Then, suddenly aware she was a woman, he tried desperately to cover his genitalia with his palms, since the dhoti was but a fragment of one.

'I am a doctor, Dr Kitteridge,' Annette said, to reassure him. 'I'm afraid that I'm trapped here . . . like you.'

'Then your k-karma is as awful as mine,' he stammered. His lips were swollen, almost black.

'They beat you, didn't they?'

He nodded. 'When I tried to protect – ' almost a whisper – 'my mother. We were some of the first of the ashram. We . . . refused to accept the change. They killed her.' His voice had become hollow, as though he was remembering an event in the distant past. 'Her karma was like mine. We have to . . .'

'Have to what?'

'Die . . . It is a sacrifice that must be accepted.' He said the words in the tone of a child reciting from memory.

Annette shook her head. If only she could clear it. The drowsiness had been replaced by a sensation of vertigo. She mustn't pass out. This poor helpless boy needed her.

'No,' she insisted, 'you mustn't believe you have to die.'

'I do. I do . . . It is the will of Kali, the Great Mother. I must be brave when it comes. I will join my real mother then.'

Never to be reincarnated again, Annette thought. So Santha had said. How to contest such a belief?

Annette tried. 'You mustn't be so resigned, don't you see? Nobody has to die. Nobody, understand? Not you, not me. You have to fight back, resist that kind of thinking.'

He stared at her. Stared and stared. His forehead finally became lined. The furrows spoke eloquently. He couldn't think it out, couldn't grasp what Annette was saying. His face broke again, sobs rose once more from that tragic well deep within him. It so affected Annette that she started to break down with him. Her hands clutched at the air like fluttering things seeking a destination. They darted expressively to his head and neck, pulled his face to her shoulder. Modesty was forgotten as her tattered blouse and bra exposed a breast, while his hands left his crotch and clung to her . . .

For dear life, she thought, dear life – poor boy, pathetic child lost with her in an infinitude of horror. Woozy as she felt, she held him, rocking him back and forth. Again like a mother surrogate. Poor lost child . . .

The sobbing increased. Her drugged consciousness tried to grasp the full meaning of the threat about them, but it fragmented. She had been led to this boy; the thought came and went like slivers of ice that soon crumbled, dissolved into her peripheral vision. It was strange as hell to see her thoughts. Images, like cold phantoms, constantly melting away. Soon, very soon, it would happen. She was trapped into the event now. It will happen, the drifting thoughts warned. Annette pressed him closer to her, held him with all her strength, protectively . . .

The air tinkled. The sound was distinctive, since the music had died long ago. She felt the boy's entire frame stiffen. Then a steady clinking, the Indian sound of many bangles striking each other.

'She who executes,' she heard the boy whisper.

Annette looked around.

'From below,' he whispered again. 'See, the snake-thing moves!'

Annette's eyes widened. Behind her, yards away, was the crevice, a zigzagging split that was at least forty feet long. Where did it lead to?

She asked, 'What is below?'

'It never ends,' he replied, his eyes big and transfixed on the spot. 'But the Master climbs down the snake-thing to a cave.'

'The snake-thing? It's not a rope?'

'No rope. See, it moves now. They are coming.' The clinking again. 'But the big woman who often executes, she is already here.'

Annette's mouth was dry, as brittle as cracked parchment. Or so she fantasized. She would never speak or scream again, since the entire lower part of her face would crumble from the dryness. She would be denied the right to protest, above all the release of screaming.

Hands were clear above the lip of the crevice. Hands gripping what the youth had called the snake-thing, the shining oily thing that hung from somewhere above and continued down, down to . . . 'It never ends.'

Now she saw the shoulders, the head of a man. His colourless hair flared back above his ears, and, even from this distance, she could feel the penetration of his eyes. His eyes were twin spells, she thought, and cursed that she was reduced to such superstition.

What spells? This was only trickery, drug-based trickery.

But the sounds turned her eyes away.

At Annette's left, the large shadow extended across the

floor and moved closer, closer, until it reached her and the boy. Annette flung herself over his body. He didn't struggle. Looking into his eyes, she saw they had glazed. He had found an escape, perhaps. She had seen the look before. He was going to cheat them of his demise, if it was to come, in the only way possible for him. He settled in her arms, his eyes, his essence, receding from contact.

The boy had descended into his tragic well.

Yet, he mustn't die. The thought exploded within her, and the mother, so denied in her, surged through every cell of her being, despite the drug, despite the terror.

Annette clung to him in her unrelenting need to protect.

Above her she could now hear feet shuffling, bangles, no longer a soft, distant clinking but a clamour, a snorting, and more shuffling, a beast pawing the ground before its strike . . .

'*Chelo!* (Get a move on!),' she heard from a growling voice. 'Don't get bobbery (angry). You leave *chuckeroo* (youngster) alone, you *sakht burra mem* (tough old memsahib) or Mrinalini then plenty doolally (mad) *goonda* (bad one).'

Annette understood none of it, but its sense was enough. Trembling, her mouth, even her breath as frozen as ever, she remained prone atop the catatonic youth.

Then another voice, almost bored: 'Separate them.'

'She make me damn bobbery. Me kick her dungy side like she good-for-nothing grass *bidi* (country prostitute).' A second later, a fierce blow between Annette's buttocks sent her into a night of swirling concentrics. When she came to again, someone with her voice was screaming.

Her mouth was wet now. She had bitten her tongue from the pain. Blood seeped along her lower lip. She was still lying across the boy. Anxiously, Annette's fingers passed over his nose, his slack jaw.

'Damn bobbery! Damn *sakht burra mem*!' The woman's voice, low, guttural, preceded more of the same pain. Again Annette pulled out of a maelstrom. This time, consciousness brought back even more agony. Her buttocks, her thighs, were a series of convulsive stabs. They wrenched through the rest of her; Annette's breathing became unsteady. She was hyperventilating. Hoarse, suffocating noises came from her throat.

'That's enough,' a man's voice commanded. 'Kick her again and you'll break her coccyx. Reach down and pull her from him.'

At that, hands seized Annette's shoulders. Flung aside, she rolled a distance. For a moment she remained on her side, then rose, bracing her weight on her elbows.

'Now,' the man from the pit directed. Stooped over the boy, a giantess in a flaming sari raised his head and placed a yellow scarf around his neck. 'Now – do it now!'

The woman pulled the scarf ends back, and the head backed with them. Back. Back. 'Please, no-o-o,' Annette wailed. One of the big woman's knees pressed on his spine. She gave a final tug . . .

Annette Kitteridge fainted at the sound of bones cracking.

18

Wayland

Santha Wrench said, 'But, Daddy, don't you see? Crazy as it sounds, I can't help feeling responsible for what has happened to Annette.' She paused, looking at the back of her hands, then at Stephen Wrench, Rama Shastri and the other men seated across the dining-room table. 'It's karma, don't you see? My destiny is tied to this godawful Thug uprising, to Kurt Leinster, even. This is twice too many times for me.'

Wrench breathed deeply.

'I don't mean, Daddy, that I'm meant to be one of them. It's that everyone I know is affected by my fate, is dragged into the confusion and violence . . . like Annette.'

Rama Shastri answered that one. 'Perhaps that is true up to a point. But one can be too resigned and do nothing. One can hide behind one's karma and become a victim.'

She nodded. 'But I already am that. It's . . . it's like having a chronic disease. It's always there, and sooner or later . . .'

Wrench's hand pounded the tabletop. 'I don't think you need to finish that.' He turned to Hanuman, appealing.

The Swami took the cue. 'Can I not ever convince you? No one of us alone is the total centre in this struggle. Listen and then evaluate objectively, Santha. Weren't your father and Rama Shastri attacked at Varanasi, lured into a trap? Was I not also attacked during my meditative trance? We are all – everyone's karma here is the centre.' He motioned to Captain Condorelli. 'You gentlemen, too. One of yours was killed, garrotted by the *rumel*?'

Condorelli grunted in assent.

'Think of that, Santha child.'

'But Kurt wants me most of all.'

'How can you be so certain? He seeks the death of your father and Rama Shastri. He seeks my destruction. He destroys even a man of the law in his quest for power. Now, you must see, *you are but part of what he wants to overcome*. Kurt Leinster, this mad Huzoor of Thuggee, seeks to destroy us because he fears our unity. That was what destroyed his efforts before.'

Santha bit her lip. 'Then, we, all of us are . . . trapped.'

'It certainly beats wasting the rest of my life as a retired, has-been law officer,' Wrench remarked with a smile for his daughter. He reached out and touched her hand. 'Santha, try to think the way the Swami advises.'

'When I think of poor Annette, I just about go crazy, Daddy. More than a week has passed, and we still have no idea where she is. Kurt Leinster couldn't have arranged a surer way to erode my peace of mind.'

'Which is precisely why you shouldn't give in. Don't give the bugger more of a victory than he already has. Am I right, George?'

'Yes. Remember, Santha, one positive thing this time is that you haven't been overwhelmed by any assaults on your psyche. This isn't the same as it was years ago. I think Kurt and his powers are limited this time.'

Like one mind, everyone turned to Hanuman, awaiting his reply. It came, and it wasn't what they expected. 'Quite the contrary, Dr Buchan. I fear they are even more powerful than before. They are certainly bolder. Not only have they come to this very spot to deliver a warning, but they also invade my master's place in the beyond. The goddess herself has tried to destroy me while I meditate.'

'But except in dreams, Santha has been left alone,' argued George.

'Have you forgotten the incident in Dr Kitteridge's plane? No, only the strategy is different. Kurt Leinster and Kunkali have learned well from the past. They've made attempts to destroy us all. Except Santha, of course. She is to be the host body for the goddess. That was one of their original intentions, and I don't believe it's changed.'

Wrench made fists with his big hands.

Thurnauer asked, 'Doesn't Leinster claim to be Kali's son?'

Again the Swami: 'And consort. Perhaps.'

'Then he thinks he's more than a man.'

'He may be by now.'

'You can't mean that.'

'Oh, but I can. I believe he was taken to Kali's abode, the plane of existence where she dwells. Some transformation of his internal nature had to occur for him to reside there.'

'You mean the guy used a heaven – or, more fitting, a hell – as his hide-out?' Jerome Abel asked. His tone was almost scoffing.

'Of course.'

Jerome kept his silence, but there was open disapproval in his attitude.

'I think I'll go to bed,' Santha announced. 'I've got a lot of catch-up work at the museum tomorrow.' She rose and bid them goodnight. For a moment, her gaze lingered on Rama Shastri, who was engrossed in his own thinking. Aware of her suddenly, he nodded, smiled. But he couldn't hide the concern in his eyes.

Heading upstairs, Santha thought of him again, how

pleased she was that he had come to America with her father. One reason was that if Indira Gandhi regained her position as India's Prime Minister, she wouldn't be able to put him in jail. The other reason was that he was her dear adopted uncle Ram, and that somehow, when he and her father were together, the universe seemed more secure. They belonged together, these two old friends, were part of the dance of life.

But if her surrogate uncle was here, why wasn't the same true of her surrogate mother? Why had Fate been so cruel? Santha fought to suppress her doom-ridden feelings and concentrated on what she had learned in the dining room downstairs. She mustn't hurt their unity by surrendering to despair.

When Santha first realized that Annette Kitteridge had been abducted, the shock drove her to bed. However, her father and Shastri arrived a day later. Their presence lifted her spirits, that and the time Hanuman spent at her bedside. Once clear of her depression, she returned to work. Things weren't exactly normal, but Santha went through the motions.

It wasn't until then that she learned of the big woman in the sari standing on the lawn. Santha had slept through the whole incident, and obviously they had kept it from her until now. Since then, Captain Condorelli had kept three men on the grounds. Only when she was at work were they away from the place. Once she had thought of returning to her Beacon Hill flat, but that urge didn't last very long. Now her life was indeed peculiar. Condorelli's men drove her to work and were waiting for her when she left. All night long, three men watched the grounds. At intervals, one even opened her bedroom door and flashed a light to make certain she was safe.

Santha hadn't dreamed of Annette. For that she was grateful. What it was like for Annette in the clutches of

233

Kurt Leinster took little imagination. Knowing Kurt as she did, Santha understood that he would try to prove to Annette how superior he was. That she was a psychiatrist would be sport for him. He would set about convincing her that she was the insane one. That would be Kurt Leinster's thinking, and Santha shed many tears about what it meant for dear Annette.

Santha walked to the bedroom window. She saw one of the detectives below. The tip of his cigarette glowed as he smoked in the porte-cochère. An overhead light, further in, cast him in silhouette with the slightest outline of light on his left side. Santha recalled it hadn't been so long ago she had observed George standing at that exact spot on a bright Saturday morning.

Everything had been so promising then. Daddy was in India chasing Thugs with Uncle Ram, but – and they had both reassured her – it was only this Ajit Majumdar and a few diehards from Kurt's old band. It had nothing to do with Leinster. Whether he was dead or alive no one knew, but that he was missing – and under very strange circumstances – was true, and that in itself was hope.

Santha began to undress, and went to the bathroom to shower. As she stepped into the tiled stall, her naked body was suffused with desire – an outpouring that could no longer be held within. She passed hands over herself while she stood beneath the water. Washing and self-caressing became one and the same thing. Oh, George, *kesari*, she thought, if only you were here.

Later, after drying herself and putting on her nightie, Santha watched the news on the small television at the foot of her bed. There had been another stabbing in Boston's Combat Zone, the part of downtown Boston filled with porn shops, nudie shows and bars. This time a man had been pulled from a car by a crowd of prostitutes; his wallet was picked, and he himself stabbed when he made an effort to stop them. The man was now at the Boston City Hospital in fair condition. The prostitutes had escaped capture, of course.

'How bizarre,' Santha said to herself. And it wasn't the first incident of its kind, she remembered. Santha thumbed the button on her remote control. The television blinked off.

She was about to put off the bedside lamp when the bedroom door opened slowly. Expecting one of the detectives, Santha yanked the covers up to her neck.

'It's me,' George Buchan said, entering and closing the door quickly. Dressed in a blue bathrobe and striped pyjamas, he crossed and sat on the edge of her bed.

'Is anything wrong?' she asked.

'Nope. I left Nirmal asleep and the Swami meditating on his bed,' George explained. 'I just couldn't sleep. Sleeping with Nirmal isn't easy, anyway.'

Santha giggled. 'Does he snore?'

'Uh-uh. But he kicks a lot. I don't think he has nightmares, though.'

'Maybe he's rock 'n' rollin' in his dreams.' Another giggle.

'I've been missing you, Santha.'

Santha sat up and pulled him to her. 'Ah, poor *kesari*.' She lowered his head to her breasts. 'Poor darling.'

'I think we'll be uninterrupted for a while.' His voice was deep, and it reverberated against her chest. 'When I passed by Annette's room, your father and Rama Shastri were in deep conversation. Your father's primed to skin Leinster alive. I guess Shastri was calming him down.' George sat up. 'I don't blame him. I want that bastard dead, too.' He checked himself. 'But it's foolish to worry. You've never been so safe.'

'What makes you so sure, George?' she asked in very sober tones.

235

'It's pretty difficult for any Thug to get on to the grounds or into this house, don't you think? Every quarter-hour or so, at least one of Condorelli's men patrols the grounds. There are thick woods on one side and at least thirty feet of lawn. As much lawn on the other side, with bordering shrubbery and neighbours just beyond that. The back is fenced in after forty feet of cleared, sloping ground, and the neighbours beyond that have two Great Danes. Only the driveway is left, and Condorelli's people aren't going to make the same mistake again.'

'Sounds great, George. But why am I so pessimistic?'

He kissed her forehead. 'It's a mood. It'll pass.'

Santha pulled his face to hers, opened her mouth. 'Here's another mood. It's hot, maddeningly hot, hot. I don't think it'll pass without help.' She met his lips. His mouth opened, and she brought him down on top of her. Simultaneously, Santha kicked herself free of her blankets. Her nightie rose to her waist as his body rubbed against her. She wore no undergarment, and now her vulva felt his erection as she spread her legs apart.

George untied his pyjamas, and they went down to his knees. Santha's arms wrapped around his back. She bunched his bathrobe up near his chest and let her hands slide down and palm his buttocks. The erection eased into her now. It seemed so large, so filled with power. In, in, it went until Santha thought it would penetrate her totally, up through the rest of her. That she was attached to him forever through the strength of the hardness.

George began to move his penis in an andante, building a rhythm that grew and grew. *Kesari*, fuck me until I dissolve in it, she thought, until every bit of me flows with the act. Until I am nothing but body blending with body.

'Oh, my!' Santha cried. 'Oh, my, oh my!'

And George continued, in and out, while her legs

wrapped around him and her nails scratched down his back. She felt so naked. Her vulva had never been so exposed. Her mind suddenly meshed with it. Santha was just cunt, she felt. She cried that out over and over. 'I'm cunt. Cunt! Cunt! Oh, my beautiful prick. I am cunt . . . Don't stop! Don't stop! Don't . . .'

Santha tensed as her body signalled she was about to come. He seemed ready, too. 'Oh, come with me, *kesari*. Come with your cunt woman!'

It happened. Santha was flung free of him, the room, the landscape. Her spirit hung momentarily on a thread as they both flowed through each other.

'I couldn't help it, *kesari*,' she said afterwards, her fingers running through his damp hair. 'It's been so long. I felt so primal. As though I was my genitalia.'

'I know, I understand,' he murmured, kissing her gently on her forehead, her cheeks. 'It was the same with me. Nothing, no thought or impression interfered with the act. It was pure – '

'Pure fucking,' she told him, and he kissed her long on the lips.

Santha snuggled in his arms. In time, she drifted into a semi-slumber.

'I'm going to my room now,' George whispered in her ear.

'Oh, must you? Your body smells so wonderful, so replete with the stuff of what is man.'

He smiled. 'That much, hey?'

'Oh, yes. You are still filled. We could do it again later, George.'

'Then what will we do when Lieutenant Abel bedchecks?'

'You can hide under the blankets.'

George retied his pyjamas, straightened his bathrobe. 'Sorry, darling, but I think it's wiser for me to leave.' He smiled at her. 'Now, no pouting. Here, I'll tuck you in.' Once she was covered to her chin, George kissed her again. Then he stood up.

'I love you, *kesari*,' he heard.

'I love you, too.'

On the landing, George started for his room, his mind preoccupied with the glorious moments he'd just experienced. Unconsciously, he pulled his bathrobe tighter around him; the house was chilly. In fact, there was a draught somewhere. George turned, saw the opened hall window at the far end and retraced his steps. He wondered briefly who had left it open, but that thought was quickly overcome by the memory of Santha in his arms, her untethered passion, her –

Passing the corridor that led through the rest of the house, George caught a flicker of movement. He instinctively swerved to face what proved to be the figure of a man. His arm rose quickly to deflect something coming at his head. The thrust was faster than his motion. A loop fell before his eyes to his neck and tightened and gagged the cry he was about to utter.

The figure moved out of range of George's bulging eyes. The Thug's scarf or *rumel* he now recognized. The Strangler had moved behind him and was pulling George's neck back more and more. The power of those *rumel*-wielding hands was beyond belief. Santha's face hovered in George's blurred vision; then faded.

The finality, the thought that he'd see her face no more, pumped adrenaline into his tall frame, and his mind screamed its refusal of death. George leaped backwards, carrying the Thug, a much smaller man, with him. They both hit the wall. Again George leaped, this time forward for about two feet, and then leaped back again, ramming his assailant against the corner of the passage. With a shuddering moan, the Thug slid down, his listless hand pulling the *rumel* free. His other hand dangled, its connecting shoulder dislocated by George's blow.

With a shout meant to alert the occupants of the house, George sprang for Santha's door and yanked at the knob. The door slammed back with a crash.

There, in the dim lighting from the curtained window, were two shadows at Santha's bedside. George flicked the lights at his left and charged at the two men, one an Indian with a hand over Santha's mouth. Her eyes met George's in an appeal for help.

He was upon them before they could spring free of his charge. George's fists were bunched at his sides, and one of them rose with all his focused adrenaline, smashing against the younger man's jaw. The Thug slumped, spun and toppled into the bedside table. The lamp fell in turn, its quartz-like base splitting his forehead.

But the Indian – a much older man, his eyes wild with fanatical fire – held his *rumel* round Santha's neck. He said nothing, but the action denoted either he be granted right of passage or Santha would die. George stopped in his tracks, trembling all over with rage. Santha's mouth was uncovered now, and her parted lips tried to form words but couldn't. George, staring at the ugly mottled hands holding the silken scarf, backed slowly.

He heard a tread behind him. From the landing, another Thug, another non-Indian, with thick curly hair like a straw cap, was set to go after him. Suddenly, from the landing to the Thug's left, a pair of *salwar*-clad legs and naked feet met his chest with tremendous force. The Thug disappeared from view as he hurtled against the window. It rattled with the tinkle of broken glass.

Hanuman stood at the threshold. A dishevelled Wrench and Rama Shastri appeared behind him. There was much shouting throughout the house and grounds as Condorelli's men sprang into action.

'Leave the room, please,' Hanuman said calmly. 'Give him room.'

George obeyed.

'Ajit Majumdar,' Rama Shastri announced and then, in Hindi, 'We are a long distance from Hardwar now.' He held a gun in his hand, as did Wrench. From the stairway, Jerome Abel and another detective climbed and sped to their side.

'Allow me to go,' Majumdar rasped, 'or – '

'If you kill her,' Shastri countered, 'you kill the Huzoor's favourite.'

'Make way for me.' Majumdar tightened the *rumel*. His eyes burned.

'What are they saying?' demanded Abel.

'Quiet, for chrissakes!' from Wrench.

'You have changed, Majumdar,' continued Shastri. 'You were your own guru for a while . . . But now you serve the Huzoor again.'

'He is the One. The Chosen. I have seen – '

'A Thug Huzoor who is not an Indian?'

'You will not fool me again. Make room. Quickly.'

Santha gave a choking sound.

'You goddamn louse!' Wrench stepped forward.

'No, Steve. Let him pass.'

Wrench, tears in his eyes, saw the wisdom of Shastri's command. 'OK, then, let's all move away,' he barked.

To a man, they did.

They waited. Majumdar appeared, arms and *rumel* still locked around Santha.

'For God's sake, don't even stir.' Wrench's words were hoarse. He was breathing heavily, his stare riveted on the Thug and his daughter. Majumdar backed to the open window. Glass crunched beneath his feet. It cut Santha's exposed feet. Blood pooled slightly near her toes.

'Tell the police to come into the house.'

'Do it,' Wrench told Abel.

The Black hesitated for a moment.

'Do it!' Wrench growled.

'Right.' Abel left them.

Seconds later, Abel called his man indoors.

Majumdar lowered himself to the window sill, making Santha bend with him. The *rumel* became very taut. Santha was gasping desperately. Majumdar placed one leg over the sill. He kept his eyes on the men. Then he quickly pushed Santha at them and jumped.

Hanuman rushed to the sill. Wrench caught Santha before she fell. 'My poor baby,' he blurted out. Rama Shastri joined Hanuman, and they both stared at the snaking thing that Ajit Majumdar had leaped to and was now sliding down.

Hanuman raised himself to the sill. His feet were bleeding, too. He prepared to dive for the strange, luminescent 'rope' that somehow stretched up from the ground. The moment Majumdar reached the ground, it dropped, however, coiled itself and disappeared.

They could see Majumdar's face in the moonlight as he looked at them one last time. He turned then and started to run towards the back of the house. He had nearly reached a wide swath of shadow when someone tackled him from behind.

'Vishnu's breath, it is my *chela*!' Hanuman cried.

Nirmal had straddled Majumdar, they could now see, and was pinning the Thug's arms to the ground.

'Quickly,' Shastri shouted to the others. 'Nirmal has caught him.' Except for Wrench, who had carried Santha back to bed, the rest rushed to the stairway.

Outside, Hanuman was the first to turn the corner of

the house. He found Nirmal grappling with somebody and it wasn't Ajit Majumdar. Further on was a figure heading for the bordering fence. Nearing the two antagonists, Hanuman kicked the Thug in the small of his back. The Thug let go of Nirmal, who jumped at him. The Thug fell prone, and Nirmal sat on him.

'Oh, Bapu,' he lamented, 'I almost had the other, but this one came as if out of the ground, and I let the other go. I think he was their guru.'

Hanuman didn't reply. He sped down the slope towards Majumdar, who was climbing the fence. Hanuman reached it, but the Thug was over it and into the next garden. Hanuman leaped, clutched the fence top and pulled himself over. Minutes passed, and he reappeared, shaking his head.

Later, Jerome Abel was at the police radio in his car, giving a description of Ajit Majumdar. Afterwards, he requested that Captain Condorelli, who had gone home early, be notified of recent events. Everyone was standing nearby, frustrated.

'Well, at least we've got four of them,' Belanger said. 'Maybe we can get them to talk.'

'Don't count on it,' replied Wrench, who had let George Buchan sit with Santha for the moment.

'What I don't understand is, when they came from the neighbour's yard, why those Great Danes didn't go after them.'

'Nobody is there tonight,' Hanuman explained. 'The dogs are gone. There is a note on the side-entrance door. The family went away to Florida. It is vacation time.'

'You mean they left just today?'

'Yes.'

'Well, how did the Thugs know they were gone? They must've been staking out this neighbourhood right under our damn noses.'

'They have ways of knowing.'

'Jeez, this is creepy. They acted after I did my rounds, I guess. I didn't see anything, and I went over every inch of that back yard. And you say they climbed something like a rope? Like in that film we've got, hey, kid?'

Nirmal nodded. He was still upset because of Majumdar's escape.

Stephen Wrench noticed, and touched his shoulder gently. 'Don't feel so bad, son. You did very well.'

'"Well" is not enough, Mr Wrench. He was a Thug guru, and he slipped right through my fingers.'

'Hell,' Wrench beamed, 'Ram and I are supposed to be old pros, and that sonofabitch has slipped through our fingers four times now.' He breathed deeply. 'The most important thing is they failed to kidnap Santha.' His voice deepened, became grim. 'Kurt Leinster is after my little girl again. That's what it was about.'

'Yes,' the Swami agreed. 'And he is bolder than ever, as I felt. He is even more powerful this time, and it will take a greater effort than before to stop him.'

Everyone looked at Hanuman, the moonlight limning his small outline. No one spoke. They settled into their thoughts instead. The only sound was the dance of the crickets everywhere.

19

The voice said softly but clearly in her ear, 'India is filled with death. The cremation pyres are burning daily every-where; but Death announces itself much more openly in the city streets. Here is a corpse, someone has died of plague; here the dogs gnaw at another, who has expired from hunger. To live there you must accept the dead, walk by them, accept them as a part of the landscape. So do not reject Death, embrace it, love its eternal link with Life; cherish the balance in all things, Dr Kitteridge, savour the rhythm, the harmony. Creation and Destruction . . .'

Her lids flickered. The ceiling was the first thing she saw, luminous, and she thought it must be foxfire, which often coats wood. But no, it couldn't be – I am surrounded by stone, she remembered.

Pain awakened with her, and at first Annette thought it was the fact that she was tied to the bed, white silken strips like bandages across her chest, her thighs, her ankles. Then Annette had the unwelcome memory of the garrotted boy and the kickings she'd received.

She moved her lips; they were cracked and extremely dry. Probably the result of the drug. Annette tried to cry out; instead, she heard a whisper. Her vocal cords seemed paralysed. She did manage to raise herself slightly and saw Mauna seated on a stool. Mauna stood up, came forward, looked into her eyes searchingly, and left.

God, this pain, Annette Kitteridge thought; God, this awful thirst and pain. And there was a voice, she recalled, a man's voice, very smooth, almost soothing, lecturing about the acceptance of Death. Maybe it means that they intend to kill me. At the moment, she was beyond caring. Death might be the best of solutions, after all. Anything was better than this pain along her backside and thighs. Tears came. She didn't want to give them the satisfaction of seeing her cry, but she couldn't help it.

Another face, a man's; pale, snowy hair; and a strange flickering in his eyes. Blue fjord eyes, very kinetic.

'Hello, Dr Kitteridge,' he said, and it was that same voice she had heard in her sleep. 'I realize that you're uncomfortable. However, this is all necessary, you see. You do understand what I'm saying, don't you?'

'No,' she whispered.

'Well, how unfortunate. I had certainly hoped we wouldn't confuse you. But let me acquaint you with the purpose of our experiment.' He paused, and for a moment the silver flickering expanded until his eyes looked totally opaque. 'Or perhaps you are already aware of where we're heading.'

She managed, barely audible, 'Brainwash . . . me.'

'That is accurate. And very perceptive. To be expected from an intelligent woman. Yes, we do intend to alter your consciousness. The term "brainwash" explains little, however. I prefer to call it a period of maturation.' His head turned to others out of her line of vision. 'Bring it in now.'

'Yes, my Huzoor.'

Footsteps fading.

'We are especially interested in acclimatizing you to Death, Dr Kitteridge. Oh, no, we are not about to kill you. It is living with Death that we are interested in . . . Can you live with Death, Doctor?'

The footsteps returned. The Huzoor moved away. Instead, Annette saw a face that was lowered to hers. The eyes were filled with shock, the mouth opened, the jaw fixed in rictus. It was the dead boy! His body was placed atop her. He was beginning to decompose, and the stench was suffocating. Annette managed to turn her head aside. 'No, please, no!' she begged, and vomit interrupted any further pleading.

The voice in her ear again: 'This is living with the dead, Doctor. When the boy was alive, you tried so hard to protect him. Now, can't you accept him in Death?'

'Inhuman . . .' Her voice sounded thick. More vomit poured down her chin. 'You . . .' Annette wanted to say something like 'fiend', but it wouldn't come. She couldn't breathe. She gagged again and passed out.

A pungency brought her back. Mauna's face formed, her hand holding smelling salts. Annette waited while thoughts, images, returned. Her nostrils cleared, and the scent of her own vomit and another lingering odour came to the fore. Annette squirmed, uneasy, remembering . . .

Nothing happened. Slowly, her breathing settled. She was apparently alone with Mauna. The girl's hands appeared near her neck. The slender fingers held a wet sponge. Mauna passed the sponge over the layer of vomit that had flowed to Annette's breasts. It was when the cold wetness touched her left nipple that she realized the breast was exposed. Annette could still feel the collar of her blouse on her right side.

The hand and sponge pulled away, and there was the noise of liquid falling in streams into a basin. Then the sound of something rising from water, which dripped back. Mauna was rinsing the sponge, she thought. The cold wetness touched her neck, shoulder and breast again. The odour this time was of a strong disinfectant.

When Annette saw Mauna's face again, she murmured a thank-you. Sleep came, a deep drowsiness preceding it.

* * *

Pain. The pain awoke her. Annette had concluded it had subsided. Now she knew it was only the shock of the boy's corpse lying across her body that had numbed the pain temporarily. A salient fact haunted her: her sleep wasn't due to drugs this last time; it had been a deep, desperate sleep.

The sleep of depression. She was beginning to sink, escape into unconsciousness. The way her clients did sometimes.

Annette winced. More pain. Also, she was hungry and very, very thirsty. 'Water.' Her lips formed the word; Annette heard no sound.

More time. A short, fitful sleep. Water. Annette wanted to rise. She was still bound to the bed. Then . . . Mauna's face looking down. A smile. Was it friendly or gloating? Water . . . Please . . . water . . .

When Mauna left, Annette was hopeful. After a while, suddenly her nose warned her. The odour rushed at her, tangible like a blow. The boy was lowered another time. This time the bearers were coughing, and they dropped the corpse on her, unable to tolerate holding the thing.

The flesh was in shreds, maggots crawled out of the cheeks and around one eyeball. Already skull bone was exposed. She vomited. God, it was as if she were bringing up her viscera. Gagging, gagging. Her last thought before blacking out was: Good, I'll die from my vomit.

When she revived, Mauna was swabbing her again. The corpse was gone. But for how long? The dread was maddening. How long? How long? She thought of the crawling maggots and choked, but there were no more maggots. I'm very dehydrated by now, she realized. No water, no food. Weak. Weak. Sleep again.

* * *

247

It was a short sleep, like a nap. Someone held her head up. Mauna again. Everything smelled of disinfectant. But there was also something welcome and new. Broth. Mauna was feeding her broth. Annette swallowed it slowly. Savoured it by letting it settle a while, as if her mouth were a cup. The broth had vegetable smells that cut through the disinfectant odour. Very nutritious stuff. Somehow, Annette knew that.

She was nearly finished with the bowl when the disembodied voice said, 'Don't you miss that dead child, Doctor?' Annette started. She could feel his hot breath in her ear but couldn't see him. 'Don't you, Doctor?'

Annette didn't know how to answer. He seemed to be waiting. Then, 'Should I order *it* brought to you?'

'No!' Rasping, her throat so sore. 'No, please! Please!'

'Will you behave, then, and do as I tell you?'

'Yes.'

'Louder, Dr Kitteridge.'

'Yes! Yes! Please don't.'

'Perhaps if you behave we'll even set you free. At least from the bed.'

She nodded faintly. There was no more voice. Mauna fed her the rest of the broth.

Screaming, not loud. Hoarse, rasping. Her own voice. Wide awake again. A nightmare: The boy was lying on her again, his eyes gone. Just empty sockets and a grinning death's head with flesh like curled peelings.

Relief surged through her. Only a dream. The pain had lessened, too. Just a steady throbbing in her buttocks now. Annette gasped, and bit her tongue. Footsteps. Were they bringing *it* back? Oh, please God or whatever controls events – no. She held her breath until she recognized Mauna's tread. The girl had brought more soup – vegetables and barley – and lukewarm tea.

But before Annette fed, Mauna freed her from her bindings. Annette braced herself on her elbow. Mauna left the food on a side table. 'Thank you,' Annette blurted out. Mauna remained expressionless. She left.

Days, nights, passed. Annette couldn't be certain. She never left the room. Her lack of strength left her incapable of the act even if she had desired to. Only Mauna came to her. She brought food and drink, nothing more. No water and soap to wash with, no comb, no other necessities.

These lackings didn't bother Annette at first, but as time went on, she asked Mauna to bring them. Mauna never did. Annette was dishevelled, hair in tangles and losing its colour, body sweaty, grimy, blouse torn on the left side, skirt stained and wrinkled from having been slept in. She was able to tie the blouse strips and cover her breasts. But the most disquieting thing was they had taken off every undergarment – bra, slip, tights, and even her pants.

Annette knew the strategy. She wished for the first time in her life that she wasn't intelligent and able to figure some of it out. Humiliation was the goal they strove for; to reduce her to something less than human by taking away all the hygienic niceties of civilization. They had succeeded to a degree. They had left her tattered and dirty, and she discovered that she had wet herself more than once while strapped to the bed.

Finally, the time came when she had to have a bowel movement. Annette requested Mauna that she be taken to the latrine. Mauna disappeared, returned with a huge wooden bowl. 'You can't be serious!' Annette protested. Mauna showed no expression. Then, 'Will you please leave the room?' Mauna stayed. 'Will you turn round?' Annette pleaded. Mauna smiled but remained facing her

249

prisoner. Rage overcame Annette. 'Turn round, you little bitch.' Mauna backed away. Her eyes held fear now. She pouted for a second and rushed from the room.

Five minutes later, Mauna was back. The Huzoor was with her, tall, lean, towheaded. He wore a white *kurta* and *cudidara* and sandals. His eyes were magnetic with those flickerings that left Annette cold. Annette forced herself to look at his chest. She knew those eyes were hypnotic.

'I want to use the latrine next time. And I want to wash, to have clean clothes and linen. I am a doctor, and this is unhygienic,' she insisted, with all the anger she could focus.

'Impossible,' she heard.

'Why?'

'We are still working on your maturation.'

'And if I refuse, you'll kill me. Then do it.'

'That's impossible, too.'

'Why? I'll never become one of you, no matter – '

'We don't intend that . . . Do you know who I am?'

'Yes.'

'Say it.'

'You're Kurt Leinster.'

'Ah, Santha Wrench told you, described me, perhaps.'

'Perhaps. I won't be treated like this. I have rights, goddammit.'

'Many areas of India have no latrines.'

'This isn't India.'

'Oh, yes, it is – in spirit, at least. You wouldn't want to upset the status quo, would you? At the moment, you are as the poorest of India.'

'Worse. At least he or she can take a bath in a stream. At – '

'Yes, agreed. Worse. But that is because you are an experiment, a – '

250

'I won't stand for it, I tell you.'

'My, how quickly one forgets. Perhaps you would rather be tied to the bed again and be visited by another corpse. We can easily provide one.'

Annette slumped on the edge of the bed. She had gone too far, and she began to cry.

'You don't want that, do you?'

'No.'

'To be seduced by Death while you are alive is horrible, isn't it?'

'Yes, yes,' she wept.

'Then be grateful you have your bowl.' His smooth voice hardened. 'You must live with your stench, Annette Kitteridge. You must lose your false vanity, your doctor fancies about hygiene. That is because you are no better than your own dung.'

'I am an identity,' she whispered. 'You will not take that from me.'

'We already have,' came the reply. 'Surrender to that, and your fate will be kinder. In time.'

At that, Annette cracked. The persecutions she had endured had already spurred the rage that brought about her scene with Mauna. This time, though, Kurt Leinster's cold, arrogant evaluation of her worth transformed the rage into action. Dung, was she? She looked for a moment at the wooden bowl she had placed in the far corner after her bowel movement. Leinster was speaking again, but she no longer listened. Annette moved without thought, propelled to the bowl with an energy beyond reason. With one flow of motion, she gripped and hurled it with every erg of strength at Leinster and Mauna.

The girl sidestepped and was only splattered with urine. But Kurt Leinster, chosen of Kunkali, Huzoor of Thuggee, was hit squarely across his shoulder breadth. Urine flew into his eyes and hair, while Annette's stools hit his neck and stuck and flowed down his *kurta* to his waist.

Immediately afterwards, Annette sensed that the earth had just split, and she was primed to fall into the crevice. His eyes had become opaque again. If any look could kill, it was that one. Annette covered her face, expecting the worst.

Time passed. Or, rather, it stood still, as it is wont to do sometimes. Extraordinarily still. The hair at the nape of Annette's head stood on end. Her legs buckled, and she sat on her bed before they gave way. Her hands never left her face.

It began low, and Annette couldn't believe it. It rose, hearty and strong, a laugh that rang and echoed slightly. It certainly was more frightening than if he had hit her. Or killed her – which was what she prayed for at the moment. It was just loud, raucous laughter. Normal, not the Devil's own laugh, as she had expected.

Annette pulled her hands away and looked. There, smeared as he was with bits of stool caking his chin, neck and tunic, Leinster was enjoying it. A madcap clown in a slapstick movie. A mental patient regressed to playing with faeces. He could have been any one of these things.

But he wasn't. The eyes were blue again, the flickerings absent. He was enjoying some private joke. Mauna alternated between worried looks directed at him and big smiles. Finally, he turned and left, the laughter continuing until the distance was too great for it to be heard.

Annette Kitteridge knew now that her fate would be worse than the death she had hoped for.

Even before Annette opened her eyes, she was certain that it wasn't Mauna watching her. *Somebody was there*, however; she was certain. Once in a while she heard breathing; the rest she sensed – an aura, vibrations of menace. Similar to an odour – sharp, cutting.

Annette had slept fitfully after a long period of imagining just how Kurt Leinster would have his revenge. Mostly, she expected to be tied down again, and visited by another corpse. But neither had happened so far. Yet.

Something heavy was on the side of the bed. Annette sat up with a start. The big Indian woman looked back at her, Annette averted her face. She couldn't bear those eyes any more than she could Kurt Leinster's. How could people possibly have eyes like that?

'Don't get bobbery,' the woman said.

Annette nodded. She didn't understand the word, but she thought it might mean troublesome.

The woman motioned she was to follow her.

Annette could barely walk. When she stood she tottered, but with an effort of will she went on. Fear of the giantess gave her momentum. Often, along the corridor, she stopped and hugged the cold walls. Then the woman would stop, always ahead of her, motion again, and Annette would continue. At times she thought it was impossible to move another inch. Thirsty, ravenously hungry and very weak, she expected to collapse any minute. It didn't happen, though. Terror of fainting while this Amazon was with her kept her effort alive.

They entered a cavern. The same vast spaciousness as before but without the white mistiness. Annette saw people here, there. They barely noticed her. Some were Indian, but most were non-Indian men and women, Americans, she gauged. The men were in chinos and open shirts, but some dressed Indian-style, like Leinster – *kurtas* and pyjama-like things that tapered at the legs. The women wore plain dresses, with a few in saris.

How Annette was able to follow the broad back in a flaming sari before her, she couldn't answer. Her terror kept her awake, alert; it even provided the motive for her actions. The thought of falling into unconsciousness and awakening to whatever punishment Leinster had decreed for her was too horrible to contemplate. Come what may, she must face it with the least vulnerability.

A sound at her side: the little man who had kidnapped her. Vic Croce stroked his beard and said, 'I see they are moving your quarters. You will be closer to the pit.'

'Pit?' Annette slurred.

'Yes, pit. All of this comes from the pit. It's like the proverbial hole to China.' He chuckled. 'Except ours is India-based.'

Annette remembered the crevice and then the unfortunate boy. Tears welled up.

'And Mrinalini is now your guardian. She is an anomaly, Mrinalini is,' Croce continued. 'They say she was possessed by demons even before . . . Well, that is not for me to tell.'

Annette had to ask, despite herself: 'What will they do to me?'

'I don't know,' she heard – and believed him. 'You are truly in the hands of the gods.' They passed another large room. Annette saw figures crowded together, many men, women, children in tatters like herself.

Croce added, 'I can tell you their destinies, though.'

'They're prisoners, too, aren't they?'

He nodded. 'They were once of this ashram. But they refused to heed the call.' His next words sounded like a quotation: '*They who deny the call will surely die.* Ah, you are nearing your new home. I leave you now, Doctor.' And he was off in another direction.

All those people – Annette had seen at least thirty – will die, she thought. The children, too. True, a mere thirty was a very small number, considering the thousands, millions, even, who died in wars. But to Annette

Kitteridge, doctor of medicine and psychiatry, it was too many. The scene of the killing of the boy flashed before her again. They were at the very spot, she realized, as her eyes fell to the crevice beyond, to the oily, dangling rope-thing.

Mrinalini turned to the far right. She led Annette to a room no larger than the one she had just left. Annette collapsed on the bed in exhaustion. She heard Mrinalini's snicker when she asked for food. The giantess left.

Annette tried to sleep. If only her mind would stop racing. Her ploy of reciting the pilot's manual to calm herself no longer worked. Her being moved to this new room close to what the little man called 'the pit' . . . What did it mean? Annette shuddered, and held her arms tight to stop shaking.

The noise of the big woman's bangles preceded her. 'Here,' she grunted. Annette saw a bowl of thick green soup and more tea. She lowered her legs over the side of the bed, took the spoon, and stirred the contents of the bowl absently. When she raised the spoon she saw it had one of the lumps from beneath the smooth green surface. Annette stared at it, shocked.

Her eyes fell to the woman's broad face. The smile was searing, malevolent. '*Sakht burra mem* like dung. She get dung.'

Annette put the spoon down in disgust. The piece of stool rolled off on to the table.

'*Burra mem* eat,' Mrinalini insisted.

Annette wouldn't. She trembled, couldn't speak, at the force of those terrible eyes. They had no silver flickerings like Kurt Leinster's eyes but were black cores to an even darker spirit.

'Eat!'

Annette shook her head fiercely.

Mrinalini Pal bent, lifted Annette from the bed and

threw her over a massive shoulder. She held Annette by her thighs. The skirt had bunched up, exposing one of her buttocks. '*Sakht burra mem* learn to do what 'lini command,' she heard. Then the giantess said no more and, with her long strides, reached the cavern in no time.

Annette squealed, pounding at the body. The giantess smelled of heavy sweat and spices, and the ghee in her hair felt greasy against Annette's exposed flesh.

''lo, up there,' someone hailed cheerfully.

Looking down, Annette saw Vic Croce with about four men. 'Going sightseeing, hey?'

Annette tried to pull down her skirt but couldn't reach it.

'Sightseeing?' she gasped, out of breath. The blood was ringing in her ears from hanging down head first.

'You're off to see the pit.' Croce was sadistically cheerful.

The pit. Annette's lips moved like a fish in air. The pit! She couldn't believe the words. She kicked her legs, but Mrinalini only tightened her grip.

Then she *knew* somehow that they were at the crevice's edge. Mrinalini jumped off, and Annette's heart seemed to rise to her gullet as she stared at the infinite drop below. The momentum stopped with a violent jerking, as Mrinalini gripped the sentient 'rope'. Annette thought she was sliding free and screamed, but the sensation left as the giantess dug her nails into Annette's waist.

Keeping her eyes closed, Annette moaned as the giantess climbed down. The moans were automatic, beyond her control, and any second she felt she would urinate. As the descent continued, she thought something fluttered past her face. The air became cooler, pleasant to breathe. Annette let her eyes open, and saw the opalescent mist again with moving streaks of silver.

Mrinalini Pal stopped. Then she began to swing to the

right. Closer and closer she swung the 'rope' to a ledge
and a cave filled with a swirling milkiness. Annette's eyes
fell down for a moment, and she almost fainted. Not only
was there an infinite drop, there were gaps like fumaroles
far, far below and what looked like stars and suns within
them. It was impossible. It was a hallucination, a dream.
Where was she? Where was this place? Annette concluded she must have been drugged again.

Mrinalini suddenly let go in mid-swing and landed on
the ledge. For a brief moment, the giantess almost lost
her balance and tottered backwards towards the drop
beyond the ledge, but then straightened and lowered
Annette to the ground.

Lying with her face flush with the white dust of the
ledge, Annette listened to the flutterings and scramblings
of life around her. At first, she thought of bats and rats,
and cringed. Then one of the ground creatures neared
and sniffed at her hair. It sounded more like a dog than a
rat. Annette raised her eyes. It was dog-like, a speckled
creature who gave a kind of bark when his eyes met hers.
Silver eyes, she saw, with a silver mouth and blood-red
tongue. Drops fell from it into the white dust. It was
blood, all right. Annette pulled up her knees and backed
away. She didn't scream this time but kept biting into the
side of her hand.

'Now you learn, *burra mem* – if Master say "Eat dung"
you eat.' Mrinalini gripped Annette's hair and dragged
her to something resembling a rock. She pressed her into
its surface, which gave, shaping itself to her body. The
rock-thing then sent out shapes like bars that wrapped
themselves around her neck, her arms and her legs, which
Mrinalini had spread as far apart from each other as
possible. The unattached ends of the bars adhered to the
'rock' face once they strapped her down.

'Now 'lini go.'

'Oh, God, where am I? Please tell me. What is this substance that shackles me?' Annette's voice was as the small voice of a child. Filled with terror. And, as if to shame her more, her bladder let loose.

Mrinalini laughed. '*Prana*,' she explained. 'All, everything, everywhere made of *prana*.'

Annette didn't understand.

'Now 'lini go,' the woman repeated, and leaped to the oily dangling thing.

'Don't leave me,' Annette pleaded as the other climbed. Laughter rumbled back to her. Annette was left alone with the fluttering and scrambling noises.

The opalescence increased. Soon Annette could barely see beyond her nose. The sounds came closer, especially the flutterings. Something perched on her forehead. It hopped on small taloned feet and fluttered its wings, driving the mist away. Annette saw a beak and unflinching silvery eyes on a small stretching neck. The 'bird' – if that's what it was – was arching from her forehead, examining her eyes. Annette became terrified it would peck at her eyes, and she closed them. Instead, there was more fluttering, and it landed this time on her breast. Then it pecked once at the fabric of her dress, hitting the nipple.

Annette screamed. The beak had cut flesh. Blood seeped from the nipple, flowing down to her abdomen. The bird's beak entered the tattered fabric again and gave a sucking noise.

It was drinking her blood! Annette could feel it being drawn from the wound. No sooner had this happened than there was more fluttering and another 'bird' landed on her other breast. Again, this creature pecked at her nipple and, along with the excruciating pain, came the reasoning that there was some intelligence behind this.

258

How else could one explain that each creature had sought out a breast?

Whatever propelled them, they were 'birds of torture' (if they were birds. She was never quite sure, because she saw only bits of them at a time) led by some unnatural Design. Annette shrieked again at the second puncture. This creature, too, proceeded to suck her blood. It couldn't possibly be coincidence. This place, the vampire 'birds', the fumaroles with backgrounds of interstellar space, was a supernatural Hell, and she was like a soul condemned to its arcane punishments.

Why? Why was this happening to her? That her life, *her reality* would change its course this way was a non sequitur, a book with two unconnected plots, where she was out of character. The bird-things had stopped drinking. She could feel them lying across her stomach as though they were lethargic, gorged with the blood.

Now the scampering was everywhere. The 'dogs' were sniffing at her, silhouettes darting back and forth in the mist. The opalescence began to settle. Snouts appeared and flashing teeth clicking against each other as they bit at air near her temples. Annette screamed again and they scurried.

A moment later the bird-things flew away.

Annette sighed. Perhaps it was over, maybe the punishment was done. 'Oh, it was enough,' she muttered aloud. 'Enough. I'll do anything I'm told.' She shouted finally, 'Anything. Anything! Can you hear me?' She didn't know if anyone else was there. The Master, perhaps. The man Kurt Leinster. She shouldn't have thrown . . . If he could only hear how sorry she was . . . 'Sorry – I'm so sorry,' she gasped. 'Sorry, sorry, sorry.' Her voice rose again. 'Sorry . . . Master. Sorry!'

Annette stopped. Something landed on her knee with a low thud. It crawled, long and many-legged. Annette began to whine. The thing burrowed into her thigh for a second and snapped at her with its pincers. Then, as if directed, it headed for her vulva. The whine changed to shrieks as the pincers bit at the vulva lips. Blood streamed through her pubic hair. The biting stopped and Annette waited, breathing hard, fearing what the thing would do next. When it moved, finally, her screams outdid any before. The thing was trying to crawl inside her.

Annette blacked out.

How long she was out was beyond her comprehension. Her confusion was intensified on awakening; nothing was as before. She was no longer shackled to the 'rock' nor were there any 'bird' or 'dog' creatures. The ledge, the cave, was a silent place. No sound. Just a gripping silence.

Annette stood up and fell down again. Her strength was gone. She sat on the ledge floor watching the oily 'rope' move lightly back and forth.

The mist, the milkiness, had also disappeared. Annette sat in the dim lighting, like an empty-headed battered doll. Then, she suddenly remembered the centipede nightmare. Annette started to shudder and sweat. God, was it still in her?

Again Annette tried to stand, again she fell. She calmed down. Moving had helped; she must keep trying to stand. Again. Again. Again. Three more times she tried without success.

It can't be in me, Annette concluded. With all this exercise, it would have come out. Annette almost blacked out again, but fought it with her will. Think of something else, she told herself. Anything.

Annette asked herself: Since there was a supernatural Hell, was there a God, too? She hadn't believed in a God most of her life, and now she was certain that she was right. No God would allow a place like this to exist. There was only Hell, then; what a cheat, how lop-sided the universe.

It happened then. Like a perverse child, whatever controlled life here summoned it forth. Inside first, sudden sharp pains, as if she held shards of glass. Annette collapsed, fell, her legs spread wide. A mock parody of birth, it came, pincers at the fore. Blood gushed out of her, splattered her vulva, her legs, in thick flowing pools. Annette watched it emerge, its blue-yellow multi-eyed head, then the long, snaking body of bilious green and black.

Annette Kitteridge was still shrieking when Mrinalini descended to her. With one punch the giantess knocked her unconscious. She lifted Annette under one arm and climbed up again.

When Annette awoke, screaming, Mrinalini slapped her over and over again, warning, 'Stop, *burra mem*, or Master say go back to pit.' The words finally penetrated. Annette, now quiet, took a fresh bowl of soup and tea. The soup was clean; there was no human waste in it.

Annette stared at the woman who had rescued her from the pit of Hell. She wanted so to please everybody. Annette tried her version of pidgin English: 'Me, *burra mem*, want say to 'lini no more bobbery. Want do right for Master and Mistress. Would eat dungy stew, even.'

''lini know,' Annette heard in reply. 'Master know. We all know. You – ours now.'

20

'Indira will be re-elected. Morarji Desai is too impotent a leader to continue as Prime Minister,' Rama Shastri told Santha Wrench. 'The internecine squabbling in the opposition coalition will bring about its downfall.'

Santha listened, yet her mind wandered to the greenhouse-style windows of Dapper Dan's restaurant in Somerville and the steady downpour that greyed the car park. The glass rattled from the wind, rain eddies flowed down its surface. They were working hard at freeing her from herself, she knew, and was grateful. She had nearly shut herself off from everybody again. Her father, Uncle Ram, George, the policeman Donahue and Thurnauer were with her.

She forced herself to say, 'If that happens, do you think Indira will continue the Emergency?'

'No, she will not. The last election proved to her that sometimes democracy works in India. Sixty per cent of the electorate voted. Approximately a hundred and ninety-four million people. The people of India put the Janata party in. That was about forty-three per cent of the ballot.' Shastri paused as he tallied up his figures. 'That's eighty-four million votes. I doubt very much that if Indira regains power she'll arouse that much opposition again. She wouldn't dare.'

'Then the Emergency is finished?'

'Yes. Indira is an acute politician, Santha. Only a fool would underestimate her. Also, I fear that she – in fact, I know that Nehru's daughter is part of the mythology of the new India. Her charisma will carry her on. Unfortunately, her son Sanjay will be with her. "The Boy", as they call him at home, is much hated for some of his programmes, like the sterilization of the poor.'

'Didn't Sanjay become suspiciously rich after building a factory to mass-produce a car he called the Masurti?' Thurnauer said. 'But production of the car never happened.'

'Sanjay's company was used as agents for foreign companies marketing lorries, aircraft, road rollers – that sort of thing,' Shastri answered. 'It wasn't illegal, but the fact that he was granted a licence was outright nepotism. Every major industry in India is licensed, you see. And Sanjay's capitalistic dreams had precedence over established industrial firms. Some think Sanjay is more powerful than his mother. The Nehru dynasty continues with this insufferably arrogant boy.'

'Uncle Ram had to flee Indira's clutches during the Emergency,' Santha informed Thurnauer proudly. 'It was his first visit to America.' She didn't add that the Thuggee cult had arrived at the same time too, and that Shastri had been on their trail then. She didn't want to talk about that.

But that wasn't news to Thurnauer, she remembered. The policeman had helped her father and Rama Shastri briefly during that period. Thurnauer was basically an undercover cop whose speciality had been infiltrating every manner of subversive group. Even the many groups concerned with Eastern religions or esoteric schools had been investigated by him. He looked like a leftover from the hippy generation. Cleaned up, in an outdated suit, charcoal grey and a bit threadbare, his trouser turn-ups too short and in the stove-pipe fashion, he looked too well dressed. His contrived long beard figuratively screamed for jeans and an open collar and checked shirt.

263

He was different, all right, and informed; Santha rarely thought of him as a policeman.

But Donahue was the opposite. He reminded her of the current danger, her attempted abduction the other night and the loss of Annette Kitteridge. Try hard as she did, his official, unsmiling manner at all times spoke in that terrible loud silence that her life was not her own.

Santha looked again at the desolate car park; then at Rama Shastri wonderingly. He had been unusually introverted when he and Wrench arrived from India, and Santha had questioned her father about it. Wrench mumbled something about Ileana Heng. So that was it, she thought; Uncle Ram's mysterious mistress had returned to him, if but for a while. Her curiosity urged her to talk to Shastri about it sooner or later. There were things unexplained about this woman – her father's strong dislike of her and vice versa. Ileana Heng had also resented, possibly hated, her mother Kamala too, Santha had heard. Once, in a rare moment of confidence, Kamala had told Santha that Rama Shastri had also courted her in the early days. Santha's grandfather, a medical doctor, hadn't believed in the childhood or planned marriages common in India, and Kamala had had the same freedom of choice about her husband as an English or American woman. Somehow, later, Ileana had become aware of Shastri's former love for Kamala and had grown insanely jealous. Nevertheless, the exotic Eurasian remained a tantalizing mystery to Santha.

That Shastri had made a difficult decision in leaving his position as Kotwal and the woman again was clear enough. But her adopted Uncle Ram felt responsible for the Thuggee presence in America again, she knew. Plus, of course, there was his deep love for her, Santha. Both as Stephen and Kamala's daughter and, she had concluded after much thought, her striking resemblance to her mother. Sometimes Rama Shastri would look at her as if he were in another place, another time. That the passage of years left people caught for a while in a memory space was a fact she had noted but never yet experienced. So that was what callow youth meant, she thought now. They had no full love memories to grieve about or learn from.

Ever the romantic, Santha Wrench drifted into a reverie, wondering what moments she would recall about George, sometimes, apparently, with more freshness than the often overrated present, the currently worshipped Now. She shrugged as if holding a conversation with herself, as if she were responding to a grim truth addressed to her with neither tact nor mercy. If she or George were alive that long. If she, especially, were not long dead at the hand of Kurt Leinster. No. Kurt Leinster would never kill her, she was positive. *He had other plans for her, and that was the most terrible fact about all this.*

Santha's eyes wandered over the room. The tables were all filled – couples, groups of men and women, business people at lunch, housewives pausing during a shopping spree. She was still, holding a fork above her spinach quiche. Eyes were staring. As the novels put it: riveted on her. Santha tracked them down. In the far corner, a middle-aged man in a three-piece suit. He was seated in a huge wicker chair. He had a goatee and white-streaked sideburns. Hooked on to an empty chair at his table was a see-through lucite walking stick. Santha frowned.

George hesitated at his trout amandine and asked, 'What is it?'

'Nothing,' she said casually.

He didn't believe her. Neither did her father. The conversation stopped. Donahue began to survey the room.

'It's nothing!' she repeated, with some irritation.

Thurnauer, who was enjoying his rosé, renewed the

conversation. He asked Shastri, 'Thugs are noted for their unusual persistence, once a victim is picked, aren't they?'

'It verges on the unnatural. It's legendary,' came the reply.

And Shastri told this factual story: During the height of the Thuggee atrocities, according to the account given by Sir William Henry Sleeman, who was responsible for an end to their practices in the last century, a Mogul, a Muslim nobleman, encountered a Thug gang one day. He had numerous servants, was courageous and well armed. Approached by the Thugs, who presented themselves as respectful Hindus on a road, he refused to converse with them, since he had heard of Thuggee. The Thugs tried to overcome his suspicions with much respect and pleasantries, but the Mogul wouldn't bend.

The next day, the Mogul and his retinue met other travellers. This time they were Muslims but also Thugs. They informed him about the dangers of the road. Travellers should band together for the sake of security, they stressed. The Mogul still refused. He wanted no strange companions and threatened them with his sword if they didn't leave him alone. Since he was also armed with a bow and a quiver of arrows and a pair of pistols, the Thugs left.

But the famous Thug tenacity prevailed. That night the Thugs stayed at the same *sarai* (native inn) as the Mogul. The Thugs became friendly with his butler and groom. The next day, on the road, the Thugs approached these two servants, who tried to intercede for them with their master. Again the Mogul refused.

Shastri sipped his tea, looked yearningly at his steak. Santha suppressed a giggle, knowing his rebellious love of beef-eating in India. He rushed to the story's end: 'One might think,' he said, 'that the Thugs would've given up at this point. But they already had a counter-plan, in case the first one failed. And they had also dug the graves ahead of time, as was their custom.

'The following day, in a vast, uncharted plain, the Mogul's party found five Muslim sepoys weeping beside what they claimed was a dead companion. He was actually one of their recent victims. They cried out that their friend had died from exhaustion. Although his grave was ready, being poor and unlettered, they couldn't repeat the funeral service from the Koran. They asked that His Highness, the Mogul, obviously a nobleman, should perform this service. The Mogul couldn't refuse. No devout Muslim would. He dismounted and, since it was improper to do the holy recitation while armed, he removed his weapons; washed his feet, hands and face so he wouldn't be in an unclean state; and then knelt, performing the service with a Thug on either side. Others were a few paces behind with the Mogul's servants.

'The Thug leader gave the signal, of course, and the *rumels* were used on the victims. Within minutes, the Mogul and his men were in their graves.'

'And I suppose if the Thugs were Hindus, as the first gang were, and it were a Hindu service, the same would've happened?'

'Absolutely.'

Thurnauer whistled silently. 'Then they don't respect anything.'

'Only their very own religious beliefs. They are fanatics. And our experience in the past' – Shastri looked at Wrench and George Buchan – 'has been that their recruits here are the same.'

Santha wished they'd change the subject. Her eyes swept back to the crowd around them, to the staring man with the lucite cane. Donahue followed her gaze. 'Is that man bothering you, Miss Wrench?' he asked.

'No . . . of course not,' she stammered.

This time from Wrench: 'He's been looking at you?'

'Daddy, stop!' she insisted. At the risk of appearing conceited, she added, 'Men often stare at me.'

'Understandable,' Thurnauer said quietly.

A chair screeched. 'I'll talk to him.' Donahue rose.

'Please don't. It's embarrassing.'

'One can never tell, miss.'

'He's probably a dirty old man,' George told Donahue. But the detective started to move among the tables.

'Damn!' Santha cried. 'This is bad form.'

'I'm afraid it's the price one pays for police protection,' Rama Shastri told her, with some irony.

'It's so stupid, Uncle Ram. Damn, he's sitting at the man's table. People are looking. I could just crawl under the table or dissolve. I'm so embarrassed.'

She lowered her eyes. Her dark lashes were moist.

'Here, hold on, dear,' her father soothed. 'He's only doing his duty as he sees it. Think of the other night when *they* tried to grab you.'

'Daddy, that man is not a Thug.' Santha gritted her teeth. 'I just can't go through life afraid that every man who stares at me is a threat like that.'

Donahue returned. He seemed disappointed.

'Well?' Wrench urged, when Donahue said nothing.

Donahue sighed. 'The guy says he's a writer. Writes books. He said he didn't mean to be rude, but you were probably the most beautiful woman he had ever seen . . .'

'Did he apologize?' Shastri asked in curiosity.

'Not on your life. When I told him I was a cop, he just stared back. He might just as well have said, "Well, you can go to hell, buddy." Excuse me, miss.'

Santha looked; the man had left his table and was moving to the exit. His stare had been neither sexist nor 'dirty', she knew.

'Well, you are very beautiful,' George suddenly

announced with a wide smile, and she could've hugged him for breaking the tension. 'I hope that guy writes about it. It should be celebrated.'

Santha thought she saw that memory gleam in Shastri's eyes again.

Thurnauer went on after the brief silence, 'I've been trying something out,' he explained, particularly to Shastri and Wrench. 'That Thug attack on that house of drug pushers. The Swami thinks it was a training stint – for the new recruits. It occurred to me that someone in that bunch was involved in the drug racket to know about that place. Well, I've been feeding names, contacts of those victims in our files, to our computer. Then I sent the data to Washington to discover whether any of these contacts was affiliated with Eastern esoteric schools.'

Both of the older men were impressed, and the matter was discussed further until everyone finally left.

Back at Annette Kitteridge's home, another group of detectives replaced Donahue and Thurnauer. They were new men, Sterns and Wicker, with Jerome Abel in charge. Although it was a Saturday afternoon, George Buchan had to see a patient at the Stillman Infirmary in Harvard's Holyoke Center. Which increased Santha's loneliness; she missed those weekends alone with George.

She moved about the big house, listless. The deep voice of her father tallying the results of a cribbage game with Jerome Abel carried along the shadowy downstairs hall. It made her smile slightly. Daddy and Detective Abel had hit it off very well with their games. She was grateful that her father had some means of easing his worries. Santha was forevermore 'his baby' or 'his precious', and she lately thought it a millstone round his neck.

She was walking past the small library near the sun room, when she saw Rama Shastri scanning book titles.

269

Santha entered. In his hand he held an old edition of Montaigne's essays. He put the book back on the shelf, and she knew at once he wanted conversation. And with her especially.

'This Dr Kitteridge has been important to you, hasn't she?' he said, a statement more than a question.

'Daddy must have told you. She filled a gap. George once wanted her to help me professionally. Luckily, that didn't happen, and a better kind of relationship developed. She always wanted a daughter, but it was impossible.'

He sat in a well-padded reading chair. 'I studied her photograph on your bedroom table,' he admitted. 'It's more than the policeman in me, you know.'

'Yes, anyone who could fill my mother's space you wonder about,' she told him directly.

He nodded. Another admission. Maybe we'll get somewhere this time, Santha thought.

But he talked of George instead. 'Thought by now you two would be married. Expected to have to fly in for the wedding.'

Santha didn't want to answer that, and she didn't know why. Shastri answered it for her. 'It's because of what happened back then, isn't it? You have never felt entirely secure since. Would Kurt Leinster return? Were you really free?'

'Uncle Ram, are you trying to psych me out?'

Shastri studied her for a moment. 'Is that an accusation?'

'Not exactly,' she replied, after thinking about it. 'But why can't we talk about you? I'm a woman now, Uncle Ram, and there are questions, things that you and Daddy have never let me know. My mother hinted at a few things once, but . . .' She now sat herself in another relaxing chair. I do have some questions,' she stressed.

'Then by all means, ask them.'

'Mother . . .'

'Kamala.' How he said that name, so soft, like a prayer.

Santha forced herself. 'This isn't easy. Did you love her? Once? Love her the way Daddy loved her?'

'Loves her still, Steve does.'

'And you, Uncle Ram?'

'Yes, it was like that.'

Santha breathed deeply. Excited, she continued: 'Very much?'

'Oh, very much, my dear.' Throughout this he had been calm, as direct as she was; but now Shastri's eyes became wistful, almost sad. 'I don't rightly know what I feel now. I don't believe in after-life, as you know. If we live on, it is in the minds of others. Some day, those others die too, and we are truly gone.'

'I don't believe that!' she snapped. 'Not a bit of it.'

She thought he laughed. 'Ah, that's exactly the way she would have reacted. I admired and loved her for that absolute ring in her voice when she was convinced about something. Strange, I find it insufferable in most people. Absolutes have done much damage in this world, my dear. Particularly religious absolutes.

'My father was a doctor, you know. Just as Kamala's father was. But Dr Shastri was a fervent agnostic, if not an atheist. Kamala's people, as radical as they were . . . they were never that extreme. I mean, in India, the land of constant God-seeking, agnosticism is an extreme. Perhaps I'm too much an imitation of Dr Jyoti Shastri.'

He was quiet. Santha waited patiently.

'Yes, she had to choose between Steve and me. Not that it ever was a choice, really. No man and woman ever loved each other more.'

'And it never affected your friendship with Daddy?'

'Of course not, Santha.'

'You're an exceptional man, Uncle Ram.'

'But isn't your father just as exceptional, my dear? He trusted me, never once doubted my respect for their love. Does that answer you suitably?'

'There's one more thing.'

'Go on.'

'Talk about Ileana Heng.'

Rama Shastri's expression changed. This time the pain was raw, if but for a moment.

'Tell me how you met her, who she is, what she means to you.'

'Why?'

'George says I'm an incurable romantic.'

'That isn't an answer. Exactly.'

'Humour me. I'm a silly girl who loves love stories.'

'An untruth. About the silliness.'

'Well, then – I know she hates Daddy. And she felt the same way about Mother, I suppose.'

'Kamala hinted that.'

'More than hinted. Besides, I've seen Daddy turn sour just at the mention of her name.'

'I'm afraid Ileana Heng isn't very highly evolved. She's more than a bit atavistic sometimes.'

'Oh, bosh. A woman is a woman sometimes.'

He looked at her strangely. 'You do understand that. Maybe that's totally you . . .'

'Not my mother.'

'Not Kamala.'

'I understand this. Some people feel strongly, and it sometimes can lead to bad, even violent results. But it's nevertheless human – to love strongly, to be possessive, even to become violent about it. Ileana strikes me as that type. Some men are like that, too. I'm not so sure they can always help it.'

'Interesting you've worked that out.'

'Tell me about her.'

Shastri's fingers groped.

'What's wrong?'

'Oh, sometimes I miss my Sher Bidis.'

'Those terrible cigarettes . . .'

He sighed. 'The lack of self-indulgence is a terrible price to pay for life sometimes.' He sighed again. Then, he began: 'A little more than twenty years ago, your father and I were in Lashio, Burma. We were connected with Interpol then, chasing an extraordinarily evil man called Feroze Surya, a drug trafficker. We entered an opium den on a tip that he might be there. He wasn't. But it was there, in a back room, that I found Ileana. She was sixteen then, which is womanhood in the Far East, as you know. She was in the lap of Morpheus from her pipe.

'Ileana is a Eurasian. Her mother was a half-Burmese, half-Chinese dancer in a Rangoon dive when she spent a night with a Roumanian jewellery merchant. He returned to his homeland the following day, so Ileana has never known her father. Anyway, she has inherited the best physical characteristics of both parents. I suppose I was immediately smitten. Despite your father's protests, I took her with me.'

'Why did Daddy act like that?'

'Ileana was an addict. Your father felt this doomed the relationship from the beginning. Anyway, despite the twenty-year difference between us, we were soon lovers. Things remained that way for the same number of years, twenty, until I was forced to leave India and come here to America.'

'Why didn't she come with you?'

'Because of her hatred of both your parents. She soon sensed what Kamala had meant to me. Kamala met her, of course, and tried her best to win her over. Ileana's crazed jealousy rejected her. Steve had already been rejected because he had never accepted her and openly showed it.'

'How unfair of Daddy. He does have his blind spots sometimes. He had no right to meddle in your affairs that way.'

'Steve was concerned for me. Too concerned, granted. But remember, Ileana is no apotheosis of compassion and understanding. She can be cruel, totally selfish, and puts on airs for having been the mistress of Rama Shastri for so long. Other times, she can be unpredictably dedicated and self-sacrificing. I mean concerning myself. She has saved my bacon a few times and in no small way.'

'Because she loves you.'

'Yes, I believe she does . . . Anyway, when I had to flee India, she wanted me to take her to Paris. I've seen to her education over the years, and Paris was the cultured place to go to. However, I chose America instead and, knowing that I would join you and Steve, she remained behind.'

'And lately . . . Daddy told me you've seen her lately.'

'She returned to me after what I considered a too-long absence. She helped us chase down the neo-Thug movement in Varanasi. It turned out to be the usual trap set by Kurt Leinster, but that wasn't her fault. And then . . .'

'Then you returned here again. Naturally, she stayed in India. You used the word "was" about her opium addiction.'

'Yes, she had broken her addiction by entering a special clinic in Kashmir.'

'That's marvellous, Uncle Ram.'

'Yes, but she threatened to return to opium if I left her again. It was emotional blackmail, and I wouldn't tolerate it.'

'Rightly so. But, my God, she was desperate, can't you

274

see? I feel she must love you, need you every bit as much as you do her. You do miss her terribly, don't you?'

Rama Shastri nodded.

'Thank you very much, Uncle Ram,' Santha concluded. 'You've explained enough.'

'You were entitled to know about these matters, Santha.'

Santha thought of her father, her mother and Shastri; of their lives, their extraordinary friendships. Her eyes moistened. Santha held back the tears and steadied her voice. 'Thank you also for your greatness of spirit and what it has meant for my parents. And me. I love you very much, Uncle Ram.'

21

Two nights later, Sterns and Wicker were on duty at the gate of Annette Kitteridge's home. The weather had cooled considerably after the rains, and they sat in Wicker's '72 Olds. Both were smokers, so the car's interior was dense with tobacco fog. The windscreen also had an outer layer of condensation, so the view, while not exactly bad, was certainly worse than it could have been.

Both detectives were college graduates, like all Captain Condorelli's picked men. Both had attended one of Boston's smaller universities while working their way up the ranks of the police force. They were basically intelligent, yet Wicker especially was at a loss concerning the Thuggee problem. If it had been a mere matter of a cult of stranglers, an abducted woman, and another attempted seizure of Santha Wrench, that would have been simple enough to understand. But the smatterings of remarks of supernatural forces, of ancient Indian mysticism, were too much, he felt. Watch out for hands that suddenly swell, for ropes that remain upright without any visible support, for appearances and disappearances unexplained, they had been told. Not by that weird old Hindu with the turban or his rock star disciple. Nor by the Indian bigshot cop or his buddy, the government guy who'd spent half his life in that godforsaken country. Nor even by Thurnauer, whom frankly everybody on the job wondered about sometimes.

No, it came from the saner element, Jerome Abel, Belanger, others. Even the captain himself.

Wicker lowered the window and threw his smoke into the night.

'I think they've just conned the captain,' he growled. 'These Hindus, they believe in any kinda crap. They still have gods with animal heads in India. Animal heads – can you beat it, Bud?'

'Stan, grin and bear it. Maybe the captain will clear up in time. When he briefed us, I got the feeling he barely believed it himself. My philosophy is, it all comes out in the wash. The captain used to be the best, and maybe he'll come to his senses. It's still better than putting drunks in paddies. This job has class. We're special, a kind of bridge between the regular police and the Feds.'

'Personally, I think we're a damn sight better than the Feds.'

'I agree, so cheer up.' There was a loud *thwap* on the bonnet. 'What the hell's that?'

'Well, it's not bird shit splattering the car, that's for sure.' Stan Wicker peered through the windscreen, then in disgust turned on the headlights. 'Will you look at that,' he said in awe, and both men got out.

Minutes later, Wicker was explaining to Donahue, the officer in charge for the night, 'She collapsed on the hood of the car, sir. Says she's the lady doctor.' Sterns, the bigger of the two, carried Annette Kitteridge into the house.

Santha, who was already in bed, reading the latest P. D. James, knew immediately that something big was going on downstairs. The many voices talking at once told her that. Her father's booming, 'Call Condorelli right away. Get a doctor, too,' brought Santha out of bed and into her slippers and dressing gown. A woman's scream then told her everything.

'Annette!' she cried out, and flew down the staircase.

There was someone on the phone, all right – Donahue mumbling Annette's name, his face sombre as usual. Then Santha swept into the living room, her body trembling with release, and there were backs before the big sofa – the detectives, Hanuman, Nirmal, Uncle Ram and Daddy, who had somehow taken command. She thought he had little confidence in Donahue's ability to organize.

Whatever the reasons, her father suddenly decided to speak to Captain Condorelli himself. He started to pass her, then whispered, 'It's not very pleasant, Santha. She's bruised and filthy, in shock, and barely clothed. Ram had the presence of mind to throw a blanket over her lower body. She only has a skirt on, dear, and it's tattered, at that. See what you can do. See if you can clean her up and get her to her room. Ram and I will move out immediately.'

'The doctor may not want her moved,' Wicker, who heard the final part, said.

'Damn the doctor!' roared Wrench. 'She's well enough to be bathed and put to bed. Here, let my daughter in. Can't you see the woman's terrified of you gaping fellows? Donahue, hold that phone. I want to talk to Vinnie.'

The 'Vinnie' had its own power. Apparently, this man knew the captain on a first-name basis. And the detectives were surprisingly at a loss, Santha discovered. It irritated her, since they must have seen rape cases in their day . . . However, when she finally saw Annette, Santha understood their reactions better.

Everything her father had said was accurate, but he had left out the most important fact: the distant, haunted expression. Probably George would recognize the same look in the eyes of the very sick, the ones who were confined until they died. They had seen the face of Hell, all right. Suddenly, Santha Wrench wanted to kill Kurt Leinster. It bordered on compulsion.

Swami Hanuman was holding Annette's hands. She had screamed for no apparent reason, Sterns reported, in a baffled tone. Hanuman had calmed her. He had sat on the sofa edge and held those long, narrow fingers. Her shrieking had trailed off at his touch. God, Santha wished George were here, but he had early-morning commitments and had stayed at Otis Place for the night.

Maybe her father was much too quick at damning doctors . . .

Hanuman measured her with his gaze, and directed, 'Give her your love and care. But be careful.' He seemed to imply there was danger, and, for a brief moment, she resented that idea. But, facing Annette now, watching the scant glimmer of recognition in her eyes, Santha welled up with what seemed the grief of the ages. What had they done to her? Santha imagined atrocities from beatings to sexual molestation. Still, none of that fitted. It just wasn't Kurt Leinster's style. Those evils were too commonplace for him. Whatever had happened, it was unusual, unthinkable . . . Santha spoke to her, softly, soothingly.

Santha's approach worked: her voice, her effusion of love and care, her touch, like Hanuman's, gentle, stroking Annette's hair, the sides of her face, as if erasing the tense, twisted lines. Annette's forehead and neck glistened with sweat. Nirmal provided a cool wet facecloth, and Santha dabbed the areas, almost whispering, over and over again, 'My poor darling, my sweet Annette. What have you been through? I've missed you so.'

It reached home. Annette listened, and finally came the full recognition. 'Santha?' she asked. Was she confronting a hallucination? Santha read the other's unspoken question. Annette touched Santha in turn. Then, 'It's you, you!'

'Yes, it's Santha.'

What followed was comparatively easy. Santha helped Annette to stand. Nirmal offered his shoulder, and, leaning on both of them, Annette went upstairs. In the bathroom, Santha sat Annette on the toilet cover, shut the door, and now, alone with her friend, quietly explained what she was going to do next. When she was convinced that Annette understood, she prepared the tub. Then she quickly rushed to Annette's room, brought back clean underwear, nightclothes, a robe and slippers. Annette was still sitting wide-eyed. 'Are you still with me?' Santha asked, worried.

'Yes,' came softly.

Santha took a deep breath and proceeded to undress her. Submissive, like a child, Annette followed the next directions and stood, wavering slightly. Santha held her up. Annette was three inches taller than Santha and only five pounds heavier, since she had lost weight during her incarceration, but nevertheless her physical weakness made her slump. Thus, her weight distribution wasn't uniform. That and the pressure on Santha's shoulder made the walk to the tub a painful struggle. Santha finally managed to lower Annette into the bath; and it was at this point that she saw the heavily bruised area at the base of Annette's spine and the two punctured nipples. While she washed her friend, tears of rage blended with the soapy water.

She had just finished giving Annette a quick shampoo when there was a soft knock on the door. Opening it slightly, she saw Rama Shastri with a bowl of bouillon on a saucer, and a large spoon. He had found the bouillon cubes in the pantry and thought the broth might strengthen Dr Kitteridge. Santha thanked him and, pulling the linen basket to the side of the bath, sat on it and started to feed Annette. But her friend took everything from her after two spoonfuls and fed herself.

Elated at the marked progress, Santha leaned forward, elbows on knees, and studied her patient. The thought trickled into her consciousness: Why had Kurt Leinster released her? Why, in fact, had he ordered his people to leave her practically at the gate to her home? The detective had reported that besides telling them her name, Annette had also stated that she had been let out of a car half a mile up the road. Annette remembered nothing else, though. Santha concluded the amnesia was perhaps merciful.

Annette raised her eyes from the bowl, said, 'Santha' in wonder, and then smiled.

Getting her to bed was much less difficult than expected. Annette stood up in the tub without staggering and was able to remain stationary while Santha wiped her body and helped her dress. Once Annette was propped up in bed, Santha combed the neck-long grey hair. The colour rinse had left it long ago.

Santha did most of the talking. Again, consoling words and sounds, little gestures of affection, like a hug and kisses on Annette's cheeks and fingertips. Annette's head finally settled into the pillow and she closed her eyes.

The doctor appeared later. He found a sleeping Santha curled up in the chair at Annette's bedside. He awoke her, and, after answering a few questions about Annette's general condition, she left the room.

Twenty minutes later, the police doctor told Santha the results of his examination. As supposed, Dr Kitteridge was in a state of shock, he began, how severe he could not estimate yet. No, she hadn't been sexually molested, but, strangely, there had been some damage to her vulva and beyond. The examination of this area would have to be done again very soon at a hospital, where there was the proper medical equipment. The doctor didn't go into detail as to the type of damage, and Santha didn't ask.

Also, there were strange lacerations on the nipples of both breasts. Fortunately, there didn't appear to be any infection. And due to kicks administered to Annette's coccyx area, there was severe bruising and inflammation. From his evaluation of the extent of oedema in the vulva and the spinal area, particularly, he would strongly recommend that she be hospitalized as soon as possible. There was also the shock to her nervous system and her mind to be considered. Whatever she had experienced, it had certainly been a form of torture. Now, if Santha would excuse him, he had to report to the others downstairs.

Santha Wrench nodded. When alone, she sat in a straight-backed hall chair and wrung her hands. Torture! Oh, God – torture! For some reason, the doctor's use of the word shattered her control. Santha pulled her robe tightly around herself and wept. It was as if every bit of pain Annette had suffered was now hers.

22

Annette Kitteridge called for Santha. It was during one of the pauses between her racking sobs that Santha heard her. She immediately fought for control to present an undisturbed face to her friend. Then she rushed back into the room, since Annette's calls had become shrill.

Simultaneously, Hanuman, who had been listening to the doctor, parted from the group. His concentration was overwhelmed by a strong need to go upstairs. The very air was afire with emanations he couldn't ignore. It seared through him as though he were in the centre of a Mind of Flame. Raging, burning . . . a pyre of concentrated hate.

At the bedside, Santha sat beside the wailing woman. Annette was struggling with something within her, Santha thought, as she stared at the writhing body. Annette's head moved back and forth constantly as if she were saying 'No' again and again. At times, she pounded the bed in frustration. But with one hand only. The other hand Annette kept under the blankets upon her abdomen.

'I'll get the doctor,' Santha told her. She was on her feet, but Annette suddenly gripped her wrist and pulled her back down.

'I'm so sorry.' Annette's look was piteous. 'I can't stop it!'

Stop what? Santha was about to ask. Annette's other hand rose free of the covers towards Santha's face. She saw that the middle finger was elongated, the skin of purest ebony, the nail very long and hooked like a talon. It dug into Santha's forehead with the sharpness of a shard of glass. Blood geysered into Santha's eyes.

283

Hanuman was over the threshold at the moment of the attack. The heels of his feet and the back of his calves acted as springs as he propelled himself at the two women. Annette had yanked Santha forward into an embrace. Her mouth was flush on Santha's in a smothering kiss. Hanuman's force broke the connection.

Facing Annette, he saw the darkening face, the kinetic, bulging eyes, heard the guttural rasp that iced the nape of his neck. Hanuman pressed the creature's head back with a football player's straight-arm thrust. The head sank back into the pillows.

Then the Swami rolled atop Santha, who was on the carpet, covering her face and screaming. Blood seeped between her fingers. With all his strength, Hanuman prised the fingers free, placed his palm flat on the wound and repeated a mantra, *sotto voce*.

Voices, shouts, heavy footsteps in the room. Hanuman watched Santha's eyes close. A second later, when he released his hand from the forehead, the bleeding had stopped, the blood had coagulated.

He stood up, and met Stephen Wrench's pain-filled gaze. 'She has the mark again,' Hanuman muttered, turning his attention to the bed. The darkness had left Annette's features, the eyes were normal, hers again, staring blankly. There was spittle on her lips.

'But how was it done?' asked the doctor when he rose from his examination of Santha. 'Where's the weapon?'

Hanuman pointed to Annette's hand. The finger was no longer ebony but a pale white. Everyone stared at the long, ugly fingernail.

'Impossible!' the doctor cried. 'She had no such nail when I examined her! It must be false!' He grabbed the hand, gasped and dropped it.

'Yes, it's fucking real,' Wrench's hoarse voice announced. He had taken something from the doctor's bag. The cutting instrument flashed in the overhead lighting. He reached for Annette's hand. 'Well, it'll never mark anyone again.'

Rama Shastri and Donahue rushed him. 'Steve, think of what you're doing!'

'My baby,' Wrench sobbed. 'My baby has the mark again.'

They dragged him away from the bed. Sterns and Wicker had joined in. Wrench continued to protest until Hanuman said, 'Observe. It is gone now.'

He was correct. The finger was Annette's again, the nail was reasonably short. The doctor, who had been studying Santha's wound, which had rapidly become a small black mark resembling a miniature pickaxe, rose, examined Annette's hand and lost control. His training couldn't accept the phenomenon. 'Did you try to use my postmortem knife on Dr Kitteridge?' he barked, taking out his confusion on Wrench. 'You ought to be arrested.'

'That's right!' Wrench replied, his rage resurfacing. 'I'm a goddamn Jack the Ripper.' The tears came back. He knelt beside Santha. 'My poor baby. Look at her.' He raised Santha, held her tight.

The doctor sobered at Wrench's grief, and calmly directed she be taken to her bed. Patting Wrench's shoulder, he added, 'I'll be with her in a moment.' He went to Annette Kitteridge. He was a long time checking her pulse and studying her blank eyes with a small light. 'Terrible, terrible,' his lips formed. 'Worse shock than ever. She's totally out of contact.'

'Her spirit had been replaced with another's.' Hanuman tried to be helpful. 'Very traumatic.'

The doctor frowned. 'Pray tell me your diagnosis,' he said sarcastically.

'There are always entities seeking to infiltrate the

human psyche. This is what happened to Dr Kitteridge, temporarily.'

'You do mean spirits, other beings . . . demons?'

'Precisely. How else can you explain the talon? You can't believe it's psychosomatic.'

'Why not? Stigmata can be caused that way.'

'Then why would Dr Kitteridge attack Santha Wrench? The doctor thought of Santha as a daughter, I am told.'

'God, man, the woman's insane. After her ordeal . . .' Hanuman shrugged.

'I must look to Miss Wrench,' the doctor snapped. He left Hanuman. Nirmal, who had been sitting quietly in the corner, asked, 'Will Kali manifest again through her, Bapu?'

'I think not. She has moved on.' He stared hard at the wall as if he could see through it to another room at the end of the hall.

There, Santha Wrench had opened her eyes. She recognized her father and Rama Shastri, and smiled.

'I'll sedate her,' the doctor announced. 'She mustn't be disturbed.' He wiped the caked blood free of the mark. Then he shook his head like an exhausted man. 'Amazing. Totally healed. What is happening here tonight, Mr Wrench?' He quickly changed his mind. 'No, please – don't attempt to tell me. I haven't yet digested what my visual sense has told me.' He stood up. 'I'll have a nurse here by morning. Meanwhile, she mustn't be left alone.' He replaced his stethoscope into his bag. 'I'll have an ambulance take Dr Kitteridge to a hospital immediately. For your daughter's sake, I suggest they remain separated for a while.'

Wrench thanked him, then went to the window as an outside light brightened the curtains and window. 'Here's Captain Condorelli at last,' Wrench said, with some relief.

* * *

Condorelli had both Jerome Abel and Thurnauer with him. Things improved considerably with his presence; Donahue was too phlegmatic to lead, and the difference was clear immediately. The captain brought an air of confidence and professionalism in with him. Rama Shastri, who understood what being in charge meant, saw smiles on the faces of Sterns and Wicker.

When the ambulance arrived, the two detectives were sent with it to the hospital to protect Annette Kitteridge. Then Donahue filled Condorelli and Thurnauer in on everything that had happened to date. The three detectives went upstairs to join Wrench, who was at his daughter's bedside. Hanuman and Nirmal were in the guest room.

'What's this mark mean?' Condorelli asked, when Wrench stepped out of the room and closed the door so they could speak at ease. Rama Shastri had entered in Wrench's place.

'It's shaped like a small pickaxe. One of the symbols of Thuggee. Santha was marked before, and it faded, in time, after Leinster disappeared. It means they now have a stronger influence over her.' Wrench's tone was even. He was calm again, but his mouth lines were tight, bitter.

'Just by marking her?'

'Trust me, it's true. Okay, Vinnie?'

Condorelli nodded. What else could he do? But he had to ask the next question. He could barely believe he was saying the words: 'And carved on her forehead by a long fingernail? The boys say they saw it disappear. Christ – a long fingernail!'

'It was more like a talon, Vinnie.'

'Holy Christmas! How do you put that in a report, Steve?'

'Just say she was scratched badly,' came the numbed reply. 'Meanwhile, just trust me, OK?'

* * *

The night led to dawn. The day progressed. At 8.05 A.M., a short, pert nurse arrived. Santha's life signs were checked. Her pulse was irregular, her temperature up two degrees.

8.52 A.M., Santha Wrench awoke and announced she was hungry. She was given tea and toast. A few minutes later, Stephen Wrench phoned the Peabody Museum at Harvard University and notified them that Santha wouldn't be at work that day. Then he phoned George Buchan and told him about Santha's condition.

10.33 A.M. Santha Wrench awoke screaming from a nightmare she couldn't remember. Her blood pressure was a touch high, her temperature normal. Once quiet, she asked for food again, and was given broth, toast and tea.

12.16 P.M. The doctor arrived. Santha seemed to be recovering rapidly. She sat up, smiled and ate more solid food: a grapefruit, toast with marmalade, milk, and two eggs that her father had scrambled.

2.10 P.M. The nurse had left the room for a moment. Upon her return, she found Santha sitting up in a chair. The nurse checked her forehead. Despite the rapid healing, a bandage soaked in diluted antiseptic had been placed on the 'wound'. She had also been given a tetanus shot. The doctor wasn't taking any chances.

2.58 P.M. Santha asked for the portable phone. When she had it, she rang George's office. She caught him just before he was to see a patient, his last for the day. George promised to come to Wayland immediately afterwards.

True to his word, George Buchan showed up at 3.57, and, before he went upstairs to Santha, he told Wrench and the others that he had gone to see Annette Kitteridge at the hospital earlier. Her condition was very serious, verging on catatonia. It was agreed that this information would be kept from Santha for a while.

At 4.22 P.M. the rains came. It was a thick, murky business. Gusts of wet leaves dotted the driveway, the roof of the garage and the porte-cochère. Santha, now dressed, sat in her bedroom window, watching the rainfall, listening to its droning patter and *r-r-rat-t-t-tatat* along the house gutters. George heard her slow, soft-spoken evaluation of what had occurred the previous night.

'They have her,' Santha concluded, 'and now they're after me. This is it, I feel it, *kesari*.'

'Feel what?'

'The beginning of the end for Kurt Leinster or me.' She faced George, her face world-weary in the grey light. 'I'm going to kill that bastard, George. For what he did to her.'

'Let it go for now,' he pleaded. 'Get well.'

She picked up a hand mirror from her dressing table. Gently, she prised up the adhesive and gauze on her forehead. The mark: it was delineated between her eyes, the dark pickaxe shape. The mark of Thuggee, of Kali Mother. Santha replaced the bandage and was quiet.

By six o'clock, Santha insisted she eat dinner downstairs. She ate well, had a coherent conversation with everybody. She was also fully dressed for the meal. She whispered to George, 'Why don't we go for a ride? I don't mind the rain, do you?'

'We're staying in the house,' George replied firmly. Pouting, Santha marched out of the room.

When George looked in her bedroom later, she was asleep. The nurse had returned from her break, and she informed George that Santha had closed her eyes the moment her head touched the pillow. 'She didn't even undress. Do you wish me to notify you when she awakes, Doctor?'

George started. So completely had he muffled his doctor role when he was around Santha that it sounded as if it didn't fit. Not here. He shook his head, freeing himself of the anomaly. 'Yes,' he said.

'Must kill. Must kill. I must kill you,' Santha repeated to the voice. She really said it to the small saffron ball. It was the only visible thing in the total darkness. The ball seemed to squiggle with pleasure, momentarily.

She heard, 'If you but follow the bouncing ball, you will find the one you seek. Remember, keep your eye on the bouncing ball.' Santha watched it until her head ached; it felt as if it had been cleaved in two parts. The pain woke her.

7.30. P.M. The world outside the curtains was dark, too. And noisy. The house creaked in the wind, and the rain added to the cacophony. The aching in Santha's head hadn't been dispelled by awakening. On the beige curtains the saffron ball danced.

Santha got out of bed and went to the window. The ball was bouncing down the lane. The lights of the porte-cochère splayed the lawn for a few feet, and the saffron ball dashed past one of Condorelli's men making his rounds.

Her nurse watched her every movement. She spoke, asking Santha how she felt. Santha looked at her, frowned, went to her wardrobe and took out her winter coat. Santha was obviously planning to go outside. The nurse, trying to be diplomatic, stated that first she must have her temperature and blood pressure taken. Approaching Santha, she heard something like a low growl. Then Santha grabbed the blood-pressure cuff from her with amazing strength and swung it at the nurse's face. The impact sent the nurse reeling. Blood seeped from her left temple and ear. She bent, covering her head with her arms as Santha swung again. Before the nurse could scream, Santha Wrench hit the woman in the solar plexus. The nurse fell to the carpet, unconscious.

7.42 P.M. A figure stealthily moved from the side door near the porte-cochère and, remaining close to the shadows against the house, eased towards the garage. In seconds' time, Santha Wrench, muffled in a winter coat and a woman's slouch hat, opened the door of her '76 VW Rabbit. She quickly turned the key and began to direct the car on to the glassy drive. Through the rear and side mirrors, the saffron ball hovered and bobbed as if eager to depart. It was bright and fuzzy-looking against the rain backdrop. Smoke enveloped the Rabbit's back window. The car had slowly emerged into the rain, and the smokiness had formed from the oil leaking into the combustion chamber.

Then another circle of light came through the thick exhaust cloud. The light suddenly V'd out into the beam of a flashlight. Her door opened. Belanger, dressed in an oilskin and a patrolman's cap from a bygone day, shone the bright spray at her face, and said, 'Sorry, Miss Wrench. I can't let you leave the grounds.'

Santha's hand was a blur of motion. She gripped the handle of the flashlight and pulled it free of Belanger's grip. Belanger gaped at his empty hands with disbelief. Then he placed a hand on the steering wheel and reached for her. Santha smashed the flashlight head on the fingers around the wheel's leather cover. With a loud curse, Belanger let go. Santha pulled the door shut and sped the Rabbit to the crossroads.

8.05 P.M. Everything on the Massachusetts Turnpike glistened – the road, the vehicles, the very night. Santha blinked, peered hard between the shush of the windscreen wipers, and rediscovered the smudge of saffron far ahead, beyond at least four cars. Must kill him, will kill, she thought.

She was amazed how Kurt Leinster had minions everywhere. That woman in the house pretending to be a nurse, the man with the flashlight. How had Kurt ever managed to get them on Annette's property? Well, she had shown them, as she would show anybody who got in her way. Must kill.

God in Heaven, the ache at her temples was unbelievable. Santha wished she had brought aspirin with her. The centre of her forehead felt moist again, but when she touched it, there was no blood. Still, it was moist and very warm. Burning, burning . . . the mark burned.

The rain was decreasing. The wind parted the downpour and they rode into the gap. Then everything was filled in again and Captain Condorelli had to shout above the din that came from the car roof: 'But where did Santha get all that strength from?'

'It is the result of the mark,' Hanuman told him. He was seated between Wrench and Shastri in the back. Jerome Abel was driving. The policemen had an ear tuned to the radio. Condorelli had just sent out a description of Santha and her VW Rabbit.

'It is more than a mark. It brands Santha as a part of Thuggee, whether she wishes to be or not. It is really a sigil. Santha's psyche is sealed by it. Somehow, the deep atavistic layers that are within us are then affected. Hence the violence and the incredible surges of adrenaline that are suddenly manifest. No doubt Santha is also blinded concerning what she has done. Her perspective is . . .'

'Warped?' From Condorelli.

'Yes . . . like that. She is being directed, not in command of herself. Similar to when she was marked years ago.'

292

'It happened before?'

'Oh, yes. That time Santha attacked my *chela*, Nirmal.'

'Why wasn't I informed?'

'I guess I blotted out the memory,' Wrench confessed. 'After all, it is my daughter.'

'It was my responsibility to warn you,' the Swami said. 'This time I haven't been as . . . objective. I have had some difficulty focusing on Kunkali's cunning. I have been strangely ineffective. For example, I became soporific a short time before Santha's awakening. I had meant to check her, but instead I slept. I fear my abilities wane . . .'

'Hey, Swami,' the captain interrupted again, 'no one expects you to do our job. We're supposed to be the pros, remember.'

'But this involves more than police work,' Rama Shastri reminded him.

The radio came to life. Jerome answered. Santha's car had been spotted, they heard; did they want her stopped?

'Christ, no,' Wrench bellowed. 'If Santha sees them, she'll drive recklessly. She can get killed on these wet roads.'

'Leave her alone,' Condorelli ordered. 'But don't let her get out of your sight.'

'Is Belanger keeping up with us?' Condorelli asked Jerome Abel. 'With his injured hand, I'm not so sure I should've let him drive.'

Abel checked his rear-view mirror. 'I see him, Captain. His hand'll be okay. It's not broken.'

'He's lucky. The nurse is, too. They both claim your daughter is shockingly strong, with a hint of more power waiting in reserve.' The captain turned to Jerome Abel. 'Get on the radio. Send out a warning. Nobody – and I mean whatever the reason – is to put a hand on that girl.'

'Thanks, Vinnie,' Wrench said softly.

'It's not to protect your girl, Steve. Hell, I've got to think of my men.'

The saffron ball was zigzagging, darting between the cars. It looked like part of the traffic. Gripping the wheel until the skin of her fingers was raw and almost bleeding, Santha Wrench spoke aloud to the accompaniment of the shushing windscreen wipers. 'Lead me on, little ball,' she told it. 'Have to avenge poor Annette. Have to find *him*. Have to kill . . .'

She was distracted. A van opposite in the next lane was keeping pace with her. Someone was looking out of the side window, a young woman's face, she thought. Why? The rainfall made the world too blurry to see the face better. The driver was a man, a shadow hulked over the wheel. What did they want?

Follow the ball, Santha told herself. Forget the people. Only the bouncing ball counts. Concentrate. Concentrate.

The Rabbit's clock read 8.13 P.M.

Belanger was delivering a monologue. His ego was hurting; his hand was a swollen, listless thing. After a few miles, he had turned the wheel over to Granger, a new recruit of a few days' standing in Condorelli's special squad. It was humiliating, that, and the fact that he'd been bested by a girl. His wife would correct him and say 'a woman'. But a girl was a girl where he came from.

They were following the captain and the others, the police radio sputtering like punctuation to his non-stop talking.

'She's crazy. Hell, her boyfriend ought to be able to tell that. He's a shrink, ain't he?' He nursed his throbbing hand – damn, he wouldn't be able to drive for days. 'You talk about power, guys. Believe me, she had force in reserve. I could sense, almost smell it. When she yanked

294

the flashlight out of my hand, I was stunned. And I thought I had strong wrists and hands. You should've seen it, you'd know better what I'm talking about. I've heard that crazy people get powerful that way. All of a sudden they can do things they normally couldn't. She was a freak, a goddamn Wonder Woman, lemme say.

'Funny, the shrink boyfriend of hers didn't spot it coming until now.' He looked at Nirmal, alone in the back seat. 'Well, love is blind, and that guy has sure been in the dark. This isn't the kind of thing that just happens.' He snapped the fingers of his good hand. 'I know that much about psychology. This has been building up in her, believe me. She's been a potential looney tuney from way back. Probably hates all men.' The rain hit the windscreen before his face in the passenger's seat like a dramatic effect in a movie. It set him on a new tack. 'Lookit that sonobitchin' downpour. Strange night. It lets up for a minute, then just when you think it's over, it comes back. Christ, Granger, did you see that fuckin' cowboy pass Cap's car ahead? Shit, with no siren or light, how's the fucker gonna know we're cops? Orders are: Don't scare her – she might crack up her Rabbit in a panic.

'So what? She's already cracked.' When no one laughed, not a chuckle, Belanger became vicious. 'Didja see the look on her boyfriend's face when he realized he couldn't come with us? Shit, someone had to take care of the nurse, and he was the only doctor in the house. Not that he could help us out here. Shit, if he couldn't spot how cuckoo his girlfriend was getting, how's he gonna help us out here? Hey, guys – you answer that . . .'

No one did.

'Cute kid, that nurse!' he continued. 'Good thing she'll be OK. She might've been killed. Mark me, with strength like that, this Santha Wrench'll kill somebody yet.

'Was on a case once. Little Puerto Rican lady, no taller

than five feet, if she was that. Thinner than toothpicks. Nice church-going, motherly type. Found her five-ten, two-twenty-five-pounder bruiser of a husband beating one of her kids to death. Drunk, understand. A sodden, boozed-up beast. She had these nails, a little longer than usual. She jumped on his back and tore out his eyes. She just stuck the nails in them and dug. Right in. No matter how much he tried to shake her off, he couldn't. Most people don't believe that when I tell it. The little lady just went crazy and dug in.'

He stopped and lit up a cigarette. The radio blared. Santha Wrench was heading for the Chinatown exit into Boston. Then Condorelli's voice, warning his cars to leave her alone until she stopped her car. Then, silence.

And more silence.

Belanger looked around him. ''s'matter with you two? Don't you have anything to say?'

8.22 P.M. Both groups, in Condorelli's car and Belanger's, listened intently to the interplay between a pair of squad cars converging on Santha Wrench's VW Rabbit. She had proved elusive. Not only had she ignored red lights but she had also skirted Chinatown by U-turns and going down one-way streets in the wrong direction. Heading for Chinatown had been baffling enough; but she now sped towards the truly unexpected: Washington Street and Boston's infamous red-light district, the Combat Zone.

Meanwhile, Santha Wrench had just followed the saffron light. It seemed to sense that she was being followed, knew which abrupt turnings, which network of side streets, would confuse the police pursuit. Even the disturbing white van that had remained alongside Santha's Rabbit right up to and down the exit ramp finally pulled away and seemed to make for South Station.

She was free at last! Free! Her exhilaration was mysterious indeed, since she had no concrete idea of what she'd been freed from. Santha hadn't seen the pursuing squad cars, not once. But the exhilaration, deeply felt, made her feel invulnerable, beyond harm from others. Santha had never felt so good, so wonderfully aggressive, she thought. This was her night.

The Combat Zone had been aptly named by the press. An area of porno stores, game and flesh arcades, all-nudie shows, and bars filled with prostitutes and pimps as well as the usual alcoholic beverages – it had an even more notorious reputation for violence. Often, gangs of prostitutes had brutalized males, whether customers or not, for their money, using knives or anything that would render the victims unconscious. Murders were not uncommon. Even people passing through in cars were dragged out if their doors were unlocked, and beaten for their money. To go there was to risk your life, the law warned the public; but people came, anyway – transients; college men on a romp; lonely, disturbed men, some married, seeking a greater sexual high.

To Santha Wrench's muddled consciousness, the Zone's bright gaudy sleaze was merely troublesome blinding lights that interfered with her search for the saffron sphere. She slowed her Rabbit to almost a crawl, peering through the scintillating drizzle. Even the slow, looping raintrails on her windscreen picked up the sparkle. Within the glare were moving shapes, many of them, closing in. A loud succession of thumps on the bonnet followed. Someone was pounding it. Santha saw that faces, all of them women, were standing before her car. She was tempted to increase her speed, felt a hot thrill at the idea, and was about to do so, when her door was opened.

Santha was seized by the shoulder and thrown into the street.

Santha sat up in a flooded pothole. Someone had already climbed into her car and put on the brake. Her eyes fell on the ring of women around her. Their faces were nothing but harsh lines and thick smudges from too much make-up. They resembled women clowns whose humour had turned sour. All the smiles were gloating ones, and the odour of strong perfume and sweat offended her already heightened senses.

There was one in particular, tall, in an open, see-through raincoat, legs in black stockings and suspenders, a skirt and tunic top of leather. The woman was apparently the leader. The rest were just as scantily clad, despite the weather, their expressions full of potential threat.

Santha stood slowly, evaluating the red-haired nemesis before her. From the others came cries, 'Take care of her, Bella.'

'Why did you do that?' Santha asked evenly. Her entire left side was wet and mud-caked. She brushed at the mess and looked at the woman again. 'Why?'

'Look, girlie, it's not personal. Business is bad tonight. We don't usually pick on women, but we need the money.'

'I don't have any,' Santha replied. She read the brief glimmer of fear in the other's eyes. Santha was calm, too calm. And, almost like an insult, her lips curling in distaste, Santha said the woman's name: 'Bella.'

The painted face emanated hate. 'Who gave you permission to say my name?'

'Oh, you mean Bella, the Bimbo.' Santha added a taunting laugh to her remark.

Again, Bella frowned. She hesitated. A pudgy woman

298

in a polka-dot mini-skirt shouted, 'Break up her face, Bella.'

Santha shrugged, grinned. 'You look like Halloween's idea of a whore. I bet you're bad at it, too.'

Bella swung, then gaped. Santha's fingers had gripped Bella's wrist before the arc of her swing was finished. Santha Wrench squeezed. 'Oh, Jesus! Oh, Jesus!' Bella howled. The raucous crowd became silent. Santha lowered Bella's arm across her raised knee. Her other hand gripped Bella's arm above the elbow. The sound of the break was like a sharp report in the hush. Bella was on the ground suddenly, passing out from pain.

Santha saw a flicker to her left. The polka-dot skirt dived forward, a blade flashing its intent. Santha backed, only two steps, but very fast and with perfect timing. The blade slashed air. Santha grabbed the pudgy arm, wrenching the knife free. It clattered along the street. No one picked it up. Santha pulled the arm backwards and up. The shoulder was dislodged. Santha dropped the woman as though she were so much refuse. The woman began to sob, her cheek immersed in a puddle.

Santha turned to the rest of the gang. The circle had widened, and now it retreated. Some of the women ran to the pavement and clustered beneath the glare of a nude show marquee, as if the neon lights were a protection.

Santha felt as if she glowed, herself. She hunched, stepped forward, and they shrieked. She knew they were not only impressed with her bone-breaking skill but that she now also exuded an ominous power that made them cringe. They huddled together like schoolgirls who had never known a moment of life on the streets. Now it was Santha who gloated, Santha who surrendered to blood lust. The heady exhilaration she felt craved, hungered for more danger.

Santha left the two broken bodies in the centre of

Washington Street and headed for the pavement like an Amazonian warrior about to engage in more battle.

As she stepped from the road, her concentration was held by a quick, familiar flash – the ball at the end of an alley leading to a street parallel to Washington Street. She paused on the corner, tugged by two simultaneous urges, unable to decide. In her intense preoccupation, she didn't notice two figures who closed in on her from a bar next to the burlesque theatre. Nor the *wheep-wheep* of two approaching squad cars.

The two figures, who were both men, a Black and a blond long-haired giant with a run of tattoos along his forearms, jumped her without warning and pulled her out of sight into the bar's interior. Santha was ready for action again, and about to strike. But the feel and smell of maleness made her change her mind. She allowed them to take her in order to see what new adrenal joys that would reveal.

On they dragged her, past customers and a female stripper on a small stage, on past the more shadowy booths where a waitress serviced with oral sex for a thirty-dollar tip, past the phone booths, the storeroom, to an office.

Santha was roughly pushed in. She heard the door slam behind her. Adjusting to more dim lighting, Santha faced two other men. Another Black, small, slim, wearing a fedora-style hat, and a beefy, swarthy man behind a desk.

'This is the bitch, Demos,' one of her muscular abductors said. Santha didn't bother to see which of the two it was. 'She left Bella and Dot out there in the street with a broken arm and shoulder. But me and Ski didn't have no trouble with her.'

'Why you picking on my girls?' the man behind the desk asked quickly. His voice was gravelly.

'Demos, I ain't finished. The cops just came outside.'

The swarthy man stood, palms bracing his weight on the desk. 'Fuck the cops. I want to know why she's beating up my girls. You better tell me fast, you cunt. I'm not a patient man.'

'They attacked me first,' Santha answered.

'That's true, Demos.'

'Let her do the talking, Neil.'

'They pulled me from the car, tried to hurt me. So I fought back,' Santha said. 'And you're a fat, ugly prick.'

The small man, who had been silent until now, said softly, 'Let me cut her, Demos.'

'Sure. Sure, you asshole,' Neil, the big Black, yelled. 'Sure, do that with the cops outside.'

Santha laughed. They stared in disbelief.

'All women are cunts to you, aren't they, Mr Fat Prick?' She raised her dress and pulled down her tights. Demos blinked. 'Look at this and weep, mister. That's pretty damn good pussy, isn't it?' Santha passed her fingers through her pubic hair. 'Weep, you fuckfaced pig, because it'll never be yours.'

'What about mine?' asked Neil. He had forgotten about the police, totally.

Santha looked him over. 'Maybe,' she replied. 'If it looks right.'

'You bet it's right, baby,' Neil told her, unzipping his trousers. 'This is one long hunk of heaven, believe it.'

Demos sat back, guffawing.

'G'wan, touch it and live, baby.'

'I wouldn't chance it, Neil,' Ski warned.

Santha placed her hand on Neil's erection.

'Go on, baby,' he purred. 'Have a taste.'

She smiled warmly and pressed with her fingers. Neil's eyes bulged. Sweat dripped from his forehead, and he shook his head. He tried to raise his hands to hit her, but she placed her other hand flush on his Adam's apple. 'Be good,' she advised. Neil tried to press his weight against her. He couldn't believe how helpless he was.

'Let me cut.' The small Black man pulled a knife.

'Yes, you do that,' Santha agreed, as she rammed Neil against the blade. Blood gushed out of his side on to Demos's desk. Demos shrieked.

'I'm getting the fuck outta here!' From Ski, who left the door open as he disappeared.

Santha straightened her clothing, hearing a loud din in the bar. The small Black was trying desperately to free himself from Neil's body, which had collapsed on him.

Santha left. She wanted to do more damage, but her senses told her she ought to move. And with speed.

Looking towards the bar, she saw four policemen. One spotted her, and the group rushed forward. Santha ran the other way. She was in a narrow corridor with graffiti on the walls. Obscene words, obscene drawings. When she reached the exit door to the alley, she took a quick look back. Two of the policemen were heading for the office, the other two were keeping to the wall of the bar. A half-second, and they'd be in the corridor. Santha pushed the heavy door open.

Thick, thick rain again. It hit the alley and rooftops hard. A mad drumming everywhere. Santha dashed towards the parallel street, where the saffron ball had been. 'Please be there now,' she told it aloud. Somehow it represented safety. The door opened behind her. 'Stop,' one of the policemen called. Santha paused, picked up a dustbin and hurled it. 'Sonofabitch!' she heard, and then the crashing noise of metal on pavement. The policeman leaped free in time and cursed again.

Facing the alley's end, Santha's heart leaped. The ball was there, waiting, dancing. Her legs pumped twice as hard, twice as eagerly.

The policemen were coming, but their pace had slowed.

They were hesitant, afraid of her power, maybe. This was wonderful. This was free. Freedom night.

She reached the alley's end. She saw the white van and prepared for more trouble. The ball bounced into the opening in the rear, however. Santha wavered for a second, heard the footsteps behind her and clambered into the dark interior. A huge shadow closed the door behind her.

The two policemen reached the end of the alley too late to see the van or its plate.

9.32 P.M. Rama Shastri phoned George Buchan about Santha's disappearance. Shastri was doing it instead of Stephen Wrench, who was too shaken to talk at the moment.

Shastri told the story before George could say much. When he had finished, George replied, 'Just before you phoned, I received a quick call. The man's voice said, "I've got her with me now. Tough luck, old boy."' George recognized who it was. He didn't have to tell Rama Shastri the man's name.

PART THREE
The Ashram

I feel sure it was the result of no mere chance that you became familiar with the terrors of what you term Higher Space; for higher space is no mere external measurement.

Algernon Blackwood, *A Victim of Higher Space*

23

The briefing room was crowded. Smoke wafted, fogged, moved in eddies. Watching the smokers with envy, Rama Shastri shifted uncomfortably in his metal folding chair. It was a way to thwart the overlay of gloom, though. These were all unhappy men, a dedicated group that felt they had failed miserably. They were used to winning, this bunch, and none had taken the abduction of Santha Wrench gracefully. But it had also developed unity. Their ranks were tighter than ever. The kind of unification that Swami Hanuman had demanded in the past, the blending as one mind that once before had defeated Kurt Leinster and Kali Ma.

So Rama Shastri was optimistic for once. The thrill of pursuit was also in the air. Something cold ran up his spine, a vibration that sensed they all felt as if they were part of a huge neural web.

Frustration, rage, then the policeman's methodology and logic combined to assist in the big chase. None of it was supernatural or the least bit arcane. It was the balance of the righteous, like a glowing fever that must work its course, a fire from the pure goodness of men that is rarely seen but sometimes springs forth when the truly Evil manifests. The uncluttered good, ancient, before religion, before perhaps even the idea of God.

Shastri smiled thinly. He had his own mysticism in his own unbelieving fashion. He blinked under the harsh fluorescents. The grim profiles of the men had a leaden pallor. Next to him, Steve fumbled with his pipe, then left it untouched. He was handling himself very well, considering the passage of time. Nearly a week and a half had gone by, and, despite a widespread and thorough police dragnet throughout New England, no clue to Santha's whereabouts had emerged.

Until now, according to Thurnauer. Which was why they were all assembled. The Swami, too, and Nirmal. Rama Shastri couldn't help but admire Captain Condorelli for being so flexible. Although Condorelli's mind still boggled at facts that shouldn't be facts but the crazed imaginings of the lunatic fringe, he nevertheless cooperated with Wrench's request that the Swami's esoteric knowledge be included. This wasn't easy for such a rational man, as Shastri knew – it had been hard for *him* in the beginning, three years ago. It was against training, against the sober policeman's perspective.

This wasn't supposed to be. This was absurd, insane, inane; it was madcap. Still, it was the truth.

The fabric of this world had been shredded, and something unearthly, awful beyond reason, had entered the cherished landscape most men called normality, reality.

Shastri's gaze darted to Hanuman and his disciple in the far corner, sitting isolated from the rest. The Swami was having a difficult time. He had explained that he felt his powers were being sapped; that Kali Ma had invaded astral regions once under the sole control of his late master, Vishnarma.

Rama Shastri had to bend his consciousness to think this way. He had a mental image of his rational self as a straight line, now bending into a deeper and deeper curve, becoming a parabola.

But past events had proved Hanuman correct. There were other 'places', planes of existence. One had to reorganize one's concept of space and time. Thinking of it that way, it was palatable. More so than the terms 'astral', 'heavens', and the like.

Captain Condorelli cleared his throat. He was about to begin, holding papers and dangling print-outs in his hands. His Calabrian features were smudges of white as the sunlight sifting through the window blinds at his left clashed with the fluorescents. It left a nimbus around his head and shoulders. He said, 'I know we've got our backs against the wall, but we've got to fight whatever despondency we feel. Thurnauer thinks he may have something new for us. But first, let's go over what we don't have, so we won't be confusing our priorities.

'First, we can pretty much exclude our Thug prisoners as a possible source of information. Experts – our medical people familiar with mind-altering drugs and types of hypnosis – say that the prisoners are operating on one frequency alone. That's a layman's way of putting it, but the terminology's over our heads. It means, simply, that anything connecting them with the Thug organization or hide-out has been short-circuited. They're not sure about how it was done, but everything seems to point to hypnosis.'

A question: 'Is it like brainwashing, Captain?'

'You could call it that. When they're caught, instead of biting into the false tooth loaded with poison, their minds automatically shut off certain memory cells. The barrier is tremendous. They even forget their identities. Besides, none of them has any ID or has been fingerprinted before, so they're all John Does for the present.

'The Thugs are from two groups: imported Indians obviously well trained as Stranglers; and the recruits, off-the-chart crazies with big grudges against society – fanatics willing to be turned into assassins for a Cause. According to the Swami, they believe that to kill for Kali sanctifies them. Yes, they think they're saintly.'

There was a long quiet after that.

Another question: 'What does that make the victim, then, a demon to be disposed of?'

'Not at all. The victim is thought of as very fortunate. Once killed by the Strangler's scarf, he or she won't have to worry about being reincarnated again. Their reward for being murdered is immediate entry into paradise.'

Someone grunted, but there was silence otherwise.

Condorelli scoured the print-outs. 'Here are the analyses from the lab reports. I'll state the highlights and let's see if we can make sense of it.

'What we did was have the lab run analyses of the prisoners' clothes and those of Dr Kitteridge. That proved to be baffling. And damn bizarre. The saner part of it was they found barnyard material: straw, chicken feed, field-mouse droppings – amazing what you can vacuum from clothing [laughter] – commercial fertilizer, beet and tomato seeds. There was also other New England stuff: a bit of hornbeam or blue beech leaf, a piece of black oak bark, a possible big clue – the rare white pine blue-green needle, found only in New Hampshire and Maine. Least-ways, in New England. Another great find maybe was a piece of smoky quartz in one man's pocket. Maybe he liked to look at it. Like when a kid carries agates. And some redstone dust. There's a Redstone Red Quarry near Redstone Station in Conway, New Hampshire.' Condorelli paused for effect. 'Sounds like we're really getting somewhere, eh? Well, let's get to the contradictory stuff.

'Here it is: specks of calcareous rock, sometimes combined with glacial ice, and the fragment of a feather in Dr Kitteridge's blouse pocket. This last material was sent to Washington. We expected we'd have to wait for weeks. You know how things are down there.'

Some nods, cynical grins.

'But Steve Wrench here called his old boss, Horace

310

Birch. Well, they say in Boston that the blue-blood Cabots speak only to God. Believe me, in Washington, they'd have to talk to this man. We were faxed the results in ten hours.

'Let me add, too, that Mr Birch offered the services of the Feds. Steve said "No"; he said our unit is the best for the job, and the Feds would only screw everything up.'

Laughter. Then, to a man, they stood and briefly applauded Wrench.

Condorelli gestured that they sit again. The noise subsided to a few coughs.

'Here's the results from Washington, boys. And how it fits in is beyond me. The lab in DC says the calcareous rock, the glacial ice and the feather fragment point to the Himalayas. The feather belongs to the' – he struggled with the word – '*Gypaetus barbartus* or', – another struggle – 'the Lammergeier. It's a bearded vulture found in southern Europe, eastern and southern Africa, and southwestern and central Asia. The lab opts for the Asian area, the Himalayas, considering the kind of mugs we're chasing. They're referring to the Indian connection, of course.

'Now, I don't know about you guys, but I'm damn baffled.' He rocked on his heels for an instant. 'Maybe, though, the Swami can help us. Please feel free, Swami – we're beyond laughing at anything.'

Hanuman stood. Slowly, he walked to the centre of the room. He seemed a wizened child among these large Western men.

'Perhaps it may occur to some of you that the Huzoor Leinster could have brought the vulture to America as a pet,' he began. 'Possible, but I believe unlikely. What is more conceivable is that he brought part of the Indian landscape here. Like the legend of the vampire in the stories, who must bring Transylvanian earth in his coffin to whatever place he travels to.'

Hanuman waited. Someone asked, 'What do you mean by "landscape"?'

'Possibly a part of the Himalayas. There is a cave where the Huzoor went to be initiated years ago . . .' He stopped. There was a great deal of shuffling, coughing. Hanuman shrugged, then, 'I don't think this is wise. Some things must be seen to be believed.' He walked off to his seat.

Stymied, Captain Condorelli scratched his head. 'It's all yours, Thurnauer,' he said to Thurnauer, who was in the front row. The detective unfolded his rangy body and stood up. In his hand were more print-outs.

'I'll be brief,' he stated. Someone applauded. 'When we discovered that the Thugs attacked a house full of drug pushers months ago, I got to thinking. First, no drugs or money was taken. This signified, the Swami believed, that it was a training stint for the new recruits. Usually, Thugs are thieves as well as assassins, but this outing was different, somehow. They didn't even bury the dead. Perhaps they knew we were watching the place and just wanted to get in, kill, and get out real fast. Which is exactly what happened.

'Now, it bothered me: Why did they pick that house? Was it an accident? Did they pick a place at random and it just happened to be a marketplace for drugs? Or was it because they knew what was going on inside and that the danger made the test more important? After all, the drug gang was heavily armed, and we were armed, too. What a stint – to kill these real bad guys right under our very noses!

'The other thing that bothered me: If the Thugs knew about the drug operation, then one of them had to have dealt with that house sometime in the past. So I got a list of everyone who was ever seen going into the place, of everyone who knew the victims in any way. Then I checked if these associates of the drug ring had ever been interested in or been connected with anybody interested in Eastern thought, esoteric schools, ashrams – things like that.

'To ensure that my data were thorough, I used Washington, too. They gave me three possibles. I believe one of them may be what we need. Let's get him on the screen.'

Moments later the group was staring at a frontal and side view of a lean-faced man with heavy lids and perfect V jaw.

'This is Alex Dyer. Abel, you may remember him from your days as a narc. He's also known as Thin on the streets.'

'Sure,' Jerome said. 'He escaped from Bridgewater about fourteen months ago. The criminally insane section. Almost killed a guard with a piece of pipe. Then he shot the manager of some twenty-four-hour-a-day store in Melrose. They never did find him after that, I think.'

'Yes, he disappeared. Everyone who knew him even the slightest was questioned. One of them, an old high school buddy, has been the head of an ashram in New Hampshire for years. I think they're heavy into Vedanta. Anyway, this Vic Croce's ashram is somewhere between Laconia and Conway.' Thurnauer took a breath, then added, 'Maybe he did hide Thin, after all. The whole ashram was searched by the New Hampshire police, but still Croce could've been hiding Thin in another place. The two were pretty close in the old days. Croce was steep into drugs, like Thin, until he found meditation and peace. A lot of these navel-lovers – your pardon, Swami – are ex-druggies . . . And maybe Thin is now a Thug, too, and maybe he tipped them off about the house.'

Belanger stood up. His hand was still bandaged. He pointed to the screen. 'He doesn't look to me like he'd fit

313

the psychological profile of a Thug recruit. Hell, he's your standard crazy hophead. A gun or a knife would suit him better than a silk scarf.'

'Yet, it may be a lead.' This from Wrench. 'The New Hampshire location fits some of the detritus found on the clothing. And the connection to the drug house makes sense.'

'Too pat, if you ask me,' replied Belanger. 'Much too obvious. Everything about this Thuggee cult has been mysterious, elusive as hell.'

'Please, excuse me,' Hanuman called. This time he stood on the chair and waved his hands. 'These Deceivers – which is what Thug means in Hindi – would use the obvious as well as the elusive, the unknown, to outwit us. It is the crafty, cunning way. Perhaps now we should investigate the very obvious. Let us go to this ashram. But first allow me and my *chela*, Nirmal, to investigate. If there is anything *unseen* in the obvious, we will find it, I assure you.'

Everyone looked at Condorelli for his reply. He frowned, then, pulling himself together, smiled broadly. 'Some decisions can't be made on an empty stomach. Right now, my mind's a total blank. Why don't we have a lunch break and return here,' he checked his watch, 'at, say, two o'clock.'

The caricature was a good one. It portrayed five-year-old Anna Condorelli standing before the fireplace with Smokey, her dog, and Cyril, the cat, who was a female.

'She was named before we checked her out,' said Pauline Condorelli, Vincent's wife. 'And the name stuck. Poor Vinnie's surrounded by us, since Smokey's a girl, too.'

Stephen Wrench handed the caricature to Anna, who bounced to her father at the fireplace. She gave him the drawing. He looked at it, laughed, and said, 'This is very good, Steve.' Anna giggled, took the drawing back and bounced again to Rama Shastri, who was seated next to a glass bookcase with thick volumes about police work. Two slender volumes at the end had been written by Condorelli. They concerned the methodology of an undercover cop and were now being used as manuals.

'I'd forgotten you had a gift for this,' Shastri told Steve as he studied the drawing. 'Remember the one you did of the leftist Krishna Menon that annoyed him so much?'

'Let's see.' Wrench closed his eyes. 'That was shortly after Nehru died in 'sixty-four. God, Ram, I don't believe I've drawn a caricature since then. Until today.' Wrench's eyes were sad. Anna Condorelli wasn't the first little girl Wrench had drawn his funny pictures for; there had been someone else years ago in New Delhi.

'Now I'll show it to Mommy,' Anna announced, and left the room, trailed by the black-ringleted Smokey. Cyril, with typical feline aloofness, had leaped to a sunny window sill and was now washing her paws.

'Four and a half years ago, Pauline and I flew to Nicaragua to adopt Anna,' Condorelli explained. 'My other two girls, Jeanne and Terri, adjusted very well to their baby sister. Things have been smooth from the start. But, as you see, I'm surrounded by females, even the two animals.'

Pauline appeared. 'Everything'll be ready in about five minutes.' When she first met Wrench and Shastri, Condorelli had quipped, 'Doesn't she look like Ali McGraw?' Pauline had blushed. Shastri, of course, had never seen the actress. Wrench grunted recognition, hiding the fact that, although he recognized the name, he rarely watched films.

Once the three men were alone again, Condorelli admitted, 'I invited you two here for more than lunch. I wanted the three of us to have a little conference. I need some guarantees before I act.' He asked Wrench directly, 'For instance, the Swami and his young friend want to be in on this New Hampshire thing. They're civilians, Steve. Can you guarantee that Horace Birch will cover my ass if I let them in?'

'Horace gave them free rein in our past encounter with the Thugs. And George Buchan, too,' Wrench replied. 'I'm positive he will again. After all, Vinnie, this case is unusual as hell. Myself, Ram, Hanuman, Nirmal and George are familiar with all its . . . well, its off-the-chart nuances. We've all seen the supernatural angles to this thing manifest in the past. We know what to expect, to a degree.'

'OK, but I'm counting on Birch to back up my report in the end. Now, do you think the Swami can do a good job?'

Shastri spoke this time. 'Swami Hanuman, whose birth name is Narayan Rana – he took the name of the monkey god when he reached enlightenment – infiltrated the enemy lines many, many times during the Second World War. He was a legend, a hero in the struggle with the Japanese. Yes, I know he can investigate that questionable ashram successfully.'

'What about the kid?'

'I would think by now that Nirmal Kapur has acquired some of his master's skills at stealth. Hanuman wouldn't want him along were it not so.'

'And Dr Buchan?'

'George will demand to be with us, if I know him,' Wrench cut in. 'He's a good man who proved his mettle in our last encounter with Leinster.' He lowered his eyes and stared at the floor. 'There's another reason why he should go. Santha . . . isn't herself since they marked her. That's obvious, considering her havoc and mayhem in the

316

Combat Zone. Witnesses described her as a fierce wild woman with superhuman strength. We saw the ones she injured, and, though God knows they deserved what they got, well, the *somebody* who did it to them just isn't my Santha. I think, I'm convinced if George is with us when we find her, he'll be able to bring her back. Somehow . . .' His voice trailed off.

Condorelli hurriedly changed the subject. 'Can any of you explain – in as simple terms as possible – what the hell the Swami was talking about? "Took the Indian landscape here to America." Was he speaking literally?'

'I'm afraid so,' Shastri said, after a moment. 'Try to keep in mind that the supernatural means exactly that. Natural law as we know it is broken. Space isn't fixed but something that can be changed or relocated. I think the Swami means that this mysterious cave that we've heard so much about, or its facsimile, is now somewhere in this country.'

Condorelli was about to say more, but his attractive daughter Terri came into the room. She had just arrived from work and was in her nurse's uniform. ''lo, Dad,' she said, giving him a hug. Condorelli introduced Wrench and Shastri. 'Joining us for lunch?' She nodded. 'Well, let's get at it,' he decided. 'It's too bad Jeanne's still at law school, then the whole family would be here.' He gestured just as Pauline called, 'Come and get it.'

'See,' Condorelli beamed, 'I knew lunch was ready.' He tapped his stomach. 'My digestive juices are telepathic. How's that for supernatural?'

24

It was the strangest captivity. True, she wasn't free, was always in the cage; but everyone had been so worshipful, so much in awe of her, never ever violent except at the beginning, when that big woman in the truck had jabbed her with a needle.

She terrified them enough, Santha knew, those times she awakened and temporarily fought off the drug. But no matter how much they cringed or backed away, they never showed any anger or hatred; some of them even fell prone before her as if she were an omnipotent queen from whom one endured any type of humiliation.

She couldn't understand why, couldn't fathom the reason. The drugs in her food had dulled her considerably. Now those moments of pure rage and strength beyond imagining were few, and she missed that wonderful wild confidence very much. It may have been a hidden, unfettered part of her, a primordial self underlying the civilized Santha Wrench of Beacon Hill, Boston, but it was she, nevertheless, not the blunted persona that now gradually predominated.

Santha had even lost her indignation about the cage.

Remembering herself at the first awakening, that self more and more like a strange being, a stalking, predatory woman who, once aware she was trapped behind bars, screamed and flung herself at them. Welling coils of hatred, life force, bursting out like a metallic spring released, pounding, grabbing, gripping, adrenaline geysering through muscle and tendon when she tried to bend the oily, glistening and increasingly repulsive rods.

The bars were of a black substance she had never seen or touched before. Inanimate in appearance, they were somehow alive, she felt. *Alive!*

They wouldn't bend or break, either. The more she made the effort, the more they sapped her strength, she found. If they could vocalize, she was convinced they would taunt her.

There was identity in those bars. There was pulse, there was quick, there was even reason.

The cage's floor and ceiling were another mystery. Although as black as the bars, they weren't of the same oily material, or wood or metal.

Every effort had been made to ensure comfort. There was a bed and a blanket, *chudders* sewn together. The temperature of the cavernous room around her was continuously moderate.

The size of the cage was fifteen feet long and ten wide, or at least that was the measurement Santha counted by placing one foot after the other as she paced. A section of it was walled off as a room six feet by eight feet. The walls were ebony and again lacked the pulsing sheen of the bars. There was a door to the room, which opened by sliding it back. Within was a lacquered eating table, a short-legged stool, and a box-shaped toilet with a pail-like insert that could be removed and emptied. There was another door in the room, opening only from the outside. The bathroom was separated from the eating area by a folding lacquered screen. The screen's surface was filled with colourful paintings of Kali battling the demon Raktavīja.

Every morning, Santha found a brass lota of scented water for bathing, ordinary soap, fresh linen towels, and a breakfast of thick oatmeal, milk, Indian chapatties and a small dish of *dahi*, a curd-like yoghurt.

At evening – these meals were the only way Santha could tell the time of day – the meal was similar, except she was given a vegetable stew instead of oatmeal. There was also a teapot of cinnamon tea and a cup and saucer.

Santha was always asleep when these things were brought in or taken away. Her sleeping periods were long and dreamless. At times, she planned to resist the drugged food, but her will was already considerably weakened. It was so since her first awakening. Apparently, the needle shot given her in the van had been very potent.

At the awakening she also discovered that she was dressed in a white sari with yellow trim. Kali colours. During two other sleeps she had been anointed and massaged with oils and given a fresh sari. Same colours, same design.

That first time, Santha had seen the giant Indian woman and flung herself at her. Now the rages were short, and she kept her distance from the bars. The repulsion, the nausea she felt from resisting was too great to endure again. What substance was this?

The other spectators, most of them dressed Indian-style, seemed to be keeping a vigil. Men, women, they sat in the lotus position on little blankets and recited mantras. Fuming braziers of incense, torches in sconces, were everywhere. Santha could just about see the chamber's walls, some portions of them glassy, reflecting the wavering flames. Santha thought she detected fear in the onlookers. In the big woman also, which pleased her. The woman must pay for what she had done, Santha strongly felt.

She wanted revenge, but that was elusive. Santha couldn't sustain the feeling or the thought. Somewhere, like a dim voice nagging, was the memory of Annette Kitteridge and someone she must kill. Each day the nagging became less and less.

Then, at last, she saw him. He came down the aisle between those in meditation. The mantras appeared to blend with the flow of his robes. Tall, a white blur from crown to foot, he carried the sacred pickaxe. Her memory fragmented, Santha had lost his name and whatever he was to her past; but her instincts still rebelled. Santha backed, a caged creature ready to pounce.

He was chanting loudly, a different mantra from the others. It was stated that only the *asuras*, the demons, could chant his mantra effectively. The silvery, static-like flickerings in his eyes were in unison with the modulation of his voice.

The Huzoor didn't stop, either. He opened the cage with one swift motion. Santha Wrench bent, facing him, her right hand extended in a clawing gesture, her lip twisted in a snarl. For a long time she remained poised in that rigid stance.

The Huzoor motioned again and again that she come to him.

The silvery flickers crossed the gap between them. The passage was invisible to the human eye, but Santha began to flinch from the effect, an icy assault that covered her eyeballs and filtered into her brain. The shock broke her poise and numbed her defiance.

Santha's body jerked. A voice – frigid with interstellar cold, inhuman and forceful – jolted her neural system. The voice commanded: *Go to him!*

Santha tried to resist. Her weakened will fought to awaken, to pull free. She had an image of Kurt Leinster as he had been years ago, and his name surfaced. Her face expressed the pain, the fury, of her anguish, and she opened her mouth to scream. Instead, a pathetic whisper: 'No!'

But when the command came again, Santha jerked

forward towards the Huzoor as if she were being pulled by a rope. After each movement, she would jerk again. Tears covered her cheeks and chin. She gritted her teeth, fighting the gelid command. Finally, her determination waned and she reached his arms.

He guided her from the cage. Head lowered, she followed him up the aisle. The alien presence in her mind was silent, and that was all that counted. The chantings surrounded her, sheltered her like a balm.

Santha was led up a dais to a couch strewn with pillows. The worshippers scattered marigolds at her naked feet – red, yellow and orange petals. They brought her scented water and sprinkled her hair, and bracelets and anklets of gold and cowrie shells. They chanted now that she was the Chosen One, the Vessel of Kunkali herself. The odour of sandalwood was almost stifling. Sitars were plucked, graceful chords fell with the petals. *Tabla* drums rumbled, a low, consistent throb.

Santha was numb, empty. She sensed she was dying, but there was no longer any sensation, no fear, no anger. Her spirit had diffused with the floating flower specks, with smoke whiffs from the braziers, with the ringing sitars.

When they brought the girdle, she wanted to deny it, to close her eyes, pretend it was unreal. The girdle was of thin hammered gold alloy with ruby inserts which made her think of blood. Attached to the girdle along its entire length were skulls, and whenever the girdle moved, they thocked against each other. The Huzoor himself attached it to her waist. He remained close to her, his breath hot on her neck, his eyes tongues of silver darting to her brain like a snake's bite . . .

* * *

Gongs. Now there were men in robes, three of them pounding the ground in unison with their *dandas*. Their heads were shaven like priests', and their bamboo staffs were decorated with white jasmine that broke free and fell to their sandalled feet. They were singing their praise of the Huzoor, that his judgment was at hand. The three were new recruits, not Indians.

But the Thug guru, old and nut brown, was. His body was gnarly in its *dhoti*, his eyes blazing from asceticism, his mottled hands like dark speckled spiders. He stood by the Huzoor's throne, gripping the pickaxe. Santha, still on her couch, watched them.

The crowd below the elevated ground waited. Stairs, at least ten, had been carved in stone leading to them. Across the dais, beside the braziers, stood Mrinalini Pal. Never once did she look at Santha. There was something about her that the woman still dreaded, Santha knew.

Figures moved, elongated, foreshortened, shadows across the wall and floor. Parodies of human forms. Like demons dancing in a magic lantern show.

Figures emerged from the veil of smoke, climbing the stairs. Three figures behind one man, holding him by the arms. The man was cursing, dressed in Levi's and a T-shirt. So out of place here. Clothing from the outside world. Santha wondered why he was present in this India-like place.

She closed her eyes to hear the music. But that ended. The gongs, the *dandas* were gone. There were no more chants, no cries of praise.

The hush made her reopen her eyes.

Santha turned on her side to see better. She watched herself turn because she was as two personas now, one dead, and one living, watching everything from every possible angle. Sometimes she observed from high above, looking down on the heads of everybody. Her limbs

323

fluttered then, and the only possible explanation was that she had feathers.

Once (and she didn't like this angle), she crawled at everyone's feet, long and black and many-limbed, she thought. Residues of her dead self shuddered, and she never looked from that angle again.

Her favourite viewing point was when she was in the shadows, stretching, squinching up, waving with the fire-light, meshing with every other shadow, visible yet hidden.

The Huzoor was speaking. 'You are the man they call Thin?' she heard.

Thin struggled with his captors.

'Let him go,' the Huzoor said.

Free, Thin rubbed his arm. 'What the fuck's going on?' he demanded, jutting his pointed profile forward belligerently.

'You are Thin?'

'Yeah. So what? What the fuck is this, anyway?'

The Huzoor held up something small and white between his fingers.

'And what is this, Thin?'

The pointed chin lowered, was tucked in.

'Ah, you don't answer. It's cocaine, and it was dis-covered in your quarters.'

Santha saw a very short man begin to climb the stair-case. He moved slowly, hesitantly.

The Huzoor stood up. He showed an accusing finger. 'You have never belonged here. Never have you been one of us.'

'I'm not interested,' Thin replied, in as defiant a tone as he could muster.

The Huzoor looked over his shoulder and saw the approaching short man.

'Victor, have you come to speak for this man? Twice

before have you appealed to me to let him remain with us. Once, when I discovered that for months before my coming you allowed him to use the ashram as a hideaway from the law. The second time when he refused to take an oath to Kali.'

Croce fell on his face. 'Forgive me, O Lord of All Thuggee, O Son of Kunkali Herself. I thought he would see the error of his ways, but he has been blinded by the things of the world.'

The Huzoor held up the small packet again. 'Things such as this? Stand, Victor, and tell us your judgment.'

Vic Croce stood up. For once, he was tongue-tied. With much effort, he began, 'When he led us to the house of drug peddlers, I believed it an act of good faith. But even then, he refused to use the *rumel*. Later, when he saved Mauna and me from the detective, I – '

'Yes, yes. But what is your judgment *now*?'

'He has desecrated our sacred ashram.'

'Say it – that all may hear.'

'He has – '

'Loud, very loud, Victor.'

'HE HAS DESECRATED OUR SACRED ASHRAM.'

'How?'

'HE HAS BROUGHT THE DRUG FILTH AMONG US.'

'And how do you judge?'

Croce wet his lips. 'I'm sorry, Thin,' he whispered.

'Judge, Victor. Judge him.'

Croce closed his eyes. His body shook as he bellowed, 'HE MUST DIE.'

'Now how do you feel?' the Huzoor asked the prisoner.

Thin shrugged. 'A man's got to die sometime. My life ain't been so great that I'll miss it. When I decided no

325

cop'll ever put me in the stir again, I set my mind for dying.'

'You're not afraid?'

'Sure, I am. But not as much as you'd like me to be. So you lose the satisfaction of seeing me scared shitless. Besides, being dead's a lot better than living with you creeps.'

'But our ways are of another world. We are supernatural. We are Heaven and Hell, can't you see?'

'OK. I've seen some weird stuff going down here. It's set my hackles on end some! But you can only kill me one way. No blood-shedding. Just a quick, merciful strangling. I've seen it done. That's the Thug's way, his sacred method of killing. So do your worst.'

Thin barely finished his speech. Nevertheless, he had made a valiant effort to appear calm. The Huzoor's hand quivered; he was in a rage. He paced before his throne. Through the murkiness, Santha saw his followers, waiting below the dais, expectant.

The Huzoor spun to Santha. He stared, and his mouth fashioned a grin, fixed like the smile on a death's head. He looked elated, inspired. His lips began to recite, to churn out a most diabolical mantra. The language was that of the ancient *rishis* who had made him what he was. And Santha understood it! The mantra spoke of the Vessel of Kali Ma, she who bore the mark, the signet of the Ages. She Who Destroys and Destroys, She of Black Kali.

'Judge,' he cried then in English. Kurt Leinster, the Huzoor, pointed at Santha and, in a resonant voice, called out the other names of Kali: 'Judge, O Devi, O Bhowani. Arise in all your beauty, O Queen of Death . . . Come, beloved. Hail to She Who Must Destroy.'

From the gathering, his last words were repeated: 'She Who Must Destroy', like a sudden wind that stirred the marigold and jasmine petals, that yanked Santha's black flow of hair until it fanned . . .

Santha rose from the couch. Bracelets, anklets, cowries, thocking skulls, made the music of her stirring. The naked feet moved on stone and the petals parted, as if in fear. The neck seemed to stretch, the eyes to bulge. A leg raised high arched before her waist and descended slowly but firmly, like the beginnings of a dance, like a statement, a deadly pronouncement. The jewelled fingers met before her face and descended, raking her sari with nails long and curled. The fabric shredded, breasts were exposed, nipples hardened, hungry with blatant lust, glistening with the sweat of transformation. Santha raked again, and the next time she raised her leg, her curvaceous thigh was exposed, and part of a buttock. The eyes wide, ever staring, pulsed for the life essence before her; the mouth grew more slack, the teeth bit into the lower lip, and blood bubbled and dripped and flowed along the breast crevice.

Clank, clink, thock, shush, the ornaments and parting flowers sounded.

Thin gaped at her. Her beauty was hypnotic, but he saw too that Death lay in it. The skulls were grinning, celebrating. Santha's eyes were black, eternal maelstroms, and her fanning hair – it spread and spread like the dark wings of Death's Angel.

Thin turned to his captors, hoping they would wield the *rumel*. No one moved. Thin looked once more at Santha coming, coming with her half-dancing, half-walking sway of hips, of breasts, of head that arched and rhythmically moved left, right, then to left, then to . . .

He screamed and screamed. His breathing became more and more difficult.

Santha, or whatever she had become, reached him.

327

Cold, gelid air clouded from her mouth into his face. His broken lips formed an oval. Thin backed. The Huzoor nodded to Ajit Majumdar. The Thug lowered his *rumel*.

25

When their meal was over, Condorelli, Wrench and Shastri loitered outside the house for a while. The meal had been very good – pot roast and gravy, boiled potatoes, carrots, onions and cabbage. Rama Shastri, who ate beef whenever he could – not often possible in India – was especially pleased. He had ignored the dessert for a second helping, while Wrench and the captain ate the home-made apple pie with the gusto of growing boys.

Now, out in the blustery day, Wrench had drifted to the edge of the hill the old house in Stoneham, Massachusetts, stood on – smoking his pipe and observing the encroaching black cloudheads in the east. Anna, with Smokey at her heels, stood at his side. The child sensed the big man's isolation and sorrow. She tentatively reached for his hand. He noticed, looked down at her with moist eyes, and let her small fingers disappear among his.

Touched, Shastri looked away. He had settled into one of his funks again. The family meal had been a welcome distraction. The table conversation had been surface and light, with Terri talking about her nursing studies and Pauline about bingo night at church, subjects like that. He wished it could have lasted longer, that idyllic family scene. But Shastri then recognized it had had its setbacks. Steve had been reminded of Santha. Mostly, the little Central American girl, Anna, had reflected those earlier days with his daughter and Kamala. They, too, had known the warmth of the family meal. Shastri remembered that more than once he had joined them in those India days; from the beginning, he had been Uncle Ram to Santha.

He blinked. It was as though she were his child, too.

The skyscape depressed him. He read ominous signs in those roiling black clouds. Shastri hated to personify Nature, but he couldn't help it. The thrill of the chase was gone, replaced now with a pall of doom.

Was Santha's possession worse than it had ever been? Shastri tore his eyes away from the sky. It was only clouds, he told himself. Clouds. Nothing but visible clumps of vapour. Dark now because of the potential storm in their depths. Think meteorologically, he told himself.

On the drive back to headquarters, Wrench expressed Shastri's fears. 'I'm praying,' he said, 'that this isn't one time too many for Santha. Captivity by that fiend has already wrecked the mind of Dr Kitteridge. This is Santha's second time in Leinster's hands. Has she got enough in her to fight back, Ram?'

Shastri thought it over, stressed, 'Perhaps she has one advantage. A slight edge, but, nevertheless, it may win out in the end. Kurt Leinster's emotions about her were always subjective. He was smitten – if it's possible to even think of him as capable of love. He seemed to envision Santha as his chosen consort. That might put her in a position of strength.'

'I'm afraid I don't understand,' Condorelli cut in. He was the driver, and, as he spoke, he turned on to the McGrath and O'Brien highways and past the Museum of Science.

Shastri explained: 'If I recall the Socratean dialogue correctly, the beloved, the ideal is always in a superior position to the lover. Of course, the philosopher is speaking of normal relationships. Anyway, I've always felt that Santha is Leinster's biggest weakness.'

'But suppose he's different than before, Ram? Leinster sure looked it when we dealt with him in Varanasi. More of a devil. Some creature more monster than man.'

'I agree, though I'm convinced there's still a human part of his personality left. He would have sought another woman to serve his needs, otherwise.'

'It's appeared to be nothing but revenge, Ram. Getting her back because he lost her last time.'

'Perhaps. But separate from his megalomania is a definite vulnerability. If only to Santha's beauty.'

Wrench shivered. 'My poor child . . .'

It started to rain.

They found George Buchan impatiently waiting with Condorelli's men. He had been telling Hanuman and Nirmal about something. 'We think this highly significant,' George said to the newcomers. 'Santha and Annette Kitteridge had a frightening experience together. They were in Annette's plane, remember?'

'Yes,' Wrench nodded. 'The engine stopped, they were being pulled to the earth by some magnetic force. Santha told me and Ram . . .' He paused. 'That cinches it, then.'

'How?' demanded Condorelli.

George retold the story up to Santha's vision of Kali from the cockpit.

'What's important is where it happened,' he added.

'It was somewhere between Conway and Laconia, right, George?'

'So there was a magnetic disruption that day – so what?'

'Not so, Captain. Annette checked later with the meteorological bureau and local geology and terrain maps. Everything possible that would prove scientifically that there was a magnetic pocket there. There was nothing. Has never been anything of the kind there.'

'So, what did it? What dragged the plane down?'

George motioned to Hanuman to continue. 'Evil – the force of Evil is a form of magnetism.'

'You believe that?'

'Yes. How else would it influence this world so much? People are attracted to it or its fruits. I'm not saying it is the same as magnetism. But it can act as a force. If a significant amount of it were in a certain area, it could act as a magnet . . .'

'Evil also repels,' Condorelli replied.

'Think of it this time as a mass. Or a centre of energy. Think of it as transforming temporarily into something physical. It could then act as a magnet.'

'Which proves the ashram is the place, all right.' Wrench was elated.

Shastri then asked Hanuman, 'Would the transferring, the repositioning of a part of India to here – as you stated earlier today – would that create such an effect?'

Hanuman nodded. 'It could. One must think of space as a material in order to understand what I mean. I'm positive that it can be proven mathematically.'

'Well, anything can be proven with maths,' George agreed, 'but is it real? Probable?'

'The manipulation of space is as possible as the manipulation of matter,' Hanuman announced, as if he were speaking of the simplest of facts.

'Like teleporting the body?' Shastri asked.

'Like teleporting space. An area. Perhaps the Cave of the Rishis in the Himalayas, where we've heard that the Huzoor Leinster first received the Scroll of Power of Thuggee. That would explain the calcareous dust, the glacial ice, even the feather of the bearded vulture. The Huzoor Leinster, with Kali's help, has moved space, the hallowed ground of the Thuggee spirit, to America.'

Shastri again: 'Is that why he wields greater power this time?'

'Yes, I believe so. I have not been able to penetrate the barrier to the Kali source as I did years ago. As long as Leinster remains in the hallowed space, he is very powerful. He strides two worlds there – the Earth and that of his adoptive mother. The only way I may possibly combat it is to go there directly, to enter that space. Perhaps then he can be stopped. Remember, however, that the Scroll must be destroyed, too. We failed last time . . .'

Rama Shastri's mind raced. He fought to curb the desperation he felt. With Hanuman so powerless, what would be the outcome? He was the mystic, not they. He understood the drama totally, knew the subtext, saw clearly what was happening in the wings. And he, Shastri, admitted it must all be real, after all. There are gods and they do mock men. It was not the type of universe he preferred.

The highway went on, lost somewhere in the thick rainfall. It had been the rainy season in Varanasi months ago, too. Shastri thought of the temple of the Thugs, of Gopal, and poor dead Shambu, who had been so proud of his ability as a tracker . . . and of Ileana Heng. Why must he hunger for her now, at this time? It was unfair. More of those dreadfully boring gods thumbing their noses at Man.

He wondered, had she followed through on her threat to renew her opium addiction? Another matter that was beyond his control. Shastri breathed in the damp air that came through the slightly opened window. The heavy scent of moist foliage came with it. On the highway sides, the billowy outline of trees trembled against a slate sky. Dusk was descending, and car lights were blurry bright discs through the streamers of rain on the glass. Tyres sloshed through pools in buzzing whishes.

Thurnauer, at the wheel, bobbed his head as he spoke. 'I got the exact location of the ashram from a yoga practitioner I met while undercover. Vic Croce's ashram has existed for nearly twenty-five years. It's pretty famous and has had open house for any newcomers until recently. Which seems damned significant. Rumour has it that the group voted to keep its population down to the existing level for personal reasons. But there's also another rumour.'

'Which is?' Condorelli asked impatiently, while Thurnauer placed a stick of gum in his mouth.

'Which is,' Thurnauer replied, fashioning the gum wrapper into a small ball with one hand and dropping it in the ashtray, 'that there was a split among the group regarding the ashram's esoteric theme. Philosophic monism, as stressed by the Vedantic school of thought – that seems to fit, too. If part of the ashram converted to Thuggee and Kali worship, then anything as idealistic and refined as Vedanta would have to go. Otherwise, it's like mixing oil and water or God and the Devil. Monism unifies as opposed to the dualistic stand of Thuggee.'

'Thank you, Professor,' his superior quipped. 'As if things weren't clear as mud already.'

'Well, philosophy is everything in this, Captain. The Vedantists are a peaceful bunch. The ashram was a self-supporting unit of dedicated followers of ancient Vedic literature at one time. They were non-violent, meditative, concerned with unifying their inner selves. That's respectable, sir, in this cockamamie schizoid culture.'

'Agreed, Thurnauer. But I hope you'll excuse me if I'm not up on my Vedic lit.'

Thurnauer continued, nevertheless: 'The Vedas are the scriptures of India, Captain. The Hindus believe that they were revealed by sound to the ancient seers, the *rishis*. Their order of utterances, their combinations of sound, their relation of letters, even their syllables are sacred. Their wisdom has influenced many great thinkers, Ralph

Waldo Emerson among them. These Vedas were the root source of this ashram's philosophy – before the change, of course.'

'I wonder how this conversion came about. If it really did, that is,' Shastri mused.

'There's talk about that, too. This Vic Croce claims he and certain other ashram folks had visions and dreams about the new Path everyone was to take.'

'But some resisted.'

'Correct.'

After that, the silence returned.

Rama Shastri imagined these once-innocent Vedantists at their meditations, blissful images of the Supreme Unity in all Existence, suddenly bombarded by Kali and her dark Faith. If it had occurred, it had been a true invasion, beyond doubt. That fierce, compelling, demonic Mother bursting forth from the underlayers of the psyche, recruiting, recruiting. Organizing her slayers of men . . .

Condorelli shook his head. 'And they think of themselves as saints. Sonofabitch.'

Yes, as saints, Shastri thought. There can be no greater evil than that which sees itself as divine.

Four other cars followed Captain Condorelli's: Swami Hanuman, Nirmal and George Buchan were in the second, with Jerome Abel at the wheel. Prior to their leaving, arrangements had been made with a motel near the ashram to use some of its space as a base of operations. They pulled into the car park just as dusk ended. Night bordered the gathering men ringed in the red flush of the motel's sign.

'I want everyone to gradually disappear into the various motel rooms you've been assigned to,' Condorelli told his men. 'Don't appear conspicuous. If you're hungry or want coffee, send one man out to any of the take-out places on the highway. Remember, nobody – no civilian – must suspect even slightly that we're the law. We're only five miles from the ashram. Any strangers we encounter might just be one of them.'

In Room 12, where he had set up his office, Condorelli said to Hanuman, 'There's to be no grandstanding. You and Nirmal are to prowl around the place and then report to me whatever you find.

'We're keeping the local police out of this, and I don't want to have to explain to them what's going on just because someone decides to play the hero and causes more trouble than necessary.'

Hanuman replied, 'This isn't likely to be easy or simple, Captain. Expect much violence. These people will die readily for their cause. But perhaps the element of surprise will be with us.'

'You don't sound very optimistic.'

'It is neither optimism nor pessimism. That is precisely why I want to reconnoitre first. I believe I can quickly discover whether we are . . . expected.'

'You think they know we're here?'

'I don't know, Captain. I believe they are prepared for almost anything, and we should always be on the alert. Remember, sir, that even without guns or knives, Thugs are extremely dangerous. They can use their *rumels* with a speed and efficiency that is nothing short of fantastic. This new breed, particularly. Their hands swell, you see, and with that their strength grows also. Acolytes, trainees, soon become expert assassins.

'I would suggest that, during our wait here, Rama Shastri and Mr Wrench demonstrate to your men what wielding the *rumel* really means.' Hanuman pulled a stained yellow scarf from within his tunic. 'I have here a . . . souvenir from our last encounter with these Thugs. It

336

can be used for the demonstration. Your men must become familiar with Thug weaponry. It is imperative.'

'I'm for it,' Wrench said, glad to have something to do. 'How about you, Ram?'

'Of course. And I would think George here would want to join us. He's had to skirmish with them before.'

George Buchan's eyes were raw. He had barely slept since Santha's abduction.

Condorelli's concentration hadn't caught up. 'Those swollen hands . . .?'

'. . . make the recruits into Thug supermen,' George stated. 'That's the way it was last time. Through some mysterious power, the newcomers become instant Thugs. A Thug strangling used to include two or three men: a Strangler and Armholders. Not necessarily so with this group. They've found a way to cut corners. One man alone can achieve deadly results. Maybe the recruits' hands are inoculated with something like steroids . . .' He never finished. He really didn't believe that.

So the interim before the attack was spent demonstrating how a *rumel* was used by a Thug. The scarf, with both ends knotted, a coin placed in one of them, was slung over the head of the 'victim' – Nirmal or Shastri – while Condorelli's men watched. Wrench demonstrated various methods of freeing oneself from the scarf: placing one finger or more between the scarf and the skin to prevent the fabric from tightening around the windpipe; kicking backwards at the Strangler's shins, which he admitted was an unlikely opportunity; throwing the attacker over one's back, judo-style; or ramming the Thug against a wall, if one was nearby, until he let the *rumel* go.

'The best way,' he announced finally, 'is to prevent anyone from getting that close to you. Shoot them without hesitation. Remember, they're not unarmed. Just because their scarves haven't the speed of a bullet, don't hesitate.

If you see one of them coming at you or behind you, fire your gun. A Thug will capitalize on your hesitation otherwise, believe me. And don't just shoot to wound. If you have to, kill the buggers.'

Nirmal Kapur pushed the brush leaves aside and a bit of a spider's web stuck to his fingers. He wiped the hand on his Levi's, then saw his master already a few feet ahead of him. Hanuman had found a ditch at the meadow's edge and was looking over its top at the house and barn of the ashram community. The trek through the meadow from the hillslope where the others waited had been slow because of the muddy ground. Nirmal's galoshes and shoes felt weighted down from the mud, in fact, and he was glad to pause to scrape the stuff off.

'Listen,' Hanuman whispered.

Sounds, cries, screeches denoting much terror shattered the night. They came from the barn area and beyond, where there was a chicken coop. The ashram had supported itself by selling fresh eggs, butter and cheese, and vegetable produce from their small farm. The sounds Nirmal identified as being from disturbed fowls, cows, a horse.

'The animals do not approve of this place. Something has invaded their territory. Something alien to Nature.' The Swami pointed around them. 'Note, too, the absence of crickets, all insect noises. Or those of the birds. The barn is the source of it all. Come.'

The small figure, lost in a peacoat and fisherman's knitted cap, rose, left the ditch and went forward, doubled over. Nirmal trailed him. He left a bed of goldenrod, the pungent odour thick in the damp air. They stopped at the foot of a silver maple, the rain following the deeply cut indentations in the leaves and dripping on to Nirmal's grey slouch hat that he'd purchased at a cut-price store months before. He tripped over a protruding root and placed his hands on the trunk's scaly bark to break his fall.

The lights of the barn entrance suddenly went on, sprawling over a suitable range. Nirmal could see his master's glistening profile now and, at his feet, the yellow of the parasitical foxgloves nourishing themselves on the maple's roots. Then, as quickly as the lights went on, they dimmed and went out. The chickens and the other animals never once stopped their protests.

'Now,' Hanuman urged, and they ran towards another tree, almost up to the barn. This one, a basswood, had branches that dipped nearly to the ground on one side. Hanuman and Nirmal clung to the shadows of the large, heart-shaped leaves. The rain pattered through the foliage, the only sound besides the pathetic cries.

Again, the barn lights went on. This time a procession of men and women came from the entrance, barely dressed for the storm. Turning the corner, they formed a front line of five people. There were at least four more lines of five each.

Nirmal could see their eyes, glassy and opaque in the brightness. 'Bapu,' he cried softly, as he spotted their hands gripping the ends of scarves as taut and as thin as cords. He reached behind him, in his waistband, took the revolver Jerome Abel had given him, and released the safety catch. 'Bapu,' he repeated, 'they come for us!'

The line spread out without warning, the lines behind moving ahead to link with the first. They were encircling the tree, shutting off any retreat to the meadow.

Hanuman tapped Nirmal's shoulder, and headed for the shadows at the barn's rear. They moved at a fast trot, ready to run at full speed when they reached the darkness. Hanuman paused as the space before them started to glow, suddenly. When it ended, the two were staring at a 'rope' reaching up as high as the barn's roof. 'Come!' Hanuman leaped for the oily surface. He grabbed it a good six feet from the ground and, while climbing, repeated, 'Come, my *chela*!'

Nirmal backed from the encroaching crowd. Three of the foremost, two men and a buxom grey-haired woman, rushed at him, their pale, lumpy hands extended. Nirmal fired. A man dropped. He fired again. The woman gurgled as her neck spurted blood. Nirmal spun, gripped the 'rope', and pulled himself up.

A hand grabbed his foot. Nirmal placed the gun's nose on the head below him, and pulled the trigger. Then he retched and dropped the revolver, as he saw the skull and grey matter mushroom. Still, he managed to cling to the sleek-textured thing dangling in mid-air. He saw the Swami dissolve into the night above and followed with all the speed he could demand from himself. He reached the top, and saw the edge of the 'rope', looking as if it had been sliced. The material made his hands tremble from the barest of reverberations. Finally, a blinding flash . . .

'Oh, Christ!' Condorelli growled. He put his night glasses down. The infra-red glare along with the unexpected flash made his eyes ache.

'Did you see that, too?' he asked Wrench, who had lowered his pair also.

'They just disappeared. A bright, blazing light, and they're gone.'

They were on the hillside, all of Condorelli's people, and Shastri and George Buchan as well.

'Well, what the hell do we do about that?' the captain barked.

The wind and rain bit at the bewildered faces. Wrench's raincoat flapped where he had lost a button.

No one answered.

26

Santha heard every word. Some of it remained vague, but enough was comprehensible, the general sense of what Kurt Leinster said was clear. Much like reading something that registers subliminally, something to return to and redigest when one is better able to concentrate.

It was important and would stay with her, she knew.

Santha Wrench was on another couch in another room. The couch was filled with cushions of many colours and had short legs like the clawed paws of some beast. The walls, at least three of them, reflected her and the Huzoor like glass. Santha lay awake but mentally drifting. She was no longer drugged, but she floated in a state of suspension between reality and a dream that could never quite develop.

'You were so very beautiful,' he was saying, 'in the power of Our Mother. My vessel-love. My wild, beautiful thing. And very soon our destinies will be sealed.'

There was a silver rapture to his words. Santha saw it in his eyes, and it trickled from his lips with each utterance. He embraced her then and poured more silvery whispers in her ear. His grip was painless but strong like the brunt of terrible winds, like the invincible lashing of tidal breakers against a lightning-blasted sea cliff that she could now see. The sky above it was filled with torrential malice, clouds carried muffled thunder. It reminded her of his voice again etched in that strange silver nimbus.

Somehow she fathomed that he was dead. Not as she had died for a while but dead as necrotic things are.

Something had decayed within Leinster, though she couldn't imagine what.

And it was attractive. Death loomed more and more, a romantic figure. Santha could envisage Kurt Leinster atop that sea cliff, his arms extended to that malignant sky, his white hair trailing.

'Now you are mine,' Santha heard, and his cold fingers brushed back the battered sari, and he bent and mouthed her nipple. 'Now I take you while they outside seek to rescue you.'

They? Who were they? she questioned silently. Santha stirred for an instant, shocked into remembering. She saw her father's face, George's eyes pleading that she not forget . . .

'No!' Kurt Leinster demanded. He slapped her.

'No,' she repeated softly.

'They do not belong here. Do you understand? They do not belong . . . Are not . . . of us.'

'Are not . . . of us,' Santha repeated.

Then Leinster stood; separated his robe. The penis was erect and huge, with an aura of primality about it that made Santha think of beasts. 'Sister,' he said, 'let us now be lovers and conceive that which will shatter the hearts of Man. With the blessing of Mother Kali, we shall conceive her – since the child can never be a him. Think now of what this child will be upon this Earth. With your beauty and my deathless lineage, with the dark power of Our Mother – think of what we will have done!'

But Santha couldn't. Her dreamlike state lingered on, and when he pressed the penis tip against her lips, she paused wonderingly. Still he said nothing, but kept his erection where it was. When she understood, finally, her lips parted. The penis entered her mouth, and again Santha had the bestial imagery. It made her shudder. This wasn't a man who so desired her, she felt, but a creature

342

created from maleficence, of energies soulless and tenebrous.

Yet she did as he bid, unable to fight back. The sucking had the gratification of womb-like comfort. Its coldness numbed her senses, and, instead of sexual fire, she drifted more. His pubic hair reminded her of damp sod, his testicles like the bulbs of a fungus flower. It was not exciting but soporific, final as the grave, as things buried.

That image made her pull away. It was unwelcome, suddenly. This was not a death she could accept.

Leinster's laughter mocked her. Methodically, as if he were following directions, he told her, 'Now we will conceive.'

When he entered her was never really clear. The pain was excruciating, the gelid sensation within her stirred her to consciousness. Santha screamed. Leinster moved himself in and out, and the cold grip from the contact diffused through her. She gagged, felt the strong urge to vomit.

'Now it will happen,' Leinster whispered. 'Now my force will enter you. My quick will be yours . . . yours . . . YOURS!' The silver no longer seeped but bubbled forth in his ecstasy. Globules of it fell on her face, lodged in her nostrils. 'YOURS!' He shouted more, his eyes opaque: 'I AM YOUR CONQUEROR. I AM THE CHOSEN LORD OF ALL THUGGEE!'

He was astride her, working to the point of coming, his voice bellowing his crazed litany, when she panicked. If he came, he would give her a child, he had said, and Santha believed him. Simultaneously, the faces of her loved ones, all the important things she had known passed before her, the last being the sight of Annette Kitteridge smiling at her that day at Lord & Taylor's.

Santha raised her head and butted Leinster under the chin. He let her go momentarily, and, lowering her hands, she grabbed his penis and wrenched him from her. Then, with a bound, she was off the couch.

Leinster stood rigid, his erection still maintained. Santha screamed and screamed her fury, lifted a stand with a flaming brazier, and hurled it at him. A blur and he was out of its path. The brazier hit the wall. Oil flowed down the room's shadowed corners and flared into blazing light.

Santha turned at a noise from the doorway. Ajit Majumdar and Mrinalini stood there. The flames and smoke snapped at their eyes. Santha saw the hesitation. It was as if she were now sacred and they were not eager to do violence to her.

Kurt Leinster nodded, aware of their thoughts. Santha's breathing was heavy, and a succession of gasping curses reflected her frenzy. She saw Annette's face again and yet again. Her hatred battered at the three of them, a palpable thing. Even Leinster tensed.

Then he found a solution, a new means to break her spirit. Like telepathy, Santha grasped this; she shivered, staring when he spoke.

'Outside, my Santha, are those who would restore you to your former self. How foolhardy, when the mark of the pickaxe is on you. It ties you to me – deeper and deeper – and once you see those others destroyed, one by one, you will realize all that is left is me.'

His tone was one of dismissal. He left, the other two at his heels. Santha Wrench sat again on the couch. The blazing oil cast a ruddy glow about the room in a final spurt of flame and then lowered and flickered softly. It reflected what was happening to her spirit, she felt.

A long time passed before the flames completely died; but then again it was only a little fire.

27

Captain Vincent Condorelli stood on the sprawling porch of the ashram house, rainwater dripping around him in long, slender cascades from the roof gutters. It was a big three-storeyed structure with five cupolas, and the porch continued round and past the southwest wing for a stretch.

He was speechless. More out of awe than shock, his gaze was riveted to the hulk of the barn across the twenty-yard dip as he listened to the agonizing sounds that came from that area.

Condorelli had just emerged from searching the house. Lieutenant Cavanaugh, Stephen Wrench, Rama Shastri and George Buchan had been in the forefront of the search with him. They had found hardly anything of interest. A bed with a tattered mattress in one bedroom, a chipped cup on a kitchen shelf, one broken lamp and the remnant of a knitted sweater in the kitchen. In the cellar was a broken hand-made tier of bunks with some very dirty bedding.

That was all.

He had barked an order that the house must be gone through one more time, to make absolutely certain they hadn't missed anything. While everyone else did this, he had gone to the porch to clear his head.

'God, I hate this case,' he said aloud and didn't realize it until Shastri replied, 'It's against the grain, all right.'

'Where are they?' Condorelli pointed to the barn. 'Are they all living in that barn with those poor animals? It's impossible. That was quite a mob I saw chasing Hanuman and Nirmal. And I'm sure there are others. Why did they leave this house?'

'Maybe it was when the ashram split on the issue of esoteric philosophy,' offered Thurnauer.

'Sure. And they took every stick of furniture, every utensil, every dish and cup except that one bit of pottery. But where to? It couldn't have been to the barn.'

'Why not? They could store everything there,' Cavanaugh said.

'I just can't believe all those men and women are sleeping with those yowling beasts. Even with a bunch of crazies, it doesn't make sense. But let's go and look, anyway.'

Word was passed to those in the house to hurry up; the captain wanted to go on.

Condorelli had been eager for action from the moment the Swami and his *chela* disappeared. Warrant or no warrant, he was determined to search the grounds and immediately ordered his men to do so. Shortly, all five cars had crossed the meadow road to the huge grounds.

Now they walked to the barn, Cavanaugh, Thurnauer and Abel in the lead with powerful flashlights.

It was very dark, the slanting rain adding to the poor visibility. A wind had risen, strong, battering, from the meadow side, and the tall grass susurrated like a ghostly presence. A handful of shingles that had blown free from the roof preceded them, scattering here and there at each whooshing surge.

'Thurnauer,' Condorelli directed, 'take some of the boys around the barn, go to the chicken coop and look that over. Everything. The farming area beyond. Make sure nobody's out there. Then come back.'

Eager to see the barn's interior, Thurnauer hesitated, then went on with six men.

'Open her up,' Condorelli told Cavanaugh.

Cavanaugh nodded to Sterns and Wicker. Wicker

346

moved faster; he reached the barn door and started to pull one of the big doors open. Sterns went to the other and did the same.

The cacophony within froze the men in their tracks.

'Something's sure got 'em worked up,' Jerome Abel said.

'Find the lights,' came the command.

Wicker, Sterns and another man went inside. It was Sterns who presently shouted, 'I have them.' First the outside lights went on. Swarms of crane flies flew around them. Then the interior lights were aglow, and Condorelli and the rest crossed the apron and began the walk down the feed passage in single file. The mangers were mostly empty, but two cows were tethered to stanchions, and, on the other side, a horse was rearing and screaming. The cows, too, were aroused. One could detect the scent of fear in the air. The horse was lathered, and all of them shivered with fear. A little way beyond the horse, they found a goat and her kid, both tethered and both near death from horror.

'Set them loose,' Condorelli ordered. 'I don't know if the weather will hurt them, but it can't do worse than what being here has done.'

Everyone scurried to do the job. They were concerned for the beasts, but also the din was maddening – they could barely hear a shouted command.

The most difficult job was handling the horse, but Wrench and Shastri, who had ridden much in India, finally managed to lead the kicking animal to the great door, where he calmed a little then sped off into the night when Wrench slapped his rump.

Then everyone searched. Some climbed into the lofts. When nothing was found, not even a hairpin, as Belanger said, Condorelli replied, 'I know my barns, all right. This isn't a place fit for groups of people. Besides, the smell of the manure gutters would've been intolerable.'

Wrench was on his haunches. 'Still, people have been in here. And a helluva lot of them. Look at these footprints and all that trampled loose hay. Everything points that they came out of here to attack Hanuman and Nirmal and then came back in.'

'But where are they?' someone asked. 'Jeez, they can't have gone under the ground.'

'Steve, Captain,' they heard Rama Shastri from the side of the barn with grain bins. They approached him. Shastri pointed. 'Many prints headed for this door. Where does it lead to?'

'Beats me,' Condorelli said. 'Can't be much more than grain or manure pits. Maybe the chicken yard. This barn has no buildings adjoining it. No smoking house and certainly no silo. I would've seen them in my night glasses.'

'It's probably locked, anyway.' Shastri turned the knob. 'No, it isn't.' He pushed. 'But the door is stuck.'

'Here, let me give it some Cavanaugh beef,' the lieutenant said. He was six-four and had been a fullback for Boston College. He gripped the knob, placed a shoulder against the door and put some force behind the push. The door opened.

'Oh, Jesus Christ!' cried Cavanaugh.

'And his mother and dad,' someone else added.

They all saw the very same thing. Yet, at times, each turned to look at the others to make certain he wasn't the only one seeing what was before them: a dimly lit ante-chamber, a cave, more than likely, judging by the rock-like walls. And a corridor slanted from its left side into what might be another cave beyond.

Cavanaugh rushed to a window a few feet from the

doorway and threw it open, shining his flashlight. He said, his voice shaking, 'I think you ought to look at this, sir.'

Captain Condorelli went over to him. Cavanaugh gave him the flashlight and their eyes met. The big lieutenant was very troubled. Condorelli leaned over on his tiptoes. After a few moments, he broke away from the window and handed the flashlight to Shastri, who was next in line.

Rama Shastri did as the others had done. The rainfall was as consistent as ever. Water streamed from a dormer roof above and splashed loudly into huge puddles that overflowed into a nearby empty pig pen. The light from the flash showed little else except a closed door to the right. The rest was barnyard leading to a fenced-in chicken area further along in the darkness. When Shastri pulled away, Wrench was waiting anxiously. And so the flashlight was passed on.

Cavanaugh finally said it: 'Captain, the door opens in here, *but outside it's closed, and there's just the barnyard.*' His voice was even, steady, despite his trembling lower lip.

'Spooks a man, doesn't it?' Condorelli asked. 'Go on, take a look, boys,' he told the others. 'Then we can all turn ourselves in at the nearest funny farm.'

George Buchan left the window. 'It's what Hanuman warned us about – the displacement of space by another space. And it only exists on this side.'

Condorelli looked at his men. They were pale, distraught. 'OK, now, let's all take a deep breath and let this settle in for a while.' He turned to Wicker. 'Go get Thurnauer and his bunch. Tell him to come back right now. Tell them everything you've seen. Prepare them for it. I'd contact them by radio, but man to man is maybe more convincing for what you've got to tell.'

* * *

No one was in the meadow, Thurnauer was convinced. He said as much to Donahue. 'They're somewhere back there, it has to be.' He meant the barn area. The frenzied chickens in the fenced-off yard had proved it. It was a mess when they reached it. Two of the hens were already dead from terror, and one was writhing on the ground, close to dying.

The rest were running about. Their screechings caused his hackles to rise, especially the rooster. He was constantly hitting the fence wire, blood from the impact oozing from his sides. At least six baby chicks had been trampled, and Donahue had found three dead from exposure where they had escaped the yard through a small hole in the fence.

Thurnauer heard the sound of the animals leaving the barn. 'Let them go, too,' he ordered, and the men went into the chicken yard to force the birds out, since they were too crazed to make the effort by themselves.

'They sense something terrible is around,' a detective named Fontaine said. 'Wonder what it is.'

'It's like in one of those horror movies,' Haskell quipped. 'You know – the animals all acting plenty scared 'cause the monster is coming.'

They had gone on to check the meadow. Wicker found them there. He quickly explained about the barn door and the mystery cave.

'It has to be under the barnyard. An underground cave,' Fontaine said. 'That's why you can't see it on the other side.'

'It's not underground.' Wicker was angry. 'It's level. I've seen it. And the door is closed on the outside.'

Fontaine laughed. No one else did.

'Well, come and see for yourself!' Wicker barked. He said to Thurnauer, 'It gives you the creeps. It leaves a metallic taste in your mouth. I haven't been this shook up

since I was shot at for the first time when I was a rookie.'
He mopped his brow with his raincoat sleeve. 'It's not
natural. It's not even real, but there it is.'

The rain beat a tattoo on their oilskins. It was the only
sound in that desolate meadow, the men were so silent.

'I think we should go in now.' Stephen Wrench stood on
the threshold. 'God knows what Santha's already
endured.' He choked, automatic in hand. He looked at
Condorelli for approval.

The captain was hesitant. 'They must know we're here,
Steve. They knew about the Swami and the kid.'

'All the more reason why we should go in two groups.
If the first walks into a trap, then the other can be
forewarned.'

'Sure. But what worries me is there might be no
survivors to warn the rest. No, we've got to have back-
up, in case.'

They waited. Cavanaugh was rubbing the soles of his
shoes against a post to scrape off the manure. 'This job.
And I thought being a detective was a glamour career. In
the movies, Clint Eastwood never steps into horseshit.'

'Cheer up,' Belanger told him. 'When I was a cop on
the beat once, this guy threw himself on the track at Park
Street Station. Me and my partner had parts of him
sticking to our shoes. We had to go down in the subway
tunnel, you see . . .'

'Jesus!' from one of them.

But it took their minds off what lay beyond the doorway. Even the grisly event was normal, at least. A few
other horrible tales followed. The topper was told by
Hernandez, who had curling moustache ends. 'Somebody
in Roxbury cut up his mother-in-law. I mean, really cut
her up, you understand. And he left all the parts of her in
these orange crates in a dump. Well, it was my job to pick

them up and bring them to the wagon. Got to have evidence, you understand.'

'Why did he butcher her up that way?'

'Well, she was a big, busty pain in the ass, he said. Even after he killed her, she looked big and formidable. So he cut her down to size, he said.'

'Jesus . . .'

When Thurnauer and his men showed up, everybody was relaxed, some laughing. Condorelli had allowed them free rein, aware of the release it gave them.

Then, 'OK, knock it off,' he said. To Thurnauer, 'Any theories, Professor?' Thurnauer just gaped at the doorway.

'Now we go in,' the captain informed Wrench. 'Let's see, first Cavanaugh, Donahue, Hernandez, Thurnauer . . .' He named some others. 'And Steve, Mr Shastri, Dr Buchan and me.' To Abel: 'Jerome, you stay here. You're in charge of our back-up. We'll keep in radio contact. And remember, leave someone out if you and your gang have to come in to help us. That's you, Belanger. You then bring in the locals. You get on the car radio fast and get them to come in. But only them. We don't want too many cooks unless we have to. Got it?'

A sullen nod. 'Yes, sir.'

'Dr Buchan, have you been given a gun?'

George said, 'Yes.'

'Are you good with one?'

'Good enough.'

'Fine. All right, let's go.'

The instant they crossed the threshold, they understood what had frightened the animals. To a man, they felt as if they were pushing through webbing; the rest was subliminal, like a subtle vibration, a threatening malignant presence. The coolest of them began to tense up; beads of sweat covered foreheads.

Cavanaugh, Thurnauer and Fontaine led the way, each with a flashlight. They went through the antechamber to a corridor with a high ceiling. It was wide enough for five men walking abreast. Behind the three lead detectives were Captain Condorelli, Wrench, Shastri and George. The captain wanted them near the front line since their familiarity with Thugs could mean they would spot anything wrong right away.

The darkness was complete now. Two other policemen turned on their lights and sent the beams along the corridor sides and behind the men to ensure that Stranglers weren't lurking in niches or creeping up from the rear. They all breathed easier when they entered a large cavern.

'There's a light ahead,' Condorelli whispered.

Slowly, very cautiously, the group crossed the great space. Nearing the light, they saw that it was bluish, that it was reflected from the walls of a smaller room. The air was temperate despite the tremendous height and vast area of the place.

'It's like the inside of a mountain. Something like that,' Fontaine said, a little too loudly.

'Part of a glacier,' Thurnauer said, as they discovered the room's reflecting walls to be of ice.

They entered, their reflections clear on both sides. The blue light was almost white. Further down was a darker gap within it. They also heard voices and stopped.

'Centre your light straight ahead,' Condorelli snapped. In the brilliant gigantic disc the combined flashlights made, they saw bars, and hands gripping them, and faces beyond.

'Prisoners!' It was Cavanaugh.

'Easy. Easy,' came the command. 'Let's keep an eye on our rear.'

As the detectives in the back did as the captain directed,

353

the rest moved forward. The cell was bleakly lit, and the odour of unwashed bodies strong.

'Oh, thank God, it's help!' a voice cried from behind the bars.

'Please release us!' A woman's voice.

'Yes, please!'

'Who are you?' asked Condorelli.

'We were once part of the ashram,' the first speaker replied.

'Vic Croce turned against us. He and his followers. Because we wouldn't serve Kali.'

'We are Vedantists, not fanatics.'

'Please, set us free.'

Rama Shastri came to Condorelli's side. 'I would be very careful.'

The bars were made of very hard wood. Cavanaugh found a lever.

'Yes, yes,' a male prisoner urged. 'Pull that down and the bars rise.'

Condorelli raised a hand. 'Hold it. I want every one of you to come near the bars so we can see you. No lagging behind in the dark, now.'

The flashlights revealed face after face. 'I count seventeen men and nine women, Captain.'

'Where are your captors?' demanded Wrench gruffly. He had been silent up to now.

'In the other chambers,' a short man replied.

'Don't they post a guard?'

'There's no need,' half a dozen said at once.

'Now, one at a time.' To the short man, 'Go on. You do the talking.'

'They know we can't escape.'

'Why aren't you all dead by now?'

'We were kept alive until their Huzoor arrived. That was only recently.'

354

'*So he is here,*' George said under his breath.

The man continued, 'We have been saved for a mass execution. They have dug what they call a *bele.*'

'That figures,' Wrench said to Shastri. 'Christ, I wish Hanuman were here. He'd know if it was the truth in an instant, with his sixth sense. What do you think, Ram?'

'I think we should go very slowly. Leave them here and investigate the rest of this place.'

'Please don't,' appealed the spokesman. 'We are hungry, crowded here. This cell has become insanitary. Some of us are ill and should have medical attention immediately.'

'It don't smell exactly like roses here,' Fontaine said. 'The humane thing to do is let them out.'

'I have no choice,' the captain told Shastri. 'OK, pull down the lever.'

Cavanaugh did. The bars slowly rose. Men and women rushed out. Shastri, Wrench and George Buchan were alert, however. 'All right,' Condorelli barked. 'Everyone keep calm. Fontaine, contact Jerome to come in. We're going to need help herding these folks out.'

Fontaine bent to his handset. The blue lights went out. Someone cursed. The flashlights were still on, however. In their beams, Shastri saw the mass lunge as one person. 'Fire!' he warned, and Wrench and George followed suit. The blinding gun flame and reverberations added to the grotesqueness of the scene. Faces fierce with blood lust turned to open-eyed shock as the bullets struck. In the struggle, the light of the flashes danced eerily. Two went out.

Shastri had seen Fontaine go down as a *rumel* encircled his neck. Cavanaugh managed a shot that sent a woman back with a scream. Only Thurnauer's light was on.

Wrench cried, 'Keep that light on, for God's sake, man!'

355

But the short man had bent under Thurnauer's arm. He bit into the wrist and the light fell. Someone picked it up quickly and it went out.

'Just keep firing.' From Condorelli.

Shot after shot ignited the darkness.

'Back up, men. Back up.'

Someone cursed again. The police were stumbling into each other.

'Find a goddamn flashlight,' bellowed Wrench. 'Isn't there one back there?'

'They took them,' a voice finally blurted. 'It was the first thing they went for. We didn't expect it.'

This was during a strange lull in the fighting. The crowd were keeping a distance between themselves and the police. Some were wailing in agony from their wounds. Especially the women.

'I had to shoot her.' Cavanaugh was breathing heavily.

'Shed no tears, lad. She'd have garrotted you, sure.'

'Keep moving back.' From Condorelli. One of the policemen was speaking rapidly into his handset. It sounded like Thurnauer, Shastri thought.

'Steve, I expect trouble any second now. It isn't the Thug way to give up so quickly,' he said to Wrench.

'They've circled us. I can hear the bastards.' It was Cavanaugh.

'Be alert. Are you all right, George?'

'Fine, Steve. They seem to be dragging something. Hear it?'

'Christ, it's dark.'

'Let's have a roll call. Cavanaugh.'

'Here, Captain.'

'Hernandez.'

'Here.'

'Fontaine.'

No reply. More cursing.

'Sterns.'

'Present.'

'Collins.' Silence. 'Collins.'

'Sorry, sir. There's some shuffling back here . . . What the fuck . . . Watch out, Cap, it's a net!'

Rama Shastri, hearing this, leaped free of the group but too late. The net was large and weighted at its ends. It flew over Shastri's shoulder and hit the floor with a metallic thunk. Shastri felt himself being pulled along with his companions. The net undulated like a snake, and what happened at one end of it affected the rest. Tighter and tighter the net became. He felt bodies scrambling over his shoulders. The Thugs were throwing their bodies on it to guarantee that it was weighted down. Other Thugs were working at the net's bindings. The blue lighting returned.

Now that they could see better, the captives sent fists and elbows, knees and feet out wherever they had the freedom to, trying desperately to get loose. They hit some of the Thugs, and a few tumbled from the pile, unconscious.

All the policemen were talking at once, it seemed, until a very loud gong sounded. Its reverberation within the cave set their teeth on edge. They became silent.

'There now,' a man's voice taunted while he applauded. 'What a performance. Heroes all to the very end.'

It was Kurt Leinster.

Jerome Abel had been listening to Thurnauer's radio summons when the door to the cave slammed shut.

'How did that happen?' he asked Wicker.

'Beats me, sir.'

'Well, open it – quick!'

Wicker grabbed the knob. After much exertion: 'It's caught, sir. It won't budge.'

357

'Here, let me try,' a bigger man said. Later, 'It's really stuck, Lieutenant.'

'Then find an axe!' Abel shouted. 'We've got to get in there and help them!'

28

After the brightness that blinded him for a while and the 'rope' had both disappeared, Nirmal Kapur said, 'Are we in Hell, Bapu?'

'If not, but a step away from it,' Hanuman replied in a strained voice.

'Are you all right, Bapu? You sound ill or very distraught.'

'I am greatly weakened, my *chela*. It has been inevitable.'

Nirmal gasped. His master lay back against the greying mist as if it were a solid wall. It held him up in a sitting position, like a small doll placed in the corner of a nursery. The squinched face was extremely pale, the eyes closed.

Nirmal gripped Hanuman's arms and started to rub them. Then, when the eyes didn't open, he shook the Swami. 'Bapu! Bapu!' he called. 'Can you hear me?'

'Yes . . . my *chela*.' Very faint.

'Do not leave me in this . . . place. Where are we, Bapu? What can I do to help?'

'Think of Vishnarma.'

Nirmal bent his ear to Hanuman's mouth. 'I can't hear you. What did you say?'

'Think of Vishnarma.'

'But I can only think of you, Bapu. What is wrong? Do not leave me alone in this . . . dream. Where are we? What is to happen to us?'

When Hanuman's lips formed the name Vishnarma

again, without sound, Nirmal sat next to him. Then he pulled at his own long straight strands of hair.

'Oh, this is too much, man,' he said to himself. 'First we play commando in that monsoon out there – wherever "there" is now – and then we climb that dangling sticky black thing – ugh, it made me think of Kali's umbilical cord – and now here we are in some space, in God knows what time, if there is Time at all . . . This is too damn much . . .!'

He rubbed Hanuman's arms again. 'Can you hear me, my father?' Nirmal's face broke until he nearly wept. 'You wouldn't die on me, would you, Swami Hanuman?' Nirmal shook his head. 'Come on, man, don't let the garbage take over. Of course he's not dead. He's in another trance, that's all. You seen him this way before. Many times, and he was OK later, wasn't he?'

Meditate on Vishnarma, he told himself.

What had jolted him so badly was the lack of warning. Here they were – Nirmal stared at the restless mist – here . . . and suddenly Swami Hanuman was very weak and out of contact. It was inevitable, Hanuman had said in fatalistic surrender. The gears ground on, the script had already been written, the natural progression – one thing to another to another. Nirmal's soul cringed at the idea. No, we make it up as we go along, baby; we innovate, we tune in and play it by ear – as it comes, as it goes, as is, as is – like with music, like it's just happening, happening, happening . . .

I should try and concentrate on Vishnarma, he warned himself.

But the funk was difficult to climb out of: Hanuman, his mentor, had always been there. Available when necessary. He was the one who had taken Nirmal into the shelter of his home when the young Indian musician was an addict years ago. America hadn't always been kind to

360

Nirmal in that time, and his rock-star fame had included the usual pitfalls – the wrong women and drugs.

Hanuman had helped to free him, through an esoteric path, through meditation and teachings handed down from the Swami's late master.

Vishnarma. Vishnarma. I must think of you.

He stared at the still figure and placed his ear on the diminutive Hanuman's chest. After much waiting, he finally caught the heartbeat. Nirmal smiled. It wasn't a time for dying.

Nor panic. What to do next, what to do?

The mist at his feet parted as if in reply. Brushing his cheek – was it a breeze? It was a breath like a breeze, and it was filled with malice, a repugnant miasma, all negative life force, all gloating and leering and proud of the usurpation of any iota of serenity left in his consciousness.

It was discordant music shattering the very scales, numbing the melodious, the tinkling, trickling notes of contemplation and peace that still remained.

'I must fight this!' Nirmal said aloud. 'May Vishnarma help me to resist.'

The mist became a maelstrom at his feet, a whirling, grey-streaked, nebula-like swirl that broke apart without warning. Nirmal could see through it then, looking at the world below.

Or was he seeing it from a distant height? From within the room itself? The angle of the scene kept shifting. Most times he was above, but now and then he was within the setting as if he were a third person standing there watching. Portions of the wall were like ice or crystals and glittered with reflections and angles of reflections. Nirmal saw that he was invisible. The reflections showed only the same two people, Kurt Leinster and Santha Wrench.

They were quite transformed. Leinster had a silvery current or something similar crossing his face – or was it his eyes? – that made him appear radically different from the man Nirmal had seen years ago.

The difference in Santha was immediately apparent in her stance. It was so aggressive that the image of a female warrior came to Nirmal's mind. All that was missing was the shield and spear, and she would have passed as a dusky Amazon. The force was latent in her limbs, her poise, the thrust of her neck and head. Her black eyes held a defiance and wrath Nirmal had never seen in her before. Her long hair splayed out, reminiscent of the fur on an aroused cat's back. She was in a tattered sari. One breast was totally naked, and its blatant beauty only added to the wildness Nirmal sensed about her.

'Stay away from me.' Santha pointed at Leinster like a sorceress placing a spell or curse. 'Stay away!'

There was deadliness to her threat.

'But you don't understand, my beloved,' Leinster taunted. 'Your father and lover George Buchan are waiting for you. They're outside, beloved. Come, you must see them. They are our guests. And I refuse to join them without you.'

Perplexity showed in Santha's eyes. She hesitated, groping to remember.

'Your daddy,' Leinster taunted. 'Daddy and George and Uncle Ram, too. Daddy – Santha – Daddy. He waits for you.'

'Daddy,' she repeated, and tears flowed down her cheeks.

'Yes, Daddy. Come, Santha – come now.'

'Daddy!' she screeched. 'George! Uncle Ram! Annette! What have you done to them?'

Nirmal's angle of view was now as if he were standing in Santha's path. He was so near to her he could almost feel her breath, he thought. Now the view shifted, and he saw Santha's legs propel her across the room in one bound. Leinster had foreseen this, however. He was already chanting a mantra in the Sanskrit of the ancient scroll that granted him the power over all Thuggee.

Santha tried to suppress the incantation. Her hands found his throat, and she pressed at the sides of his windpipe. 'Good for you, baby!' Nirmal rallied, slipping into the American slang he liked so much.

Kurt Leinster's blue eyes disappeared, and, with only the whites showing, he was now a total albino. There was something twice as chilling, even more ghoulish, about him. He didn't struggle with her but allowed her powerful fingers to press harder. The fingers seemed to sink into the sallow flesh, deep hollows of pressure that promised to crush his windpipe any second.

His mouth remained open, the colourless lips curling grotesquely like strips of rubbery fungus. A wispy blackness poured from his gullet, and at first Nirmal thought it was a snake or some other slithering creature. It thickened gradually and twisted and turned around Santha, a smoke ring or the like. It passed before her eyes, broke her concentration. She backed, releasing Leinster, transfixed by the wavering inky trail that expanded and formed in mid-air the outline of a face, a black fury of a woman's outline with eyes like pinpoints of sparkling energies that bore and bore into Santha. Nirmal bent forward to see the smoke form better. He recoiled. It was Kali's face in its most hideous aspect, and, as quickly as it manifested, it dissolved and flowed quickly into Santha's open mouth.

Nirmal found himself in Santha's mind at that very moment, and he shuddered, then wept at what he felt. His consciousness leaped free again with a repulsion that left him breathless. Santha in turn covered her face; her cries were piteous. When it ended, when she lowered her hands, Nirmal wept again. The scene dissolved, the mist rushed across it like a curtain.

Nirmal turned to Hanuman and saw there had been no change. The Swami was as still as stone.

'What am I going to do, teacher?' Nirmal wailed. 'You are no longer with me, and Kali has seized the spirit of Santha. Who among us but you could prevent this? I'm helpless, my master, and am now overwhelmed with grief and despair. Why am I left alone to witness this?'

'She is mine,' he heard then, and it set him to looking at the swirling mass again, like clouds parting at his feet.

A king of rooms surely was before him. The place had no boundaries, he thought. A room? A cavern, more like, with stalactites and stalagmites everywhere and a pit with one of those 'umbilical cords' hovering down, down into the pit's depths.

The view shifted. He was being directed to new scenes. It could just as well have been a movie, except that what was happening was real. There was a dais, and the pit with tendrils of fumes was in the background to the right of the Huzoor, who stood in the centre of the dais. On both sides of him, near surges of more wisps from brazier incense, were a man and a woman. The man was old, in a turban and *dhoti*, but his eyes held a young fire. He was a man constantly revitalized by a passion, a fanatic's dream. One could read it in his gaze, a guru Thug. Ever eager to use his *rumel*, to kill, to kill, to kill . . . for Kali Ma.

On the Huzoor's right was the giant woman. Her madness needed no reason, no meaning. It was instinctual, had always been with her. One could tell by her placidity at the moment. Somehow, that held more threat of terror than even the guru.

'She is mine,' Leinster, the Huzoor, announced to his followers below the dais. 'Mine! Mine!' Now to those behind the bars of a big cage in the distance to the far left of the platform.

Santha emerged from the mesh of torch smoke and

364

incense traceries. There was much noise from the cage. The view closed in on the faces of the captives: Wrench was shouting; behind him were Shastri, George, Captain Condorelli, his men. Trapped, prisoners of the Huzoor.

It was too much for Nirmal. It hadn't occurred to him, not once, that they would all fail. Stephen Wrench, Rama Shastri and George Buchan were part of the group who had defeated Kurt Leinster before. When he and Hanuman had fallen into this trap, he had believed the rest still to be too formidable as a group to fail. Certainly never to the point where everyone was taken prisoner.

Hanuman had been correct. His theory was that as long as the Huzoor remained on sacrosanct ground – namely, this 'imported' space from India, this cave or cavern of the ancient *rishis* – then Leinster would be stronger, more capable, than ever before.

Thus Hanuman and his link with Vishnarma, with the various aspects of Vishnu, had not been enough. He had been outclassed, as the American sportscasters called it in boxing. Kurt Leinster had become a heavyweight with a knockout punch.

Not so, came a nagging thought.

But the events below commanded his attention. Stephen Wrench kept seizing the bars, then letting them go as if he'd received a tremendous electrical shock. Captain Condorelli, Shastri and the others were trying to hold him back. But Wrench had snapped at the sight of his daughter. He was bellowing, calling her name, threatening Kurt Leinster. Nirmal couldn't quite hear the words; they were muffled for some reason. Only the Huzoor's words had been clear, distinct.

Each time Wrench received a shock he nearly collapsed. The bars were obviously dangerous. The detectives finally overwhelmed him, but even then Nirmal detected Wrench squirming, trying to kick himself free of the weight of their bodies.

Leinster was speaking. The view shifted. The men in the cage might never have existed, the shift was so abrupt.

'Kali Ma is merciful, and in great wisdom she determines that all things are in their proper order. Thus do we, her supreme children, rule and are thereby sanctified. Therein were we chosen for saintly acts. The sacred duty of the Thug' – he held up a *rumel* – 'is to take lives.'

'Kill.' From the congregation.

'Yes, kill. Kill for Kali.'

The gathering parted. Among them were the handful of Indian Stranglers Leinster had brought to America. As they parted, two lines of men and women and children were exposed to everyone's sight. Their hands were bound behind them, and they were on their knees. Some were weeping, some cursing, but none was very energetic, since they had been ill fed and, at that, the food heavily drugged.

'These . . .' Leinster accused, his voice ringing like a mad prophet of old, 'these are the members of the ashram who rebelled against the coming of Kali Ma and against the revelations of myself as Lord of all Thuggee. Having refused the quick of new life, of a new path, they are now as dead. And it is fitting their bodies shall establish our new *bele* that we have prepared, far, far out in the meadow where even these intruders' – he pointed towards the cage – 'couldn't find it. They, too, will be part of our *bele*. But first the ashram must be cleansed.

'Oh, do not pity them secretly in your hearts, my brothers and sisters. They were properly warned. They had their choice and didn't heed it. Not once. So let us not hesitate. Let us begin . . .'

He spun around and faced Santha.

'Come, Vessel of Kali Ma, O Radiant Flower of Thuggee. Come, lead them, inspire them to do what must be done.'

Then the hush settled. More than the hush of people becoming silent, the hush permeated everything, an invisible gripping of sound before it could set itself into motion. Had water been trickling there, it would have done so in silence.

The cavern waited breathlessly.

Santha had been an unclear vision, bits of flesh, sparkles of jewellery, murmurs of essence, behind the veil of smoke and incense wavelets.

Now she stepped into the centre of the lighted dais. Now the inexplicable gathering of glowing brightness was filled with her nubile body. She wasn't naked, but as near so as to suggest beauty beyond measure, a loveliness meant for goddesses.

Santha was an impossibility, a dream, a wish – and a painful, excruciating, tragic blend of the awesomely pleasurable and the most hideous Evil.

There was no deformity, nothing physically repulsive. But there was.

And it was all in the perfection. The methodical, preconceptualized motion that verged on the mechanical.

Since Santha Wrench was now possessed.

She walked, moving as Kali would walk, would move. The spasmodic jerking of head, arms, legs added to the menacing effect. Her accoutrements clinked, chocked, tinkled and shushed along with her. The eyes, wide, black, quick, never still, boring into others, speaking in their energies – I am Kali, you do aught but submit to me since I am indeed *She Whom All Men Fear*.

And, as out of the distant reaches, a voice calling in the wilderness, her father shouting her name, desperate to break the spell – *Santhaa-a, Santha-a-a.*

367

She didn't hear. Nirmal, seeing she didn't hear, struggled with a grief he couldn't explain except that there were universal chords all humanity responds to . . . He knew Stephen Wrench, he knew his daughter – it was his pain, too!

Down the dais the vessel came. Her naked flanks, her naked breasts, her lower lip heavy, blood-red with atavistic longing . . . the fanning hair like black wings, the clatter of her skull girdle, the clicking rattle, the necklace of bone . . .

. . . the *shwish*, the *swush* as the hair battered the air, as the neck nodded left, right, the arms and hands and fingers, too – left, right – pointing as she passed down the aisle between the kneeling victims.

The standing Thugs behind them heeded the gesturing commands. The *rumels* fell over necks. That day Vic Croce disposed of his wife, who had protested against Kali so strongly in the past. And Mauna of her younger brother, who refused to change his belief in non-violence.

Many who died were related to those who killed.

Nirmal Kapur whimpered, biting the side of his palm as he watched each victim fall.

The scene became milky, the grey mist again blotted the great room out of sight.

Nirmal Kapur moved away from the spot, on his haunches, as if he feared he would be contaminated by what he'd seen. He dragged the prone Hanuman along with him. Self-pity welled up in him, a tidal wave of depression and despair: the emotions he had suppressed for so long under the Swami's tutelage. Of what use was he now, to what purpose could he serve and do that which he must or everyone was lost? It was an unfair responsibility, meant for heroes. Why, he was only a boy, nearing thirty years as he was, a boy with enough musical talent to charm the *devas*, true, but nevertheless a child yet to be a man.

And without the Swami he was younger still.

This was not a place to be, not a situation for him to be in; and, although he knew he wasn't a coward, there was the insecurity, the lack of belief in himself, that made everything so cruel and unfair.

He wanted to be back among the blue mercury tubes and pinkish neons, the strobes flickering his face and his guitar into scatterings of incandescence. He wanted music, but there wasn't any. After all, his soul was nothing but G clefs and flats, saptaks and ragas.

And – this he hadn't felt for a long, long time – he wanted that hypodermic elixir, to feel the heroin jolt that eased all sorrow.

So Nirmal prayed. It wasn't much of a prayer but a part of what he had been trained to do; it came automatically.

If only as a diversion, he thought.

But there is Vishnarma. 'Oh, yes, there is – let us not forget,' he said aloud to himself. *Vishnarma.*

Think of him, my chela. *Think of him.* It was as if Hanuman were speaking the words now.

Nirmal Kapur closed his eyes. He sat in the lotus position and made the effort. *Vishnarma, Vishnarma, Vishnarma* – like notes afloat on the scale of Eternity, drifting down the frets of Time . . . low notes, barely audible, like a sonic whisper . . . *Vishnarma.*

The nimbus moved over the body and hands and arms and face of the saintly guru, rippled with the life that moved and spoke. 'Climb that.' The voice meant the black wall, the towering vault-like structure before Nirmal. 'Use the tree as your master before you. Go to the garden of Kunkali the Sleeper, the astral Dreamer,

369

she who seldom wakens. The matrix of the goddess that must dream of the countless realities. Go.'

Nirmal stammered, 'But what must I do when I find her?'

'You will know.' An implosion.

His trance had burst, an eruption of brightness that hurled him back . . .

Nirmal stood up. For a brief moment he stared at Hanuman, then left. The Swami must already understand why he must go. Must – no doubt of it.

And Nirmal moved. Without thinking, he went on. He had meditated, after all, and been successful. He urged himself forward, forced himself to advance through the cloudiness that, as if heeding his telepathic command, parted and parted.

Until he arrived at the great wall, darker than nightness, and the tree of ebonywood whose uppermost branch reached out to the wall's edge. Reached with an uncommon gnarliness, like splaying long fingers ever clutching.

Nirmal started to climb. The tree slanted like a toddling, drunken thing about to go into a convulsion; and he was almost able to run up the weaving trunk in the beginning. But soon the climb became arduous . . .

There were obstacles. Minor setbacks, true, but already they were nibbling at his new-found convictions. The tree breathed. It heaved in and puffed out, and the effect was unpleasant. Nirmal experienced some vertigo before he'd finished moving on foot and had to descend to his hands and knees before he fainted.

To touch the bark wasn't much better. That the tree was like a gigantic lung with bellows pumping air instead of sap made Nirmal cringe every time a wheeze or a massive sigh came from the multiple knotholes.

Also, the higher Nirmal went, the more the tree

moaned. It was a protest; the louder it sounded, the more he envisioned Kunkali awakening in her bower. He wished he could stop up those holes with leaves, but when he saw their fungoid patches, Nirmal soon retreated from that idea.

At last he scaled the extending limb and let himself fall free. He landed on the wall's top and waited. Below, the garden was both shadowy and very silent. No bird songs, no buzzing of insects, no flutter of wings; the shadows moved in soundless undulations. Pockets of light were apparent, then quickly darkened. Nirmal had glimpses of sepia hollows, little more.

He paused. Here he was to venture into that forbidding place without even a weapon. Then he wondered what weapons would suffice against any of the creatures that lived there. It was a moot point.

This quest began to resemble an initiation. Was this to be Nirmal's rite of passage? If so, again, its unfairness dismayed him. Didn't his master's master understand that he was but a lowly *chela*?

Ah, well, Nirmal decided, if he was to save Hanuman and the others – such an arrogant supposition – he must go on as before. Besides, the branches of the tree, those finger-like extensions, were rustling as if eager to pluck him back. Nirmal dived for a tree on the other side of the wall with a scaly, piebald back. His hands held fast to the tree when he hit it. Too fast. His knees and ankles had also met the rough surface, and now he couldn't move any part of him that had made contact.

'Vishnarma,' he called, 'can't you see that I'm stuck? The least you could do is release me.' He tried to will his fingers free and managed to raise them enough to see the thin layer of resin that held them.

He heard a flapping. Wings! Nirmal groaned, raised his eyes and saw a bright blue wave descending to the bark a yard above his head. Then it disassembled into thousands of – he could only describe them as 'wormlets'. They formed a blue band a foot and a half wide around the tree and progressed downward to where he was. Close up, he saw that they were actually little crawling curls of blue light that in worm-like fashion were eating up the resin. In no time, Nirmal was sliding down the trunk to the ground.

It was much too fast and, unprepared, he landed with a thud. He stood, rubbed his backside and laughed. Some hero.

But laughter was a relief more than a luxury. Nirmal soon set his jaw for whatever lay ahead. Gone was the panic, the self-pity. He had Vishnarma with him now, and the memory of the event that he'd witnessed back there in Kali-space; of Stephen Wrench and all those brave and noble men in that cage; of Santha Wrench, not only perhaps the most beautiful woman he had ever seen but now perhaps the most tragic too.

That motivated him most of all. If there had been one gain Nirmal had discovered in America, it was a paraphrase of 'suffer not witches . . .'

– suffer not Fate and its fickle finger.

Since the philosophy that had led him to drug addiction was one of fatalistic resignation to whatever happened, Hanuman had taught him – but in an esoteric fashion, not a pragmatic one – that Man can control his stars.

Now that teaching stirred again within his neural being, his musculature. He moved along a path through the clusters of sepia ferns ahead, allowing, trusting, his instincts to guide him.

When the fern overhang finally ended, he found that a natural pool cut through the path. He would have to go round it; and, sensing that this might be another trap, he

372

moved cautiously, keeping a wide distance between himself and the pool edge.

The water concerned him. Standing on his tiptoes so he could see the surface better, he immediately noted that it didn't reflect the world above it. Instead, the surface appeared to reflect something within the pool itself and, at that, almost obliquely and in two angles, as if the water turned inward at the centre as in a whirlpool or a maelstrom. This drove Nirmal to approach the edge to see what these two angles reflected.

The first thing he saw was the backs of two naked men, one in each angle, which were in turn separated by a thick silvery line that held no reflection at all. Then both angles lifted into the air as if they were mirrors and, with great splashes, deposited the two naked figures on the pool's stone borders.

Their backs were still turned to Nirmal. There was something familiar about the lean olive-coloured men with wet, lank, shoulder-length hair.

Something tugged hard at the heels of his feet, and, looking down in bafflement, Nirmal saw his shadow stretching and stretching itself in an effort to pull him from the spot. Streaks of blue shot through the grotesque shadow like miniature lightning. Recognizing Vishnarma's energy sparklings, Nirmal jumped backward in sudden fear.

Too late. The figure nearest to him pressed one side of his head against Nirmal's right side. Nirmal gave out half a yowl, since the creature had no face whatsoever, before it pressed itself against his cheek; but now he saw and felt that half taken away. Before him stood a Nirmal with a half of the left side of its face, the same right side that had detached itself during the contact. The half-mouth before him completed his yowl.

Nirmal's fingers roamed over his right jaw. The cheek,

the mouth were gone. The fingers darted upward, and of course the nostril and eye and ear on that side were missing, too. All Nirmal felt was a smooth, fleshy surface. He emitted a despair-filled sound. The figure finished it for him.

'You've taken . . .'

'. . . my face,' the figure completed.

A sudden black blur, and he thought everything had turned to night. Now he had no eyes. But no, the blur was to his left. It had pulled the faceless creature away. Nirmal stared, puzzled, looking behind him, then back to the dark outline of a man who gripped the faceless thing by the wrist and swung it into his companion. The other doubled, holding its facsimile of a stomach. The black blur then flew to its side, ripped free the missing half-face and, bounding to Nirmal, bowed and slapped the half back where it belonged.

Nirmal blinked. His shadow bowed again, took his arm and dragged Nirmal as it ran at top speed. Looking back at the pool, Nirmal saw half a dozen more faceless facsimiles of himself leap out. He immediately complied with the shadow's urging and ran harder until they were side by side. Then Nirmal passed it. That was when the shadow became a part of him again.

How long and how far he ran was beyond his understanding. Time doubled up on itself in this unholy garden, and what might have been a great distance lost its great depth and seemed to shrink. The only thing he could rely on was that he was winded, and he willingly collapsed in a fern-enclosed nook and waited for his breathing to become regular.

That he was no longer chased by the pool beings, he knew for certain. He could tell from his shadow's behaviour. It was reacting normally, totally in sync with his movements.

Nirmal was staring at nothing in particular when something wobbled past at least ten feet in the air. It looked like a gigantic bubble with a sickly, bilious tint. Large enough to hold several big men standing, it wasn't empty. Squinting hard, he recognized his beloved Hanuman, still prone, eyes closed, just as Nirmal had left him. Jumping to his feet, he left the nook, following the bubble in grief.

He was almost back on the path through the fern jungle when there was a resounding cracking and a tearing-of-fabric noise, and Nirmal was gaping down at a wide crevice that had suddenly appeared before his toes. Even then, he was so eager to reach his teacher that he nearly toppled into what seemed to be, as he peered over the brim, depths that had no end.

The strange bubble started to disappear behind an arch of great fern leaves. The thick sepia haze settled over the bubble's face, and Hanuman's still form was lost from view. Nirmal stamped his feet, pulled his lank hair. He shouted Hanuman's name two, three times.

The edge of the crevice began to crumble. Black sod and purplish grass broke free beneath his feet. Nirmal backflipped, landed on his feet, and yelped, as even more of the ground broke away.

He also saw that the crevice had spread to both sides of where he stood, and, from the noise behind him, he could tell that the fissure was continuing there, too. It was like being stranded on an island in the midst of space.

Nirmal pulled his tresses again. His eyes were moist from frustration. 'Bapu, forgive me. I've failed you,' he cried out, across the great rift.

He felt then a tapping on his shoulder. Nirmal turned and was nose to nose with his shadow. Within the interior of the head outline, blue threads sparkled and leaped into the chest area. 'Vishnarma! You have come to my aid again.'

The shadow nodded, held up an index finger and left Nirmal. It walked to the crevice's lip. Its chest expanded as if it were taking a deep breath; then began to stretch and stretch until it bent over the abyss like a black rainbow. Then it gradually flattened itself into a bridge to the other side.

Spirits buoyant, Nirmal ran along the stretched right shadow leg as if he wore seven-league boots. Nearing the waist, he made the mistake of looking over the edge and almost fell off. He caught his breath, relaxed and set out again. On both ends, front and back, there was more ground crackling, but the shadow only stretched itself more. Running over the chest area, narrow pillars of blue life force geysered around Nirmal. It was like a victory celebration. Nirmal raced up the left arm, then over the back of the hand and the long thumb, and once again stood on solid ground. Nirmal turned to the bridge, but it was already gone. Looking to his side, he saw that the shadow now belonged to him again.

Nirmal ran on. A breeze of images passed through his head. Vishnarma was communicating with him. The bubble was a dream of Kunkali, the Eternal Sleeper. It was not Hanuman, the physical shell, in the bubble's confines but, worse still, his very essence. Somehow, *she* had been able to take it from the Swami in his weakened state and was bringing it, willing it to *her*, to partake of it.

To eat it.

Nirmal shuddered. 'Vishnarma, light of my master, save him!' Nirmal prayed, and he ran faster, searching the grey shroud of sky as he did so.

He saw the bubble at last. The bile colour had increased on the surface. It looked a bloated, decaying thing, a floating disease-ridden membrane.

But how to get to it? It was at least fourteen feet above the ground at the moment. He left the fern cover, entered a clearing. He heard the cracking noise again, and his heart pounded in his ears.

There was a massive dome-shaped rock ahead. Nirmal leaped up its side and neared the top. He was moving instinctively, without thought, sensing that Vishnarma would find a way, trusting that he would succeed. The bubble was slightly beyond the rock.

Nirmal suddenly slid. The rock had shifted, and he saw extending from its base a curving trunk-like extension. At its end was a head the size of a kettle drum. The eyes, menacing, bloodshot ellipses, ran along the circumference like the digits on a clock. The centre was a round maw with thousands of filaments reaching for him. Blobs of saliva drooled from their tips, hit the dome surface and sizzled. The fumes rose to Nirmal's nostrils, and he screamed from the burning pain . . .

He was suddenly touched. Gentle fingers touched him, and the pain lessened, then left entirely. Simultaneously, he was lifted, raised, and he knew it was his friend the shadow. His legs had bent and straightened, and the shadow's had done the same as it held him close like an embrace, and they leaped or sprang or, better still, flew up, up . . .

When they reached the wobbling membrane, the shadow stretched a rigid finger to the green, black-veined face, and it parted as if the blue – the very bright, almost whitish blue – of the shadow's fingertip had made an incision in the surface. They rushed in, and, as quickly as it had parted, it closed.

In the murky twilight dream there was a glow. It emanated from Hanuman like a pulse, a man's eternal self. Nirmal's breathing had turned inward, he knew, since there was no air to breathe here. There was only the substance that was Evil, the atmosphere of unlife, or unlove, but powerful, nevertheless.

Nirmal continued to let himself be directed. He touched the glow that was Hanuman. It fused with him as Vishnarma had fused with his shadow, and the three essences began to pulse brighter, ever brighter.

The bubble sank. The brightness of the three lit up the Bower of Skulls below. It splashed forth through the membrane, splayed the sleeping goddess. Skulls connected to their vine shoots clicked their jaws in agitation. Skeletal hands crawled up her blood-stained divan. They resembled fungoid crabs scurrying along a vermilion beach. The Sleeper had her eyes open. It was always so when *she* slept. Golden ellipses. They would turn to silver immediately if *she* awoke. Her mouth was also open, and drool with red traceries seeped between her fangs to her pendulous breasts. Kunkali was expectant. Her dream offered three to partake of, three to devour . . .

Now, Vishnarma commanded, and the thought was all radiation. It suffused Vishnarma-Hanuman-Nirmal. The membrane sizzled, ignited, was as blinding as phosphorescence. The dream imploded. Nirmal hurtled through concentric azure rings that pushed him further and further from a shriek of black rage that pulled Space into itself.

In his arms was his master's light, as tangible as any body. Even before he awoke, sitting bolt upright, staring into Hanuman's smiling face, he knew they had won.

'Was I dreaming, too?' he asked.

Hanuman shrugged, and pointed to a break in the mist. There, a rope-thing led to the ashram cavern.

'We may leave now,' the Swami announced.

29

Nirmal Kapur was still euphoric from his experience in the Garden of Kunkali, the Sleeper. That he had done something very exceptional, he was convinced. He no longer felt that he was just a *chela*. He was different from before, had faced obstacles he believed would destroy him. Vishnarma had helped him, true, but nevertheless Nirmal had done his part.

Rapidly, he told Hanuman what had happened while the Swami was in stasis. 'You have done well, my son,' the Swami replied. He looked at the world below, the gap through which a rope-thing hung. 'And how convenient that this has opened above the secret cavern. We are in control at last.'

'Then our combined power zapped Kunkali with enough force . . .'

'Yes, *she* is incapacitated. But only for the moment. Come, we must hurry.' Hanuman entered the gap and started to descend.

Nirmal looked down. The height was considerable. He bent, gripped the 'rope', and followed his master, trying to keep his eyes level as he did so.

It was a descent through a series of clouds. Nirmal searched for the source, and saw a quartet of fumaroles high, high above in what must have been the cavern's ceiling. Nirmal wasn't sure, but he thought he saw star constellations when the mist cleared from the fumarole openings. Quickly, he lowered his eyes, since looking into that spatial vastness made him feel that he was falling upwards.

Hanuman disappeared into a cloud cover beneath him. Nirmal also entered the cloud, which proved to be moist and warm like steam. For a long time, he continued to descend in a blinding swirl of meshing woolliness.

Nirmal's limbs were becoming heavy; pain shot through his back, from his shoulder blades to the upper musculature of his arms. His deltoids were stretched beyond endurance, he thought. Brief memory flashes of what he had already undergone passed through his mind; this was certainly no time to fail himself. Nirmal willed: Don't stop, just go on, and don't think about the pain. He passed through more cloud cover and was suddenly startled to find himself totally exposed in the next moment.

He had only about twenty feet to go. Hanuman was already waiting at the bottom. For an instant, Nirmal paused, surveying his surroundings. To his left, almost parallel with the 'rope', was a pit, a crevice that reminded him of another split in the ground earlier. He could barely see within it. He was positive that it was another vertigo-inducing endless drop like the fumaroles. Steam or fog or whatever it was seeped from the pit edge. Looking over his right shoulder, Nirmal's hackles rose. Through the roiling haze he saw a dais and the back of what he knew had to be the Huzoor. There were others with him. He recognized the big Indian woman who had come to the Kitteridge place and tried to set up Hanuman for a *rumel*'s loop. On a backless divan, lying on pillows, was Santha in a sari, her eyes closed.

The Huzoor was speaking. Beyond the dais, visible in small rents in the brazier smoke, was his audience, the ashram Thugs. And further to their right was the cage. Nirmal started to move down again.

On the ground, he paused, waiting for the pain in his limbs to subside. Hanuman touched him gently. He pointed to a pile of guns and ammunition near the crevice's lip. It had to be the weapons belonging to the detectives. They were obviously placed there to be thrown into the pit. Thuggee had no need of guns.

But the detectives did. Nirmal and Hanuman rushed to the pile and proceeded to gather the weapons, putting them in jacket pockets, waistbands, wherever possible. There were too many of them to take all at once. Hanuman then pointed towards the cage and led the way.

Cautious, moving on cat feet, they kept as much behind the roiling smoke wall as possible. An automatic fell from Nirmal's pocket. The sound was muffled by the mob's chanting; fortunately, the gun's safety catch was on. Nirmal picked it up, took a deep breath and continued.

Rama Shastri mentally reviewed the plan. He didn't like it, but he had to admit it was the best and only one that could be developed under the circumstances. The rage that had spread within these men was truly something unforeseen. Professionally, they were all smarting; but that had become the least of their grievances.

Worst was the massacre they had been forced to witness.

All those victims, like lambs lured to slaughter; weak from hunger, undermined by the oppression, a kind of slavery based on the denial of basic necessities. Perhaps death had been welcomed by some, especially those victimized by their own former loved ones.

Even to his mind, the Thugs were no longer human. Monsters, demons – any antonym of 'human' fitted.

Stephen Wrench was probably the most affected. Shastri was more worried about him than the plan. Since the killings, Wrench had been mumbling to himself like a man deranged. Shastri, after much effort, managed to make sense of the barely audible words running into each other. The shocking meaning had Shastri's head spinning:

'I've got to destroy her,' he had heard. 'I've got to destroy my little girl.'

Pulling George Buchan aside, Shastri revealed what he'd heard. George listened; he was extremely pale. 'I must confess it's turned me, too!'

'Santha isn't responsible,' Shastri retorted. 'You've heard Hanuman explain why she's so vulnerable. She's like a receptor . . . her psyche . . .'

'It's difficult to believe she's somehow not responsible. Some unresolved area, some psychological susceptibility to . . .'

Rama Shastri walked away. It had disturbed him as well, Santha coming down from the dais and gesturing that the *rumels* were to be used. But one look at her face had been enough to convince him. It was Kali, all right, acting through Santha's body. No more than that.

Steve – well, he probably thought that the only way to save his 'little girl' was through her death. The big man had snapped. Rama Shastri next enlisted the help of Captain Condorelli, who understood. He agreed to keep an eye on Wrench, too, if they ever escaped.

Assessing George again, Shastri thought: So much for psychiatry. Then, no. George had been more than loyal to Santha all these years. It was little more than a momentary reaction.

The men moved about restlessly. Of the fifteen who had gone into the cavern, only one was dead. Although some of the detectives had been quick to point that out, most realized that they had been spared for further 'sport'. In short, it had been a bad show for the pros, Shastri thought. He realized that crooks in general were stupid; not anywhere near as innovative as Leinster. Not as bizarre, nor as sadistic, nor as evil, nor as . . . Shastri shook himself; thinking was an ordeal at the moment.

All these men – closed in; sometimes it was a distraction: their chatter, whispering mostly, with bursts of anger, a curse . . . still, it was nervous talk all around him. And the flocculent grey swirls were oppressive.

Every so often, someone touched the bars, only to pull his hand away rapidly. Even Shastri had been curious after seeing Wrench almost lose consciousness when he gripped them in his earlier frenzy. He had touched the bars, too.

The sensation wasn't anything so blatant as an electric shock. What passed through his body was much more subtle. Similar to a sickness that comes on in waves: weakness, nausea. Chiefly revulsion towards the black substance.

That it was similar to but different from the rope-things was obvious. The 'ropes' were touchable, or nobody would have been able to use them. At first, he thought that only the Thugs were allowed to grip them but then recalled that Hanuman and Nirmal had been successful. He wondered about those two, amazed they weren't in the cage, as well. Where were they? Were they still alive?

The bars, black as the 'ropes', were different in that they pulsated a poisonous rejection. That was the way Shastri pictured it, as if they were live things, sentient and poisonous with hatred.

He forced his mind to wander, studying the cavern again. The vastness was overwhelming. If he brooded on it too long, he felt reduced to a microcosmic scale. Medieval churches gave him the same feeling. That he was neither underground nor above ground in the heart of a mountain, but instead in space displaced from thousands of miles' distance, made it even more evanescent.

Leinster was speaking from the dais now, and it caught Shastri's attention. The tone of his voice more than the words informed him of what Leinster was saying. He was rallying the gathering for another massacre; and, remembering those faces responding as one mind earlier, Shastri shuddered. A crowd, a mob, to be more precise, was indeed a most terrible beast.

The murkiness had increased everywhere, he noted. Smoke from braziers and torches and then again the billowing steam from the pit and the fumaroles. Were they the result of volcanic roots? But how? There were no volcanos in the Himalayas. It was perhaps the displacement that caused it – all those energies unleashed in the process of moving a piece of the East to the other side of the world.

Leinster's voice was even louder, his followers were chanting in reply. They would be coming to the cage soon. Then, the plan – to rush the Thugs the moment the cage was opened. No weapons – just muscle and brute strength. Condorelli's men felt they could possibly win in that kind of struggle.

But Shastri, thinking of the phenomenon of the swollen Thug hands, swollen through supernatural influence and power, wasn't so sure. Hands so influenced had the strength of two men, easily.

There was a commotion behind Shastri, at the rear of the cage. Hernandez hurried to Condorelli. 'Captain, Captain – it's that swami and the kid.'

Condorelli followed him, Rama Shastri behind.

Cavanaugh and Thurnauer were holding guns and bullet clips that Hanuman and Nirmal were handing to them between the bars.

'Where have you been?' Shastri whispered.

'That is for a later telling,' the Swami explained. 'Heed my words. Notice. The multitude is silent. They are meditating. Kali will grant them the force to kill successfully. Be prepared for such power. I must leave now. There is something I must do immediately. Nirmal will bring you the other guns.' The Swami turned, and disappeared behind a series of pillars.

'Have you seen Santha?' Wrench demanded.

'She's on a divan on the dais,' Nirmal explained, handing a gun to Shastri, a Mab autoloading pistol. Wrench already had his Browning .38.

Wrench grunted.

Condorelli said, 'See if you can hurry with the rest of the stuff. This only arms seven of us.'

'I'll try to do it all in one trip,' Nirmal told him.

'Hurry! Those guns are essential.'

Nirmal went.

They all listened to the silence.

'When the meditation ends, they'll come for us.' It was Thurnauer.

'Tell me something I don't know,' snapped the captain.

'Remember,' Shastri cautioned, trying to get the attention of every detective present, 'they acquire great power from this meditation. Kali infuses them with great power, skirting the usual Thuggee training period. Their hands become overdeveloped, weapons in themselves. That force goes behind the *rumel* when they wield it. You've heard all this before, but it can't be repeated enough. Be very, very careful.'

Later, Hernandez checked his watch. 'Six minutes. The kid's been gone six minutes.' A murmur from the meditators. 'Holy Mary, they're coming out of it. Where's the kid?'

'Here,' Nirmal told him. He had taken his jacket off, filled it and tied it up like a sack. 'This is all of it,' he added.

'Did you arm yourself, kid?'

Nirmal, wincing at the 'kid', nodded. 'I've got to join Swami Hanuman.' He didn't wait for the murmurs of 'thanks' that came from the men.

'If I survive this, remind me to buy all his recordings,' Hernandez said.

'I guess Jerome couldn't get to us,' Cavanaugh said.

'Yeah,' Condorelli replied, 'we've already discussed that, too. Can't anybody be original?'

'Sorry, Cap, we're all on edge.'

'Me, too,' Condorelli admitted.

'I meant, Jerome could've got some of the SWAT team stuff, the rifles, the tear gas . . . We left them in the cars.'

Captain Condorelli made a wry face.

'Kurt Leinster would have found a way around that, too,' Rama Shastri told him. 'Don't blame yourself. At least, we have our handguns back.'

'Thugs die from bullets like anyone else,' Wrench informed them all. His tone was grim. 'Count on it.'

Finally, seven members of the cult, all men, approached the cage. One of them, massive, bearded, and Indian, held a torch. They were led by Vic Croce.

He stared at them.

'Look at the smile on that bastard's face,' growled Wrench.

If Croce overheard him, he didn't show it. He continued to stare. Every prisoner was in sight, since the small room for Santha's privacy when she was trapped there no longer existed. Also, the one door into the cage was now in the front – large and, as before, opening from the outside.

'Gentlemen,' Croce said at last, 'the time has come. I have been observing you at my leisure, savouring every suspenseful moment you endure awaiting your doom. It must be a mental torment all by itself. And the humiliation – imagine: Boston's Finest helpless at the hands of a group of unarmed civilians. That is, unarmed except for these.' He showed them a *rumel*.

'Yeah, we know,' Condorelli said. 'You're a hotshot Strangler. But you're also a maggot, in case you didn't know.'

'Captain, Captain. You would probably call a drug pusher or a rapist the very same. Surely – '

'I can do him one better,' Wrench cut in. 'You're an impotent little toad getting his hots off playing Thuggee. You didn't strangle your wife a while ago because of any deeply felt religious belief. You just killed her because you couldn't fulfil her like a man could.'

When Croce's smile dissolved, the detectives cheered.

'You hit home, Steve,' Condorelli said.

Croce's fingers went to his beard. He tugged at it. 'You will see what inspiration is,' he vowed. He shaped a swollen hand into a fist. 'I was the first to hear the call of Kali in my dreams. I was the very first of the ashram.'

'Bullshit,' someone said.

'Yeah, sell it somewhere else.'

'You're first, all right. A number one asshole.'

Laughter.

'You think to rush us when we open this cage,' Croce shouted. 'But we have prepared for that emergency. Only a few will be released at a time. The rest will have to watch their comrades die. And so it will continue until you are all . . . fit to fill our sacred *bele*. Then I will laugh and celebrate, eat and drink while sitting on your grave. It is a Thug custom, you know.' He nodded to one of his men and to the torchbearer. 'Begin. Our lord awaits them.'

The Thug bent and released the lock to the cage, the torchbearer at his side. Everyone in the cage was silent as if holding their breath. The Thug pulled the door open.

Wrench, who was in the lead, stepped out, then Condorelli, Cavanaugh and Shastri. The torchbearer stepped forward, holding the flames in the faces of the rest. The torch burned hungrily, the flames stretched, jumped at them.

'These will suffice for now,' Croce was saying.

'You think,' Wrench said calmly, and he pressed the trigger of his Browning. He held it in his topcoat pocket. A muffled report, smouldering fabric, and the torchbearer fell. Wrench fired again, this time with the gun exposed, and another Thug fell, blood gushing from his throat.

Condorelli meanwhile was on one knee. The Thug who had opened the cage door had pulled him out by the arm, and the captain had slipped and fallen. Then, when Wrench fired his first shot, the Thug flung himself on Condorelli's back, sliding his *rumel* over his face. The *rumel* tightened immediately. Condorelli grabbed for the scarf with his free hand; his gun was still stuck in his jacket pocket with his other hand. Pinioned as he was, he couldn't pull his arm free.

The world about him turned into jolts of light against a black background. He was slipping fast, he knew, but, try as he would, he couldn't stop the pressure against his windpipe. He faded and woke a second later, coughing sputum on himself. 'You OK, Cap?' he heard, and he slowly focused on Hernandez's face. Apparently, the rest of the detectives had escaped from the cage, and one of them had saved him. He nodded, staring at the scene before him.

They were surrounded. At least five Thugs were dead at his feet. A short distance to his right lay Sterns on his back, another loss.

The encircling Thugs were separated from Condorelli's group by a few yards. Vic Croce, he saw, had retreated to them, and they stood waiting, silent and expectant. Stephen Wrench suddenly jumped forward. Both his hands were busy, one with his gun, the other with the torch. Taunting and cursing them under his breath, he kept moving and they kept backing. Rama Shastri stood to his left, keeping pace with every step. Wrench lunged again. This time the edge of the flame caught Croce's beard; he screamed, beating at his face. A woman pulled him to her, lifted her dress, and so smothered the fire.

Wrench was chuckling under his breath. George Buchan rushed to his right now. He and Shastri were there to protect him, since the big man had gone berserk. Cavanaugh joined Buchan, and snarled back to the men, 'Get in here, you, Donahue, you, Collins. Don't let him do it alone.'

Every one of the men had seemed stunned without the captain. Condorelli cursed; they were trained better than that. Yet, he understood. These criminals were extremely different. He could count six, seven, women among them, one elderly.

He found his voice. 'Don't forget how easily they killed those other folk. Even kids, they wasted,' he rasped.

That spurred them. And it was at just the right moment, too. The circle around Wrench and the rest was expanding.

Shastri didn't hesitate. He steadied his pistol with both hands. One, two, three of them, men, went down wounded.

'That's the idea!' Condorelli urged. 'Incapacitate them. Let 'em sink in their own blood.'

He was able to move faster now. Hernandez nevertheless stayed with him in case he was needed. Condorelli tried to shake off the fuzziness in his head. The jolting flashes lingered, although they weren't as strong now.

Condorelli had just about reached Cavanaugh when a wild shriek turned his blood cold. Gunfire echoed and reverberated enough in this vast place, but that was very bearable compared to the shriek. It was a banshee's cry magnified ten times ten. The crowd of Thugs split apart as it neared, and Wrench and the rest saw Mrinalini Pal charging at them. Both her arms were extended as she held two braziers of oil and coals aloft. Wrench cried out a warning, and fired. If he had hit her, it didn't slow down the charge. She continued to plunge into the fray. Then, when she was near enough to them, Mrinalini paused and hurled the braziers.

'Cover your heads!' Condorelli commanded. Topcoats, jackets were yanked up. The contents of the braziers – burning oil, blazing coals – descended like a torrent from Hell.

Nirmal, aware that there was no time to spare, hurried along beyond the dais. There were columns, as in a temple, that he was able to speed to and hide himself behind until the next rush into the open. Also, a wall of basalt bordered the rear of the dais, and he was thus invisible to anyone on the other side. Nirmal reached a column to the right of the dais and searched for his master.

The stillness of the multitude had ended. The Huzoor was asking for the prisoners. Ajit Majumdar stood with him. Both had their backs turned from Santha on her bed of pillows.

The roiling smoke had spread, a grey wash over the scene. Nirmal's eyes smarted. The figures on the dais were delineated for a second, then became silhouettes, then were clearly visible again. Close by, where Santha lay, the shadows were even darker. Nirmal thought he saw movement there.

He did. The outline of Hanuman rose from the floor and was bending over Santha. The Swami had crawled along the dais until he reached her. Nirmal pulled his revolver from his waistband – the one he had lost earlier outside the barn and found again in the weaponry pile. He gripped it firmly, and lowered himself.

Keeping to the floor and the shadow splotches, Nirmal crawled to join his master. Slowly, he edged along on his elbows and knees, pausing now and then to see what the Huzoor and his leading Thug guru were up to.

So far, they hadn't turned in the direction of Hanuman and Santha.

Nirmal was about to rise at the Swami's side when he heard the shots. Hanuman had been chanting in a low voice in Santha's ear, and he didn't even hesitate when the sounds of the battle rang out. He continued to speak to Santha, whose eyes were closed as if in sleep.

Again Nirmal turned to see what the Huzoor was doing. The fierce, sullen giantess had appeared, and the Huzoor was giving her commands. She nodded, took two of the braziers and hurried towards the din.

Nirmal was now on his feet. There was only one torch, in a wall sconce, on this side of the hall, and there was much darkness.

'Now you may release the breath of Kali. The Sleeper has been confounded in her bower. Her force has lessened for a time,' Hanuman was telling Santha. 'I summon you, entity of Kunkali, leave this vessel immediately, by the name of Vishnu of the many incarnations, by Matsya the Fish, by Kūrma the Tortoise, by Varāha the Boar, by Parasurāma Rama with the Axe, and by the prince of the Ayodā. *Leave her now!*'

Santha's eyes opened wide. Her mouth opened also, lips forming a circle as if she were blowing out air. Hanuman motioned to Nirmal as he backed away. They were to keep their distance. From Santha, black tendrils poured; they curled and slithered through the air. To Nirmal it looked like the ectoplasm of the darkest of spirits.

It continued to weave and snake across the room. More and more poured forth until the darkness grew thick and viscous.

The din of battle continued to dominate everything. Now the Huzoor's ranting could be heard thundering: 'It had to be the Swami and the *chela* who brought them their guns. How did those two escape Kali Ma's trap? Where are they now? Search everywhere . . .' And, with that, Nirmal saw him spin to point at the space beyond the dais. The Huzoor saw then the black tendrils. His eyes traced the source; he shouted, 'There they are. Kill them, my noble Majumdar! Kill in the name of Kali!'

Screams, curses, bellows. The screams were by far the most disturbing, as they were made by otherwise hard, brave men. The coals burned through heavy, thick material, even the leather of gloves, but they were the least deadly.

It was the burning oil that played havoc with everything that made a man; it seared flesh and splashed into the most cherished parts of the face. Hernandez fought with only one eye functioning after the oil landed; Donahue was victimized by so much of it that the *rumel* death he met seemed welcome. But, instead of cowering, Condorelli's people reacted twice as fiercely. No longer were there restraints on their instincts because some of the enemy were female.

Mrinalini Pal had ensured that. She'd stripped the female image of the Thug women down to its predatory heart. Bullets hit the mark or ricocheted like a hailstorm of lead. Skilled in sidearms, most of the detectives fired automatically, despite burning fabric or hair or even bodies. They had sensed rightly that the Thugs would rush in immediately after the brazier contents landed. It became a matter of shoot now and self-repair later.

It was a fortunate reaction. The aisle through which Mrinalini had raced closed after her attack, with the result that Thug after Thug collapsed on one another as they fell wounded or dead.

Yet some broke through, which was how Donahue died. Cavanaugh was nearly the next victim, but Thurnauer used his gun butt on the head of the Thug, a portly man with a size seventeen neck. The *rumel* loosened, then retightened. 'Christ,' Condorelli cried, 'shoot him!' and fired into one temple. Simultaneously, Thurnauer emptied one of his automatics into the other side. Blood and grey matter mushroomed on to all three policemen. Some of it sizzled in the burning patches of their clothing.

Stephen Wrench, still the berserker, was firing and smashing and butting his way through, seeking a way to the dais. Shastri had been left behind where he stood over George Buchan, who was recovering from a glancing blow of the brazier against his neck. As he knelt, he was still able to shoot at the swarm of legs and hit at least three. Shastri meanwhile held his own, a strange sight – his eyebrows had been completely singed.

'Go on ahead, help Steve,' George told him. 'I'm OK. Seeing one of everything now instead of two.'

Shastri bounded into the gap, sidestepped a shrieking woman who held a *rumel* in a blood-covered fist, fired down at a hand that gripped his ankle and immediately let go, and scrambled up the dais. He heard Wrench shout, 'Santha!' and saw the big arm rise, the gun at its end. Shastri threw himself at him. The shot went wild.

'You fool, can't you see Hanuman's with her?' Shastri screamed. 'She's free now. He released whatever was gripping her soul.'

Eyes glazed, tears streaming, Wrench said, 'She's better off dead, Ram. After . . .'

'You crazed fool – it wasn't her fault. Stop and think, man!'

But there was no time. Mrinalini Pal emerged from the murky screen and charged again.

Nirmal fired and missed Ajit Majumdar. Until the incident at the barn, he had only fired a gun twice before, and that was at his father's home on the fringe of Bombay years ago. That he was a terrible shot, he well knew; he decided to conserve his bullets and wait until the Thug was so close he couldn't miss.

The Huzoor summoned Majumdar back, however. Nirmal began to follow Hanuman as he led Santha away from the dais.

Then came Wrench's call. Stunned as she was, Santha had turned and headed back.

The curlicues of grey and black closed in. Wrench's view of Santha misted over, but another opening had formed, exposing the crouching giantess, Mrinalini. The war cry, a growl that rose to a high frenzy, came from her lips like a sonic wave. The two men stood rooted to the spot for an instant, while the sound plucked at their ganglia. Both knew fear then, and they were not men to feel emotion easily. Mrinalini's *rumel* flapped like a batwing in the long reach of the woman. It was around Wrench's neck before he realized what had happened. Shastri sprang at her, his gun directed towards her stomach. Her foot rose, she kneed Shastri in the groin, and he fell back.

His rush did save Wrench's life, however. Her grip on the *rumel* had weakened for a fraction while she concentrated on Shastri, and Wrench capitalized on it. Both his arms rose, and he pushed his elbows back hard. Mrinalini grunted, and the *rumel* fell free.

Wrench grabbed at her but she evaded him. Her teeth

sank into the wrist of his gun hand, and his gun clattered to the floor. Mrinalini interlocked her fingers, making her big hands into a weapon. She swung her double fist like a sledgehammer at Wrench's jaw. The blow drove Wrench staggering across the dais. Mrinalini leaped at him with her *rumel* again.

'Daddy! Daddy!' Santha said softly, then louder. Nirmal tried to stop her, but she disappeared in the cloudiness. 'This fog is unnatural, Bapu,' he said then. But when he looked for Hanuman, the Swami was gone.

Santha emerged from the density. The Huzoor's throne was ahead and, leaning against it, the sacred pickaxe. Santha, hearing a sound, went forward and seized it. She turned, and saw Majumdar before her. His feral eyes gleamed for a moment as they met hers, but then he backed away. Santha was holding the pickaxe high, threatening with every motion of her body to use it.

The sight of the sacred object, of the vessel of Kali wielding it, gripped his superstitious soul. He turned and ran into the mist.

Santha pursued. Something deep in her urged her to do so. She was afire; the restored self within her drove her across the dais. She ran blindly but saw within a hazy image of her father. 'Daddy,' Santha whispered. She heard a gunshot nearby and increased her speed.

Santha broke through into a clearing. She saw Mrinalini's broad back as she lowered her *rumel* to Wrench's neck. Santha swung the pickaxe, swung it with all her strength, that it would drink deeply.

Rama Shastri crawled; the pain was excruciating. He had seen the giantess heading for where she had sent Wrench reeling. He finally managed to stand, and moved slowly, the Mab pistol dangling at his side.

A figure bounded into the small clear area ahead. It turned, and Shastri faced Ajit Majumdar. The Thug saw that Shastri was in pain, that he doubled over with each step.

Majumdar's jagged teeth showed as he smiled. 'Ah, so it is destined,' he said with confidence, and approached, the yellow scarf taut.

Rama Shastri shot from the hip. Majumdar's body jerked. He stared with disbelief at the spreading red stain across his tunic. 'Nothing is destined. Ever,' Shastri told him.

Majumdar fell back into the roiling barrier.

Another area cleared suddenly and Shastri groaned. He had been much too slow. Mrinalini was bent over Steve, who was trying to rise. Her *rumel* was already around his neck. Shastri quickly raised his Mab, hoping he wasn't too late.

He held his fire when he heard a crunching, then a sloshing noise, and saw blood gush from Mrinalini's mouth like vomit. From the dense smoke wall behind her emerged Santha.

Mrinalini's chin dropped, the blood pooled at her feet. Her eyes were childlike, as if she had spilled something and was watching it spread. Then came the splosh of her inner organs pushing forth through her torn sari. Santha had put more weight on the axe handle and forced the point down into the abdomen.

Wrench rolled away from the blood and gore. Mrinalini's eyes became opaque. She fell; her face thudded against the floor. She bounced slightly and was finally still.

Stephen Wrench's smile spoke loudly. A great burden had just left his shoulders. Santha had demonstrated that she was free, was herself. He reached for her and held her close.

Feet pounded behind Shastri. George Buchan appeared. 'There she is, old man,' Shastri said. Santha saw him. She left Wrench and came forward. Again the fog curtain parted, hands appeared, grabbed, pulled her in. Santha's cry was immediately muffled.

Kurt Leinster's voice spoke from behind the veil of churning, threading fogginess. 'How tragic. Again the two lovers are separated.' His laughter was like a blow. To a man, Wrench, George and Shastri winced.

'What is this soup?' It was Condorelli, who was suddenly at Shastri's side with a few men. 'Smoke, steam, fog – Christ!'

'All you say and more,' Shastri murmured. 'Leinster's powers control the elements here.'

The voice spoke again, at a further distance. 'Please, gentlemen, please come and witness our departure.'

And the density separated, exposing what appeared to be a way through it, like a tunnel.

Wrench and George went in. Shastri moved very slowly; he was preceded by the captain and the two detectives.

'I hope that you're following, especially George,' the voice goaded. 'You always were the prince of idiots. So faithful and true, like one of those stock heroes in the old melodramas. Not a treacherous cell in your body. The good man, the caring doctor . . .'

'That's correct – everything you're not, you fucking creep,' George shouted. 'Why don't you show yourself? Or are you afraid of me, Kurt?'

'Now, that's so damn obvious, George. Using your bag of psychiatric tricks to lure me into a trap.'

'His voice is fading!' Wrench cried.

'Yes, *Daddy*.' Kurt said the word with mockery. 'Don't you understand, Santha and I are going away for a while. Together. Together. You hear that, George?'

'Show yourself, you bastard!' George screamed.

'Easy, boy. Careful,' Condorelli told him. He had just joined them. They all waited in the silence. The air was dense again. Everywhere. They could barely see each other.

'Christ, has he gone? Is she . . .?' From Wrench.

'No, *Daddy*,' they heard then. 'We're still here. Santha isn't speaking right now. I've gagged her, you see. I'm afraid you're stuck with little old me.'

Wrench swallowed. 'Look,' he pleaded, 'take me instead. Take my life. It's lives you want, essentially, isn't it? Kill me instead and let my daughter go. Please, man, if you have any soul left in you.'

'Touching.'

'Is that all you can say?'

'You'd really like to see her. Just one more time, hey?'

'Consider what I've said, man.'

'I'll give you one last peek, I'm so touched.'

Wrench held his breath. The air became more and more transparent.

'The soup's dissolving,' Condorelli whispered in awe.

Then they saw Leinster before his throne. Santha was bound and gagged, propped up against a pillar. Ajit Majumdar, his tunic torn at the shoulder, a tourniquet fastened near his wound, was standing a foot below his Huzoor.

Leinster held a scroll in his hand. 'This is what defeats you each time,' he ranted. 'This is my power source.'

'He mustn't read from it,' Shastri stated. He had finally reached the others.

'You have failed this time,' they heard. 'Santha will be taken with me, and we will return again – reborn with the sacred quick of Kali Mother.'

His eyes lowered to the scroll, his lips moved. Wrench,

Shastri and the others started to run forward. There was still half of the dais to cover.

The shot rang out. It ricocheted off the stone backdrop behind the throne. The Huzoor raised his eyes . . .

Nirmal, who had come from behind the wall and fired, stood now before Leinster. He aimed again. Leinster looked up, his lips still moving. The cavern trembled. Nirmal lost his footing, slipped to his knees. Ajit Majumdar bounded to Nirmal's side. His *rumel* rose.

Rama Shastri had limped forward. The quaking had stopped those around him in their tracks, but he had continued. Now, he too stopped, and held his Mab steady while he aimed. Very swiftly he did this, since he was a crack shot in nearly all conditions. He fired. Ajit Majumdar's forehead burst open.

Kurt Leinster, the Huzoor, Lord of all Thuggee, knew he had no time to read his scroll now. With long strides he left the throne area and sped beyond it. The fog had descended again, a great pall that spread within seconds.

'He's heading for the pit!' George Buchan shouted. He was the first among those in pursuit.

At the pit's edge, Leinster looked back, the silver in his eyes like static. He held the Rishi Scroll of Power in one hand. The pursuers saw him leap with tremendous agility to the 'rope' above the abyss. Then he proceeded to climb it, his laughter resounding behind him.

George Buchan, others, fired their weapons. No one seemed to hit the mark.

George groaned, then, looking again, cried out, 'Look!'

They froze, staring at what was happening with disbelief. Hanuman had appeared from nowhere, it seemed, and, with the agility of the Monkey God whose name he'd taken, leaped at Leinster's legs. He was now working his hands up to Leinster's waist and, once there, in one motion lifted himself to the other's back. The Swami chopped with his free hand at Leinster's wrist. Leinster's eyes bulged as the scroll slid from his numbed fingers.

Leinster started to chant then, rushing the mantra words as fast as possible. Hanuman chopped at Leinster's throat, slid down to Leinster's legs again and somersaulted in mid-air to land on the pit's edge.

Above him, Leinster was holding his neck, desperately gasping for air. He tried to keep his legs wrapped around the 'rope', but his lack of balance defeated his effort. The legs fell free. Wrench, George and Condorelli reached the edge in time to see Leinster fall and fall, to be sucked through a fumarole into the interstellar reaches.

'Now we must leave this place with much haste,' Hanuman announced.

They didn't have to be told twice. A tremendous rumble ran through the entire cavern. Santha was quickly untied, and she was able to move as rapidly as anybody.

The only laggards were Shastri, Hernandez and Thurnauer, who had been wounded. The two detectives were soon freighted by Jerome Abel and his group, who had suddenly turned up. The door of the barn had burst open when the quakes began, allowing their entry.

Stalactites fell everywhere behind them. The detectives had one prisoner, the only survivor of the Thug cult willing to leave. The rest – nine of them – chose to stay with Vic Croce, who sat among the bodies and detritus like a forlorn dwarf. The willing survivor was Mauna, who, breaking her vow of silence, begged the detectives, 'Help me.'

They made the barn in safety. As the door shut, those who looked back saw the walls of the alcove chamber dissolving. Wrench lowered Shastri from his back. He had carried his friend all the way.

'The phenomenon of the displaced space is over,'

Hanuman stated, staring at the door. 'It will now open to the world as we know it to be.'

Some of them nodded in agreement. The rest sat there looking at the Swami and then towards the door. They sat or stood and rested and waited until they were breathing normally. No one ventured to test Hanuman's theory, however. The door remained shut.

30

The woman didn't move. Santha Wrench suppressed a sob for what seemed to be the nine hundredth time. The woman sat in her nightdress and bathrobe, her clipped grey hair now swept back above her ears in neat brushed strokes. Santha had just finished brushing it, chattering all the while as if everything were normal.

Annette Kitteridge hadn't even blinked. Her gaze was on a point somewhere beyond time or place. She was totally out of contact, as the hospital staff described it. Various medications had been attempted, and shock therapy; nothing had helped.

Would she ever come back? Santha forced the question from her mind. Annette had to return to life, to be restored, be whole again. To fly again, soar in her Beachcraft Bonanza as if she were queen of Heaven and Earth. At the controls, Santha repeated, at the controls, at the'. . .

Santha pulled up a chair near her friend, took the long, narrow fingers and gripped them tightly. The action was desperate. It held a wish dream of healing, as if her touch were enough. Santha knew this, but it was founded on the logic: *Maybe she'll feel my love and that will be enough.*

But love could no more heal than any touching or tears. Annette Kitteridge was catatonic. She had to be washed, dressed and undressed, fed, and taken care of in every way.

God damn Kurt Leinster, Santha raged. She had seen him fall into the crevice months ago. Those present at the edge of the drop had told her he had fallen into an endless abyss, doomed to wander in an unimaginable interstellar reach. Somehow, it didn't seem to be punishment enough.

If only I had been able to do to him what I did to Mrinalini Pal, she thought. The strong atavistic feelings had left her, but she felt no guilt whatsoever about the deed. After all, she had saved her father's life. But it was more than that, she knew; she had finally grown up: there were times when killing was justified. Nature's blessing was behind the act, and, in its way, that was a kind of morality.

Strange, she realized, I will never understand the motivations of Kurt Leinster and his followers. Why such evil exists in this life is as much a mystery as Creation itself; but it does, and, by that fact, it must be dealt with, unpleasant as the task can be.

Santha looked into Annette's eyes. They were still focused on that private place that kept Annette a prisoner.

'Oh, sweet, sweet dear,' Santha began, 'I don't think you can hear me, but I must tell you anyway.'

Santha paused. The sunlight from the small room's window seemed to illuminate Annette's face. Outside the room, Santha heard the food trolley coming down the hall and the clatter of trays. It was the lunch hour, nearly noon. Soon she must leave for the airport.

'I'm going away, Annette,' Santha began. 'To India. And I'm not sure why. Lately, my sweet dear, there are so many, many things I can't reason out or explain. But I'll try. I'll even write these ideas for you later in a letter, and maybe some day you'll understand.

'I must go. It hasn't been an easy decision. There's George to think of, after all, and Daddy. You see, they won't be coming with me. Oh, Daddy will come to India to see me – that's if I stay any length of time, of course –

but George, well, I don't know exactly how that's going to turn out, Annette.

'Don't misunderstand me – I still love him. But things have changed since . . . It so happened that back there in that terrible cavern, George saw me transformed. I remember how I looked and what I did, too. This time it's perfectly clear, but as if I am observing someone else when I remember it. *And it was someone else*, Annette, just like it wasn't really you who attacked me.

'We were possessed, and, because we were, it is understandable. To us.

'But to George it made a difference. Oh, I realize that it's unfair to expect otherwise just because he is a psychiatrist. He is, after all, a human being first and then my lover, but it nevertheless affected me very badly. I especially needed his love – well, after it was over – but he couldn't help me for a while. He kept seeing Kali in me ordering the execution of those poor ashram folk.'

She shuddered, and bit her lower lip.

'His reaction set me to thinking about things. About why I was always so vulnerable to possession, matters like that. Swami Hanuman, bless him, has told me I am merely more receptive than most others, that it has nothing to do with the good or the bad of me. I am psychic, I suppose, but I'm afraid this trait has worked against me.

'Now George claims that his revulsion is over, that everything is as it always was. But *I'm* not convinced, Annette. I must regain a belief in myself. Even stronger than before, if possible. I need some distance from everybody and everything here. So I've decided to return to India. Perhaps there I can acquire some perspective.'

Santha stopped talking. For a long time she stared at Annette, hoping.

At last, with a sigh, she concluded, 'I'm leaving now,

sweet dear. I must get to the airport. George arranged that I could see you at this hour, and it's been . . .' She struggled with the tears that were coming. Quickly, she went to Annette, hugged her, kissed her hair, her cheeks, her eyes. She couldn't speak another word. Taking her bag, Santha rushed from the room.

Santha had just arrived in the cab, Shastri saw from the waiting room. She was smart in not allowing George to drive her. He might influence her at the last moment, and Shastri felt it was imperative she take this trip. Yes, George might stew for a while, but it would be good for him, too. Wasn't there something about absence making the heart grow fonder?

He thought then of the letter in his pocket. Yes, sometimes that really worked.

Besides, what a send-off, considering it was supposed to be for just a handful of months. Or would it? Did they all sense that she would remain in India longer than that?

Shastri watched almost every male in the place stare at her as she entered. He would have to get used to that. Santha was so striking that men couldn't resist gaping. She was to stay at his home in Jaipur, Rajasthan, and he was certain she would have the same effect on men there.

Shastri stood now, from the chair he had been sitting in, watching the hubbub outside the massive terminal window. He went to join the rest, using his cane. The doctors had estimated it would be another month before the bruising around his groin would lessen.

It was a marvellous send-off, he thought again. Steve and George were present, of course. But Nirmal and Hanuman were also here. And surprisingly, considering their busy schedules, Captain Condorelli, Cavanaugh, Thurnauer, his arm in a sling – broken during a struggle when he fell down the dais steps – and Jerome Abel.

Shastri knew these lawmen had come to show Santha that they thought her innocent. He felt grateful. George, pale, the side of his neck still bandaged from the blow he had received, and Nirmal helped carry her luggage in.

'Remember, old friend, I'm counting on you to keep an eye on her,' Wrench muttered under his breath.

'Steve, I mustn't be imposing. I'll watch her, but I must respect that Santha . . . She's a grown woman now.'

Wrench grinned slyly. 'You've never been in a fatherly position before. Odds are, you'll be as much of a pain in the ass at it as I am.'

Shastri started. He hadn't thought of it that way. He had always been the observing adopted uncle before. He frowned.

Captain Condorelli approached him. He extended a hand. 'I've enjoyed working with you, Rama.'

'And I with you, Vinnie,' he replied.

Condorelli looked at Santha. 'Think she'll be OK? I mean, after . . . what happened?'

'I believe she'll be.'

'Hell, it could've been one of my daughters.'

Shastri nodded. Secretly, he thought it was very unlikely. Santha had been chosen by the Huzoor because she fitted certain requirements. A major one being her Indian side.

He heard Hanuman say, 'You are loved, Santha, as you can see. Justifiably so. Remember, my master, Vishnarma, will be with you as he is with me always.'

George and Nirmal returned from depositing the luggage. Santha approached Nirmal. Shastri thought he saw both of them start. Something magnetic had passed between them. She had been holding his hand, but now, despite herself, she hugged him.

'Now, there's a lad who became a man overnight,' Cavanaugh said.

Shastri had noticed that, too. But it was more than his manhood Nirmal had discovered, Shastri concluded. Nirmal – the being who faced Santha Wrench now – had been forged in the fires of the gods.

'Yes, we have all changed,' he mused aloud.

The detectives were silent, thinking of the dead – Fontaine, Sterns, Collins, a few others – and the half-blind Hernandez. It hadn't been an easy battle.

Then Thurnauer did the unexpected. And Shastri found himself stammering. Pulling a small book with an embossed cover from his pocket, Thurnauer opened to a blank page and held up a pen. 'Could I have your autograph, sir?'

Rama Shastri was greatly relieved when he and Santha were on the plane. He always felt awkward at departures like this. He sat next to the window and reread the letter he had recently received from Bombay. Santha meanwhile dabbed her eyes with a handkerchief. She had been alone with George Buchan in the end, and it had been very painful.

Rama Shastri read:

Mongoose,

I believe you are alive and in good health or Gopal would have heard and thus notified me. This is to assure you that I am also well and that I await your return with all the enthusiasm you should expect from me who have been your ardent lover all these years. I have pondered again and again the storm-tossed events that keep us apart. I must confess I bear some of the guilt for this. My once addiction to opium was always an impenetrable barrier between us in the past; and it was unjust of me to threaten to return to my pipe if you went to America. Alas, there was nothing I could do about your choice of friends, but in the matter of the pipe – this is to assure you I have refrained from partaking of its deadly ecstasies.

Is not my written English better? I am almost capable of *le mot précieux*.

Now I am residing in Bombay in wait for you to seek me out and gather me in your arms as you did in Lashio long ago. Yes, I say – fie and a pox on all those obstacles between us. Love conquers all.

Enclosed below is my address in Bombay.

Shastri grinned broadly. Yes, yes, fie and a pox, indeed. But how would Ileana react to Kamala's daughter? Shastri thought of Santha lowering the pickaxe into the back of Mrinalini Pal. He doubted after that if Santha would be afraid of his mistress. In fact, Ileana might have to change, become a bit more mature, too.

He looked at Santha's profile. Kamala's spirit was with her always, he concluded, in that memory place where the dead live on in the minds of loved ones. He would be helped, caring for Santha in India.

But the most gratifying thought was about himself. Yes, Ileana Heng was waiting for him. Besides that, though, Santha – and Kamala in her – would be caring for him as well. That was the grandest thing about it all.

He, too, was loved.

Glossary

angya kurti	blouse-waistcoat combination for women
ashram	monastic shelter for practitioners of Eastern thought
asura	demon
babu	native clerk
bangri	necklace of glass beads
bapu	old person, father/mother
bele	burial ground sacred to Thugs
bheesti	native water-carrier
Cages, the	red-light district in Bombay
chapatties	unleavened bread
charpoy	wooden-frame bed with webbing
chee-chee	derogatory term for Eurasians; derived from their sing-song speech
chela	disciple, pupil
chudders	bolts of cloth, sheets
cudidara	pyjamas with tapering legs
dacoits	robbers
dahi	curd-like yoghurt
danda	bamboo staff
dassis	streetwalker
deva	good spirit
dharmsalas	shelter for pilgrims
dhoti	draped loin cloth worn by men
fakir	religious mendicant
ghat	wharf; used for bathing, funeral pyres and sacrifices to gods
ghee	clarified butter
godown	storage room or shed

goor sugar	coarse sugar
guru	spiritual teacher, master
Huzoor	Lord
Kali	goddess of destruction
Kali Ma	Kali Mother
karma	destiny brought about by one's own acts
kesari	lion
kotwal	senior policeman
kotwalee	police station
Kunkali	a name for Kali; the Maneater
kurta	long-sleeved tunic for men
kutcha butcha	half-baked bread; derogatory term for Anglo-Indians
lammergeier	bearded vulture
linga	phallus
lota	small brass water pot
maharajah	great ruler
mantra	chant, spell or prayer
mozzinet	mosquito net
nais	barbers
patka	man's sash or belt with decorated ends
prana	life force or basic life substance
raga	melodic scale pattern
Raj	rule
Ramasi	secret language of Thuggee
rishi	seer, usually the most ancient; believed to have been present at the Dawn of Time
rum-johnie	prostitute
rumel	scarf or cord used by Thugs to strangle victims
sadhu/sadvi	holy man/holy woman
sahib-logh	Europeans
salwar	loose pyjamas gathered at ankles

saptak	in music, equivalent to the Western octave
sarai	native inn
sari	woman's draped garment
Shakti temple	temple dedicated to the worship of Kali
shaluka	coloured vest for men
Sher Bidi	brand of Indian cigarettes
sitar	plucked seven-stringed instrument
tabla	hand drum
Tagore's *Gitanjali*	*Book of Song Offerings* by India's greatest poet
teen pao	three-quarters; derogatory term for Anglo-Indians
tikka mark	vermilion cosmetic mark on the forehead
tilak mark	spot on forehead, supposed to cool the brain; placed on participants during religious and other ceremonies
Vishnu	the second god of the Hindu trinity
yogini	female practitioner of yoga